CONTENT WARNING!

PLEASE READ!
DO NOT START THIS BOOK WITHOUT
READING THIS FIRST!

YOUR MENTAL HEALTH MATTERS!

This story may trigger those that suffer with **heavy grief** surrounding the **death of a child.**
While I want everyone to read my books, I absolutley don't want my readers to put themselves in a situation that will stir up pain and anguish suffered. If you are not in a good headspace, then please **do not attempt to read this book** until you are.

This is just a book. A story. It's written for readers of dark romance that enjoy the thrill, suspence, and emotional damage that the characters suffer through on the road to their HEA.
YOU ARE MORE IMPORTANT THAN THIS STORY.
So why do I write such stories?
Because sometimes, pain and suffereing needs to be acknowledged. It needs to be shared. It needs to be understood.

FOR THOSE THAT DO DECIDE TO READ THIS
BOOK

Yes, there is a cliffhanger, but I swear, this time, it's one that brings hope!

TRIGGER WARNING

The Secrets & Scars Series is a dark MF contemporary MC age gap romance that contains subjects that may be triggering to some readers, and this thrid book comes with an additional warning.

Subjects included but are <u>not limited to</u>:

- Emotionally dark and traumatic.

- Abuse from parents,

- Graphic violence,

- Drugging,

- Non-consensual acts including rape outside the relationship,

- Demeaning acts,

- Suicidal thoughts & self-harm,

- Kidnapping,

- PTSD Trauma,

- Trauma from Religious Extremism,

- Exposure to cultish situations,

Beautifully SHATTERED

Secrets & Scars Series

—Book Three—

SARAH JD

Cover by Nat at DAZED Designs
Many thanks to my Alpha & Beta Readers: Gini, Anoesjka, Melissa, Stevie, Tiffany, Cheria, Tamarra, and my alpha & proofreader Jen.

- Emotional & physical blackmail,

- Explicitly detailed sex scenes,

- Killing, brutality and gore,

- Backstory includes stillbirth,

- Pregnancy trauma,

- Birth trauma,

- Death of a child/infant,

- Extremely heavy grief.

STILL WITH ME?

Get the tissues ready and get comfortable.

This is a heartbreaking, but still truly beautiful story, so buckle up and hold on tight. You are about to meet a whole new side of Abbey!!!

DEDICATION

To those who have lost someone,
and losing them utterly broke you.

There is truly nothing more emotionally painful than grief,
and sometimes, surviving it feels impossible.

This story was written with tears and heart shattering pain,
deep within the dark trenches of misery
that feels impossible to climb out of.

If you have survived this sort of suffering,
then I dedicate this book to you.

You are the epitome of strength.

1

RINGO

The room is too quiet. Too heavy with crushing devastation as I lift my Angel's hand in mine. It's lifeless, cool, and feels like it weighs nothing as my big hand swallows it whole.

Her ring is gone. The black band I gave her on our wedding day probably ripped off by those fucking cult cunts! It doesn't matter though, because my name is there, inked around her slender finger, screaming to the world that she's mine. That I'm hers.

There's no pink left in her hair now. I'd noticed that the night I came home to her. Our last night together. Right now, I kinda wish it was pink again. Then at least there'd be some colour in her.

She's deathly pale. Her lips fade into her skin, the only colour left is from the purple bruises someone fucking gave her.

Fuck!

I grit my teeth, my breath hitching as I fight for control, and lower my forehead to her hand, hoping the skin on skin contact will anchor me.

I want to hunt down those fuckers, right fucking now, but there's nothing on this Earth that could make me leave my Angel's side. Not again. Not ever.

A savage, unrelenting pain carves through my chest as images I know I'll never outrun flood my mind for the hundredth time.

Her, lying on the ground, so fucking fragile, drowning in pain as she gave birth… and I couldn't do a fucking thing to take away her agony.

And little Bobbi…

Fuck!

"Ringo?"

My head snaps up, tears sliding down my cheeks as my eyes lock onto the caramel stare I wasn't sure I'd ever get to see again.

"Abs," I choke out, needing to clear away the lump in my throat as it thickens with emotion.

"Where am I?" she breathes, her lids heavy as she blinks, her fingers curling weakly around mine as her body slowly wakes.

"Fox Pines Hospital." I stroke my thumb over the back of her hand, studying her face closely as a frown pinches her brow.

Fuck. I don't want her to remember. Not any of it. But I can tell, from the way her eyes focus on something that's not here, that she's piecing things together.

Her gaze starts darting from side to side, like she's watching a movie trailer behind her eyes as her mind catches up, likely reliving the nightmare I'd give anything to erase.

What I'd give for her to forget. To not fucking remember any of it.

"Ringo…" She stiffens, her eyes meeting mine again. "Bobbi… where's Bobbi?"

Jesus fucking Christ. I can't do this. I can't be the one to shatter her heart, but fuck, I sure as hell won't let anyone else do it either.

She tries to sit up, so I press my free hand gently to her shoulder, urging her to stay down.

"Angel. You can't get up just yet. You need to stay there."

She's already shaking her head before I even finish.

"No. No! Where's my little girl?" Her frantic gaze scans the room, probably searching for a crib or some sign of her baby.

But there's nothing, and when she sees that, her sharp, panicked glare snaps back to me. "Where is she?!"

I swallow thickly, not even sure where the hell to start. Not sure I'm ready to be the one to destroy her whole world.

"Why are you looking at me like that?" she snaps, ripping her hand from mine like she already knows what's coming.

I open my mouth to speak, but the words practically choke me.

"Ringo! Where is Bobbi?!"

"Shit, Angel… she was just too little. They said her lungs couldn't cope. And not having the right equipment when she was born meant she couldn't get the care she needed."

Anger twists her face, even as her eyes brim with tears.

"Why are you talking about her in past tense?" she sobs. "Stop talking like that. She's okay. Just take me to her!"

Abbey tries to get out of the bed, but the rail on the far side slows her just enough for me to catch her in time.

"Abs, stay there. You can't get out of bed."

"Like fuck I can't!" she snaps, swinging her legs around with pure rage etched across her face as she bares her teeth at me. "Take me to my baby!"

"Mrs Musgrove." A nurse bursts into the room, rounding the bed in a rush. "Please, lay back. You've lost too much blood. You need to rest."

Abbey's sharp glare whips to the nurse. "Then bring me my baby!"

The nurse stiffens, her eyes darting to me, and all I can do is shrug, because what the fuck else am I meant to do? This is fucking soul-crushing.

"I'm sorry, Mrs Musgrove. I wish I had better news. But under the conditions your baby was born in, and being so far from the hospital… well, we just weren't able to keep her alive. I'm so, so sorry."

For a long drawn-out moment, Abbey remains deathly still, staring blankly at the nurse. Her chest rises and falls in shallow, rapid breaths, but other than that, she's frozen. Locked in some kind of trance.

Then, she gives her head a little shake, her eyes still pinned on the nurse.

"Please bring Bobbi to me. I need to feed her."

I stiffen, and I can see the flicker of sympathy flash across the nurse's face.

"Why don't you lay back down, and I'll see what I can do."

The fuck?!

I'm about ready to rip the nurse a new one when she gently helps Abbey to lie back, my Angel now calm, like she didn't just hear her entire world collapse.

The nurse looks at me and jerks her head towards the hallway.

"I'll be right back," I tell my wife, who just nods, settling back under the sheets like nothing happened. Like she wasn't just told that her baby died.

Following the nurse out, I close the door and round the corner before the nurse sighs and turns to face me.

"She's in shock. The denial you just witnessed is her brain's way of protecting her."

"But…" I huff, raking my hand through my hair. "She's expecting you to bring her baby to her."

"Yes. She is." The nurse nods, glancing at her watch. "I'll let the doctor know what's happening and see what she wants to do."

"What the fuck do I do in the meantime? Just go along with it? Lie to her? I'm not fucking doing that."

The nurse shrugs. "Maybe steer the conversation towards her recovery. Try to shift her focus."

I scoff. "There's nothing else on this Earth that will interest her more than her child."

"I'm sorry." The nurse offers me a soft, sympathetic smile. "I don't know what else to suggest. Let me speak to the doctor."

Grinding my fucking teeth, I watch her hurry off, leaving me alone to face the wreckage.

Fuck. I just don't want to make things worse.

I stare at the door for a few beats, part of me fucking terrified to go back in there and face my wife. Face whatever questions she's about to throw at me.

But fuck, I love her. I can't turn my back on her. She needs me more than ever.

Slowly, I drag in a deep, steadying breath, bracing myself.

When I step back into Abbey's room, she's sitting up in bed, anxiously biting at her nails.

"Will the nurse be long?" she asks, her eyes bright with anticipation, and my fucking heart sinks to the pit of my gut.

This is so fucking cruel.

"I'm not sure," I grit out, my voice rough as I fight back the kind of emotions I've never been good at dealing with.

Nodding, Abbey's gaze drops to her stomach as she pulls back the sheet.

"It's hard to believe how much my belly has gone down already," she says with a soft grin. "It's kind of like a deflated balloon."

"Yeah." I force a smile as I retake my seat by her bedside, watching her jab a finger into the hospital gown where her bump used to be.

"How long have I been here?" she asks, settling back into the pillow before a yawn engulfs her.

"A bit over a day," I admit, tracking every flicker of expression on her face like it might be the one that shatters her.

"Have I been asleep this whole time?"

"Not asleep," I pause, dragging in a steadying breath as the memory of blood haemorrhaging from her sends my heart into a full-blown panic. "More like passed out. Like the nurse said. You lost a lot of blood."

She nods slowly, like she's letting that sink in.

"Bobbi will be starving, then. I want to try breastfeeding her. Make sure she gets all the good stuff."

Fucking hell. I can't do it. I can't fucking lie to her.

I'm about to open up her emotional wound when the door swings open, and the doctor walks in, smiling warmly at Abbey as she rounds the bed.

"Abigail. I'm Doctor Madden."

"Oh, hi." Abbey smiles, sitting taller in the bed, the exhaustion she wore moments ago falling away. "I'd like to see my baby, please. She must be hungry, and I'd really like to start breast-feeding her."

Dr Madden doesn't miss a beat, not even flinching at my Angel's request.

"I'm sorry," she says gently, "but I'm afraid I can't bring Bobbi to you."

Abbey's face falls. "Why?"

Dr Madden reaches out, taking Abbey's hand between hers, the warm smile fading into something softer, full of sympathy.

"Abigail... Bobbi didn't survive. She fought as hard as she could, and we did everything in our power to resuscitate her... but we weren't able to save her."

Abbey's eyes flood with tears, her gaze snapping to me.

"But... she was alive. I held her," she whispers, yanking her hand from the doctor's and pressing both palms to her chest, right where Bobbi had rested after the birth. "She made the cutest little sound, and she squirmed on me. I *felt* her."

Dr Madden nods. "Yes... you were lucky to have those few precious moments with her. I wish you'd had longer together, but I'm afraid there was nothing more we could do."

My Angel's hands stay glued to her chest where I know she still feels her baby girl's warmth... even if it's only a memory.

She shakes her head, her eyes snapping to mine, full of betrayal.

"I asked you to keep her alive. To give her my blood. To *make sure* she lived."

"I tried," I choke out, my fucking eyes burning as I fight like hell to hold my shit together. "I'm not a doctor though, Angel."

"I'm afraid there was nothing your husband could have done." Dr Madden cuts in gently, redirecting Abbey's attention back to her. "We had a team working on her, and a team working on you. I wish I could tell you something different, but Bobbi just wasn't strong enough to survive the conditions she was born in. And you… well, honestly, with all the blood you lost from the placental abruption, it's a miracle we didn't lose you too."

A sob rips from Abbey as she shakes her head.

"Why would you save me? Why would I want to be here without my little girl?" Her tear-filled eyes lock on mine, broken and furious all at once. "I don't want to live in a world where men think it's okay to rape and beat women. Why would I want to live when those are the only memories I *HAVE*!?"

The scream that tears from her throat has Dr Madden flinching, and Abbey fists her hands in her hair, glaring at the doctor like she's ready to burn the whole world down.

"YOU SHOULDN'T HAVE SAVED ME!"

"Please calm down, Mrs Musgrove, or I'll have to get someone from psych in here."

"Get the fuck out!" I'm on my feet in an instant, and Doctor Madden jolts at the lethal edge in my voice. "You bring psych anywhere near her, and I'll fucking gut you, and them." I jab a sharp finger towards her, fury cracking beneath my skin. "She just learned that her baby died. Her fucking reaction is valid!"

"But… she might try to harm herself."

I shake my head. "You don't fucking know her. She would *never* do that."

I point to the door, my stare daring her to say another word.

She gets the message, holding her arms up in defeat as she backs away and leaves the room, and fuck, I don't even know if I believe what I just said.

The only thing that ever made Abbey fight was to keep her baby safe.

Now Bobbi is gone.

Now the one thing she was fighting for is no more.

I wish I could say that what we have is enough, but what if… it's not?

As the door swings shut, it flies open again, and the moment Abbey locks eyes on her best friend Lexi, I crumble to my knees.

Lexi is on the bed in an instant, wrapping her arms around Abbey as they fall into each other. Their guttural cries fill the room, raw and broken, and I know then that my beautiful Angel finally understands her daughter didn't survive.

Any chance I had at holding back my own pain is ripped straight out of me as the sound of Abbey's grief, laced with such agony, tears my fucking heart from my chest.

2

ABBEY

Nothing feels real. Not this hospital, not the staff, not even me. It's like I've slipped into another dimension. A place built from nightmares, where the sun never truly rises and the moon never truly beams. A world ruled by pain and suffering, where any trace of happiness is ripped away the second it dares to appear, like it was never real. Just a tease. A cruel reminder that you'll never crawl out of Hell.

They've wrapped me in heated blankets, but nothing can melt the ice in my veins. They can't stop the trembles that wrack my body as Ringo pushes me in a wheelchair. Lexi walking beside me, her hand in mine, offering support, but her hold feels like disintegrating mist. It's there… but not.

All I can feel is this brutal grief, squeezing my heart with so much force I'm certain it's about to explode.

I wish it would.

I don't want to do this… but I have to. I won't be able to make sense of anything until I see Bobbi with my own eyes. Maybe that's the moment I'll snap awake. Maybe this whole thing is just a fucked-up dream.

God, I want that maybe to be real.

The sight of Doctor Madden standing outside the door with 'Morgue' written across it has my stomach roiling.

I want this to be a dream, but I know it's not. Even though nothing feels real, everything also hits with a vividness that guts me.

Dammit. I don't even know anymore. My head is all kinds of wrong right now.

The doctor gives me one of her fake sympathetic looks again, and I just glare at her.

She should have saved my daughter. She doesn't deserve my decency. Not even a slither of it.

I'd been waiting for them to bring my little girl to me, swaddled in a blanket so I could hold her, but maybe that's just the way it's done in movies. The doctor insisted that I had to come down to this eerie basement. Said it will be easier for me this way.

Nothing about this is easy.

"You ready?" Lexi asks, and I glance up into her blue eyes, swimming with tears.

None of this was real until she stepped into my room. One look at her, and I knew. I knew Ringo, the nurse and the doctor weren't lying.

My little girl was gone.

I nod, even though I'm not ready. How can anyone be ready to see someone they love dead?

But I need to do this. I have to see Bobbi with my own eyes.

If I don't, I'll spend the rest of my life wondering if this is just some twisted dream. A nightmare too brutal to even comprehend.

The doctor pushes the door open, and inside, a man stands by a row of stainless steel doors that look like something out of an industrial kitchen.

Shit.

I guess it is. A fridge for the dead.

I shake my head, ready to tell Ringo to turn the wheelchair around, panic clawing at my insides as my stomach lurches.

"I'm going to be sick." I croak just as someone shoves a vomit bag in front of my face, catching the first expulsion.

Behind me, Lexi holds my hair back with one hand while rubbing my back with the other, and I heave and heave, like if I just vomit enough, maybe I can throw up the grief too.

But it's no good.

It's still there. Heavy and crushing.

I can't do this.

When I'm finally done, I wipe my mouth with the back of my shaking hand, and Ringo's hand moves into view, reaching for the bag.

"Let me take that for you, Angel."

Shit. Why is he being so gentle with me? I practically blamed him for my little girl's death.

Do I blame him?

Maybe.

I asked him to save her, and he didn't.

Was it his fault? Probably not. But I need someone to blame. I just have to.

Right now, aside from the doctor, he's the only one here my fury knows how to aim at. There's this wall of madness around me, thick and suffocating, and I don't know what to do with it.

I'm so full of hate I can taste it. So much that I'm scared even Lexi might catch some of the blast.

I let Ringo take the bag from me, unable to meet his eyes. I'm too angry, too close to breaking. But I keep it bottled in, needing to get through this moment.

"Show me." I force the words past my lips, my voice raspy and barely there.

The older man in the white medical coat nods and opens one of the lower doors before sliding out a metal tray, and on it… a white sheet covering a very small lump.

My heart just about stutters to a stop, and I watch frozen as he slowly peels back the sheet.

A sob rips from my throat as I reach for the wheels of the chair, taking over to move myself closer, coming to stop beside her… beside the lifeless, impossibly still body of my baby girl.

Shit.

This is real.

Bobbi's gone.

My little girl is dead.

Cries fall from me, tears tracking down my cheeks in a never-ending river, but my eyes never waver, taking in every inch of my Bobbi.

I didn't get a good look at her out in that pine forest. She was messy, and I was crying then too, but I was also struggling to stay conscious.

Now that I think about it, that must have been from the blood loss.

Reaching out, I glide my finger gently over her tiny digits, her fingernails tinged blue, matching the rest of her skin.

"Hey, l-little o-one." I sob. "I'm s-so s-sorry I couldn't p-protect y-you."

I trace her eyelashes and brows, barely there, both so light in colour. I wonder if she would have grown up to have blonde hair like me.

I guess I'll never know.

"She's beautiful, Abs." Lexi kneels beside the wheelchair, and we lock eyes.

"She kind of l-looks like an a-alien," I admit, the words stuttering out between sobs, and Lexi's lips kick up in the smallest smile.

"An adorable alien."

I nod, fresh tears falling. "Yeah. My l-little adorable a-alien."

Reaching out, Lexi gives my shoulder a gentle squeeze that nearly anchors me, like she knows I'm barely holding on.

I can feel Ringo on my other side… quiet, but there.

I don't want to drag my eyes away from my little girl for even a second, but when I hear him quietly sniff, I risk a glance.

Tears wet his eyes as he stares down at my baby, his jaw moving, clenched tight like he's fighting to keep it together.

Shit.

I didn't even think about what this might be like for him. He's probably remembering Hope.

I know I'm angry at him. At everyone. But I'm not so far gone that I don't feel the punch of his pain. It hits me hard. Right in the centre of the thing that's broken.

My heart.

I want to ask him to come closer, but that wall of madness is still here, so impenetrable I can't seem to break through it.

So, I turn my eyes back to my little girl, for one last look.

She's right here. I can see her, lifeless, blue and cold, but my heart refuses to believe she's really gone. Not when she still feels so alive in my heart.

I can feel it then. My heart. The beat faint at first, starts to thump harder, and with it, something inside me begins to stir.

It's not light.

It's not warmth.

But something so much darker.

Something heavy and primal, unfurling in my chest like a wildfire.

I should be scared. But I'm not.

No.

There's no room for fear anymore, because I've just realised something.

Now I know why I didn't die.

Leaning forward, I pull myself up on shaky legs, my body trembling under the weight of everything I'm carrying.

Lexi and Ringo steady me, one on each side, and I lean down, pressing my lips to my little girl's stone-cold forehead.

My tears spill onto her delicate skin, and for a moment, I let myself wish we were inside a fairytale, where a kiss or the drop of a tear could magically spark her little heart back to life, sending blood rushing through her veins again.

A fairytale where there's always a happily ever after.

But my story doesn't end like that.

No.

Mine ends in violence and blood.

"Mummy will get them," I whisper, knowing Lexi and Ringo can still hear, but the man standing off to the side can't. "I will make every single one of them pay. I won't stop until they are all dead."

Using my thumb, I gently brush away the tears clinging to Bobbi's skin. A soft touch that feels like both a blessing and a curse.

"That's one promise I know I can keep, Bobbi." I straighten, my heart shattering all over again as I look down at her one last time, and swear one last promise. "And once they are all gone... Mummy will join you."

3

RINGO

A bbey's parting words to her little girl are haunting me. Echoing in my head, refusing to let go. What gets me isn't just the words. It's the quiet certainty in her voice, like she's already made peace with them. Like she's decided on an ending she won't come back from.

Lexi West

She's grieving. She just needs time to heal.

I keep staring at Lexi's message. She sent it after leaving last night. After spending the whole damn day holding her friend close as she unravelled. I watched Lexi hold her together through every drop of the emotional rollercoaster Abbey is suffering through.

Today, Abbey's a ghost. Quiet. Still. Sometimes she cries, but it's so soft I wouldn't even know unless I caught a glimpse at her face.

And even then, I've got to fight to see it, because that face is rarely turned my way anymore. Like she can't bear to look at me. Like she hates the very sight of me.

Fuck… I can feel her slipping through my fingers.

I think I'm losing her.

Standing from my chair, I round the bed so I can see her, and the moment she clocks me getting close, she turns her head, shutting me out once again.

"I know I'm an ugly fucker, but you never used to have trouble looking at me."

She scoffs, but that's it.

Rounding the bed again, she starts to turn her head away, but I lurch forward, gripping her chin roughly.

"Stop trying to ignore me."

Her eyes flare, hot and wild, like she's two seconds away from punching me.

Maybe she fucking should.

"I know you're angry, bu—"

She scoffs again, louder this time, rolling her eyes like I'm pathetic.

"What? You don't think I understand the fucking pain you're in?" I shove back from her, releasing her chin, my fists balled and teeth gritted as I itch to break something. "You don't think I know what it's like to see my dead daughter? To hold her? TO FUCKING GRIEVE HER!"

Abbey flinches, tears quickly pooling in her eyes, but still, they hold nothing but fury as she glares at me from under her lashes, like she's imagining my death in vivid detail.

"You want me gone, Angel?" I ask, holding my hands out at my sides, not fucking sure what else I can do to get her to talk to me. "You wish you'd never met me?"

"Yes!" she snarls, sitting upright as she bares her teeth. "I wish Maggie had never found that pregnancy test and told my mum! I wish Tahli had never reached out to Lexi for help! I wish Lexi had never asked you to kidnap me! I wish everyone would just leave me alone!"

I nod, knowing she doesn't really mean her words. She's angry. She's lashing out. She's hurting beyond belief and doesn't know where to direct it.

I can fucking relate to that.

"How fucking awful that your little sister cared so much about you that she reached out to your best friend for help." I roll my eyes, knowing it will piss her off, but at least she's not silent anymore. At least I've managed to crack something open. "How fucking unbelievable that Lexi would reach out to me knowing I could do what she couldn't, even after everything you did to her to push her away."

"Fuck you!" she snarls.

"You wanna hit me, Angel?"

"Yes!"

I chuckle darkly. "Have at it." I hold my arms out again, daring her, but she doesn't move. "What's wrong? You don't think your anger can make your swings hurt? Because your words sure hit the fucking mark."

Her face falls, that tough mask starting to crack as her lower lip starts trembling, yet her glare remains.

"You wanna hurt the people that care about you the most? Then come on. I'm right fucking here, Abbey. Loving you despite the hate you glare my way, like you wish I was the one that died."

"You should leave," she snaps, and again, I chuckle.

"No way in fucking hell am I leaving you. You're fucking stuck with me, Angel. Whether you want me or not. I meant every goddamn word of our vows." I raise a brow. "Do you remember them?"

"I don't care about them," she bites back, and I shrug, even though her words fucking sting.

"Pity. Because I do. I vowed to honour you, and respect our differences. I swore I'd cherish the good times and ride out the fucking storms. Hand in fucking hand, Angel. Side by fucking side." I step closer, and my chest tightens when she doesn't try to shift back, not taking her eyes off me, where before, she couldn't even bear to look at me. "This is one hell of a massive fucking storm. So even if you scream for me to go, I'm not leaving your side."

For a long beat, she just stares at me, her brow starting to furrow with each passing moment.

"Our marriage isn't real," she spits, and this time I scoff, fucking done with that lie.

"Isn't it?" I growl. "It sure felt real to me. You fighting your demons and giving yourself to me on our wedding night sure felt fucking real, too. So did the days that followed. The way it fucking hurt both of us when I had to leave you at my ma's to go and do club shit and start hunting the bastards that raped you. *That* was fucking real, Angel."

I sit back in the chair, dragging it closer, not taking my eyes off her as her glare starts slipping slightly.

"How about the video calls each night?" I lean forward, resting my forearms on my knees. "You falling asleep mid-call while I spent most of the night just staring at the screen. Watching you snore and drool."

Her anger finally crumbles.

She's so young. So innocent. She hasn't deserved anything that's happened to her. And fuck, those big doe caramel eyes are like a window into her shattered soul right now.

"How about when I came back and found you out in the storm?" My voice softens as I see a glimpse of the girl that I first met. "You fucking ran to me, Abbey. You were as desperate to be in my arms as I was to have you in them. There's nothing fake about that. Not a single fucking thing."

"I don't snore," she whispers, and my lip kicks up at one corner.

"You do. And it's fucking adorable."

She shakes her head, her eyes dropping to her fidgeting hands.

"I'm angry," she whispers.

"I know."

"I want everyone to hurt," she admits quietly.

"I know, Angel."

Her caramel eyes flick back up to mine, wounded and raw. "How can you love me when I'm so nasty to you?"

Shifting forward, I take her hand in mine, half expecting her to pull away. But she doesn't. That alone nearly knocks the wind out of me.

"Because I know you don't really mean it. What you're feel-ing… it's natural. Wanting someone to pay? That's normal."

She shakes her head slowly. "I want *everyone* to pay. I want to grab a flamethrower and burn the entire world down until there's nothing but ash."

I nod, because *fuck,* I remember that. I remember being so full of fire I could have destroyed cities.

"In time, that rage will redirect to just those who actually deserve it."

She considers that for a few long beats, gnawing on her lip while she thinks.

"What do I do with the anger until that happens?" she asks, her caramel eyes wide and wrecked, like she's drowning, and she doesn't even care.

Fuck.

What I would do to carry her suffering for her.

"You need an outlet." I hold my arms out again. "Use me as your punching bag all you like."

Rolling her eyes, she falls back onto her pillow with a sigh. "I'm not going to do that."

"Why the fuck not?"

We stare at each other for a long, loaded moment before she finally answers.

"I don't really want to hurt you."

Fuck. Hearing that is a fucking relief.

I'd been bracing for the worst, thinking maybe I'd already lost her. But perhaps not.

"I know, Angel."

Her tears finally spill over, sliding down her temples and into her hair as she stares up at the ceiling, her hands pressed to her chest.

It takes me a moment, but then I realise… the way her fingers curl like she is holding something fragile… like she's holding Bobbi again. Just like she did in that pine forest. Only this time, Bobbi isn't here. She's holding nothing but a ghost.

"I think…" she chokes out, her voice barely there, "I think I'm angriest at myself." Her eyes flick back to mine, wet and full of unimaginable pain. "I wasn't strong enough to protect Bobbi."

Her hands fall to her sides, releasing something that was never really there.

Shaking my head, I stand and climb onto the bed next to her, tugging her into my arms. She shifts to give me room without hesitation, letting me pull her close. Finally letting me hold her like I've been dying to do.

"Don't talk like that, Angel," I whisper into her hair. "You've done nothing but fight for her. And you still are." My throat tightens, thick with emotion. "I heard what you said to her."

She presses in closer, curling into me, and fuck, it feels so fucking good to feel her hand on my chest and her breath on my neck as she finally lets me get close to her.

"I meant what I said to her," she admits into the crook of my neck, her voice husky and raw from her own emotions.

"I know."

"All of it." She pushes the point. "I meant it."

I know what she's getting at.

She's not just grieving. She's planning her exit.

She wants me to understand that when her vengeance is done, she doesn't want to keep going.

She wants to leave this world. To rest eternally with Bobbi.

The thought has invisible claws tearing through my chest, shredding everything on the way to my fucking heart.

"I know," I whisper, my voice rough as I stroke fingers through her hair, holding her tight against me. "But maybe… when that time comes, you'll see it differently. You'll see that moment as the start of something new, Angel. Not the end of everything."

She sobs again, finally breaking completely in my arms, and I hold her, even as my own eyes sting and my chest threatens to cave.

She cries for what feels like hours, and all I can do is let her purge the pain like this. There's nothing else I can do.

I can't bring Bobbi back.

I can't erase the hell she's been through.

I can't fix this.

But… I *can* be here.

A warm embrace. A shoulder to cry on. A safe place to land.

A human punching bag, if that's what she needs.

Whatever she needs, I'll give it. Over and over until the day she wakes up, and the pain isn't so suffocating.

It'll never leave her. But maybe one day she'll learn how to live with it.

And that… is probably the hardest part of all.

Eventually, Abbey falls into a deep sleep, and I manage to slip from the bed without waking her.

My phone has been buzzing non-stop in my back pocket, so I duck out of the room and hit redial, calling Smitty back.

"Bout fucking time," he answers, and fuck, if I could reach through the phone and strangle him, I fucking would.

"Insensitive much?" I snap, and he sighs.

"Sorry. Fuck. How is she?"

"Bout as fucking good as anyone in her situation."

"Yeah. Poor kid. She's too fucking sweet to be facing this sort of shit."

I grunt, mainly because him calling her a *kid* just rubs me the wrong fucking way.

She's not a kid. She's a goddamn warrior. A mother who lost her baby.

"You called?" I bite out, not in the fucking mood for Smitty's usual brand of chaos.

"Yeah. All the funerals are set for Wednesday. Just wanted to check if your woman wants to have her kid's funeral at the same time."

"No," I snap, ice in my voice as fury lights up my fucking chest.

The fuck is he thinking?

Does he believe she'd want to lump Bobbi's farewell in with the rest? Like it's just another fucking name on the list?

She's not just grieving. My Angel is gutted.

And he fucking thinks she'd give a single fuck about anyone else's funeral right now?

"My wife will arrange her own funeral for her daughter."

"Yeah. Okay. I figured, but... well fuck, I dunno."

He sounds unsure for once, and it almost makes me feel bad.

"Where are the funerals taking place?" I ask instead of ac-knowledging his insensitivity.

Is it even insensitivity? Or am I just looking for someone to throw my own rage at?

"At the new compound," Smitty responds. "We've set up a memorial area. Our fallen will be cremated before Wednesday, and their ashes will be placed in the memorial wall during the ceremony."

Shit.

I rub my hand down over my face.

I need to get my head outta my arse.

People fucking died.

Good people.

Important people.

People who wore our patch and called me brother.

People I fucking cared about.

My gut twists, the weight of it finally catching up with me.

So many have died.

For my club.

For me.

For Abbey.

"I'll be there," I rasp, hating how obvious the emotion is in my voice. "Just text me the time."

"And will your wife be there?" he asks, like her presence is expected.

"If she's well enough," I mutter. "I'm sure Abbey would want to go. She built close ties with a few of them."

Fuck. How's she even going to handle that news? Grieving her daughter and now fallen friends, too?

The weight of it all presses down, getting heavier by the fucking second.

Glancing up, I stiffen as my eyes lock onto a group of people coming my way.

"Shit, Smitty. I've gotta go. I've got company."

4

ABBEY

Yawning, I stretch, my whole body aching as my sore muscles instinctively send my hand to my bump to check on my little bub… only… my bump is gone.

I gasp, eyes snapping open as reality slams into me like a freight train.

Oh. My. God.

Little Bobbi… is gone.

A sob claws up my throat, pain slicing through my chest like a blade.

For the tiniest moment, just a heartbeat, when I woke, everything felt normal. I was still pregnant. Bobbi was still safe. Life was still hard, but there was hope.

That's what my brain clung to… that fragile, cruel lie. But then, like some twisted Groundhog Day, I have to relive it. Again. The moment I remember Bobbi is gone.

She's… dead.

I choke on my sob, my eyes flicking around the hospital room to find it empty.

I can't do this. I can't be here. I can't breathe in this life. Not without Bobbi.

"My wife will arrange her own funeral for her daughter."

Ringo's voice floats through from the other side of the closed door, his words stopping my tears in their tracks.

Who is he talking to?

Bobbi's… funeral…

I have to arrange Bobbi's funeral?

"Where are the funerals taking place?" he asks, and since I can't hear anyone else talking, I have to assume he's on the phone.

Wait.

Funerals? As in plural?

My already shattered heart plummets to the pit of my stomach as memories come rushing in.

Ringo got called away because the new compound was under attack.

Me outside, in the rain, crying under the Jacaranda tree.

Lightning.

Men running over the ridge.

Screams.

Gunshots.

Yelling.

Jols…

"I'll be there. Just text me the time." Ringo grunts, his voice clipped and sharp, like he's a second away from losing it.

But of course, he's pissed. He's stuck here, dealing with me, while people are dead.

Stoner… Tucker…

"If she's well enough. I'm sure Abbey would want to go. She built close ties with a few of them."

No…

No!

Jols!

Shit, no. Not Jols, too. Please, not Jols.

"Shit, Smitty. I've gotta go. I've got company."

My heart thrashes wildly in my chest. Images of Jols getting shot slamming into me.

Her body hitting the wall. Sliding down. Leaving a trail of blood.

God, *why*? *Why* would you do this?

How could I be so selfish, caught up in my own pain when Ringo has lost people too?

What about Mule? And Brody?

Oh my god. Poor JD. Is he now mourning the loss of his little brother? Of Jols?

Who else died? What the hell happened at the compound? It was under attack. That's why Ringo left.

"Guys, now's not the best time," Ringo growls, his voice edged with fury.

"Just because you married her, doesn't mean you can shut us out."

Jared?

"Has she been able to eat yet?"

Lexi. I'd know her voice anywhere.

My friends are here.

"Step aside, arsehole."

Shit. Marcus.

The door swings open, and I swipe at my wet cheeks as my friends stroll in, most of them glaring at Ringo as they pass him, still standing out in the hall.

"There she is." Simon's smile is forced as he steps in, shouldering past everyone to get to me before sinking onto the edge of my bed. "Can I please hug you?"

My lip wobbles as I nod, drawn to the way his hazel eyes shimmer with worry.

He wraps his arms around me without another word, and I fight to keep myself from falling apart.

I should let it all out. Every scream. Every sob… but I don't. Something in me is refusing to crack in front of my friends.

For some reason, I want to be alone in my grief.

When Simon pulls back, releasing me, my gaze shifts, drawn like a magnet to Ringo as he finally steps inside.

Now with so many people in here, the room feels like it's closing in.

Ringo's dark eyes lock with mine, and he mouths '*sorry*', leaning against the wall, arms crossed, keeping his distance as my friends draw closer.

I want to tell them to back off. Their nearness is suffocating, making me too anxious, and dread still sits heavy in my gut at the guilt of knowing people died… because of me.

"Is there anything we can do, Abs?" Lexi asks, rounding the other side of the bed, taking the seat there.

I shake my head, parting my lips, but nothing comes out. I don't have anything to say to her right now. Only to Ringo.

Darting my eyes back to him, I clear my throat in the hopes my voice actually works when I try to speak.

"Who are the funerals for?"

Ringo's brows hitch. "You heard my phone call?"

I nod. "Some of it. Who died?"

His lips press into a thin line, his gaze flicking to my friends before landing back on me.

"We'll talk about it later, Angel. Your friends are here to see you."

He's deflecting. Holding something back.

Something he doesn't want to tell me.

My heart kicks up again, beating hard like it's trying to escape, but it's trapped, and it starts struggling.

My hands fist the sheets as my lungs seize, suddenly refusing to pull air in.

"Hey, are you okay, Abs?" Marcus asks from behind Simon, his voice tight with concern.

I can't answer. I just shake my head, my eyes locked on the stark white sheets spread over my lap.

"Abbey. What can we do?" Lexi asks, and I catch movement from the corner of my eye as she stands, moving closer.

This is too much. Too many people. Too many deaths. Too much pain.

It's unbearable.

Suddenly, Simon gets shoved off the bed, and Ringo is there, his big palms framing my face as he forces me to look at him.

"Angel. Listen to my voice, okay?"

I try to nod, but his grip makes it near impossible to move.

"Think of the last place you felt safe. Where was that?"

My lips part, the words sticking, yet somehow, I force them out.

"Your home."

He nods, his whiskey eyes locked on mine. "Good. Think about that. Picture it. What do you see?"

When I think of his place, one room lights up in my mind like a flare.

"Your room," I whisper.

"Good. Stay there. What do you see in it?"

"Your guitars," I breathe, the tight coil in my chest easing slightly. "The window that overlooks the barn and pond. The couch…" I trail off, not wanting to admit what comes to mind when I think of his couch. What we *did* on it.

But a small smile tugs at Ringo's lips, like he knows exactly what memory crashed into me.

"When you feel panicked, think of that place." His thumb grazes over my lips, and for a moment, I forget we're not alone. "Or any place that makes you feel at ease."

I nod slowly, my eyes locked with his, sinking into them like they are the only thing keeping me afloat.

Slowly, his hands fall away, and I immediately feel their absence, leaving me cold and alone once again.

"I just…" I start, heat pricking the backs of my eyes as I remember what had me spiralling briefly. "I just need to know who died."

He nods. "Soon, Angel. I have to take care of something. I'll be back in fifteen." His gaze shifts to Lexi. "Stay with her until I come back." Then he glances around the room. "All of you."

Everyone nods, and his eyes fall back to mine as he lifts my hand and presses his lips to it.

"I'll be right back."

I nod, even though I don't want him to go, and I watch him stand, hurrying from the room.

I'm more than curious what is so urgent that he has to rush off, but then, the reason why I'm here in this hospital bed hits me again, and I just want to shatter.

Bobbi.

My friends talk to me about what? I can't tell. Their words drift around me like static, their worried gazes flicking to me, but their voices… well, it's all just white noise right now, because all I can hear is the blood in my veins, thundering like a stampede of elephants.

They ask me questions, but I can't even summon the energy to listen, let alone answer.

I know they mean well, but I just want them to leave. I want everyone to just go away and leave me alone.

I don't want to be here.

It would be better for everyone if I just go. The amount of suffering I've dragged into their lives, either directly or indirectly, is why I can't stay. They'd be better off without me. Then they can finally breathe. Live a life free of worry. Free of the rapists hunting me. No more crooked cops to worry about raiding them or kidnapping anyone. No more Southern Sadists risking their lives for someone who's not even worthy of their protection.

"Hey, Abs." Lexi's voice pierces through the armour quickly moulding around me, her touch gentle as she gives my shoulder a squeeze.

I blink at her, the sound of the room rushing back in, which is when I notice there's only Lexi, Jared and Marcus left in here with me.

My oldest friends.

"Sorry for bringing everyone. They were worried, and I thought seeing them might perk you up a bit, but I can see now it was too much."

I nod. "Yeah… I'm not good company right now."

"We don't have to talk, Abs. We just want to be here for you." Marcus lowers himself to the end of the bed, his eyes meeting mine.

There's no pressure in them. No judgment. Just… love.

But I can't take it.

"I think… all I need right now is to be alone."

Marcus flinches at my admission, but he shakes it off a moment later.

My voice is flat and clipped. There's bitterness lacing my tone, yet I can't find it in me to check myself.

I'm nothing but toxic energy after all.

Bad things happen to good people when they are around me. Maybe it really would be better if they just leave.

If Jols hadn't been babysitting me at Ringo's house, she'd still be here. Alive.

Stoner too.

Shit. Even Millie got shot.

Did she survive?

The door creaks open, and everyone's heads snap towards it as Ringo pops his head in.

"I need everyone to leave. We need to speak with Abbey."

Shit.

This is it.

He's going to tell me what protecting me has cost his club. Cost him.

How can he even stand to look at me?

I half expect my friends to argue, but they don't. They just nod and exit, Lexi pressing a kiss to my forehead before retreating, too.

Well… I wanted them to go. And now they have.

So why do I want to scream for them to come back?

Because you're not strong enough to hear the truth fall from Ringo's lips.

Remaining in the doorway, Ringo talks quietly to Lexi, who nods and glances back at me, offering me a small wave before leaving.

And then… just like that. We are alone.

No.

I don't want to hear this. I can't take any more bad news.

I need to go.

Throwing back the sheets, I swing my legs over the side of the bed when Ringo's voice interrupts me.

"What are you doing?'

"I need to leave. I can't do this, Ringo. I can't bear to hear what you have to say. I know I wanted to know, but now I know I'm not strong enough to handle it."

Ringo sighs. "You can't leave. You have a guest."

I shake my head, lowering my feet to the cold floor.

"No more visitors. I don't want to see anyone."

"Seriously? You're really going to turn me away?"

The voice from the doorway hits me like a lightning strike, and I swear, time stops.

My eyes snap up, locking on the wheelchair gliding into my room, pushed by JD.

I barely register him, because in that chair is someone I was sure had died.

"J-Jols?"

She giggles. "Yeah, I don't look that bad, do I? Am I really that hard to recognise?"

Tears explode behind my eyes, spilling down my cheeks as I stumble off the bed, my knees nearly buckling beneath me as I take my first step.

Ringo is right there, catching me before I hit the ground, his powerful arms helping me close the distance.

I crash into Jols sitting in the wheelchair, clinging to her like I'll never let her go again.

She hisses, and I jerk back, my eyes going wide as I take her in.

"Shit. Sorry," I gasp, panic rising as my gaze snaps to JD, but he just smirks like he expected this.

"It's okay," Jols half laughs, half groans. "I'm on the mend."

She's wearing a hospital gown like mine, but I catch a dressing peeking past the neckline.

"You got shot… I thought…" The lump in my throat swells. "I thought you were dead."

She shrugs, like that little detail is barely worth mentioning.

"I've been shot before. It doesn't hurt as much as you'd think."

Ringo scoffs from behind me. "That was your body going into shock."

Jols just shrugs, shooting me a lazy grin.

"I'm not so easy to kill."

I stare at my friend. The one who reminds me so much of Lexi.

Her long, dark hair is braided back messily, like someone tried but didn't really know what they were doing.

JD, probably. Or a nurse who gave it a half-arsed go.

But her eyes? That sharp, striking blue is still there, and her cheeks are rosy. Alive. Glowing like the fight never left her.

It makes me wonder what I look like, and for a brief moment I worry, but then just as fleeting, the care slips from me.

Nothing like that matters anymore.

"I'm so sorry. It's all my fault."

Jols scowls. "Uh-uh. I won't let you do that bullshit, Abbey. It's not your fault. My fault. Or Ringo's fault." She stabs a finger in my direction. "The men who did this? It's *all* on *them*. The fuckers that raped you. The cops who ignored your statement and dragged Allen into it. Every last bit of it is on them."

Slowly, I nod, knowing she's right, but still, it's all centred around me.

My head starts to swim, a wave of dizziness washing over me, and I stumble.

Ringo is right there again, his hands strong and steady as he guides me back a few steps and lowers me into a chair.

"Take it easy, Abs," he mutters quietly, concern lacing his voice.

I nod, but don't meet his eyes, the familiar feeling of grief curling back inside my chest once again.

None of this is fair.

I love Jols. I really do. But she got shot and she's still alive, yet my little Bobbi… she's not. She's dead.

I don't want to be here.

"Can you two helicopters give us some girl time?" Jols asks JD and Ringo, and they lock eyes before nodding, their gazes landing back on me.

"Will you be alright for a bit, Angel?" Ringo asks, and I nod, not knowing the real answer to his question.

Will I be alright?

Probably not.

Nothing is alright.

Nothing will be alright ever again.

I barely notice Ringo and JD leaving the room, my thoughts swallowing everything as I stare at nothing.

"Talk to me."

Jols' voice slices through the fog, and I blink up, meeting her stare.

"I'm glad you're okay."

She frowns. "Don't talk about me. Talk about *you*. What are you thinking?"

Why does she want to know that? She can't change anything. Can't bring my baby back.

"I think I want to be alone."

She quirks a brow. "Pushing people away won't help."

"I dunno. Kinda feels like it will," I mutter, my voice flat, and Jols sighs.

"Ringo's worried about you." She wheels her chair closer, boxing me in, giving me nowhere to look without it looking obvious that I'm avoiding her eyes.

"He should stop."

"He blames himself, you know?" She reaches up and rubs her collarbone like it's hurting.

Is that where she got shot?

I shrug, not answering her question, and I catch the frown pulling at her features.

"You blame him?"

"I made him promise to save Bobbi before saving me," I snap, the words ripping out like they've been burning my throat all of this time.

Her brows shoot up, and she stares at me in disbelief.

"You made him promise something impossible," she snaps. "How could he ever know what was going to happen? He's not a medical professional, Abbey. He's just a man. A man madly in love with a woman, trying to do everything in his power to protect her."

The words slam into me like a truck, and I break, fat tears bursting from my eyes, burning a trail down my cheeks.

"He shouldn't have made the promise then."

The words leave my mouth, knowing they are selfish, yet I can't make myself take them back.

For a long, drawn-out moment, Jols just stares at me.

Her silence is unforgiving.

I want to ask what she's thinking, but also, I don't, because what does it matter?

Nothing matters anymore.

"Turn the tables," she finally says. "Put yourself in *his* place. Helplessly watching the person you love in pain, dying right before your eyes, making a declaration of love, and begging you to do something that even God himself couldn't do." Jols shakes her head, her glare burning as she watches me. "You fell, Abbey. That fall caused you to go into early labour. Your placenta was damaged or whatever the hell it was. You were in the middle of *nowhere*. No doctors. No equipment. Just the earth, the trees, and a bunch of Marx medics trained to handle war wounds, not internal placental abruptions and babies born ten weeks early."

Jols huffs, her chest rising with the anger of having to spell it out to me.

"Nothing could have saved Bobbi. Even if she'd been born in this hospital, there's no guarantee she would have survived." Reaching forward, Jols picks up my hand, wrapping both of hers around it. "Sometimes, bad things happen that are out of everyone's control, and I'm so extremely sorry, Abbey. I'm so sorry you have to go through this. I can't even imagine what you are feeling. But even so, one thing I *do* know is you're going to need me. Your friends. Ringo. Leaning on us is the only way you get through this."

I shake my head, easing my hand from hers and rising to my feet, the action forcing her to wheel her chair back to give me space.

"You're wrong." My voice is cold. Dead. "The only way I get through this is by killing the men who did this."

Her face pales.

I don't think it's because she's shocked, but more like she knows just how true my words are.

The door bursts open as JD hurries in, fear etched on his face.

"Fuck. We've gotta go!"

I snap to attention, watching as he takes out his phone and calls someone.

"What's going on?" Jols asks, but his answer comes when whoever he calls picks up the phone.

"Satan's Rebels are heading this way. Get out of the pissa!"

5

ABBEY

"**W**ho are Satan's Rebels?" I ask, catching the panic rolling off Jols and JD as they lock eyes.

"They're a rival club," JD barks, slipping his phone in his pocket and taking out his gun, checking it for something. "They've teamed up with Ian Allen and that cult church your olds are tangled up with."

My eyes go wide.

A rival club?

Ian Allen is working with a different motorcycle club?

"They were the ones that hit the compound," JD continues, "caused a distraction to pull Ringo away from you so Allen and his crew could move in and take you."

The room tilts.

This really is all because of me. Without a doubt.

"Where's Ringo?" Jols asks, her voice light with panic.

"He'll meet us out in the hall. He was taking a piss," JD snaps, cracking the door open and peeking out. "Fuck. We have to go. *Now.*"

I rush to Jols' wheelchair, watching JD hand her a gun without hesitation.

I'm about to ask if he has a gun for me, but he's already swinging the door open and stepping out.

Gripping the handles of the wheelchair, I push it, moving us out into the hallway in the direction he points. His eyes are panicked when they flash in the other direction, and a shiver ripples up my spine.

"What fucking room is she in?!" a male voice bellows from somewhere behind us, and I nearly let a squeal escape, fear slicing through me.

"I'll take Jols. We have to hurry." JD urges me aside, taking control of the wheelchair and pushing it faster. My feet scramble to keep up as the voices grow fainter behind us.

But then, something warm starts oozing down my leg, and my feet slow as I try to see what it is.

Bright red blood streaks down my calf, despite the thick pad I'm wearing beneath my underwear.

I'm bleeding.

I'm bleeding because I'm not pregnant anymore.

Because I gave birth… and my baby died.

I'm bleeding because those Satan's Rebels pricks teamed up with Officer Allen and made sure I was left vulnerable enough to be taken.

A kidnapping that led to the fall. A fall that led to premature labour.

The labour that led to Bobbi's death.

Suddenly, JD and Jols vanish from my sight as red rims the edges, and rage wraps around my heart like barbed wire.

I turn.

I start walking back.

Back towards the voices.

Back towards the threat.

Back towards the nurses being bullied for information.

I don't try to hide the blood running down my leg.

Let them see what *they* did.

Let them see what *they* caused.

Let them bear witness to what *they* created.

"Are you looking for me?!" I yell, storming straight for them, adrenaline pulsing through my veins as I take in the four guys wearing leather vests, covered in the tackiest tattoos I've ever seen.

"Shit! No! Abbey!" JD's voice comes from behind me, but it's far away. He must not have noticed I'd stopped and changed direction until he heard my voice.

"Damn. Yeah. You're the bitch we are here for." The skinhead sneers, eyes lighting up as he pulls out a gun and aims it at me.

"Yeah? You here to kill me?" I ask, closing the distance quickly, my actions causing a slight pucker between his brows, which only deepens when I step right up to him. So close that I lean forward and press my forehead to the tip of his barrel. "Do it. Pull the trigger."

His jaw ticks. "I fucking wish. Sluts like you deserve to die, but my orders are to bring you in."

"A Sadist is coming!" one of his buddies hisses behind him, drawing his attention, and his gun dips.

I move, my eyes trained on the gun, my hand wrapping around the barrel, yanking it from his grip before he even knows what's happening.

"What the…" he trails off as I level the barrel between his eyes.

"Angel!" Ringo's voice booms from somewhere, but I ignore him and the nurses scurrying to hide, my focus on the gun and its heaviness as I jam it harder against the man's forehead.

"Because of people like you, my baby died," I deadpan, my voice flat.

There's no pain in it. No fear. No anger.

Just cold, and dead calm.

I've accepted his fate, and now it's time for him to accept it too.

"So now," I inhale, my finger tightening. "You have to die."

I squeeze the trigger.

The explosion is deafening, a thunderous crack that echoes up the hallway, making my ears ring. I stumble back, the kickback of the gun jolting my arms, and blood hits my face in a hot, red spray.

A shower of crimson bursts out behind him, splattering across the hallway and painting his brothers in gore.

As if in slow motion, I watch him drop to the floor, his eyes still wide, a bloody hole between his eyes as he stares up at nothing, the stark hallway now painted red.

I'm too dazed to react in time, too caught up in the silence behind the gunfire when the other three men pull their guns on me.

I don't have time to react. Time to move. But before they can fire, a shower of bullets pelt into two of them, tearing up the hallway.

Their bodies jerk and twist as lead rips through flesh, spraying more blood as they collapse with heavy thuds, and I'm still standing in the middle of it.

Panic ripples through the last man standing, his aim faltering as he steps back.

But shit. He can't leave. He doesn't get to walk away.

Not after what they did.

He has to die too.

Lifting my gun, my aim locks on his chest before rough hands grip my shoulders and yank me backwards.

"Abbey, stop!" JD's voice roars in my ear, and before I can blink, he's wrestled the gun from my grip as the other man turns to run.

"No you fucking don't!" Ringo growls, charging past me and into my line of sight.

Even though JD is tugging me backwards, my eyes stay trained on Ringo, a beast unleashed, fury burning through every step he takes towards the fleeing man.

Catching the guy mid-sprint, Ringo grabs him from behind and slams him to the floor.

He mutters a plea to Ringo, but he doesn't care. He just sneers, raises his gun at the man and fires.

The shot cracks like a whip, snapping me out of the haze of bloodlust, the sounds of screaming nurses and patients filling my ears as the world rushes back in.

The smell of gunpowder and blood overpowers the usual hospital smell, and for a long moment, I just stare at the carnage.

The four dead men sprawled on the floor. The pools of blood puddling the linoleum. The patterns of blood splatter on the walls and doors.

Then my gaze finds Ringo. Tall. Muscles coiling beneath his vest, his arms weapons of their own.

He's something else.

Something beautiful and vicious.

Something deadly.

The moment his glare snaps to me, I flinch, feeling the lethal threat behind his eyes.

He's pissed. At me.

I realise I'm no longer being dragged backwards, and I can't feel JD's presence at my back. He's left me to fend for myself with his best mate, and I get the feeling I should be terrified.

But I'm not.

Because I know that monster.

He's mine.

Even as Ringo steps over the dead bodies and storms towards me like he wants to tear me to shreds, I don't flinch.

"You could've gotten killed!" he snarls, and I huff.

"*You* could have gotten killed."

His furious eyes narrow. "The fuck is wrong with you?!"

I shrug, cold and detached. "Ohhh, I don't know. I'm kinda feeling a bit pissy since, you know, *my baby died.*"

Ringo shakes his head, and for a flicker of a moment, I see it in his eyes.

Disappointment.

"*This* isn't you. You're not this person, Angel."

"Aren't I?" I shrug. "Kinda feels like a good fit to me."

A deep, menacing growl reverberates in his chest, but I ignore it and spin on my heel, walking away like the blood painting the floor means nothing.

JD and Jols are frozen, staring wide-eyed at me like I've grown horns.

And maybe I have.

"I assume we're leaving now?" I snap, brushing past them and hearing JD mutter a faint, "Yeah," like he's not sure if he's talking to me, or the monster I've become.

6

RINGO

Five days. That's all it's been since Bobbi died, yet it feels like weeks, because every passing minute that my Angel isn't herself is another minute I'm watching her slip further away.

She has every right to be angry. To want vengeance. To demand justice.

But I never imagined those broken words she whispered to her dead baby meant that she was literally going to take that justice into her own hands. I figured she'd want someone else to do the killing for her.

Shit.

I was expecting some sort of remorse after killing that Rebel. Tears. Guilt. Something for taking the life of another human. And while she *has* fallen in a heap, it's not because she killed that Rebel fucker.

It's because I won't let her leave. Because I refuse to let her go out and kill more.

"She talking to you yet?" Jols asks, handing me a steaming cup of coffee as I sit on the deck of the lake house we've been hiding out in.

It's a Marx safe house, just a few doors down from Griffin's digs.

Redfield Lake is calm. There are no boats on the water nearby. Probably because it's fucking cold out here.

But fuck, it's colder inside. Colder in the bedroom upstairs. The one I'm supposed to be sharing with Abbey.

"Barely." I grunt, blowing on the steam before taking a scalding sip.

Fuck, Jols makes a good coffee.

"Maybe after Bobbi's funeral, she'll start to come around." Jols offers a glimmer of hope, but fuck, I'm just not sure there is any.

"What if she's gone?" I rasp, dragging my gaze from the still water to where Jols sits in the other rickety deck chair, sipping her own brew.

She takes a long moment to respond, her eyes dropping to her cup as she considers my question.

"It hasn't even been a week. She just needs time."

I grunt. "How much time?"

Her brows hitch. "I don't know. How much time did you need?"

My gaze falls away from hers at the reminder. "There's no amount of time."

Sighing, Jols settles back into the chair, ignoring the way it wobbles like it's ready to give out.

"Exactly. This isn't something you recover from. She'll be forever changed because of this."

My eyes flick back to hers. "I don't want her to change. I want my sweet wife back."

Sympathy washes over Jols' face. "This isn't about you, though. This is about her. What she lost. Her grief. How she comes out on the other side might be influenced a little by those who rally around her, but ultimately… it's all on her."

I stare at my friend for a long moment.

How the fuck is she only twenty-four? She's too young to have this sort of life knowledge, but then again, you don't run with an outlaw MC unless you've had it rough.

I know she's had a fucking tough time of it. Her attack and the medical issues that followed. Learning how to trust men again after being torn apart.

Why the fuck is life so hard?

"So you think I should let her go on her so-called killing spree?" I ask, the thought alone making me want to fucking puke.

"Hell no. She'll get herself killed in the first five minutes." Jols scoffs, taking another long sip of her steaming drink. "But maybe it's worth thinking about inviting her to go with you."

I shake my head, eyes drifting back to the lake.

"I don't want her to kill anyone else. One day, she might snap out of this rage and drown in her regret." I glance back at Jols. "She's got a big heart. Too big. She'll never be able to forgive herself for taking lives."

"So don't let her. Do the killing yourself, or most of it, anyway." Jols shrugs, voice calm like we're talking about groceries instead of murder. "But let her see it. Let her know it's happening. Give her the closure she thinks she needs."

I nod at that. It's a better option than her pulling the trigger again, yet I can't help but worry.

What if, when her head clears, she looks at me and sees the man who became her weapon?

I guess that's still a better option though.

Better for her to hate what she sees in *me* rather than what she sees when she looks in the mirror.

Finishing my coffee, I head back inside, taking a moment to rinse my cup and leave it on the dish drainer before heading upstairs.

There are two bedrooms up here in the attic-style house.

One room Jols is using, and the other is meant to be for me and my wife… But in the three days we've been holed up here, there's been nothing remotely marital about it.

As I always do, I tap lightly on the door before slipping inside. I don't know why I do it. It's my room too, but fuck, I don't feel welcome in it.

My eyes fall to the bed, and the lump under the blankets.

Abbey is hiding again. Wrapped up tight like the world can't touch her if she stays buried deep enough.

She's been sleeping her days away. Or at least, pretending to so she can avoid interacting with everyone.

With me.

I get it. I really fucking do. But watching her disappear like this is fucking breaking me.

I don't want to lose her. Not when I only just found her. Not when, for the first time in years, she's the reason I feel *alive*.

Jols is right, though.

This isn't about me.

This is about Abbey.

Her pain. Her way of coping.

Moving around the bed, her face is mostly hidden under the blankets, eyes closed, but her lids are twitching, like she's really awake and is pretending to be asleep.

Sliding down the wall, I sit on the floor beside the bed, my back resting against the cool plaster as I stare at her face.

Then she sighs and slowly blinks her eyes open.

"I can feel you staring."

I smirk, but it's barely there. It's too fucking hard to pretend right now.

Her caramel stare is lifeless. Like the light in her orbs has been snuffed out.

"How are you feeling about killing that man?" I ask quietly, and she rolls her eyes.

"The same way I felt the ten other times you asked me," she mutters, shifting slightly under the blankets, and for a second, I think she is going to roll away, but all she does is bunch the pillow under the side of her face a little more.

Good. She's not pushing me away just yet.

"Do you understand *why* I'm asking you?"

She just shrugs at my question.

"The Abbey I knew a week ago would be struggling with taking someone's life." I point out, my voice soft, but the truth of it hits hard.

"The Abbey you knew a week ago is gone." Her tone is flat. So matter-of-fact. And fuck, her words slice through me like a fucking blade.

My face falls at her honesty, but I don't like it one fucking bit.

"So what?" I snap. "Now human life is worthless? Expend-able?"

Again, she rolls her eyes. "Of course not. Only the ones that deserve to die."

I lean forward a little, my tone low and steady. "And who deserves to die?"

She sits up quickly, taking me by surprise, and starts reeling off the names like she's been keeping a list in her head.

I guess it's no different from the list I asked her to write out for me when I first took her.

"Ian Allen, Donny, Daniel, maybe his dad, Darnel, Minister Banes, all of Ian Allen's cronies, the Satan's Rebels… oh and my mum, maybe my dad and sister Maggie."

Fuck.

She has put way too much thought into this.

"You want to kill your sister?"

She nods. No hesitation.

"Mags is too far gone. Her first instinct was to drug me at that chapel so I'd stop fighting when my mum wanted to shove me into a wedding dress. She *helped* those men hold me down so my mum could get it on me." Her voice is low, fast, and dripping with venom. "I tried to tell her the church is a cult, but she wouldn't hear it. She's just like my mum. Doesn't see what Daniel and his friends did as rape. And then…" She throws her arms up in the air, her eyes wide in disbelief. "Then she offered herself up to marry Daniel instead of me after they found out I was already married. There was this whole weird discussion on bloodlines, and who the real father is… like they need to know who he is because *only he* can marry Maggie in my place, since Maggie shares the same blood as me."

"The fuck?"

"I know, right?" she snaps, eyes blazing.

As fucked up as this conversation is, my heart fucking thrashes just knowing she's finally talking to me.

"None of what that church has done is right," she says, voice shaky but gaining strength, "but it wasn't until I heard that conversation that I really realised it's truly a cult. And they wanted my baby, Ringo. They wanted her for whatever fucked-up ceremony they were talking about. And I don't think it was a wedding."

"What?" I frown, shifting to my knees, moving to the edge of the mattress. And fuck, when she doesn't shift away, that gives me hope that what we had is still there. "Do you think they were talking about… some sort of sacrifice or something?"

"I don't know." Her voice trembles as her gaze falls distant, like she's trying to recall the memories. "Maggie said she'd sacrifice herself for the family…" Her eyes go wide and her breath catches. "You don't think she meant… I mean, I thought she was referring to becoming a wife, but what if it was more than that? What if *I* was meant to be the sacrifice… or Bobbi was?"

I stare at my Angel for a long beat, my eyes wide with the horror of what she's saying. It's just too unbelievable to even consider, but fuck, isn't that exactly how cults work? Twisting the sickest shit into some kind of holy order?

"I want to say it's absurd," I admit quietly as our eyes meet, "but the truth is… I don't fucking know."

She nods. "Same."

Her brows pull together as she sinks into thought again.

"I wonder why they're still after me," she murmurs. "They came to the hospital to take me, not kill me. But why?" Her voice cracks. "Do they know Bobbi is…"

She doesn't finish that sentence, and I don't blame her.

Even on the best days, saying the words out loud is like a fucking knife to the centre of your chest.

"Whatever. It doesn't matter," she mutters, voice flat. "They are bad people. And they must die."

Staring into her caramel gaze, I watch as whatever light had flickered in there moments ago, snuffs out again.

"I agree." I nod. "They must, which is why I have a proposal for you."

Her brows lift slightly, the smallest spark of curiosity catching in her eyes.

"I know you want to kill them yourself, but it's too dangerous. So here's what I'm thinking. You use *me* as your weapon. We hunt them down *together*. And you watch while I make them pay. Every last one of them."

She's silent for a long beat, just staring at me. Her caramel eyes remain fused to my face like she's trying to read between the lines. Trying to figure out if there's a lie in them.

Then she speaks.

"I want to be the one to kill Daniel, Donny, Darnel and Ian Allen *myself*."

"But—"

"Take it or leave it," she cuts me off, and I frown.

"I get Daniel, Donny and Darnel. They raped you. But why Ian? Why *him* too?"

The moment her eyes cloud over, glassy and distant, my gut fucking sinks.

Dread barrels into me like an eighteen-hundred-pound bull.

"We can add him to the list of my rapists now," she says, voice trembling, yet her glare is pure ice. "He told me he wanted to know what all the fuss was about… then tag-teamed his nephew in to have at me next."

My blood turns to fucking ice.

"No."

"Yes," she snarls. "They all wanted one last piece of me before I was married off to Daniel." She shivers, full-bodied, like the memory is crawling across her skin.

A roar rips from me as I lurch to my feet.

Abbey gasps, whimpering, and scurrying back on the bed as I spin and slam my fist into the wall, the plaster crumbling from the force of my punch with a sickening crack.

I spin, storming across the room to the chair I've sat in every fucking night, trying to keep myself from crawling into bed with her, to give her the space she needs, and I heft the fucking thing up, and hurl it across the room.

It shatters to pieces, slamming into the far wall, splintering wood and tearing through the plaster like paper.

The bedroom door bursts open, and JD hurries in just in time for me to take a swing at him.

He ducks my fist, but I don't stop.

I can't stop.

I need to hurt someone, and I need to fucking hurt them *now*.

7

ABBEY

S tanding by the windows in the living room, I stare out across the deck of the lake house to the twin rustic bathtubs, both of them occupied, a man in each soaking in steamy sudsy water like it's perfectly normal to take a bath outside in full view. Their backs are to me, and I can hear the deep baritone of their voices as they talk and laugh.

One of them is Brody, and to be honest, I'm relieved to see him. I had no idea what happened after Ian Allen drugged me in Ringo's bedroom. For all I knew, they'd killed everyone before taking off with me.

But here he is. JD's little brother, laughing and joking like the world isn't shattering around us.

I guess it isn't shattering around him.

Only me.

There's nothing right about any of this. That's the only thing I know for sure.

The other guy, I'm pretty sure, is the one who tattooed our names on our fingers on our wedding day. Vender, I think his name is.

There's another guy I don't recognise, sitting out on the deck, handing Brody a beer from a cooler, and the rest of the men are sprawled out, talking shit and acting like this is just another typical Tuesday.

Stocky, Murf and Trunk are among them, and seeing their familiar faces is the slightest comfort.

Mule isn't here, though. The man that watched over me when Ringo left me behind at his family home. My silent shadow. I wonder where he is. Did he get out unscathed, or is he… one of the dead?

The thought makes me feel sick. No one deserved to die, but some did.

I just don't know who. I haven't made the effort to ask, and I don't know if it's because I just can't bear any more suffering, or if I just don't care.

I guess I'll find out tomorrow when we go to the compound. When the club will gather to farewell their dead in joint funerals.

I don't really want to go, but I probably should. They died because of me. The least I can do is honour their sacrifice.

Ringo hasn't noticed me standing here, watching them like they're characters on a TV screen.

He's over by the railing, his knuckles still torn up, dried blood crusted over the scabs forming after he lost his shit yesterday.

I don't blame him. I'm not angry at him for losing control like that. I'm kind of jealous I couldn't do the same.

He didn't like hearing about what Ian did to me, and well… I didn't like living through it.

Just another memory I have to try to suppress I suppose.

JD has a bruise blooming under his left eye from one of the few hits Ringo managed to land. I'd been worried they were about to have a full punch-on, but JD simply tried to wrangle his best mate, and with Murf's help, they dragged him off somewhere to cool down.

I haven't seen him since… until now.

Maybe… maybe the thought of how many men have fucked me is too much for him.

Maybe I'm nothing but damaged goods, and now he's trying to figure out how to cut his losses.

Maybe he's finally realising I'm not worth all the shit I've brought down on him and his club.

He'd be right.

"You gonna go out and join them?"

Jols' voice startles me, and I spin to see her taking the last step down from the staircase.

I shake my head.

"Don't worry about Brody and Vender. You've seen both of them naked before at the Western," she points out with a shrug, and I turn back to peer out at Ringo.

As if he can feel me watching, his eyes flick up to lock with mine, and I wait for some kind of emotion to show on his face.

There's nothing… Just a blank, unreadable stare.

"I think I'm gonna go lie down," I mumble, turning away from the dark gaze I wish could still love me despite everything. Despite how tainted I am.

As I pass Jols, her hand snaps out, gripping my arm and stopping me in my tracks.

"I'm not gonna pretend I know what you're going through," she states, levelling her blue eyes with mine. "But remember back at the Western? When you realised there was something I *could* understand? That I'd been through something similar, too? That we bonded over it?"

Slowly, I nod, the burn at the back of my eyes threatening to give me away.

"Yeah. So?"

"Well, I might not understand what you're going through right now," she releases my arm, turning to face me fully, "but there's someone who does. Maybe not exactly, because everyone's experience is their own, but he's standing right outside."

Her gaze flicks to the window and mine follows, landing on him.

Ringo.

"Ringo's been patient with you. He's taken care of you. He's fought for you. He knows what it's like to lose a child. He had to bury his little girl. Had to witness the vulgar way she was brought into this world. He never got to hold her while she was still alive." She sighs, her eyes falling distant, like she's remembering a time a few years before I even met him.

"I'm not saying his situation is more tragic." Her eyes shift back to mine as I try to swallow the thick lump forming in my throat. "But I am saying that he knows. He understands. And he loves you. Ringo would do anything for you. But he can't if you keep pushing him away."

"I'm not pushing him away," I snap, frowning, but then, a twist of dread coils in my stomach. "Am I?"

"You are," she says without hesitation. "You're drowning in your anger. And yeah, it's fucking valid. Without a doubt. But just don't forget that you've got people who care about you. People who *love* you and want to help." Jols rakes her fingers through her sleek, dark hair, another sigh escaping her like it's been trapped in her chest for too long.

"Life is fucking hard on a good day, Abbey. And what happened to you… well, there aren't words big enough for how incredibly unfair and tragic it is. For the way your parents have treated you. For what those men did to you. And now, losing Bobbi too? That's a different kind of hell." Jols pauses, her eyes softening, and it's not until now that I feel tears trickling down my cheeks.

"But life can still be good. Just look at Ringo. He somehow managed to keep going after Hope died. He found a purpose. Something to live for, and he held on with both hands, even when he thought he wasn't strong enough anymore. And then… one day, out of the blue, he kidnapped a blonde girl covered in blood." Her lips twitch into a ghost of a smile. "And he fell in love with her."

My throat thickens as fresh tears well in my eyes, my heart hurting for a different reason. A reason that isn't all about Bobbi.

"So maybe you could take some time to focus on what you *still* have." She nods her head towards the window, and my gaze follows, landing on Ringo again. "You've lost something massive, Abbey. A piece of your heart that will never heal, but you still have something worth living for."

She points out the window before reaching down to give my hand a squeeze, the simple gesture nearly breaking me.

"You still have friends. You still have a little sister who needs you. There's a whole world waiting for you… if you'd just let it in."

Shit.

She's right. I know she is, yet I can't make myself admit that out loud.

Tahli still needs me. She's not safe with my parents. Not in that church. Not with Maggie so brainwashed, determined to sacrifice everything for the cult.

I've got Lexi, and Jared, and Marcus. And the other guys, too.

I have new friends I never expected. Like Jols, standing right here, refusing to let me hide.

And then there's Ringo.

He's something else entirely.

"Where did Ringo sleep last night?" I ask instead of admitting my feelings, and her brows shoot up. "Because after he lost it, I didn't see him again. Did he leave? Go somewhere?"

Her face falls. "JD and Vender took him to Griffin's. A few houses down."

"He hates me now," I whisper, my eyes dropping to my feet like maybe the floor will swallow me whole.

"No, he doesn't. He's not avoiding you because he hates you," she says softly. "He's avoiding you because he thinks *he failed you*. He blames himself for not protecting you. For putting the club first."

My eyes flick back up to hers.

"He didn't know what was going to happen."

"No, but it doesn't make him blame himself any less." She reaches out and gives my shoulder a squeeze.

"You two need to talk. I think you'll find you're actually both on the same page."

Is she right?

Are we on the same page?

Does he still… care for me?

A few days ago, I would have said it didn't matter if he did or not. I was too far gone after waking up to learn about Bobbi's death. Too far gone when I switched something off inside me and killed a man.

But seeing him flip out yesterday, and having this conversation with Jols… well, now I'm not sure about anything I thought I knew.

When Jols excuses herself and heads outside to join the guys, I consider following. Just walking out there and pretending I'm part of their world again… but my feet won't move in that direction.

There's music and chatter and laughter, and I just can't be around happiness right now.

What is there to be happy about?

Why is the world still turning when my version of it has stopped, frozen in time, caught in the vicious loop of memories I can't outrun?

Holding my little girl… and then being told she is dead.

It's a never-ending reel in my head.

Not able to deal with anything else right now, I go upstairs and sleep most of the day. It's easier than sitting in silence, trapped in my own thoughts.

I want to go on a killing spree and tear the world apart. But I know I'm not ready.

Not physically, at least.

I'm still bleeding. My breasts are sore and engorged, because even though Bobbi died, my milk has still come in, and I don't know what to do about that.

Who do I even ask? Should I even do something?

I've thought about asking to borrow someone's phone to call Ayden's mum, Andrea, but I just can't bring myself to go through all the questions or hear the sympathy in her voice.

I just… can't.

So instead of dealing with all of that, I sleep.

It's a little after 11pm when I wake again, hungry, but not enough to want to eat once I remember Bobbi is gone, leaving me to live in this harsh reality.

The room is empty. Ringo still hasn't come to me, and I'm beginning to think Jols didn't know what she was talking about.

If he truly cared, he'd be here… right?

Shit, what do I know?

Getting out of bed, I check over the black clothes Jols gave me yesterday to wear to the Southern Sadists' funerals tomorrow. Now that my bump has somewhat deflated, it's easier to fit into her things, even though they are still a little snug and nowhere near the style of anything I would normally choose for myself.

But as I look at the black leather, I have to admit, right now, they match the darkness swirling through my veins like thick, suffocating smoke.

Black is the colour of mourning, after all.

Moving to the window, I glance down at the far corner of the back deck to see if the guys are still out there, but it's all dark and silent, like everyone has already gone to bed.

My heart sinks.

Ringo's not here.

He's not sleeping with me again.

Maybe I really have pushed him away for good.

That thought cuts deeper than I expected. More painful than I can handle, and I realise I really do *need* Ringo.

I need his love. His strength. His stupid protective growl and the way his hands soften when they touch me like I'm something fragile.

I need him.

Even more than that… I *want* him.

"Where are you?" I whisper into the dark room, and as if I've conjured him out of thin air, I spot the silhouette of a man standing down on the bank, by the water.

My heart does a little flip. The kind I felt weeks ago when my world hadn't completely crumbled.

But then… it sinks to the pit of my gut as I watch him stagger to his knees like his legs aren't strong enough to hold him up anymore, his hands fisting in his hair like he's trying to rip the strands from the roots.

I spin, my heart hammering as I run from the room, taking two steps at a time, ignoring the snore coming from the couch as I dash past.

My fingers fumble with the latch on the glass door a few times before it releases, and I slide it open, bolting out into the night.

My heart, the one I thought dead only minutes ago, thrashes wildly in my chest as I race across the deck and down the steps, the icy chill of the damp grass soaking my bare feet as I start running across the yard.

As I get closer, my feet slow. The sound of gut-wrenching sobs rips through the quiet, so raw and broken as he kneels, slumped and defeated on the sandy bank of the lake.

This…

This is pure heartbreak.

My own sob works its way up my throat, but I hold it in, totally crushed to see… to hear the strongest man I know, completely falling apart.

Did I do that to him?

Did I break his heart?

"C-Cam?" I breathe, but he must hear, his panicked, tear-soaked eyes snap up, locking to mine just a few metres away.

"Angel?" he chokes out, and the sob I was holding in rips from me as I launch forward just as he stands.

He catches me, like he always does, wrapping me up as I throw myself into his arms.

"I'm so sorry." I cry into his neck, clinging to him like I'm drowning. "I didn't mean to be such a bitch."

My legs wrap around his middle as he lifts me, holding me like he'll never let go.

"I'm sorry I'm so *damaged*. Please don't hate me. Please don't give up on me."

"*Fuck,* Angel," he rasps into my hair. "I love you. I'll never hate you. I'll never give up on you."

I pull back, stunned by his declaration.

"You… you really love me?" I ask, not sure if I heard him right, because surely he doesn't.

Not after everything I've put him through.

He holds me tight, one arm locked around me, the other hand cradling my face like I'm precious.

"I really fucking love you, Abbey. I know it doesn't make sense. The short time, the age difference… fucking everything that's happened. But fuck, why does it have to make sense? It feels more right than anything I've ever felt."

Tears pour down my cheeks as I stare into his eyes, or what I can see of them in the faint light coming from the jetty.

"I love you, too," I whisper. "I think I have for a while now, but I was too scared to tell you. I thought you'd just see me as young and dumb."

"Fucking never," he rasps, shaking his head. "There's *nothing* dumb about you. You're fucking *everything*."

Another sob lurches from my lips, right before he claims them.

It's a wet, salty kiss, laced with grief and suffering, but also, a thread of something else too.

Something like hope. Like maybe we aren't too far gone.

Our tongues clash, hungry and desperate, like they're fighting for more.

More of what? I don't know, but I just know I need him.

I need to crawl under his skin, wrap myself around his soul, and *stay there*. Forever.

When Ringo pulls back, I whimper, and his thumbs brush over my cheeks, wiping away the mess of tears like he wants to erase my pain.

"Can I come to bed, Angel?" His voice breaks as he speaks, his emotions still raw. "Can I hold you in my arms tonight?"

I nod frantically. "Please."

"*Fuck*," he breathes, pressing his forehead to mine. "I thought I'd fucking lost you. I didn't know how to get you back."

"I'm sorry," I whisper. "I'm still here. Kind of."

Easing back just enough to see my face, he nods.

"I know things aren't the same. Your life has changed forever. But maybe… hopefully, we can find a new normal. Together."

I gulp.

I want that. I want him. But every time I think of Bobbi, I can't see how I'm meant to go on.

So, I just nod.

Not because I'm trying to reassure him… I can't. But because I simply don't know what my future even looks like.

Right now, there's nothing but darkness. And it's hard to see a way out of that.

But here with him, there's a spark of something I'm going to hold on to.

I have to do that.

For him.

For Bobbi.

For myself.

Carrying me across the grass in silence, Ringo takes me back inside and up to the bedroom. I reluctantly release my grip around his neck as he lowers me to the bed, watching his large frame move quietly through the room as he retrieves a towel.

His eyes meet mine as he kneels at the edge of the bed, before drying and cleaning my feet like I'm something sacred, and once he's done, he helps me slip under the blankets.

I watch him in the faint glow coming from the night light in the corner, my eyes transfixed on him as he toes off his boots and strips down to his boxers before crawling in beside me.

I'm nervous as he settles in, worried he might want more. That he might want sex.

I just gave birth six days ago, and from the little I *do* know, I have to wait at least six weeks for that.

Will he feel like I'm pushing him away again if I refuse him?

I don't want him to feel rejected, but thankfully, he doesn't try anything. He simply pulls me to his side, tucking me close, and wraps his arms around me.

Even though my heart mostly hurts like a dagger keeps stabbing it over and over, when I'm with him like this, it doesn't hurt quite as much.

"Cam?" I whisper as we lie tangled together, our foreheads nearly touching.

"Angel?"

"I know Bobbi is gone… but it doesn't feel real." I glance up, finding his eyes already on me. "I still feel her…" I take his hand and press it to my heart. "Right here."

"Because that's where she lives now." He gently strokes the valley between my breasts where I held my daughter just days ago. "She will always be there. No matter where she is, she will always be wrapped in your love."

"Yeah," I breathe. "I guess you're right." I leave my hand over his as he strokes the skin over my heart. "Cam?"

"Yeah, Angel?"

"My tits really hurt."

He stiffens, and I glance back up at him, catching the look of mild panic in his eyes.

"My milk has come in… and I don't know what I'm meant to do about it."

"Oh." He shifts slowly, pulling his hand away. "Fuck… I don't really know about any of that stuff."

I nod. "Me either. I thought about calling Andrea, but I just can't deal with having a conversation about everything. I don't want to hear her say how sorry she is." I swallow thickly. "Does that make me a bigger bitch?"

"*Fuck no*, Abs. You're not a bitch at all. Not even close." He pauses, clearing his throat. "How about I give her a call in the morning? I'll do most of the talking."

My lips twitch a little wider, and shit, I think it's a hint of a smile.

"Thank you."

"Of course, Angel."

We fall silent, but we continue to stare at each other.

I know he's years and years older than me, but he doesn't make me feel it.

He makes me feel like his equal. Most of the time.

And God. The things he's done to protect me. To save me. To *kill* for me.

"Were you crying because of me?" I dare to ask, remembering how he fell to his knees out by the lake, like life was too heavy to carry.

"Truth?" he asks, his eyes searching mine, and I nod.

"Please."

"Yes, mostly."

His head dips, eyes falling like he can't stand for me to see the truth on his face.

"I'm sorry," I whisper, feeling the stab of guilt. "I never meant to treat you so badly."

He shakes his head, jaw tight.

"I can handle you lashing out at me, Angel. What I couldn't handle was knowing I failed you. Knowing that cunt Allen, raped you."

My throat locks up, burning, and it takes me a few tries to swallow it down, just enough to speak.

"You didn't fail me," I say, my voice scratchy, but he just shrugs, eyes still cast down.

"I just want to protect you. Stop all this bad shit from happening, but I can't seem to get a grip on anything long enough to make it stick."

His eyes flick back up to mine, and there's something dark in them now. Something I don't recognise.

"I… need to tell you something," he rasps, his voice rough as his brows pucker, and I stiffen.

I don't like how that sounds, and I know whatever it is, I'm not going to like it.

"Tell me what?" I manage to ask, even though my heart is hammering.

He sighs, remaining quiet for a moment like he's stalling, or trying to figure out how to put his words together.

Shit. Maybe I *don't* want to hear this.

"I found out who gave up your location to Allen. The one who set the ambush on the compound in motion. And your kidnapping… all of it."

I bolt upright in bed, my eyes wide as I stare down at him.

"*Someone* gave up my location? I thought… I just assumed they tracked me somehow."

I'd never really thought about it before. I just knew Ringo left, and they came.

"Yeah. They found you because of…" he trails off, and rage flares in my chest, my fists clenched tight as I fight the urge to punch the truth out of him.

"Who?" I snap. "Who was it?"

He sits up, although he takes his sweet arse time, shifting back to lean against the headboard.

"Cam?!" I practically yell, my voice breaking with frustration.

He blows out a breath and sighs, his eyes deadly serious as he parts his lips.

"It was Wendy."

I stop breathing.

I don't move.

I just stare at him.

Because did he just say…

"Wendy?" I echo, my voice a little screechy.

"Yes, Angel. Wendy called the police tip line and got put through to Allen."

For a long, drawn-out moment, all I can do is stare at him, completely stunned.

I knew she didn't like me. The feeling was mutual, but oh man, I didn't think she'd ever stoop to *that*.

But shit. She did. She actually did. That's what he's saying, right?

Wendy told Officer Allen where I was.

She gave me up to get me out of the way.

"Are you… fucking serious?!" I snarl, rage bubbling in my gut, fighting to be set free.

"Yes, Angel. I'm so fucking sorry." He reaches for me, but I shrug back, too consumed by my fury.

"Where is she?"

His hand drops heavy to the bed, his body sagging with exhaustion, like talking about her drains the life out of him.

"She's chained up like a dog at the compound."

Is he… serious?

"She is?"

"Yes," he nods.

"Like a dog? Like, actually chained up on all fours?"

"Yes."

Jesus… that's… wait.

Why is she still alive?

"I thought you would have killed her," I admit, my eyes dropping to his fists, twisted in the sheets like he's struggling to hold himself together.

"Trust me. I fucking wanted to."

I study him for a long moment.

This big, broody man who wants to protect me so fiercely. The man who nearly lost his shit on our wedding day when he found out the lies Wendy spat.

The man who *wanted to kill her*.

"Why didn't you?" I ask, trying to pull back on my snappy tone.

"I'll tell you, but can you at least come here?" He pats his lap. "I can feel you pulling away again."

Frowning, I glance down at the mattress, to the space I've put between us.

Shit. I didn't even realise I'd moved.

I hate that I did it. Hate that my head is so messed up that I didn't even notice.

Crawling forward, I straddle his lap, feeling his strong hands grip my hips like he's scared I'll disappear.

Eye to eye, we stare at each other, my hands gliding up his arms to settle over the thick, tense muscles of his biceps.

"I'm sorry," I murmur. "I'm here. I promise."

Leaning forward, doing what he loves to do, he presses his forehead to mine.

"I've fucking *missed* you."

Shit. The pain in his voice is like a punch to the chest.

He must have been frantic when he found out I was taken. He must have felt so helpless.

"I've missed you too," I admit, and he pulls me in for another hug.

His arms squeeze me to him, his nose nuzzling in my hair, and I think I hear him sniff me.

Under any other circumstances, I'd call him out on it. Tease him a little. But that's not where we are at right now.

Right now, we are sharing the darkness.

After a moment, he eases back slowly, like it physically hurts to let go. Then he clears his throat, those dark eyes locking with mine.

"There were a couple of reasons I didn't kill Wendy," he starts. "The first was because I needed to make sure the location she gave us to find you was legit. She was our only lead. I couldn't risk it. I had to keep her alive until I had you back."

I nod. It makes sense.

"And after you knew she told the truth?" I press. "Why didn't you kill her then?"

"I've been keeping her alive for you," he admits, his hands slowly roaming over my back like he can't handle the idea of not touching me. "Killing her… that would have been easy. And a quick death would have been a mercy. She doesn't fucking deserve mercy."

A chill ripples up my spine at the venom in his tone. Sometimes it's easy to forget that Ringo is a killer when he can be so gentle with me.

"I needed her to live in pain. To fucking feel it. Every day. So, I kept her alive for *you*."

"For… me?" I echo, and he nods.

"Yes."

"Why?" I ask, completely confused.

"So you can be the one to kill her. If that's what you want."

I blink, and my heart stumbles.

"But I thought you insisted on being my weapon?" I frown, my head tilting as I study his face.

"I did. But I didn't want to take that away from you if it's something you *needed* to do." He sighs, blowing out a breath, his fingers grazing up my back until his hand cups my nape. "But Angel, I don't want you to do it. Killing someone… It's something you can never undo. You'll live with it for the rest of your life. Shit… just knowing I couldn't stop you from killing that Rebel at the hospital…" He trails off like he can't fathom what will happen to my soul now.

His grip on my nape tightens, and a low growl rumbles in his chest.

"I need to be the one to carry that burden for you, Abs. That's what I'm built for. Please let me kill Wendy. You can watch. You can tell me exactly how you want it done. I'll make her suffer for what she did. But I just don't want you to have to carry something like that."

It's too late for me. I already killed that man at the hospital, and honestly, I'm not even sorry.

Maybe that makes me a bad person, but I used to be good. I used to be fair and kind, but those parts of me died with my daughter.

Nodding, I lean in closer, nestling into his chest, soaking in his warmth as his arms come around me.

"Okay," I whisper.

It's a lie.

I love Ringo for trying to save my soul, but the truth is, it died last week with Bobbi.

Wendy *will* die tomorrow, and it *will* be by my hands.

8

RINGO

"The Rebel isn't talking, but one of the pigs has started squealing." Griffin smirks, his stance wide and arms crossed over his chest as he stands next to me.

Four black SUVs sit in the driveway, and Marx Security hang back on the sidelines while I chat with Griffin. His crew has been working in the background, interrogating a Rebel and two dirty cops who won't see the light of day again once they're done.

They were grabbed by Griffin's security team at that cult chapel we raided to get to Abbey, and after everything that went down with Abs… well, I was fucking grateful Griffin's team offered to take over. It gave me the space to focus on my Angel and her grief.

"What did he say?" I mutter, flicking a glance over my shoulder at the lake house, waiting for Jols and Abbey to emerge.

"He coughed up the location of a safe house Allen has been using. I've got a team monitoring it now, but so far, there's no movement." Griffin's gaze shifts past me, his brows hitching. "Fuck. That your girl?"

I glance back over my shoulder as Jols steps down from the porch with Abbey trailing behind, and for a fucking moment, I swear, everything stops.

"My wife," I correct absentmindedly, and Griffin mutters a quiet, "Yeah."

I've got tunnel vision. That's the only way I can fucking explain how everything else around me fades until all that's left is my blonde Angel.

Although the sweet girl I call Angel looks more like a sinner right now, dressed head to toe in black. Leather pants slick and tight like they are painted on, hugging every curve. She's got more meat on her now, the little pregnancy weight she carried only making her more woman than I've ever seen.

How the fuck didn't I notice that before?

Sure, she's been in sweatpants and drowning in my oversized t-shirts since we left the hospital, but fuck, I never pictured this.

"Close your mouth. You're drooling," Jols snickers as she passes me, snapping me out of my fucking trance.

"Pretty sure every man here is," Griffin chuckles, and my fucking scowl cuts straight to his security team, who are, in-fucking-fact, practically drooling.

"Eyes off!" I bark, and they all stiffen, snapping their heads away as boots crunch over gravel, getting closer to me.

"Why are you yelling at them?" Abbey asks, and my eyes find her sharp glare.

Fuck. Even her glare is hot.

She looks so fucking different wearing the gear Jols gave her. Leather pants. A black tee stretching a little too tight over those huge tits, engorged with milk—still can't wrap my head around that fact. And a black leather jacket that seals the whole fucking look.

Not to mention the boots. A pair of Jols' riding boots. Black. Stopping halfway up her calves, thick sole, chunky as hell, and fuck… has there been anything sexier?

Sure, stilettos and leather scream, fuck me, but a woman dressed to ride? That's fucking tough. And right now, my Angel looks like the sweetest sin there ever was with her blonde hair straight, but not too slick.

It kinda has that *'I didn't really try look'*, or *'I've just been fucked and didn't put much effort into fixing it'* look.

Fucking sexy as fuck.

"That's right, Angel. I'll yell at any fucker who drools over what's mine."

Her brows shoot up, like she's fucking surprised anyone would, but before I can say more to reassure her, JD clears his throat, butting in.

"Gotta hit the road, man."

I nod, clenching my jaw as Griffin lifts his hand, signalling his crew, and one by one, they pile into the SUVs.

"Do me the honour?" JD asks Jols, nodding to his hog.

She has her own ride, but club rules are club rules. Only brothers and prospects ride today, so she nods, and the two of them head over to his Harley.

"Saddle up, Angel," I rasp, needing to clear my throat, because fuck, I can't stop staring.

The way she looks dressed like this is fucking hot. Dangerous.

Nodding, Abbey grabs the helmet waiting on the back of my bike, slipping it on.

But fuck, I can't move… because my eyes drop to her arse in those leather pants, tight enough to have me about fucking ready to drop to my knees and worship her. My cock jolts awake for the first time since she was taken. Nearly two fucking weeks ago.

She spins, catching me staring as she fastens the helmet.

"What?" she snaps, still in the same mood she was when I woke this morning.

I'm not sure she even slept.

"Oh, nothing… just admiring how fucking edible your arse looks in those pants." I smirk, stepping over to my hog and grabbing my own helmet.

She rolls her eyes. "You wouldn't think that if you saw the nappy-sized pad I'm wearing to soak up all the blood I'm still bleeding."

I flinch.

Shit.

I hadn't thought about that at all. Very fucking far from it.

That alone would put anyone in a shit mood, let alone after everything she's been through.

"I'm sorry." I step up to her, fisting the front of her helmet near the mouth vent and tugging her closer, loving the little squeak of surprise that slips past her lips. "You're still fucking delicious, Angel. Now, be my good girl and get on my hog. I wanna feel you snuggled up behind me, pressing those tits against my back."

Her cheeks flare to life, and for a second, I catch a glimpse of my old Angel. The one from before. The one I used to talk dirty to without guilt clawing at my chest.

"What if the nipple pads Andrea dropped off this morning don't hold up? What if I start leaking milk?" she whispers, eyes darting around us like someone might hear, and I fucking grin.

"I'll lick you clean, Angel."

Her mouth forms an O as she stares, wide eyed at me, and I hope like hell Andrea was right when I spoke to her on the phone this morning.

She told me the best thing I can do is treat Abbey how I normally would. Don't treat her like she might break. Save that for the moments she does. She needs to feel some sort of normalcy to be able to get through each day, even if nothing is normal for her anymore.

It sounded like good advice at the time, but now I'm wondering if maybe I took it a little too far...

Did I really just tell her I'd lick up her leaking milk?

Fuck.

I did.

And fuck.

I don't exactly hate the thought of it.

Fuck... now my cock is like stone.

Pretending like I'm still that cocky fucker she met weeks ago, I shoot her a wink, and the corner of her mouth twitches, a slight grin tugging at her lips like muscle memory. But then, like she realises she was about to smile, it's gone. Her face drops, and she ducks her head, pretending to double-check her helmet.

Andrea told me that might happen too. And fuck, I get it. I remember that feeling all too well.

At first, I couldn't fucking fathom how anyone could laugh or joke or even enjoy a single fucking thing after Hope died. Then came the moments where I laughed or made a joke. Fuck, the guilt hit like a sledgehammer. How the fuck could I feel happy?

So I understand that part, and I hate that my Angel has to suffer through that as well.

We mount up, our hogs roaring to life before we follow two of the SUVs, JD's hog next to mine with Jols on the back like that's exactly where she belongs.

Trailing behind us are Vender, Trigger, Brody, Trunk, Murf and Stocky, with the last two SUVs coming up the rear.

It's a twenty-minute ride from Redfield Lake to the new compound on the fringe of Fox Pines. We have a smooth run, not encountering any issues like rival clubs, cops, or fucking pandemic roadblocks.

The fucking urge to just keep riding is a huge fucking pull. What I'd give to be done with the bullshit of life and just hit the open road with my Angel's arms wrapped around me.

Fuck, we probably wouldn't get far if she was dressed like she is now in all that leather.

But today isn't about me.

Hell, it's not even about her.

Today is for the Southern Sadists MC, and our fallen brothers.

The Marx escort pulls up outside the compound gates, where they'll hold position for the day, clearing the road for us to enter.

Abbey's fingers dig into my cut as she stiffens behind me, and I can tell she's taking everything in as we ride down the long driveway in a silent procession. A low rumble of grief and honour.

The space in front of the barn, which we now call the yard, is packed. Club brothers are everywhere, all in their cuts, their bikes in a line on the far side, settled under the huge trees, out of the sun.

But it's the eight bikes parked in a row in the centre of the yard that hits the hardest.

Seeing them… remembering who we are here to farewell… puts a huge lump in my throat.

Fuck.

Pulling up, we park our rides with the others, our engines falling silent, one by one.

Dozens of eyes land on us as we dismount, and I see Abbey tense, her shoulders stiff the second she feels the weight of the crowd.

Lifting the visor, her tear-glazed eyes lock with mine.

"I don't know if I can do this," she whispers, and I step in close, making sure I'm the only thing she sees right now.

"Angel, you don't have to. If at any stage it gets too much, you can bow out. No one will question it. You can go inside the barn if you prefer."

Her lower lip trembles, and she shifts, peering past me towards the sea of Southern Sadists.

"They must all hate me," she whispers again, one tear escaping before she swipes it away through the visor.

"Trust me, they don't," I say, hoping she can hear the truth in my tone. "They are your family now, Angel. They've been worried sick over what happened to you and…" I trail off because fuck, even I can't bring myself to speak about her baby today.

She blows out a breath… and then another, like she's trying to gather every broken piece of her heart.

When her eyes lock with mine again, she gives me a nod, climbs off my hog, and tugs off her helmet.

Fuck me. What is it about a woman taking off a helmet and letting her hair tumble free?

"Where will they be buried?" she asks, setting her helmet on the back of my bike.

"No burials here, Angel. Our fallen have already been cremated. They'll rest forever in a memorial wall, just over by the big oak tree." I gesture across the yard, past the pool, to the massive tree.

"Oh…" she murmurs, and I turn to catch the frown pinching her brows. "I assumed your club would do a whole burial thing."

Leaning in conspiratorially, I smirk at her. "Cremation burns the evidence. No bodies. No DNA. No loose ends. No digging up our dead, Angel."

"But wouldn't you want the police to have the evidence to find whoever did it?"

I shake my head. "Yeah-nah. That's not how the Southern Sadists roll. We take care of shit ourselves. No pigs involved."

"You have them as allies, though. Like that police officer in Fox Pines." Her frown deepens, and fuck, it's cute.

"We've got some in our pocket. But we're outlaws, beautiful. We live by our own set of rules. Not theirs." Reaching out, I graze my fingers over her cheek before brushing her soft blonde strands behind her ear. "Sure, the pigs help when it suits us, but justice?" I shrug. "That's ours to serve."

Her caramel gaze flicks up to mine, and something like understanding flashes behind them.

She's starting to get it.

"Come on. I've got something to show you before the service starts." I take her hand, ignoring the stares we're getting, and lead her to the scrubby patch near the barn that reeks of stale piss.

She smells it immediately, pinching her nose as she cringes.

I chuckle.

"Are there no toilets here?" She sounds nasally with her fingers still closing off her nose.

"There are, but this is the sacred spot my brothers love to piss. Right where we usually keep the mangy dog tied up."

Her brows hitch, and she drops her hand from her nose, her eyes snapping to mine.

"You've been keeping Wendy here?"

I nod. "She gets this sweet aroma, day in, day out."

Abbey scoffs. "I wouldn't call it sweet." She shivers with another cringe. "It's fitting for that bitch, though."

This time, it's my brows that hike up, taking in the fire in her eyes as she glares down at the chain looped around a tree that Wendy is normally locked to.

The old Abbey would find this unacceptable. Probably would've lost it over seeing this, her soft, gentle heart not able to take such inhumane treatment. But that girl is gone now. I need to keep reminding myself of that.

A bike horn blares, and we both turn as the crowd starts moving around the motorcycles parked in the centre of the yard.

"Service is starting," I mutter, glancing down at my wife. "You wanna go into the barn?"

Eyeing the crowd, she pauses for a moment before shaking her head, and fuck, I didn't realise just how much I wanted her to stay. To stand beside me and honour my club brothers.

"They're dead because of me," she says, voice flat. "The least I can do is farewell them, too."

I want to correct her. They aren't dead because of her. I hate that she's blaming herself, so really, she doesn't have to farewell them out of obligation. But I'm a selfish fucker and reminding her that there's something bigger going on might talk her out of joining me for the service, meaning I'd be alone.

I never used to be bothered by that, but since meeting her… since marrying her, I realise I want her by my side for everything from now on.

I don't have to do things alone anymore.

So, instead of talking her out of it, I reach out and take her hand before leading her into the yard.

Joining my club, I feel Abbey's grip tighten in mine as Doxies offer her warm but sad smiles, and my brothers bow their heads, like she's royalty.

She's not the queen of our club, but she's my fucking queen, and they all know it.

They all respect it.

And they'd all bleed for her, because she's part of the Southern Sadists family now. And that fucking means something in this found family of ours.

Up the front, Smitty stands with his wife, Jols' mum, Maureen, and next to them, Spud has his arm wrapped around his old lady, as the two women quietly cry.

As we approach, Jols steps up and hugs her mum, her eyes finding us as she pulls back before doing a quick, quiet introduction.

"Mum, this is Abbey."

My Angel offers a nod. The kind that holds warmth and sympathy and a helluva lot of respect.

How she manages it given her own grief, I have no fucking clue.

Smitty and Spud each offer their condolences to my wife, pressing respectful kisses to her cheek.

Her palm is sweaty in mine, her grip tight, and there's a slight tremble running through it.

I can feel how on edge she is. I bet she's thinking about fleeing.

I wouldn't blame her. Her fucking daughter died a week ago today. The fact that she's even here says everything about how fucking strong she is.

Behind us, the eight motorbikes roar to life, and Abbey flinches, glancing over her shoulder, confusion pinching her brow.

She has no clue what will happen at a Southern Sadists funeral, but she doesn't ask any questions. She simply shifts a little closer and takes it all in.

Another engine fires up in front of us, and we glance past Smitty to see the hearse bike.

There are no coffins in it, only boxes. Eight of them. Holding the ashes of our fallen brothers.

Abbey's trembling grows stronger as the reality of today's events sink in, so I tug her closer, keeping her hand in mine as her other hand reaches across her body, clinging to my arm.

This is exactly where she should be. Right here next to me.

Always.

The hearse bike slowly idles forward, and we trail behind on foot, rounding the pool area until we reach the oak tree, and the new wall, freshly built from stone.

The eight bikes of our fallen idle behind us in a tight formation, ridden by their closest brothers, breaking off as they reach the tree, and parking them at either end of the memorial wall, before draping the cuts of our lost over the handlebars.

Abbey is sniffing, clutching onto me as she trembles from the wave of emotion that flows through the crowd.

Jols steps up on my Angel's other side, offering a tissue before running her hand up and down Abbey's back in comfort, and we watch on silently as the riders who brought the fallen's bikes move over to the hearse, each one retrieving a metal box.

Each urn is stamped with the Southern Sadists MC death head, road dust worked into the design like scars around their names.

They carry them with reverence, placing each box gently on the boulder in the centre of the memorial site, before Smitty steps forward and turns to face our club.

"Club brother, Stoner. Otherwise known as Theo Watson." Smitty calls out the name of our first fallen, his voice steady but hard with grief.

Every club brother thumps his hand to his heart.

"Club brother, Tucker. Otherwise known as Freddie Tucker- son."

Another round of thumps fill the air.

"Club brother, Mule. Otherwise known as Jamie Halley."

More thumps, but this time, Abbey's knees buckle next to me, and a strangled sob escapes her.

I catch her with both arms, holding her up, and Jols moves quickly to steady her from the other side.

Fuck.

Jols told me about the bond Abbey had formed with Mule. He was the one I'd ordered to be her shadow and watch her back while I was away. I hadn't told her he was one of the dead. Mainly because she didn't ask, and I didn't have the fucking balls to add that to the weight already crushing her.

"Club brother, Kite. Otherwise known as Rory Stein."

Another round of thumps.

"Club brother, Roadie. Otherwise known as Tim Vega."

Thump.

"Club brother, Barts. Otherwise known as Darryl Martin."

Thump.

"Club brother, Bowey. Otherwise known as Ray Bowey."

Thump.

"And lastly, club brother, Zeus. Otherwise known as Kevin Leeds."

Thump.

The air is thick with grief. Whimpers and sniffles fill the crowd behind us, mostly from Doxies, but some of the men, too.

Even tough bastards break when it's one of our own.

Smitty gives a nod to the side, and Celina, Casey, Nola and Helina step forward, each carrying trays lined with shot glasses.

They move through the crowd, offering one to each club brother, and to any Doxies, wives or old ladies who wish to raise a glass.

At the front, Smitty lifts his shot high, and Vender steps up beside our Prez, his voice rough as he speaks a few kind words about Stoner.

Then he raises his own glass.

"Stoner's drink of choice," Vender calls, his voice cracking with emotion. "Tequila."

We all lift our shots, and beside me, I can feel Abbey taking everything in, her head moving from one side then the other.

"We toast," Vender calls, and we all chant.

"One for the road, brother."

We all slam back the foul tequila, the burn cutting through the lump of grief clogging my throat.

Fuck, that shot is harsh. Fucking fitting for today, if you ask me.

The Doxies return, offering another round. We swap our empties for full glasses as Spud steps forward, this time, sharing a story about Tucker that has us snickering at the old guy's antics, before we fall silent and Spud raises his glass.

"Tucker's drink of choice. Jimmy," Spud calls. "We toast."

Again, we all chant. "One for the road, brother."

Since I'm not much of a drinker these days, the bourbon burns, but it's fucking welcome, warming my chest as it settles.

Next, Mex steps up, shot already in hand, his story darker and violent about Mule, our silent predator. The man who kept to the shadows, suffered in silence, but fucking always had your back.

These stories aren't sugar-coated. They're not about painting saints.

They're about honour. Truth.

About the men who lived and bled beside us. Who died protecting what we stand for.

Their sacrifice will never be forgotten.

As Helina passes with the tray, I swap out my glass, and Abbey grabs one too, her tear-filled eyes flicking up to meet mine, her cheeks flushed and wet.

It's like she's silently asking if it's okay for her to take a shot. Asking for permission.

Right now, her submissive side is present. It's probably the closest she's been to the old Abbey as she stares up with those big doe eyes, seeking approval.

She doesn't need my permission to have a drink, but fuck, if she needs it, I'll give it, so I nod, watching her submissive gaze lower as she bows her head, her shoulders relaxing before turning her attention back to Mex.

"Mule's drink of choice. Bundy," he announces, and we all raise our glasses as he finishes. "We toast."

"One for the road, brother," we chant, then down the rum.

Fuck. That shit is like rocket fuel.

Naturally, my gaze drops to my Angel to see how she's faring after the rancid shot.

She hasn't touched a drop since I've known her, given she's nothing like Kylie, and would never risk harming her baby. But she's not pregnant anymore.

She shudders, her pretty face twisting as the Bundy hits her, trying to shake off the strong molasses burn, coughing a little as her watery eyes dart up to mine.

I offer her a small smile, taking her empty glass just as the next tray makes its rounds. Clearing her throat, she hooks her arm through mine, holding on like she's scared I'll vanish into thin fucking air. And fuck, it grounds me feeling her tight grip.

Things between us have been tense up until the late hours of last night, when I thought we had somewhat figured ourselves out… but her coldness this morning has had me on edge again.

I need to remember what Andrea said and give her the space to go through each emotion that hits her and be there ready with open arms when she needs me.

Like right now.

Fuck, it feels good to be wanted by her.

We go through the ritual for each of our fallen, shot after shot, memory after memory.

It's brutal. Crushing. A stark reminder of how precious life is.

Once all the empties have been set aside, Vender opens each urn, scooping a small portion of ashes from each one and places them into a single stone bowl, mixing them together.

Eight lives.

One brotherhood.

Glancing down at my Angel, I notice her curiosity and remember what she said the day we got married. That us bikers were poetic.

And fuck, maybe she's right, because what we're about to do next is sacred. It's not something you'll see at any civilian funeral.

9

ABBEY

I've never known a funeral to be like this. There's so much honour. So much grief, yet also so much celebration. This service is, well… unexpected, but utterly beautiful, and for the first time since Bobbi died a week ago, I let myself think about how I'll honour the few minutes she lived.

It's something I've been avoiding. When Ace called Ringo a few days ago and asked if I needed help choosing a casket, I completely shut down.

All I wanted was to smash the vase on the table, straight into Ringo's skull, and that… terrified me.

He was just the messenger, and Ace was just trying to help as well.

But my rage has been consuming me. I haven't even *tried* to fight it, if I'm being honest with myself.

Why should I?

Why should I push it down just to make other people more comfortable?

They don't know what this is like. They haven't lost a child… Except, that's not true, is it?

Ringo has.

Jols was right. Our experiences aren't the same, but he knows this kind of heartache.

I have to keep reminding myself of that. Remind myself that *he loves me*. That *I love him*. That he'd do *anything* for me.

Because sometimes, the rage inside me wants to take over. It wants to destroy. It wants to make this whole world suffer.

And sometimes, I want to let it.

Music starts playing from a hidden speaker, and my brows shoot up when the heavy beat drops.

"It's a playlist of their favourite songs," Ringo rasps quietly in my ear, picking up on my confusion. "Today, their music is the only music we'll hear."

Ohhh. I love that.

That's so special.

My thoughts shift to Bobbi's funeral, and my gut twists.

She never got to listen to music. Never got to decide what she did and didn't like.

Does that mean her funeral will be silent?

"Hey." Ringo's warm palm comes up to cup my cheek as he shifts in front of me. "What can I do?"

Shit.

I bet he knows I'm thinking about my little girl. He's so perceptive. Especially when it comes to me.

It makes me feel guilty for the real reason I agreed to come today. I hate myself a little for it, but I'm also glad. It's what got me here today. Because as hard as this is. I needed this. The reminder of how fiercely the Southern Sadists take care of their own.

"Nothing," I breathe. "I'm okay. Promise."

He doesn't buy my lie. I see it in his eyes, almost like I've let him down.

Did he want me to ask him for help?

Maybe.

But I just can't.

Not right now.

Not yet.

Leaning in, he presses a kiss to my forehead, his beard brushing my skin, and my eyes flutter closed, soaking in the feel of him. His scent wraps around me, and for a moment, I'm cocooned in the safety of his presence.

"Come on, Angel." He eases back, his dark eyes locking with mine the second they blink open. "Let's go."

I frown but let him lace our fingers together and lead me to a line forming by the boulder where Vender is now sitting. The familiar buzzing sound instantly takes me back to our wedding day, when Ringo got my name tattooed on his finger, and I got his forever etched into mine.

It's a tattoo machine.

"What's happening?" I whisper, rising on my toes to get a better look past the wall of the bikers already in line.

"Vender has mixed the ashes with ink," Ringo says quietly. "And now, each club brother will get our fallen brothers' names inked on them."

My brows shoot up in surprise.

Yet another truly honourable thing to do.

God, all we do at funerals is pray to a made-up deity, and talk about the dead like they were saints, even if they weren't. We drop flowers into their graves, then eat and drink, and move on.

Okay, so maybe that's a slightly jaded summary, because obviously it's more meaningful to those that are closest to whoever died, but still. We don't do stuff like this.

As we move up the line, I get a better view just as Mex takes his turn. He shrugs out of his vest and pulls off his shirt, revealing a torso of art already inked into his skin, but on his side, there's a blank patch, and I realise it's under what looks to be a list.

"All of my club brothers have a list inked on them somewhere. A list of fallen men they called their brother at some point over the years." Ringo's voice is rough, laced with emotion as he speaks quietly beside me. "Some lists are longer than others, depending on how long they've been patched in… but today, that list grows. Substantially."

I glance up at my husband, his eyes trained on Mex, his expression filled with sorrow.

"Eight names. Eight lives lost in one night. Eight brothers we'll never ride beside again."

Hot tears sting my eyes, and guilt nearly has me collapsing. But I force myself to keep it together, because this isn't about me. This is about Ringo. About his club. And the men he loved like brothers.

I turn back, watching Mex's face as Vender tattoos the names into his bronze skin. He doesn't flinch. Doesn't even look like he's breathing. But when it's done, he and Vender clap hands and pull into a rough hug, before Mex steps aside, making room for the next man to take his place.

When it's Ringo's turn, he takes me with him, passing me his vest and shirt before linking our fingers again and tugging me close on one side. On the other, Vender gets to work on the list.

Ringo doesn't flinch as the needle scrapes ink into his skin. He just stands there, silent and patient, soaking in the pain, like he deserves it.

In a matter of minutes, Vender is finished, and Ringo releases me, clapping his palm with Vender and pulling him in for the same bro-hug Mex gave.

When they pull apart, Ringo takes my hand again, leading us off to the side. His eyes fall to his ribs, scanning the list I hadn't realised was a list until now.

But now it's longer.

Forever etched into his skin. Eight new names added to it.

Stoner

Tucker

Mule

Kite

Roadie

Barts

Bowey

Zeus

It's permanent, and poetically brutal.

Reaching out, I run my finger gently over the names, feeling the skin raised beneath the black ink.

"I'm bound to them now. Through blood and ash," he chokes out, clearing his throat as our eyes meet. "It's how we keep our fallen brothers with us. Always."

I swallow hard, my vision blurring my view of his ruggedly handsome face.

His hand dives into my hair, tugging me against the heat of his bare chest, and I wrap my arms around him, never wanting to let go.

He turns us away from the crowd, shielding this moment of raw grief. It gives us a sliver of solitude to mourn a tragedy that should never have happened.

We stay wrapped in each other for a long time. The music changes from heavy to soft rock, then to something quirky I've never heard, before we finally ease apart.

"I've been pissed at Smitty lately… for trying to drag me back into club business." He trails off, his eyes drifting over my head to the gathered crowd beyond. "I didn't want to think about any of this," his gaze flicks down to me, "because I wanted to keep my focus on you. My beautiful, grieving wife." He brushes my hair back with both hands, cradling my face between his rough palms. "You're my number one priority. I'll do anything for you…"

He trails off again, and I blink up again, my stomach knotting as dread seeps in.

"But?" I ask, because it sounds like there should be a but.

He sighs, bringing his forehead to mine in that way he loves, so close now that I can see flecks of black in his whiskey eyes.

"But they're my family. And *you're* my family." He eases back slightly, his gaze flicking to my lips before returning to my eyes. "Somehow, I've got to figure out how to make that fit together."

I frown, not sure where he's going with this, but he keeps talking, like the emotions of the day have cracked him open, and now the dam inside him is pouring out.

"Men like me don't get much by the way of happiness during our shitty existence, Angel. We get fleeting moments, few and fucking far between, and most of us don't ever find real love."

My heart flips, his thumb brushing over my cheek as he looks at me like I'm the most precious thing on Earth.

"Instead, I found acceptance. Community. In the club. In my brothers. A found family, built not by blood, but by choice and loyalty. For a lot of the guys, it's the only family they've ever had." His gaze shifts over my head to the crowd again, but his hold on my head never wavers. Like he's afraid if he lets go, I'll run.

He knows me too well, but I'm done running from him.

"Me… well, I've got my ma and sisters. I've got the club, and my fucking ride-or-dies in JD, Murf, Trunk, Stocky and Jols." His whiskey eyes lock onto mine again. "And now I have you."

I nod against his hands, and he releases my head, one arm sliding around my back to hold me close, all while his eyes stay locked on mine as I crane my head back to meet them.

"You *do* have me."

"I don't know that I deserve all the love I'm getting, Angel," he murmurs, his voice hoarse. "But I'll fucking take it. Because we both know too fucking well, how fast it can all be ripped away."

My lip trembles as I give in to my own emotions.

I think he's trying to make a declaration. Trying to say what he can't quite explain. How torn he is between me and his club. Two polar opposites. Two worlds that were never meant to blend.

But here's the thing… The violence that runs through the veins of the Southern Sadists is now coursing through mine, too. I'm not the same girl I was a week ago.

Now, when I close my eyes, I picture violence. Blood and gore. It's always there now, lurking under the surface like it's always been there waiting. I just couldn't see it until now.

Hell, I dream about things I've only ever seen in horror movies.

Because I'm *that* angry.

At the world.

At the arseholes that raped me. Tormented me. Traumatised me.

At my parents and sister.

At *everyone* really, even if I shouldn't be mad at them.

"Have I made you feel like you have to choose between me and your club?" I whisper, scared my voice might crack if I try to say it any louder.

Ringo shakes his head, his thumb gliding over my lower lip like he can't stand the thought of not touching me.

"No, Angel. It's more like I dread dragging you deeper into this world. I dread tainting you. Ruining you."

"I'm already ruined," I deadpan. "That's something no one can save me from now."

"Fuck. I know." His jaw ticks. "And I fucking hate that."

"Can you love me the way I am now?" I ask, needing honesty more than reassurance, and he jerks back, scowling at me.

"I can love you *any* way you are, Angel. But you'll heal. The anger you carry won't always burn like this."

"And if it does? Can you still love me if I'm a heartless bitch?"

His lips kick up into a smirk. "The answer is *fuck yes*. But just so we're clear. I don't think you are, or could *ever* be, a heartless bitch." He leans in slightly. "Besides, I could always demand you to behave."

My heart does a little somersault at that, because damn him, the submissive in me is *still* lurking.

It never used to be obvious to me, but it is now that he pointed it out weeks ago.

"I'd like to see you try," I tease, pushing the boundaries just enough to test him, and for a moment, something inside me lifts.

The heaviness in my chest eases. That one moment of banter feeds me.

"Hmmm. There's that brat who only shows her face every so often." He grins right as the music fades behind us. "Shit. Come on. We've got to get back to the wall for the last part."

Ringo releases me, quickly slipping on his t-shirt and vest, which he calls a cut, before taking my hand and leading us back into the thick of the crowd.

We watch as Smitty steps forward, carrying each metal box holding the essence of each fallen Southern Sadist to the memorial wall. And one by one, he slots them into the opening in the stone.

Spud steps up next, securing metal plates over the front of each opening, engraved with their names.

For a moment, Ringo's breath hitches, his shoulders go tight and his eyes gloss over with welling tears.

The sight makes my chest ache. I *hate* seeing him in pain. Just like last night by the lake. Seeing him shattered like that was torture.

It's easy to forget he's human.

When you look at him, with those thick corded muscles, wide shoulders, and towering height… well, he doesn't look like he can break. He looks like he was built to *carry* pain. Not *feel* it.

But he does.

And when those wet eyes drop to mine, and he pulls me close, burying his face in my hair, holding me like he'll drown if he lets go… I know without a doubt that this man feels it all.

"Life is a fucking gift, Angel," he murmurs so only I can hear. "It's so easy to take it for granted. So fucking easy to forget that in the blink of an eye, it can all end."

I don't know if he's reminding me or himself.

Maybe both. But either way, it doesn't matter. I believe him, even if the idea of life being a gift makes me feel sick.

My life doesn't feel like a gift.

But those few minutes of Bobbi's life, when I held her to my chest, felt her tiny warmth, the soft squirm of her little body, and heard the faintest sound slip from her lips… well, that was surely the greatest gift of *my* life. Even if it was only a moment.

Instead of speaking, I just hold Ringo tighter, gripping him like I can transfer everything I feel through that squeeze. I can only hope it's enough to show him that I care.

When he pulls back, threading his fingers through mine, our eyes lock, and we just look at each other.

He's still hurting. I see it in the dullness of his eyes. The way they aren't lit up with his usual fire.

Lifting our joined hands, I bring his to my lips, pressing a kiss to his knuckles.

"Fuck, I love you." His voice is low, but sure, and for a split second, that fire flickers back to life in his eyes.

I can't say the words back right now. It's not that I don't *feel* them. God, I do. But they get stuck in my throat. So instead, I lower his hand and press it to my chest, right over my heart.

It's been cold there since Bobbi was lifted off me. Since I lost her. But last night, when I did this with Ringo as we cuddled in bed together, something shifted. That warmth returned, and it's back now, the empty ache slipping away.

Like he senses it, Ringo pulls me into his arms again, crushing me to him. He buries his nose in my hair like he's trying to breathe me in. Memorising me.

I do the same, pressing my face into his chest and inhaling that sharp, masculine scent of his. Spice and sweat and safety.

It grounds me. Makes me feel at home. Making it feel like *he* is my home.

We stay in each other's arms as Smitty says a few more words, his voice carrying over the crowd. Then, one by one, the club brothers climb onto the motorbikes that belonged to the fallen.

With my cheek pressed to Ringo's chest, I watch the men start up the bikes and steer them off to the side.

A moment later, the engines roar to life, a thunderous growl that tears through the silence, and in perfect unison, they take off, kicking up a cloud of dirt and smoke.

It's a send-off. A tribute. A final burnout in honour of their dead.

Exhaust smoke fills the air, choking the sky like the grief swelling in their chests.

In *my* chest.

"Southern Sadists!" Smitty bellows as the engines shut down a moment later. "We chant!"

I straighten in Ringo's arms, but he keeps his arms locked around me, holding me still as his voice rumbles against my cheek, through the wall of his chest.

"May the road rise up to meet us.
May the wind be always at our backs.
May the sunshine be warm upon our faces.
May the rain clouds never be black.
We are the Southern Sadists MC.
Ride 'em high.
Ride or die."

God… these men and their club… it's so beautiful. So poetic. Their unity is everything I've craved in my life.

People who have my back. Who love me even if I'm broken.

I get what the Southern Sadists are now. And I want that.

I only hope what I'm about to do here tonight is something they can forgive.

10

ABBEY

I was expecting glares and even harsh words from the club brothers and the Doxies today. After all, eight of their own are dead because of me. But not one person has been cruel. Instead, I've been met with quiet sympathy, gentle hugs from Doxies, and more whispered condolences than I know what to do with.

I should feel anything but this rage that is waiting to explode from me, yet its claws are in deep, not letting me go. It doesn't matter how many people offer their respects. It won't bring my Bobbi back, and it won't sate this violent beast unfurling inside me.

The sun is setting now, the club gathered around a furious bonfire, music of the eight dead still playing over the speakers. The motorcycles of the fallen are parked off to the side, their leather vests draped back over the handlebars, like each man is still sitting there, watching on from the afterlife.

No matter how many times I try to look away, my gaze keeps falling to Stoner's and Mule's bikes. Tucker's too.

They died at Ringo's house trying to protect me.

No matter how many times I try to tell myself it wasn't my fault, my brain comes to the same conclusion.

I was the reason they were there.

I was the reason Ian Allen and his men stormed the property.

I was the reason Ian arranged for the rival club to ambush the compound.

All of it… falls back to me.

A gunshot suddenly cracks through the air, making me jump. Ringo's arms give me a reassuring squeeze as Smitty's voice booms over the chatter, my eyes darting to him to see his hand raised, and in it, the gun pointing towards the sky.

"They rode hard. They died harder." He lowers his gun, pointing it at the grass by his feet. "Now they ride free. In Valhalla. In the wind. In us."

Someone hurls fuel into the fire, and the flames explode higher as heat licks our skin, even at the distance we are standing.

Some in the crowd cheer. Others weep. A few shoot bullets skyward, while others mount their bikes and rev their engines before tearing around the bonfire in donuts that kick up dust.

"You doing okay, Angel?" Ringo's low rasp brushes my ear as he leans down, and I pull back from his chest to nod up at him.

"I'm okay…" I bite my lip, my eyes scanning over the chaos unravelling around us. "I guess this is kind of like a wake?"

His lips kick up slightly as he brushes some of my hair back behind my ear.

"Yeah. This is the part where we celebrate them. The life they shared with us."

I nod, even though the word *celebrate* feels wrong. I know this is a normal process of farewelling someone who has died, but it's hard to understand how anyone can smile, let alone laugh, at a time like this.

"What's going through that head of yours?" Ringo asks, eyes locked on me, always observant.

"I guess… I just don't get how they can laugh right now."

He watches me for a beat, the fire casting shadows across his face, one side lit in gold, the other cloaked in black. His thumb grazes my cheek, warm from the flames that feel closer than they are.

"Well, Angel. It's a form of honouring our dead. They aren't here anymore, so we have to live for them." He glances up, eyes skimming the groups around us, each one wrapped in their own conversations. Their own grief. "They're telling stories. Laughing at the stupid shit they did. Remembering who they were. Keeping them alive by speaking their names, because today is about them. Our dead." His eyes flick back to mine. "Grief is a fucking bastard. It's messy and loud and confusing as hell. But if you let it run through you. If you stop fighting it… that's when you start to get stronger. That's how the healing begins."

"I still stand by what I said on our wedding day." I grin up at him. "You guys are poets. Nothing you say can change my mind about that."

His lips stretch wider, a real smile tugging at the corners this time, and for a moment, we just stare at each other. Then, his smile fades, and his eyes turn more haunted than I've ever seen them.

"Thank you for coming today. I know it's been hard."

Reaching up, I cup his jaw, loving the feel of his beard against my palm.

"I thought I was just coming for you," I say softly, "but I quickly realised I was here for me, too."

He nods, probably thinking I mean saying goodbye to his club brothers. And yeah, that's part of it, but it's not the whole truth.

I came here today to seek justice. That's all I had on my mind when we left this morning. All I thought about as we rode up the long driveway of the compound.

But witnessing the funerals here today... I realised I wasn't just here to seek justice for Bobbi... but now I want it for the eight men now nothing but ash in a box, too.

"Are you two ever gonna let go of each other?" JD snickers, deliberately shouldering into us, and I step back as he slings an arm around Ringo's shoulders. "Come join us. I was trying to tell Brody about that time Stoner picked up that chick in Adelaide, and you ran into her in the pisser, nearly fucking choking on your saliva when she whipped out a dick and started pissing in the urinal next to you." JD cackles, smacking Ringo's back. "Come on. You tell the story so much better."

A genuine smile breaks out across Ringo's face, and wow, I love seeing it. Just for a second, the weight seems to lift off his shoulders.

"Fine," he laughs, as JD pulls him towards the others. "You coming, Angel?"

This is it. My chance. It's now or never.

"I'll join you in a few minutes." I flash him a small, fake smile. "I need to pee, and…" I point to my engorged boobs, and his brows shoot up.

"Oh, shit. Yeah. Of course."

He looks a little nervous, which is odd to see, but this whole milk in boob situation is new for the both of us.

Andrea sent me some links to watch instructions on expressing some of the milk by hand to give a bit of relief. Maybe I should have shown Ringo too. It could help him understand better.

That will have to wait though. I have other matters that need tending to first.

"I'll be back soon." I wave him off, and for a moment, he hesitates.

His feet stop moving, and I worry he can see straight through my lie, but I shoo him with a flick of my hand, and he smirks, shooting me a wink before jogging to catch up with JD.

Not wanting to draw attention, I head to the barn, slipping inside where I know there's a toilet the Doxies have been using.

The barn is empty and quiet, so I linger in the doorway, peeking back out at the crowd, noticing everyone is busy talking, drinking… grieving.

My gaze flicks over to the shipping container that sits alone. It's on a patch of dirt, bald of grass, and the door is slightly ajar with a spray-painted warning on it.

Southern Sadists Only!

I know what's under it.

The dungeon.

It used to be part of the old Vixen's Lodge before it burnt down. The dungeon is the only thing that survived, hidden under the rubble, its metal walls cased in concrete protecting it from the inferno.

Jols gave up the details about it easily this morning, probably not realising I had a plan. Not realising I wanted to know where they were keeping their dog while the funerals were taking place.

Sucking in a breath to steady myself, mostly because I'm desperate not to get caught, I slip out of the barn and into the shadows, darting from tree to tree until I get close enough to the shipping container and slip inside.

There's a hatch in the floor, and I flip it open, surprised it's lighter than it looks.

Hovering over the opening, I stare down into the black void, and regret still not having a phone… again.

It'd be great if people would stop kidnapping me so I can keep a phone longer than five bloody minutes.

Glancing around the dim container, my eyes catch on a tangle of wires snaking up the wall to a switch. Rushing forward, I flick it on, and the space floods with harsh light, but so does the opening in the floor, illuminating a steep staircase that travels down to a metal door.

The dungeon.

Just knowing this place exists creeps me out.

I remember reading about it in the newspaper last year, back when the investigation blew open a trafficking ring and the illegal sex club operating out of the house. The dungeon was put in by the owner, who called himself Master, and the evidence they found in there was damning.

That gives me the ick, but the fact it's currently holding someone I want dead is enough for me to step down under the earth. Because it's time for some justice. Or vengeance. However you want to look at it.

The metal door is bolted shut, but I quickly slide it across and shove it open.

The room is already lit up, probably controlled by the switch I flicked on upstairs, so I quickly scan the space.

This end holds a table, some tools, and a couple of chairs. At the other end… a naked woman with dark short hair, sticking up in wild clumps, is curled in on herself.

Closing the door, I watch her flinch, but she doesn't look up. She doesn't know it's me.

Chains rattle at her wrists as she shifts, stretching out to the wall and bolted in place.

She's not going anywhere.

In the corner is a bucket, and I cringe as I realise the pungent stench that nearly has me gagging is coming from it.

Urine. Faeces. Vomit.

A vile shiver ripples through me.

"Because of you, my baby is dead."

My words come out loud, echoing off the walls, and in an instant, Wendy's head jerks up, her dark eyes locking with mine, wide with shock. She stares at me before glancing behind me like she's expecting Ringo to walk in.

Tough luck, bitch.

"My husband said he kept you alive for me." I step forward, surprised by how steady my voice sounds.

I should feel nervous right now… right?

Shouldn't I be freaking out? Shaking? Crying?

I'm not, though.

What I feel is colder than that. A cocktail of numbness, and something that tastes almost like anticipation.

Wendy scoffs. "You think he kept me alive for *you*?" She shakes her head slowly, a bitter smile twisting her sunken face. "If that's what he told you, then he was lying. He kept me alive for *himself*. I told you. He likes his sex violent. But you wouldn't listen."

She pushes herself up with effort, her legs trembling beneath her. Her naked flesh clings to her bones, every rib visible. Every joint too sharp. She's malnourished. And broken.

But not broken enough.

"He kept me alive so he could fuck me like *this*." She gestures to her frail, ruined body, and I frown before I can stop myself, her eyes flaring with victory.

But I'm not buying her bullshit.

"More lies," I deadpan, and she laughs manically, the high-pitched sound grating on my nerves like nails running down a chalkboard.

I know that laugh, though. The unhinged sound used to throw off your enemy.

It's the same one I used at the chapel, when my mum and Minister Banes thought they were going to force me to marry Daniel.

That kind of laugh isn't about joy. It's pure madness wrapped in defiance.

"How can you be sure?" she snarls at me, and it really shocks me that she has the audacity to continue with her twisted charade. "You hardly know him. You've got no idea who the man is that you married."

That hits a nerve.

Not because I believe her. But because I've asked myself that exact question before.

Do I really know Ringo?

Still, I know better. She's baiting me.

I've seen Ringo with Jols. With his mates. With his club. Hell, I've witnessed his mum tear shreds off him while he just took it.

Ringo is a monster, but not the kind she's trying to paint.

"You just couldn't handle it, could you?" I cross my arms over my chest, smirking at the bitch. "He chose *me*. After all those years you begged for his attention, and he barely even looked at you. Then out of nowhere, he claimed *me*." I shrug, like it's no big deal. "Guess your dirty cunt wasn't as good as you thought it was."

Her mouth drops open in a gasp, eyes wide in disbelief. Probably because I've never spoken like this to her before.

Maybe I should have.

Then, she starts *screeching* like a banshee, yanking on the chains and fighting against them like a rabid animal, while I start laughing.

The sound of her breaking is like music to my ears.

"Just admit it, Wendy. You fucked up. You got sent away. Banished from this chapter, and your bruised ego couldn't take it. So you decided to take me out of the picture."

She bares her teeth at me, pure hatred dripping from her glare.

"Why won't you just die, you fucking cow! You're not good enough for him or this club! You're worthless, used-up trash!" She seethes, spittle flying from her cracked lips. "I did Ringo a *favour*! He didn't want to raise another man's kid! And now he doesn't have to!"

I snap.

Spinning on my heel, I storm to the table by the door, my hands closing around a pair of spiked knuckledusters. I don't hesitate, sliding them on as I turn back to face her.

"Say it again, bitch."

Wendy's eyes gleam with malice. She knows exactly what she's doing. She knows exactly how to get under my skin.

But fuck her. How dare she speak about Bobbi's death like it was a blessing.

She snickers, eyeing the flash of metal shielding my knuckles. "Now he doesn't have to raise someone else's kid!"

"And why is that?" I urge, needing to hear the words no mother wants to hear. But I need them. I *need* her to say it so I can finally let go and unleash my pain on her.

The moment her lips part, I know she's going to give me exactly what I need.

"BECAUSE YOUR BABY IS DEAD!"

Red. Hot. Rage.

It bursts from me. Violent. Pure. And unrelenting.

I hardly realise I've moved before I launch myself at her. One second I'm standing over her, the next I'm on her, my fists flying, the spikes biting into her skin as I swing at anything I can reach.

I've never fought anyone like this before. Never even been taught how to throw a punch. But it doesn't matter. It's nothing but raw instinct right now, and I give in to its pull on me to swing hard. Faster.

Each blow lands heavy, fuelled by grief and fury, shredding her arms, her chest, her face, any part of her I can get to as she screams and thrashes beneath me.

When she tumbles to the floor, I go with her, straddling her bleeding and broken body, my fists never stopping.

Her blood coats my fists, warm and sticky, but still, I don't stop.

I can't.

I pound the spikes into her until her struggles weaken. Until her screams fade into whimpers. Yet still… I'm not done.

Animalistic screams fill the room, and it takes me a beat to realise it's coming from *me*. But still, I don't stop.

My eyes are trained on Wendy, watching as her skin splits with each blow, her blood spraying across my face, dripping from my chin as I tear her apart.

"ABBEY! STOP!"

The roar slices through my frenzy, and I jerk upright, chest heaving as I turn and hiss, baring my teeth at my husband as he stops dead in his tracks, just inside the doorway.

His eyes lock on my blood-coated fists, and the spiked knuckledusters that now look like they're a part of me since no skin or metal can be seen.

Only blood.

"Fuck," someone mutters behind him, probably JD, but I don't look away from Ringo.

"She's *mine*," I growl, like a wolf snarling over its kill.

Every part of me is wound tight, ready to pounce again if anyone so much as tries to take this from me.

"She's nearly gone, Angel," he says carefully, holding his hands out in front of him like he's trying to tame a beast. "Let me finish it. You don't want to carry that."

My husband is a beautiful monster, made up of sharp lines, rough edges, and so much lethal control simmering beneath the surface.

I know he could put me down in an instant. But still, I shake my head.

"No!" I snap. "I need this, Cameron. Her death is *mine*."

My voice doesn't sound human anymore. It's husky, and primal, laced with savagery I didn't know I had in me.

"I don't want *you* to carry that burden, Abbey." His voice softens even though his eyes are still hard as they pin me in place. "You think you want it now, but later… it'll eat you alive."

"I appreciate your concern, but this isn't up to you, husband." I bite back, and Ringo exhales hard, running a hand through his hair.

Then he turns to JD. "I'm gonna need your help, man."

Help?

My stomach drops.

He wouldn't… *would he?*

Shit. They're going to overpower me. I can see it in their eyes. Two men with strength I can't outmatch even if I tried. They're going to take this from me. Take what's rightfully mine.

I don't even think. I react.

The moment Ringo turns his back on me again, I lunge forward, my fingers curl around the grip of his gun, yanking it from the back of his pants before he even registers what's happening.

By the time he spins, eyes wide, I've already got the gun pointed at him.

"Her death is mine. Now get out of my way."

"You seriously pointing *my* gun at me, *wife*?" he snarls, his lip curling with rage.

"You can punish me later," I snap, barely hearing Wendy's blood-soaked gurgles behind me. "Just move out of my way."

"Punishing you later is a fucking *understatement*, Angel. You sure you wanna push me on this?"

"Never been more sure of anything in my life."

We stare at each other for a long beat, neither of us flinching, the heat between us laced with danger.

Then JD clears his throat. "Ringo, man… she's right. It's her call. If she hates herself later, that's on her."

I raise a brow at my husband. A silent challenge, and he snarls again, jabbing a finger in my direction.

"I'm trying to *save* you."

"I don't need saving. *Not anymore*."

"Yeah," he scoffs bitterly. "That's what I'm fucking afraid of."

"Riiingoooo… helppp…"

I spin, hearing Wendy's gargled voice, her eyes barely cracked as she tries to reach for him.

I stomp on her hand.

Hard!

A sickening crunch follows, and her scream dies in her throat, choked off by her own blood.

"Don't fucking speak to my *husband*!" I scream, my voice ripping through the room so loud, I almost don't hear the fast footsteps coming my way.

I spin just in time, gun up in an instant, aimed right at Ringo.

He skids to a stop, freezing in place, surprise flickering over his expression at being caught attempting to take me down.

"Stop!" I yell, angry tears bursting from my eyes. "Whose side are you on?!"

"Yours, Angel. *Fuck*. Always *yours*." His voice breaks, laced with pain, and I know I'm the one that put it there.

I swipe at my face, nearly grazing my cheek on the spiked knuckles, smearing more of Wendy's blood across my skin.

"*JD!*" I bark, not taking my eyes off Ringo. "Unchain her."

JD hesitates, but only for a moment before he slowly and carefully moves past Ringo, giving me a wide berth as he heads for Wendy. Then I hear the clink of the chains, and the sound of metal against metal as he does what I asked.

"What are you doing, Angel?" Ringo asks gently, his hands raised again, like I'm a wild creature he doesn't want to spook.

I guess I *am* the beast in this story.

"Vengeance," I snap. "Justice. Call it whatever you want."

Behind me, the chains hit the concrete floor with a heavy clatter, and I know Wendy is now free.

Such a pity she's in no state to run.

Glancing over my shoulder, I eye JD closely, ready to turn on him too, if I have to. But he just gives me a nod and backs away, leaving Wendy sprawled in a slick pool of her own blood.

"Leave," I tell Ringo, but he shakes his head.

"Nope."

I huff, frustrated, but not surprised. "Fine. But don't touch me. Don't *try* to stop me."

He holds his hands up in surrender, but his jaw is tight, and his eyes stormy. He hates this. Every second of it.

For a moment I wonder if this is it.

The moment he stops loving me.

The moment he realises I'm too far gone. That I'm not worth the trouble.

"Help…" Wendy's gurgled plea floats up to us, and I spin, dropping to my knees, gun still in my left hand as I slam another flesh-tearing punch into her already mangled face with my right.

Ringo and JD curse behind me, but they don't move. Not when I stand, my fists bloodied, and start dragging Wendy's limp body across the floor.

Not even when I grab her under the arms and start hauling her up the stairs.

My lungs burn, and muscles scream from the effort, and fuck, my gut aches, a round of cramps clawing at me, reminding me that my little girl is no longer growing inside me.

I drop Wendy at least half a dozen times, cursing myself, because shit… I didn't think this through.

I'm not strong. Not like this. Maybe it's the adrenaline making my muscles work harder. Or maybe it's the weight she's lost, making her lighter. But eventually, I get her to the top of the stairs, dropping her with a thud as I heave in air, staring down the stairs at Ringo and JD at the bottom, staring up at me like I'm something holy. Or monstrous.

Probably the latter.

"Please… Don't…" Wendy starts to beg, weakly struggling as I lift under her arms again, and drag her across the filthy floor of the shipping container.

She's too weak to put up a fight, still, I punch her again, just to shut her up.

"Shut up," I snarl, dragging her again. "You don't get to speak or beg for your shitty life."

I kick the container doors open with one boot, the night air hitting me like a slap as I haul her out into the flood-lit yard with JD and Ringo slowly following.

"Do you think those men stopped raping me when I begged them to stop?" I hiss, dragging her through the gravelly sand, her skin scraping raw as her blood-soaked eyes blink up at me. "Do you think they *cared* when I fell and went into premature labour?"

Gasps ripple through the air like a wave, the Southern Sadists' and Doxies' attention now turning to me before the music cuts off, leaving only the sound of the crackling bonfire and Wendy's gurgled breaths.

"Do you think anyone could save my daughter when I begged them to? Even when I begged a god I don't believe in to save *her* instead of *ME!*"

My scream echoes up into the night sky as I keep dragging her into the centre of the yard, beneath a tall light pole that illuminates us for everyone to see.

Then I let her go.

Her body hits the ground with a sick thud, her skull bouncing off the dirt.

"Maybe…" Wendy rasps, coughing, the sound horrid and wet, "maybe you deserve… everything you get."

I scream again, pure unleashed fury ripping out of me.

Even now, knowing she's about to die, Wendy can't stop being a spiteful bitch.

I hit her again.

And again, blood spraying across the sandy ground, soaking in like a stain as tears stream from my eyes, hot and fast.

Then, I spin, facing everyone watching on. Their eyes wide. Their bodies frozen.

Including my husband.

"She's responsible for their deaths!" I yell, my voice cracking as I jab a finger towards the row of motorcycles, and the eight leather vests. "And she's responsible for the death of MY BABY!" I cry as the unbearable pain shatters my heart. "*Bobbi Cameron Musgrove!*"

They need to hear her name. I want the world to remember it. Remember her even though she never got a chance at life.

And then, I turn back to the woman who took it all from me, and lift the gun, aiming it at Wendy's head.

"See you in Hell, bitch," I sneer, before I pull the trigger.

11

RINGO

The loud crack of the gun rings out like thunder, echoing far longer than it should as I stare at my wife. She's completely unhinged. Tainted far more than I fucking thought.

My chest rises and falls in sharp, panicked bursts. I wanted to stop her, but the look in her eyes down in that dungeon fucking terrified me.

That wasn't my wife. That was someone else entirely.

Don't get me wrong, I love a strong woman. But this? This is something else. Something I know she'll never recover from once the veil of her fury lifts.

"JD," I rasp, keeping my voice low so I don't startle my Angel, standing in the centre of the yard, still holding my gun.

"Yeah?" he asks, standing by my side, shoulder to shoulder.

"What's Smitty doing?" I ask him to look because I can't.

I won't take my eyes off my wife. I can't let her suffer through this alone, and this brutal, fucked-up moment is the only way she's letting me be a part of it.

Watching on helplessly. Letting her do the one thing I know will leave a permanent scar on her soul.

"He's, uhhh… grinning."

I blow out a relieved breath, because fuck, I didn't know how this would go down. We've got a code. No killing on the day we honour a fallen brother. And yet, here she is. My wife. Not just killing the woman who set this whole nightmare in motion, but doing it right out in the open for everyone to see… on the day we remembered eight of our own.

She just murdered a woman in front of over sixty witnesses.

Fuck.

"I need you to do damage control for me," I mutter. "Please." I add, because fuck, if he were a smart man, he'd distance himself from me right the fuck now.

Smitty might be grinning, but that doesn't mean it's good.

"Of course." JD claps a solid hand on my shoulder before leaving my side to try and get a handle on how this shitshow is landing with Smitty. With the crowd.

Abbey's arm is still outstretched, the barrel of the gun still locked on Wendy's head, but I spot the weakness to her hold. She's starting to fade, and fast.

Moving up behind her, I clear my throat to let her know I'm there.

"Angel. I'm here. I'm going to touch your shoulders now," I say quietly, but she still tenses the second my hands gently land on her.

She starts trembling, and her shoulders sag, yet she doesn't move. Doesn't speak. Doesn't tear her eyes off Wendy's bloodied corpse.

"I've got you," I murmur into her ear, pressing my front to her back, and sliding my hand down the length of her outstretched arm. "I'm going to take the gun now."

This time, she nods, the tremors wracking through her increasing.

The moment my hand wraps around the gun, she releases it, spinning, and burying her face in my chest, her hands fisting my cut in desperation like she's drowning, and I'm the only thing keeping her above water.

She's back. My Angel is back, but I've got no idea how she's going to react when it hits her. When she realises she just killed Wendy.

Somewhere behind me, someone starts clapping, and then more join in as it spreads through the crowd. Shoving my gun into the back of my pants, I keep my hold on her with my free hand, never wanting to let her go.

She stiffens in my arms as the applause builds, like she's only just hearing it now, and then, Smitty's deranged laugh cuts through the noise.

"Now that's justice," he cackles, striding up to us as Abbey pulls back just enough to glare at him.

I shift so I can see him too, and his grin is fucking huge and obnoxious. He looks like a fucking proud dad who just watched his kid win a fight.

"I always thought there was a feisty killer in our little charity case," he snickers, winking at her. "How does it feel?"

Stepping out of my arms, Abbey levels a death glare at my Prez, her top lip curling in disgust like she's seconds away from spitting in his face.

"How do you think it feels?" she snarls a rhetorical question. "I just beat another human within an inch of her life, dragged her out here, and killed her in front of everyone to get justice for my little girl! And you know what?" She steps right up to my President and sneers in his face. "It hasn't changed a damn thing. My baby is still dead!"

She's still wearing the spiked knuckledusters when she shoves him, daring to lay a hand on a man who doesn't take kindly to disrespect. A man who on more than one occasion, hasn't thought twice about throwing fists at an unruly woman.

Smitty staggers back a few steps, and gasps spill from the Doxies' lips as Abbey continues to glare at him like she's daring him to do something.

My body fucking tenses, ready to move, ready to throw myself between my Prez and my wife, consequences be fucked.

But then Smitty starts fucking cackling like a goddamn lunatic.

"She's fucking delightful!" he practically sing-songs, throwing his head back with laughter.

A few of the drunker brothers cheer, while others just shake their heads and laugh at our unhinged king.

"Tell me, Charity," he grins, eyes wild as ever. "Shall we burn her corpse on the bonfire?"

My fucking brows hitch, my eyes cutting to my wife as she glares back at Smitty.

"My name is Abbey. Stop calling me Charity," she hisses through clenched teeth, stepping back and glancing down at the woman she just killed. "I'll let Celina decide what to do with the body. I don't believe in desecrating the dead."

With angry tugs, she frees herself from the metal weapons on her hands and lets them fall to the ground with a heavy thud.

Her tear-glazed eyes dart up to me, and fuck, the trauma in her eyes is hard to miss, but there's also something harder. Strength.

The tough woman she's had to become in the blink of an eye is mixed with the sweet submissive soul who walked into my life a few months back. They're at war inside her, and neither one is winning.

"I'm ready for that punishment now."

Fuck.

I was furious with her before. For pointing a gun at me. For defying me. For making me feel like I'd lost her for good.

But now, all I want to do is pull her into my arms and kiss the weight of the world off her skin.

My gaze scans over the blood smearing her face, like painted evidence of what she's done.

I need to clean her up. If we were to leave now and get pulled over by the cops, she'd be totally fucked.

And then I'd have to kill them, too.

Giving my Angel a nod, I mutter a quiet "excuse us" to Smitty, then start leading her away. Shielding her from the whispers and stares. From the aftermath.

Finding JD on the fringes of the crowd, I lean in as we pass. "Give me a couple of hours in the bungalow."

He nods, saying nothing, as the crowd parts, not for me, but for my wife.

Once we break free through the thick of it, I scoop her up in my arms, cradling her to my chest as I carry her off into the night.

She doesn't protest, snuggling into my chest, her body limp like she can no longer bear to function. She doesn't ask me where I'm taking her. She doesn't need to. She trusts me, even after the showdown we had minutes ago.

And fuck… when she had that gun on me, I didn't know if lunging for it would end with a bullet in my chest. I couldn't read her. Couldn't be sure. There was a very real chance she would've pulled that trigger.

So I didn't move. Didn't push, because this unhinged version of my Angel is uncharted territory, and I needed her to know I meant what I said. That I wouldn't stop her. Even though everything in me was fucking screaming to.

Fuck.

Carrying her down the dark trail that weaves through a tree-lined path before opening up to a small clearing, I find the row of shipping containers that have been converted into small bungalows with two double beds and a tiny bathroom in each.

Climbing the steps of bungalow number three, the one JD and I share when we're on the compound, I gently lower my wife to her feet.

She stiffens a little, like she's only just noticed we're somewhere new, and I reach over her head, my fingers feeling along the top of the door frame until I find the key. I quickly unlock the door, putting the key back before I push the door open and reach in to flick on the light. She doesn't say a word, stepping over the threshold, her eyes tracking everything from the two beds, only a few feet apart, to the open door at the other end that leads into the bathroom.

"This is where you were staying," she says quietly, moving further in, recognising the familiar space I showed her on one of our video calls.

"It is, yes." I shut and latch the door behind me before shrugging out of my cut and hanging it on the hook by the door.

Abbey's eyes fall to the two beds, and she studies them for a moment before pointing to the far one by the bathroom entrance. "That one is yours?"

"It is," I rasp, toeing off my boots, and her eyes find me over her shoulder before she frowns.

"I can't have sex yet."

I smirk. "I know, Angel."

Her frown deepens as she turns to me.

"Then what's my punishment?"

"There'll be no punishment tonight." I start lifting my shirt, watching her track the motion.

"But…" her voice wavers slightly, her caramel eyes flicking up to mine. "Why?"

Pulling my shirt over my head, I toss it to the side, enjoying her eyes on me as they track down my bare chest, and even after everything we've been through, how her cheeks still flush like it's the first time she's seen me this way.

"Because, Angel." I step closer, my voice dropping low. "When I punish you, I need you strong. I need you healthy. I need you to be able to take it."

She visibly gulps.

"Now, be a good girl and strip for me."

She shakes her head, worry flickering over her face. "But I can't—"

"You're covered in blood, Angel." I cut her off, and her lips part in an O as the realisation hits. "We're going to clean you up."

Her eyes widen, flicking towards the open door of the bathroom, worrying her lower lip between her teeth.

"I can wash myself." She glances back at me with a half-arse smile.

"I'm not asking for permission, Abbey. I want to wash *my* wife clean. That's all there is to it."

"But…" she trails off, her eyes darting past me, towards the door.

Is she seriously thinking about running? Surely we're past that bullshit now.

"But what?" I growl, and her caramel eyes snap back to mine.

"Well, for one… I'm still bleeding." She gestures between her legs, and I shrug.

"I'm not afraid of blood, Angel."

She shoots me a 'really' look, brows raised, eyes glaring at me like I'm talking shit.

"It's *menstrual* blood. Or whatever you call it when you've pushed a baby out of your hooha."

I smirk. "It's a pussy, Angel. I thought we'd already been over that."

She rolls her eyes. "Not when we are talking about childbirth, it's not."

Shit. I guess she has a point.

"Fine. But I'm not afraid of menstrual or post-birth blood either. So get naked and get your arse in the shower."

As my hands move to my belt, her eyes follow, watching quietly as I start stripping down.

She doesn't make a move to do as I've demanded, and I wonder how far I can push her, given her fragile state.

"Why are you still dressed?" I ask, tugging down my fly.

"I want to wash myself."

"Not happening. But how about you tell me why, all of a sudden, you don't want me in the shower with you?"

She sighs dramatically, throwing her arms up, turning around on the spot like she's searching for an escape route.

She won't find one. There's only one way in and out of this shitty little bungalow, and she knows it.

"Angel. Talk to me," I demand, and she whirls around, fire blazing in those big doe eyes.

"My body isn't the same, okay?" she snaps, her chin jutting as her voice trembles with frustration.

"Okay. I figured as much, Angel. You gave birth a week ago. You were thirty weeks pregnant. I might look it, but I'm not an idiot. I know your body's gonna need time." I take a step towards her, reaching down to hook my finger with hers. "And for the record, I don't give a fuck if you've got stretch marks, or fucking love handles, or a jelly belly. None of that matters to me."

Her brows shoot up at that comment.

"Yeah, I know about the jelly belly, Angel. And you know what? I don't fucking care about anything but *you*. Because I fucking *love* you. Every messy, scarred, changed inch of you. They're battle scars. Wear them with pride. They're a part of you, and I love every single fucking piece of you. You're perfect to me."

Her lip starts to tremble as her eyes fill with tears.

"You shouldn't. I'm a horrible person."

I'm shaking my head before she even finishes her sentence, and I step up close, feeling the heat coming off her body.

"No, you're not." I run my hands down her arms, lacing our fingers together. "Now get naked. We need to get you clean, and get you some new clothes."

She nods, staring up at me like she's trying to work something out in her head. There's a long beat where I think she's going to say something, but nothing comes. Instead, she steps back, bends down, and starts unlacing her boots.

While she strips, I shoot Jols a message to arrange some new clothes for Abbey, and when she's finally naked, I gather up the blood-soaked leathers and leave everything but her panties out on the porch for Jols to burn.

Taking Abbey's hand as I pass, I lead her into the bathroom, and she takes over, reaching into the shower and flicking the water on, holding her hand under the stream until she gets the temperature right.

I don't take my eyes off her as I peel off my jeans and follow her into the tight space. Moving up behind her, I press my bare chest to her bare back, and fuuuck, she melts right into me despite her earlier insecurities.

Since there's hardly any room, I leave her to it, watching over her shoulder as she drenches her face and hair, working in the soap and shampoo to rinse away the blood. She scrubs what's left off her hands, which is when I catch sight of grazes on her knuckles. They are small, but angry, and must fucking hurt, obviously left behind from those brutal metal weapons she wore.

Fuck. I honestly never thought she had it in her.

Never imagined she'd look at a table full of weapons and bypass the knife, and even the gun.

A gun is too quick, though. And loud. It would've alerted me sooner.

A knife would have been a better option. Less effort needed to do damage.

But no… she didn't go for the easy kill. She chose the weapon that requires maximum effort. All the strength, and all the energy.

You only choose that weapon over the others when you have rage to get out of your system.

And fuck, I watched her get it all out.

My heart aches for her.

For the pain she's drowning in. The trauma she's barely surviving.

I'd take every ounce of it if I could. I'd fucking bleed for her. Burn for her. I'd fucking die for her.

When she's done scrubbing her skin, she leans back against me again, and I slide my hands around her waist, tugging her close, my palms flat against her stomach.

Just like that first night when I took her from her parents, I can feel her ribs again.

I loved seeing her pregnant. Even though Bobbi wasn't mine, I imagined she was. That my Angel was swollen with my baby inside her.

Now there's no bump. Just soft skin and prominent ribs.

My gaze drops down her front, but fuck, I can't see anything past her huge tits.

Fucking hell. I knew they were bigger than before, but this? I had no fucking idea.

"Angel," I rasp into her hair, unable to tear my eyes away from the way the water cascades over her full, heavy tits, trickling over her swollen nipples, dark and peaked and… fuck… fuck… is that…

"Yeah?" Her voice cuts through my aroused fucking thoughts, my cock already hard, pressed into the small of her back.

Fuck, why does she have to be so short? If she were taller, my cock would be in just the right place to… *shit. No. Fucking stop. She can't have sex so soon after giving birth, you fucking pervert!*

Abbey shifts a little, turning her head to the side, waiting for me to say something.

Fuck. Just say it. Just tell her what I'm seeing, for fuck's sake!

When the hell did I become such a chickenshit?

"Don't freak out, okay," I mutter against her ear, and she stiffens, so I quickly finish. "I think… your tits are leaking."

She gasps, her hands flying up to cover each nipple, and fuck, doesn't she know how hot that is to see her touch them?

"Shit, I'm sorry," she whimpers in embarrassment. "I'm gonna need, like ten minutes to… you know."

She tries to shift away, but I hold her firmly against me, which is when I guess she realises my hard cock is digging into her back, because she stiffens again, and fuck, all that does is press harder against it.

"Angel, you don't need to apologise. I'm not freaked out by it. I only said something because I knew *you* would be. The last thing I ever want is for you to feel embarrassed by your body." I nip at her ear. "Your fucking stunning body."

"Too late," she whispers, her voice strangled, like she's wishing the earth would open up and swallow her.

"Beautiful," I breathe against her ear. "I don't ever want you to be embarrassed in front of me. I'm your husband. I'm here.

For good. To worship the ground you walk on. To worship every fucking inch of you.”

She whimpers as I glide my hands up, wrapping them around her wrists and slowly tugging her hands free, releasing her tits from her grip.

She resists at first, but the moment I draw her lobe between my lips and gently suck, she surrenders, dropping her hands to her sides as she stares down at her full, aching rack under the spray of water.

“Look how fucking beautiful they are.” I breathe into her neck, my gaze locked on her nipples as they pebble even tighter, knowing I’m watching.

“They kinda hurt,” she admits, and fuck, I bet they do.

The skin is stretched so tight. Almost like they are engorged.

And I guess they are. Engorged with milk.

Slowly, I graze my fingers back up her ribs, tracing the curve beneath each tit, pressing my thumbs to the soft swollen flesh, testing my Angel to see if she’ll pull away, or ask me to stop.

But she doesn’t, so I take the risk, and gently cup them.

A sharp hiss falls from her lips, and I freeze, but don’t remove my hands.

“Does that hurt?” I ask, and she nods, but then shakes her head.

“I don’t know.”

I can’t help but grin to myself. I fucking love how honest she is with me, even when she doesn’t want to be. It’s one of the things I’ve noticed about Abbey.

For the most part, she doesn’t lie.

She holds back, yeah. Keeps pieces to herself. But if you ask for the truth, she gives it.

Which is why her actions tonight shook the hell out of me.

She said she was going to use the bathroom, but instead, snuck into the dungeon and beat Wendy nearly to death.

I keep turning it over in my head and can't help but think she planned it.

It's definitely something we'll be talking about. But not now. Not tonight.

Tonight, I need to remind her that she's loved, because when the guilt hits… when it really sets in, my love is all she's gonna have to grasp onto.

With each of her swollen tits in my hands, I lift them slightly, surprised by how heavy they are. We both watch as more white milk beads at the slit of her nipple, mixing with the water as it flows down her body.

"Angel," I whisper. "Can I do it for you?"

I expect her to stiffen. Maybe call me a pervert. But instead, my wife surprises me.

"Only if it's something you want to do."

Fuuuck. Doesn't she feel my rock hard cock grinding into her back?

Yeah, I fucking want it.

"Of course I do. I'd do anything to make you feel better."

She nods against my lips as I nip at her neck, and fuck, my kiss has her arching, pushing her chest forward with need.

She's turned on too.

Fuck, is this a kink? Swollen, engorged, milk-leaking tits?

If it's not, then it fucking is now. And later, I'm abso-fuck-ing-lutely looking that shit up online.

But for now, my Angel has given me the green light, and I'm not about to fuck it up.

"How do I…" I trail off, realising I've got no fucking clue what I'm doing.

I've never done this before. Never even thought about it before tonight.

How the fuck do you express milk from a woman's tits?

Taking the lead, Abbey places her hand over mine to guide me. Even with the size difference of our hands, it still works, and her fingers settle over mine, putting them in place. My thumb on one side and fingers on the other.

Then slowly, she shows me.

Starting from the outside, we gently squeeze the plump flesh, working in towards her nipple.

And fuuuck… milk doesn't just bead… it squirts from her.

My dick jerks, and she groans.

"Shit, am I hurting you?"

Fuck… is this wrong?

She shakes her head. "The let-down feeling… it's relieving."

Again, she guides our hands, repeating the motion, getting the same result.

Another soft squirt, and another sigh from her lips.

After a few tries, she drops her hand, leaving me to it, and fuck me… as horny as this is making me, it's got nothing on how good it feels to help her like this.

There's nothing hotter than easing her pain with my own hands.

After a few minutes of attention on one side, I switch to the other, careful not to grind my cock into her back again, even though every groan from her has me on edge.

Never in a million years did I think I'd be doing this. Helping my wife express milk from her tits.

Some might think it's fucked up. Others would probably be just as turned on as I am.

But to me, there's nothing vulgar about it. This isn't about a baby, even though that's technically why it's happening. But right now, it's about my wife. The woman I love. The woman who's been through hell, suffering in pain both physically and emotionally.

I'll do whatever the fuck I can to get her through this for as long as it takes, until hopefully, one day, the physical pain fades, and the emotional scars start to heal. Even if it's just small stolen moments of peace.

After a while of expressing the milk, the tightness on Abbey's tits eases, so I stop and gently turn her in my arms.

Her eyes meet mine, tired and glassy, but shining with something like gratitude as she looks up at me. I cup her cheek, staring into her stunning caramel orbs that still aren't as bright as they used to be.

"I love you, Abbey. Nothing will change that, okay?"

Her lips kick up a fraction, but not enough that you'd call it a smile.

"Not even when I point a gun at you?"

I smirk. "Especially not then. Just remember if you do that again, I'll consider it foreplay."

She lets out a soft, one-breathed laugh, like that's all she can manage, yet fuck, at least it's something.

"Was this foreplay?" she asks, and I know she means everything that's happened since walking into this bungalow.

"If you're ready for it to be, then yeah."

"I can't have sex yet," she repeats what she said earlier, and I let out a sigh.

"I know. That's not what I'm talking about."

Frowning, she pulls back a little, and I'm not even mad, because it gives me a better look at her tits.

Fuck… would she let me kiss them? Suck on them?

"What are you talking about then?"

"You can still climax, right? That part of you still works?" I ask, and she frowns, her eyes dropping to my chest as she considers my words.

"I actually don't know."

"Well, if you're game, we could try and find out."

"I still have a… graze down there."

I cringe because, fuck that sounds brutal.

"Is it on your clit?" I ask, having no fucking clue about that stuff, and she shakes her head.

"No… It's right… inside."

Fucking hell. If any bloke thinks he is the more superior sex, then he needs his head checked.

A woman can grow a life inside her and then push it out through a tight channel and survive all the pain and trauma that comes with it. As far as I'm concerned, women are the strongest species on this damn planet.

"I only need to touch the outside, Angel. Your sensitive little bean." I smirk, and her cheeks flush red.

"I'm bleeding."

"Nothing wrong with blood. That's actually a kink well known in motorcycle clubs. Ever see any of my brothers wearing a red wings patch on their cut?"

Her brows shoot up. "You're not serious?"

"Deadly, Angel. But tonight, given everything, I'll just use my fingers. How's that sound?"

12

ABBEY

'm lost for words, because since… Bobbi… I've felt only a few emotions. Fury, grief, and numbness. But now… now for the first time since Bobbi, I feel hot, achy in all the right places, and I'm desperate for Ringo to touch me, even if I don't know If it's right.

The press of Ringo's fingers to my clit has me jerking, and in an instant, I forget everything but him, me and where he's touching me.

"I fucking love the way your body responds to mine," Ringo rasps, leaning in, his lips ghosting over mine. "And this little button here," he circles my clit, robbing my brain of every coherent thought, sending electrified heat straight between my legs. "It's all mine. To touch. To lick. To *suck*."

My hips thrust forward, my lids falling shut as his words flood my mind with images that ignite my arousal into an inferno that only *he* can tame.

Then he kisses me.

I moan into his mouth as he parts my lips with his tongue, leaning back against the tiled wall, completely forgetting that we're cramped in a tiny shower. Forgetting *everything* except the way he makes me feel.

His kiss is gentle yet devouring, much like his fingers, quickly pushing me higher. It feels so good, heat licking over my skin as I writhe under his touch. I surge my hips forward, getting lost in the pleasure as it draws closer to that edge that usually has me tipping over. Only this time, I can't quite get there.

Shit. It's just there. Why can't I...

I suck on his tongue, a desperate yearning inside me now, chasing that intoxicating feeling like a crack whore ready for her next hit.

'Come on. Take me there!' I scream in my head at my own stupid self, the sensation of ecstasy climbing but staying out of reach.

I whimper, tearing my lips from his, letting my head fall back against the wall, and refusing to open my eyes, too scared I'll see disappointment in his.

But then I feel him shift, and my eyes spring open, finding him kneeling awkwardly on the floor.

"What are you doing?"

"Whatever I have to do to bring you pleasure, Angel," he rasps, his lust-drunk gaze burning into me. Then his eyes drop to my breasts.

Given my short height in comparison to him, his lips are level with my nipples, and he lets out a hungry growl before leaning in and flicking his tongue over one very tight, needy peak.

I gasp, and his eyes flick up to mine like he's checking if I'm okay with what he's doing. When I don't say anything, he does it again, this time, his fingers return to my clit.

I cry out, my nipples more sensitive than they've ever been, and he growls again, flicking his tongue faster in sync with his fingers working me between my legs.

This… this is doing something to me.

Before I even realise, my hands are fisting in his hair, gripping hard as I drag him closer, arching into him. Another low, animalistic growl rumbles from his chest, and I feel it against my nipple just before he closes his mouth around it, and then… ohhh… ohhh… he *sucks*.

I should stop this. I should pull back. But I can't even think straight. Not with the friction of his fingers against my clit, and the way he draws on my nipple, his hot tongue lashing over it…

"Cam!" I cry out, breathless and desperate, my eyes squeezing shut before I force them open again, needing to watch him. "Oh my God… are you…"

I nearly scream as he sucks harder, his fingers working over my clit at a relentless pace, and in a blinding explosion that I'm not prepared for, I shatter into a million pieces in one of the longest, most intense orgasms of my life.

Oh. My…

The moment the enormous wave starts to fade, my knees buckle, but Ringo stands, catching me easily, holding me up as I bury my face in his chest.

For a long moment, I stay quiet, my panting breaths the only thing I can hear as the weight of embarrassment settles over me at what we just did.

I just… let him *drink* from me.

I shake my head against his chest, but his big hands come up, gripping either side of my face, gently tipping my head back so I have to look up at him.

"I should've asked if you were still green. I'm sorry, Angel."

Shit. The colour system.

It's easy to forget in the heat of the moment, but the truth is, I would have stopped him if I really wanted to. And that's the problem right there.

What I needed to get over the line isn't right. Is it?

"I wasn't red." I breathe my admission, still flushed with shame at what I just let him do.

Did he do that just for me? It obviously worked, but at what cost to him?

Does he find my boobs vulgar now? Does he think I'm disgusting?

Did my milk taste awful?

"Were you orange?" he asks, his dark eyes dancing between mine.

"Were *you*?" I scoff, and he frowns.

"Fuck, no, Angel. I was, and always will be, green when it comes to you."

Pressing my hands over his, I peel them from my face and shake my head, dropping my gaze to his chest.

"But you… that… I should have…"

His low chuckle pulls my eyes back to his.

"If you think for one fucking second that your tits and milk are a turnoff for me, then you are *very* fucking wrong. That was one of the hottest things I've ever done." He runs his hands over my soaked hair, his eyes piercing mine with fierce determination. "But I probably should've asked first. I'm sorry about that."

I worry my lip between my teeth, considering his words.

If he *had* asked permission to… drink from me, would I have said yes?

Probably not, if I'm being honest with myself. Not because the idea of it wasn't a huge turn on, but because… it's wrong, isn't it?

Right now, my breasts are a *baby* thing, not a *sex* thing… or are they?

Shit. I don't even know.

The real question is, did I like it?

Who am I kidding? Of course I liked it. It was erotic as hell. It felt so good, and even though I felt a bit crampy, it seemed to heighten the pleasure somehow.

Jesus, I don't understand any of this.

"I think… I liked it." I cringe, and his brows shoot up.

"You *think*, or you *know* you did, but you're feeling weird about admitting it?"

I purse my lips. "The weird one."

He smirks.

"Hopefully next time, you'll feel better about it."

"Next time?" I squeak, and he chuckles, nodding.

"There's definitely going to be a next time, Angel."

"Oh," is all I can manage, and he chuckles.

"So, I've gotta tend to this." He gestures down, and my eyes follow, latching onto his very hard dick, jutting out in front of him. "Do you want to step out and dry off while I fix this?"

"No." I shake my head, peering up at him through my wet lashes.

He growls and grins at the same time, bracing one hand against the tiled wall over my head, his other wrapping around his thick length.

"Fuck, Angel. You give me the best spank bank material," he rasps, and for the first time in… I don't even know how long, a giggle slips past my lips.

As he moves his hand up and down his shaft, his eyes drop between our naked bodies, so mine follow, and I see blood swirling on the floor, getting washed down the drain.

Once again, my cheeks go up in flames. This time, from pure humiliation.

"One day, I'm gonna earn my red wings with you, Angel."

My eyes snap to his, my lips parted, ready to protest. But the moment I see his eyes glazed over like he's in a trance, I know there's no way I'll ever deny him what he wants. No matter how dirty it is.

Hell, I'm beginning to wonder if I might not be just as dirty.

That thought has butterflies surging in my belly as courage I don't normally feel has words falling past my lips.

"Yeah? Are you gonna eat my bleeding…" I trail off, because shit, I'm not good at dirty talk. Not like him.

"Finish the sentence," he demands, his hand working faster on his dick, his voice grittier, and his breathing more ragged.

Shit. Can I really do this? Talk super dirty and not sound like a complete dork?

"Finish it," he hisses, his hand moving in a steady rhythm, so I suck in a breath, hoping for courage.

"Are you gonna eat my bleeding… pussy?"

He groans with pleasure, his free hand dropping from the wall and fisting my hair as he chases his release.

"Yeah, Angel. I'm gonna eat your bleeding *cunt*."

I stiffen at the word I struggle with, but then quickly relax because *this* is Ringo, and the word means something different coming from his mouth.

It's not an insult or used in a vulgar way, so I clear my throat and give him what he wants.

"You gonna stick your tongue inside my bleeding… *cunt*?"

The word burns on my tongue, but the second I see that familiar pleasure-pained twist in his face, my shame melts.

"Fuck yes, Angel. I want you to ride my tongue with your bleeding cunt."

Something inside me snaps at his filthy words, the image of me straddling his face flashing through my mind. In an instant, my hand wraps around the tip of his cock, feeling how hard the rim is.

I really love that part of him where the tip flares. It has my mouth watering, and I consider dropping to my knees so I can run my tongue over it.

But I haven't done that with him yet, and the memory of the way Donny used to… nope. No way. That memory is not welcome, dammit!

Ringo's pleasured grunt has me focusing back on him, and he moves his hand away to make room for mine, so I slide my grip lower, feeling the bulging veins that creep up his shaft.

Oh, I like those veins too.

"Grip me tight." His voice is strained, his hand coming over mine, squeezing, making our combined grip like a vice as he takes control, pumping his dick.

"I'm gonna sit on your face." I breathe, my voice husky, and oh my God, I can hardly believe these filthy words are falling from my lips.

"Fuck, yes," he growls, moving our hands faster. Harder.

There's almost a franticness about it now, his breaths quicker, the muscles coiling up his arms rigid and tense.

He's close. So close.

I want to make him come.

"I'm gonna grind on your face and smother you with my blood."

"Yes!" It's a strangled sound, his head thrown back.

"Come all over me!" I practically yell, and he roars, his hand stopping our assault to squeeze around mine, and I feel his dick pulsing under my grip as hot white ropes of cum start spilling from his tip.

Some of it lands on me, but the water quickly washes it away, and I'm kinda disappointed. I wanted to see the evidence of his climax for a bit longer.

And just like that… I'm horny again.

Watching him come apart is something else. To know I did that to him, that I'm his spank bank material, makes me feel important. Special. And despite how aroused I am, without warning, tears spring to my eyes and I burst into tears.

Ringo curses under his breath, peeling our hands off his dick. But I'm already inconsolable, the reality of my world crashing back down on top of me, shattering me.

My legs give out, but as always, Ringo catches me, and I start blubbering, nothing making sense. Not even the thoughts in my head.

Bobbi is gone. Dead.

Others have died fighting for us. And tonight, I killed a second person. But this time, the satisfaction wasn't what I thought it would be.

It didn't feel like justice. It didn't feel like enough, or maybe it felt like too much.

Oh. My. God.

I have killed *two* people.

Maybe Bobbi was taken from me for a reason. Maybe I'm too much of a monster to be called a mother.

I'm not worthy.

Even though I'm a snotty mess, Ringo still scoops me up, carrying me out of the shower and dries me before slipping one of his tees over my head.

I don't deserve his love. His affection and care, but I'm too selfish to walk away.

I know I still have friends. And my little sister. But Ringo? I need him like I need air. Without him, I don't think I can get through this.

Carrying me to his bed, Ringo's voice is gentle as he says over and over, "I've got you."

There's so much pain inside me. So much guilt and disgust swirling together. It's unbearable, and I just want it to stop.

I want *all* of it to stop.

Sliding into bed with me, Ringo cocoons me in his arms, and I soak in his love, even though I don't deserve it.

Eventually, I cry myself to sleep, drifting into a space of nothingness where time doesn't exist. Pain doesn't exist.

I don't exist.

When I wake later, Ringo is still awake, running his hand over my hair in slow, soothing strokes. He's still here with me despite my breakdown. Despite me pushing him away so many times, I've lost count.

He's here. And that means something.

"How long was I asleep?" I croak, my voice raw.

"Only thirty minutes, Angel. You should try to get some more sleep." His lips press to the top of my head, and I burrow closer, clinging to his warmth, his scent helping to keep me together.

"Are we staying here tonight?" I mumble into his chest.

"No. The wake will end at midnight. We'll ride home after that. But we can rest here until Jols brings you some new clothes. I'm not taking you out there wearing just my t-shirt, Angel."

A small smile tugs at my lips, but then guilt instantly stabs me.

I need new clothes because the ones I had on were soaked in Wendy's blood. There's nothing funny about that.

Sure, she deserved to be punished, but did she deserve *that*?

Who have I turned into that can do that so easily? That I can smile right now? That I could beat her to a pulp, drag her before an audience, and shoot her?

I cringe inwardly, self-hatred sinking its claws into my chest.

Did I really just smile, the thing I can rarely do lately, because I killed another person?

I consider that and replay Ringo's words in my head, only to realise, the moment I smiled, I wasn't thinking about Wendy and all the blood. I was thinking about what we did in the shower, and perhaps that's a bigger reason to feel guilty.

I let myself feel good.

I shouldn't feel good.

Nothing about what I did is good.

Sharing that kind of moment with Ringo almost feels wrong, because there's nothing right in my life anymore.

"Wanna tell me what's going through that head of yours?" Ringo asks, and I shift, peering up at him to find those whiskey eyes full of love.

How can he love me after what I did? After the monster I became, not letting him help me… and pulling a gun on *him*.

He should hate me.

"I'm afraid if I tell you, you'll send me to a psych hospital."

His lips kick up. "I'll never fucking send you anywhere. You're mine. And I'll look after you until our dying day."

Shit. He sounds like he means it, although after everything tonight, I don't know why.

Still… it's comforting to know someone cares that much about me.

My parents didn't, yet here is a man, fifteen years older than me, willing to *risk everything* just to give me whatever pieces of himself he has left, even after the unrecognisable person I became earlier.

I don't deserve him.

"You'll get sick of me before that happens." I scoff, and he just shakes his head, leaning down to press a soft kiss to my forehead.

"Never." He shoots me a wink as he settles back against his pillow. "Now, tell me what's going on up here." He taps his finger gently to my temple, and I sigh.

"I feel... guilty. And confused," I admit, my gaze dropping under the weight of my shame.

"Hey," Ringo rasps, hooking his finger under my chin, coaxing my eyes back to his. "You've got nothing to feel guilty about."

"That's not true," I whisper, sucking in a breath to keep my tears at bay. "I feel guilty for... enjoying myself in the shower with you."

Tenderly brushing his thumb over my cheek, he offers me a small smile.

"That's gonna happen sometimes. It's normal to feel guilt when happiness sneaks in. But don't forget, it's part of healing."

I wonder when *his* first moment of happiness was after Hope died.

"I also feel confused... about Wendy," I admit, needing to get this off my chest. "I wanted her dead. I was sure that's what I needed to feel better."

"Only it didn't, did it?" There's no judgement in the deep gravel of his voice. No hint of *'I told you so'*.

So, I shake my head, needing to give him this truth.

"I told Bobbi I'd kill them all," I admit, the image of my daughter's lifeless body flashing before my eyes. "I made her that promise at the morgue. But it doesn't feel like enough. Killing Wendy didn't feel like enough. I don't get it."

Squeezing my eyes shut, I see Wendy's eyes right before I pulled the trigger. Her fear. Her acceptance that death was coming for her. The hatred she wore like a second skin, right up until her last breath.

"That's the thing, Angel. Nothing will be enough. Because nothing can bring Bobbi back."

Hot tears sting as they fall. I have no control over them as Ringo's words settle deep into the hollow ache inside me.

Nothing I do will ever bring Bobbi back.

"It hurts so much," I whimper, and Ringo's hand slips behind my head, guiding me to his chest, holding me tight.

"I know, Angel. I know."

I feel like all I do is cry lately. Like every tear is laced into every breath I take.

It was there before Bobbi died, but since then... I fear I'll never stop.

My husband holds me through it, neither of us saying a word, the silence a welcome comfort. A safe place for me to fall apart.

I ride the emotional rollercoaster I can't seem to find a way off of, wondering if there will ever be a day where the pain doesn't strangle me.

By the time my tears dry up, I'm drained, and my drowsy eyes flutter closed, chasing a reprieve.

"Ringo?" I murmur against his chest, and he grunts in response, so I continue before I lose my nerve. "When are you going to get mad at me for killing Wendy?"

"Not tonight, Angel. But make no mistake. We're going to have a very fucking serious talk about it," his voice rumbles. "About how I get the feeling you planned to take things into your own hands all along."

I stiffen at being caught, but then he presses his lips to my hair in a soft kiss, and I know that even though he's mad, he still cares about me.

It feels very... unconditional.

Something I'm not used to.

"Right now, though, all I want is for you to remember what it feels like to be safe in my arms." He strokes my back in comfort, and I nod against him, tightening my hold around his middle, burrowing into his side.

At some point, I must drift off again, floating through a weightless, dreamless space… because the next thing I know, I'm rousing to what sounds a lot like… panting.

Tensing, my eyes snap open to find myself spooned back against Ringo's chest, and only feet from where we lay are two figures writhing in the other bed.

"Shhh." Ringo's hot breath fans quietly over my ear. "They think we're asleep."

As the sleep clears from my eyes, I blink until the figures make sense.

It's JD… and Jols.

Oh.

Snapping my eyes shut, because now I feel like a peeping Tom, my heart races at the sight of watching other people together despite all the sex I've seen play out at the Western.

But this is different. We are in an enclosed space. This feels private. Intimate in a way that feels like we're trespassing.

And then, just when I think Ringo is surely going to pull the blanket over my head and cut off the sight, he leans close and whispers in my ear.

"Keep watching, Angel."

13

RINGO

A grin pulls at my lips as my Angel obeys my words, slowly prying her lids apart to watch our friends entangled in a frenzy like they can't fucking control themselves.

I know the fucking feeling.

Abbey had been asleep for a while when I heard their boots on the porch. She'd rolled over, and I'd kept her close, wanting her to feel my arms around her, even in sleep. She didn't even stir when they came into the room, Jols whispering and giggling quietly.

So naturally, I closed my eyes and pretended to be asleep.

It was purely for Jols' benefit. I've seen JD fuck more times than I can count. Hell, for the last couple of years, he's been my own live porn star, putting on private shows with women so I could jack off in peace, without the Doxies trying to get a piece of me.

Whereas Jols has never done anything but stand on the sidelines and watch the orgies at the club. Never participating.

"I'm gonna eat your sweet cunt, Babydoll," JD whispers, trailing kisses down over Jols' bra-clad tits, which is the only thing she's wearing now.

Babydoll… I'll have to remember to give him shit about that later.

Abbey's legs squirm a little under the blanket, and from where I'm propped on my side with pillows behind me, I can see her eyes are still on them. Locked on the show unfolding in front of us.

My eyes flick back to the couple, lost in their own world. JD's head is now buried between Jols' thighs, and Abbey's breathing deepens as we watch Jols arch her back, her hands fisting into JD's hair, her lips parting in a silent moan.

I'm horny as fuck. My release in the shower earlier only scratched the surface, barely taking the edge off. And now, as my Angel squirms again, clearly turned on by what she's seeing, I decide we can take a little of *our own* pleasure from this moment.

Sliding my hand from Abbey's stomach, I graze my fingers down to her panties, my eyes on the side of her face as she bites her lip, before pressing my fingers over the fabric. Right against her clit.

Well, there's a sanitary pad in the way, but I can still feel her through the padded barrier.

Abbey stiffens, but a moment later melts against me, shifting her top leg wider to give me better access, and I fucking smile.

My Angel is horny again.

Even through the barrier, I can feel her little nub is already swollen with need, practically matching how fucking hard my cock is, pressed firm against her arse.

Fuck. I'll never get enough of her.

JD's hand shifts between Jols' legs, and when she arches again, slapping her hand over her mouth, I know exactly what my best mate is doing to her.

His fingers are inside her. Deep.

Grazing my digits lower over my Angel's panties, I feel the heat radiating off her and bite back a fucking groan, because I bet her arousal is already making her slick.

"Your panties are hot. Is your pussy wet for me?" I breathe quietly against her ear, and I swear my words work like fire, her body turning into an inferno against me.

A whispered, strangled sound escapes Jols' lips, drawing my attention to see her body going rigid as she comes, and my Angel's hips drive forward, seeking more friction.

"Fuck, Angel. Does that make you want to come too?" I whisper as JD draws Jols' orgasm out, and Abbey nods slightly, holding her breath as my fingers move faster over her.

Coming up for air, JD grins wickedly up at Jols before his head turns in our direction.

Jols is too busy panting through her aftershocks to notice me watching, and JD shoots me a wink, his lips stretched in a fucking cocky, toothy smile beneath his scruffy beard.

Not wanting to alert Jols to her audience, I swallow my chuckle, my eyes dropping to Abbey's face to see her lids are shut, faking sleep like a good girl.

JD raises his brows as he nods towards Abbey, and I nod back, silently confirming that she's awake.

What he does now is all on him.

With my fingers still slowly circling the fabric over Abbey's clit, I watch JD shift over Jols, whispering to her, this time quieter, making it impossible for me to hear.

He shifts back, his hard cock jutting out in front of him as he reaches to the side, fishing through the pockets of his jeans, probably searching for a rubber.

"Open your eyes, Angel," I whisper, watching her until those long dark lashes flutter open to see JD kneeling on the bed, still searching for protection as Jols quickly shifts, sitting up and taking his cock into her mouth.

My cock fucking jumps at the sight.

Not because I'm aroused by the sight of Jols or JD, but because watching a woman's lips wrap around a man's cock always gets me off.

"Fuck, Babydoll. You suck me so good," he whispers, though fuck, it's hardly a whisper. He knows we're watching, and he's not holding back.

Abbey's hips start gently rocking against my fingers, building a rhythm that has my cock weeping at the tip. Without meaning to, I grind the hard fucker against the valley of her arse, and she tenses, but it's short-lived when my fingers move faster, and her lips part, a soft pant slipping out.

Finally finding a condom, JD tears the foil packet open with his teeth before gripping Jols' head, and pulling her away.

"You're hungry tonight, Babydoll."

She nods, watching him roll the condom on, and then he pushes her back to the mattress, hovering over her before slapping his cock over her mound.

Fucking cocky prick.

The move makes Jols giggle, and she quickly slaps her hand over her mouth, and this time, when they both look our way, I close my eyes.

Would Jols stop if she knew we were watching?

I'm not actually sure. This is a side of Jols I've never seen. She's never risked being caught like this before.

I suppose she knows I won't rat her out to Smitty, her overbearing stepdad, but still, getting caught by someone else is a huge fucking risk. Especially with so many people on the compound. Anyone could've seen her sneak in here.

The thing is, death and funerals have a way of making you reassess what actually matters. So maybe Jols doesn't care anymore.

Too bad it's JD that'll pay for it.

Rustling on their bed pulls my attention, and I crack one eye open.

They're not bothered with us anymore, their focus now back on each other.

"Watch them, Angel," I urge quietly, pressing my hand to Abbey's mound and grinding the heel of my palm against her as I start rubbing over the padded fabric that covers her entrance.

Her eyes fly open just in time to see Jols hook her far leg over JD's shoulder, his hand pressing her wide open in a way that we can see nearly everything as he lines up his cock and slowly sinks it in.

They both groan, and now I'm the one shifting, fucking aching to feel Abbey wrapped around me.

I knew she was struggling to come in the shower earlier, which is why I knelt down and did something I hoped she'd like.

Something I knew might push the line, but would snap her out of her head and away from the weight of her broken heart.

With that in mind, and my need to feel my cock close to her entrance, I release her pussy, feeling her stiffen as I quietly shift just enough to free my cock, and slide it between her thighs.

"Keep your legs tight, Angel," I whisper against her ear, pushing my cock as far as it'll go as she closes her thighs around it. "I'm gonna fuck them until I come."

A faint whimper falls from Abbey's lips, her legs flexing, sandwiching my cock with warm, perfect pressure, and I quietly groan against her ear.

My hand returns to her front, skating over her mound, now pulled tight to accommodate my cock, and I start pumping my hard fucking rod as I kneed her clit once again.

Our ragged breathing syncs, both of us locked in a quiet rhythm as we watch our friends fuck.

They're too lost in each other now to care if they wake us, their moans growing louder as they chase their highs.

Dry fucking between Abbey's thighs is gonna leave me with a sore cock later, but right now, I'm too far gone to care.

As I pump my cock between the press of her skin, her fingertips graze over my tip, feeling the fat head of my cock as it pokes in and out.

Groaning in her ear, I nip at her lobe, my eyes no longer on my mates, but focused on the side of her face and her parted lips as her cheeks flush from her arousal.

She starts writhing against me, grinding her clit harder against my fingers, even as she grips my cock between her legs, shifting it higher until I'm not just fucking her thighs, but grinding against her panties too.

"Fuck, Angel. I want to dirty your cunt with my cum, and mix it with your blood."

She doesn't stiffen like I expect her to when I say the word *cunt*. Instead, she moves again, frantic now, tugging her panties aside until my cock slides through her slick folds.

We both moan, and if she notices, she doesn't let on, panting loudly as the fat head of my cock glides over her clit with each slow grind from behind, while my fingers rub her needy bud harder, matching the rhythm.

We're both gonna end up painted in her blood, but I don't give a fuck. If she wasn't grazed inside from giving birth, I'd already be buried deep inside her.

It's JD's and Jols' cries of ecstasy that finally push Abbey over the edge. Her climax ripping through her so hard I can feel her cunt pulsing against my fingers and my cock as I thrust from behind.

"I can feel your pussy throbbing," I rasp, my voice strangled as my nuts draw tight and pleasure detonates inside me.

A second later, hot jets of cum shoot from my tip, pulsing against Abbey's clit and drenched folds.

"Enjoy the show?"

JD's voice is what snaps me out of my haze. That and my Angel stiffening against me before she squeaks and yanks the blankets up to cover her head.

"As always," I chuckle, tightening my arms around my embarrassed wife as she hides, while Jols giggles in the bed next to us.

"You two are secretly gay lovers, aren't you?" she teases, not the least bit embarrassed that we just watched them, and got off to it.

"Nope," JD chuckles, pinching Jols' nipple, which has her gasping and slapping at his hand. "But Mr *Celibacy until Abbey came along* used to love watching me fuck. It's been a while, but I gotta say, tonight was my favourite."

"I was more into how my Angel got so turned on. Not you two ugly fuckers." I snort, and then quickly duck, covering Abbey protectively when Jols tosses a pillow at us.

"Just remember. You never saw me. I was never here," Jols deadpans, and I hold a hand up in surrender.

"Yeah, yeah. I know."

"Ahhh, is Abbey alright?" JD asks, peeling off the cum-filled condom from his now lax cock.

Stiffening under the blankets, Abbey grips my hand like she is silently begging me to make her invisible, and I can't help but grin.

"She's okay. Probably just a little mortified."

The moment the words leave my lips, Abbey's elbow jams into my ribs, and I wheeze out a cough as Jols and JD laugh at my expense.

"Come on, Babydoll. Let's take a shower and get cleaned up." JD grins at Jols, and I can't help but notice the smile they share.

It's weird seeing them like this. Jols with her walls down, and JD actually giving a shit about a chick. There's more than lust in their eyes, and although I kinda knew something was going on between them, I hadn't realised it had gotten this serious.

Casting my eyes down to my blanket, I give Jols and JD a sliver of privacy as they scramble off his bed and he chases her into the bathroom.

I noticed her bullet wound is healing near her collarbone. It's going to leave one hell of a scar. Despite her injury, she's recovering quickly, but I'd bet my money the drinks she's consumed today are the reason she doesn't seem all that bothered by it.

Tomorrow will probably hurt like a bitch, though.

"Are they gone?" Abbey whispers from under the blanket, and I chuckle, peeling it back to see her hair plastered to her sweaty forehead.

"They're showering," I confirm, brushing the damp strands off her face. "I dirtied up your pretty pussy."

She giggles at my words, but a second later, her smile slips, and I know exactly where her mind has gone.

Back to her fucked-up reality.

"You did. I guess I got you dirty too."

Her voice is quiet, almost hollow. I fucking hate seeing her like this. It's so fucking cruel.

"Once they're done, I'll get you washed. But for now, this'll have to do."

Reaching behind me, I snatch up the towel from earlier, and ease my cock out from between her thighs, and we get to work, cleaning ourselves up as much as we can, my cum and her blood already sticky and drying in some places.

Abbey doesn't speak, her eyes fixed on the floor like looking at me might make her break.

This isn't about me, though. It's about her and the unthinkable pain she's choking on every second she remembers what she's lost.

She moves to sit at the end of my bed, wearing nothing but my shirt, her drenched panties now wrapped up in the towel, forgotten. She stares at her feet, blankly, saying nothing while she waits.

"Can I get you anything, Angel?" I sit beside her, but she shakes her head.

It's fucking hard not to take her silence personally. I wish I was enough for her. Enough to glue her broken heart back together and bury the ache in her chest.

Nothing will ever be enough to fix that kind of pain.

With my hands resting on the tops of my thighs, I sit beside her in silence, letting it stretch, giving her the space she needs right now without making her feel alone.

Running my hands over my legs a few times, my pinky brushes hers, and before I can move it away, she hooks hers with mine, like she needs that simple connection.

I'll give her whatever she needs, no questions asked, so we sit in that quiet silence, only this time, our fingers are linked together.

When JD and Jols finally emerge from the bathroom, with steam billowing out behind them, their grins drop the moment they take in the sombre mood of the room.

Moving to Abbey, Jols lowers to her haunches, getting in Abbey's line of sight.

"I've got some clean clothes for you." Jols gestures to the chair in the corner. "One of the old ladies had a spare pair of leathers, and Casey gave me some underwear for you in case you needed it."

"Thanks," Abbey whispers, and Jols reaches up, taking her other hand.

"I'm sorry we... you know, went at it with you guys in the room. I've had a few drinks, and well... it felt like a good idea at the time."

Abbey's head lifts, a small smile tugging at her lips. "I'm sorry for watching."

Jols shrugs, a cheeky smile lighting her face. "I don't mind a bit of exhibitionism. Just not in front of my stepdad. That's just creepy."

They both laugh, and for a second, the room feels lighter.

My eyes shift to JD's, finding him watching on with a flicker of sympathy in his expression.

Today has been a-fucking-lot for everyone. Heavy as shit.

"How are you feeling after earlier?" Jols asks, her voice soft before Abbey sighs.

"You mean after I beat Wendy to a pulp and then shot her in front of everyone?"

Jols nods slowly, her gaze laser-focused on my Angel like she's assessing everything she does, and Abbey shrugs, taking a moment to clear her throat.

"I'm not sure I know who I am right now, to be honest."

Reaching out, Jols rubs Abbey's arm in support. "That's totally understandable. You've got a lot going on, and now you're trying to find your footing in a world that doesn't look the same anymore. You're not going to be the same person you were before. And that's okay. It's gonna take time…" Jols trails off, because she doesn't need to spell that out to Abbey.

She knows my Angel is suffering through every brutal second of it.

"Thank you," Abbey whispers, her voice tight like she's barely holding it together. "I just hope I'm someone still worthy of your friendship when I come out the other end."

Jols smiles. "I've got no doubt we're gonna be the best of friends. How could we *not* after you just watched me have sex?"

"Oh my God," Abbey groans, burying her face in her hands as JD and I start laughing. "I blame Ringo. He told me to watch." She waves a frantic hand in my direction, which only makes me laugh more.

She's so fucking adorable when she's flustered.

"Angel, I'll happily take the blame."

Her head snaps in my direction, a grin tugging at the corner of her lips as she tries to glare at me.

"On that note," JD chuckles. "We are gonna clear out before you two start having angry sex."

"We will not ..." Abbey trails off, clearly realising arguing is pointless as JD leads Jols out of the cabin.

"What were you saying?" I smirk, and she stands with a huff.

"Shut up."

I follow my exasperated wife into the bathroom and join her in the shower again, both of us washing away the blood and cum. This time, we manage to keep it G-rated, drying off and getting dressed before leaving the sanctuary we found inside my room.

It hits midnight as we rejoin the party, most of my club brothers fucking hammered, slurring and swaying, and laughing like they haven't seen death up close tonight.

The Doxies are nearly as bad, hardly able to hold each other up, half-sprawled on the makeshift seating around the dwindling bonfire.

A sharp whistle slices through the noise, drawing attention to Smitty, standing tall on a massive cooler with a beer in hand, the fire casting shadows across his face.

Then he clears his throat.

"To our brothers who rode harder than hell, who took no shit and gave no mercy. You weren't saints. You were sinners with steel in your blood. You fucked up, fought hard, and always had our six."

Slowly, Smitty raises his beer to the sky, eyes locked on the stars, and mine follow, watching the embers from the fire drift up like the souls of my brothers are leaving the Earth.

"They say the road doesn't end, it just curves where we can't see. So wherever you are now, brothers, I hope the beer is cold, the bikes are fast, and the bastards you owed are burning instead of you."

Smitty clears his throat again, struggling to keep it together, and lowers his beer, pointing it towards the row of eight hogs lined up, with a cut hanging from each one.

"I ain't gonna lie. This world is colder without you ugly fuckers. But we Sadists, carry your names, your scars, and your sin. And through us, you'll live on until the day we go down swinging."

My brothers roar with a cheer, some thumping the centre of their chests as Smitty continues.

"And when my fucking time is up," Smitty bellows over the crowd, beer raised high as tears streak down his cheeks, "I'll ride into the fire of Hell with my head high and my fucking middle finger raised!"

I fucking shout with my brothers, my throat burning, and my chest tight with the weight of the grief in the air.

Abbey snuggles in closer, tucking herself into my side, not out of fear or sadness, but because the brutal wave of brotherhood wraps around her too.

With his beer pressed to his lips, Smitty drains it before turning and tossing it into the fire, his silhouette framed by the flames as he holds both arms up in the air and yells at the top of his lungs.

"Ride easy, brothers! We've got the watch now!"

Beer bottles go flying into the air, glass smashing all around us as the crowd turns feral.

Brothers turn and find the closest Doxies, and it's like a fucking free for all as clothes are torn off in a frenzy.

That's my fucking cue to leave.

Steering Abbey out of the fray, JD is quick to follow with Jols, while the other guys shacking up with us at the lake stay behind to enjoy a night of sin.

"You okay to drive?" I ask JD as we reach our hogs, and he nods, gesturing to Jols.

"She's the one who had too much to drink tonight. Not me."

She rolls her eyes but doesn't deny it, and I leave them to get prepared, turning back to help Abbey into the helmet and then onto my bike.

Leaving the madness of the party behind, we cruise up the long driveway to the entrance. The Marx security detail is already in place, and as two of their SUVs take the lead, we fall in behind, while another two tail us.

It's pitch black out in this part of the countryside. The clouds have started to close in over the valley, thick with pending rain, casting an eerie weight over everything. Our headlights slash through the dark, lighting up the pine trees as we whip by at high speed.

Rounding a descending bend, we barely have enough time to brake when the two lead cars slam on their brakes, their tyres squealing as they fishtail before finally grinding to a stop.

My hog wobbles hard, and I fight to keep control of it as Abbey screams behind me, her arms clamping tight around my waist. My bike slides sideways, too fucking fast and sharp, and I hold the fuck on, bracing as we skid towards the SUV.

I fucking hold my breath, my heart in my throat, but we stop mere inches between us and the fucking car. The squeal of tyres doesn't end there, my eyes darting to the side to see JD closing in fast, and Abbey screams again, as my best mate careens towards us.

My eyes are fucking wide, a cold spike of dread rushing up my spine as I brace for a second time, but by some fucking miracle, JD, with Jols on the back, stops a breath away from clipping us.

"Fuck. That was close." The crazy fucker laughs, but my eyes are over his shoulder now, hearing and seeing the SUVs behind us struggling to stop in time, too.

JD stiffens, and Jols tucks her head into his back, and I wonder for the third fucking time in a matter of seconds if we're about to become roadkill.

For a few long beats, all I hear is my own breath before my surroundings come rushing back in to hear yelling and car doors slamming as a few of the Marx crew leap from their cars with their guns raised.

"Why'd we stop?!" one yells from the back.

"There's something blocking the road!" another yells from up front.

"Angel. Are you okay?" I ask, my eyes flicking around, because fuck, something doesn't feel right.

"Y-yes," she stammers, her dainty fingers digging into my sides as she trembles.

"JD?!" I yell over the chaos, and he grunts.

"We're fine. I need a new pair of boxers, though." He laughs, but I can tell he doesn't find this the least bit funny.

"Uhhh, guys?" Jols' uncertain voice has us all alert. "Something's not right."

My exact fucking thoughts, but before I can do anything about it, the loud crack of gunfire starts piercing the air.

14

ABBEY

"**H**old on!"

I barely catch Ringo's shout over the sharp crack of gunfire, a squeal leaping from my throat as he takes off, the sudden force nearly throwing me off him.

The roar of his engine smothers some of the chaos as we swerve past the SUVs and men firing into the pine forest. JD is right on our tail, and as we clear the last vehicle, a massive BOOM explodes behind us.

Whipping my head around, I catch sight of the rear SUV engulfed in flames, and a man running blindly, his whole body on fire, screaming in agony.

"Oh my God!" I cry as bile rises up my throat.

"Don't look, Angel!" Ringo yells, gunning it as we speed past a cluster of rusted drums scattered across the road.

It's not hard to tell that they were deliberately placed there, leaving no space for a car to get through, but enough room for a smaller vehicle… like a motorcycle.

Shit.

"I think it's a trap!" I shout close to Ringo's ear, hoping he'll hear, and when he nods, I know he has.

"Fuck. I think you're right."

"We've got company!" JD bellows, coming up beside us, and I don't need to look back to see, because the headlights in the rearview mirrors show me.

"Fucking Rebels!" Ringo roars, pushing the throttle harder as a pack of motorcycles chase us.

I cling to him, my muscles tight as my heart hammers, terrified we are going to lose control and crash, but as we round another bend, and Ringo starts slowing, I risk a look ahead.

There's another roadblock, and this time, it's a wall of bikers with their guns pointed right at us.

"Fuck, Angel." Ringo's hand grips my thigh, giving it a firm squeeze, and my heart sinks.

He knows we're trapped. He knows there's no way out of this.

We slow to a stop, and the motorcycles behind us do the same, staying back as a man up front steps forward wearing a cut the same as those guys we killed in the hospital.

Satan's Rebels.

"Give us the girl and we'll let you live!" he shouts, and a whimper slips past my lips before I can stop it.

Ringo's hand tightens on my thigh, silently telling me he won't let that happen, before he opens the visor on his helmet to respond.

"I'll never give her up!"

The Rebel laughs like Ringo just told him a joke, and the rest of his men copy.

"We gotta go bush." JD's low voice draws my attention, but Ringo doesn't look his way. His gaze remains on the Rebel still laughing.

Flipping open my visor, I glare straight at the smug Rebel, hoping my voice comes out stronger than I feel.

"What do you want with me?!" I call, and he grins wide, eyes gleaming as he finally focuses on me.

"It's nothing personal, darlin'. Just business. If we bring you in alive, we get a good fuckin' payday."

I scoff. "Do you still get paid if I'm dead?"

His smile drops. "No. So rest assured, we ain't gonna kill you."

"Might play with you a little first!" some random Rebel yells from behind the guy up front.

I feel more than hear the low growl that rumbles in Ringo's chest at that.

"Who's paying you?" I shout, and the Rebel answers easily.

"Some fucker called Dudley Banes. A man of God, apparently."

I stiffen.

Minister Banes is paying a motorcycle club to hunt me down and kidnap me.

"Aren't you working for Ian Allen?" JD asks, and the Rebel shrugs.

"Allen is a fucking snake. Yeah, we've dealt with him, but he's not the one writing cheques. That prick's got his own agenda, and unless he can top two hundred grand, then he's worth shit to us."

"Two hundred thousand dollars," I mutter in disbelief.

"I'll pay you more to walk away," Ringo calls.

"Wait. No!" I hiss, but Ringo squeezes my thigh again, a silent warning to stay quiet.

The Rebels burst out laughing.

"As tempting as that is," the lead Rebel's smile drops, "we don't do business with our rivals. But I'll gladly take your money after we have your girl and you've got a bullet in your skull."

A gasp escapes me as Ringo revs the engine, and a second later we lurch forward, tearing off towards the shadowed pine forest off to the side.

Another squeal bursts out as I clutch him tighter, my body getting jostled like a rag-doll as we leave the road for grass.

I'm too scared to look back, but I can hear the roar of bikes chasing us, and I guess I have to be thankful they want me alive, otherwise I'd be riddled with bullets by now.

"Fuck!" JD and Jols yell in unison as their bike slams into a rock, nearly throwing them off. But JD wrestles it back under control, speeding up again to catch us.

"Ringo!" I cry out in panic, because shit, I don't see a way out of this.

If they catch us, they will kill him. I know it!

"It's okay, Angel!" he calls back. "I won't let them have you."

He doesn't get it. He doesn't get that *his* safety is what I'm worried about. Not my own.

It's then that I see the flicker of flames up ahead, and I realise we're heading back towards the first ambush and the Marx security team.

Gunfire cracks ahead, but it's less than before, and as we draw closer to the treeline, I see the carnage that's been left in the wake.

There are bodies. So many scattered on the ground. Still and lifeless. Most wearing Rebel cuts, but some dressed in the Marx black uniform.

We hit a bump, and I bite back my squeal this time, until I realise the bump was actually us driving over a leg, and then I squeal for a different reason.

Shit. Shit. Shit.

That was a leg. Without a body attached to it.

I need to keep it together. Now's not the time to freak out.

These arseholes played a part in Bobbi's death. I shouldn't be running *from* them. I should be running *towards* them, with a gun in one hand and a knife in the other.

Breaking through the treeline, several Marx security spin our way with guns raised, but when they see it's us, their aim shifts behind us to the swarm of Rebels closing in.

The Marx team starts firing into the trees as Ringo and JD swing their bikes around the SUV and pull to a hard stop.

Jumping off quickly, they draw their guns and start shooting into the treeline, using the SUV as cover.

"Abbey!" Jols hurries to my side, helping me off the bike, my legs shaking so bad I can barely stand. "Keep your helmet on. Let's go!"

She drags me across the road, into the other line of trees, and I panic when we get further and further from my husband.

"I don't want to leave Ringo." I snatch my hand back when we're a few metres in, the forest ahead looking pitch-black and unforgiving.

"We won't," she promises. "We'll just hide back here."

Drawing her own gun, Jols holds it steady in front of her, scanning the chaos unfolding on the road.

Suddenly, rough hands grab me from behind, and I scream as I get dragged backwards into the shadows.

Jols is right there, her gun trained on whoever has me.

"Let her go or I'll shoot!" she snarls, and the man scoffs.

"I'll take my chances you're not that good a shot."

I claw at his hands, but he's wearing gloves, and it barely fazes him. I'm too preoccupied trying to get myself free to notice until it's too late, when a man comes crashing into Jols from the side.

I scream again, the arsehole dragging me deeper into the darkness, my heart thundering in my chest.

They said they wouldn't kill me, but they also said they might "play" with me.

I know what men like them consider play, and I'd rather die than let another man use my body for his sick pleasure.

Suddenly, the man stumbles, and we start falling backwards. We hit the ground hard, a loud "umph" ripping from him as he takes the full impact.

I don't waste the chance, and slam my elbow into his ribs, his grip loosening enough for me to roll off, and quickly scramble to get up, so I can run.

I make it two steps before his hand snaps around my ankle, yanking me back down, my body slamming into the dirt hard. I claw at the earth, digging in to pull myself forward, but he's strong and fast and annoyingly determined.

I kick back, my boot connecting with something solid, and he roars in pain, making me grin.

I hope that hurt, arsehole.

He's not done, though, on me again in an instant, crawling up my body as I twist and fight to get away.

Knowing I can't out-muscle him, I change tactics and stop trying to drag myself away. Gripping my helmet, I hurry to tug it off, holding it like a weapon, and when he rolls me over, I swing.

The crack is loud as my helmet smashes into his skull, and he tumbles off me with a thud.

Rage explodes through me as I straddle him, seeing his glazed eyes blinking at me, completely stunned.

With both hands locked around the helmet, I swing again, driving it down into his face with everything I've got.

I scream and I swing. Again and again. The feeling of his bones crunching spurring me on.

I keep going, smashing it down, caving in his face until all I can see is bone and blood.

I refuse to stop. I need to make sure he can't hurt me. Can't hurt anyone ever again.

"Angel!"

Ringo's bellow cuts off with a thud, and my eyes snap to him, now on the ground, only metres away with a man on top of him, trying to force a knife into his chest.

The noise that rips from my throat resembles a feral war cry, and I charge without hesitation, my sights locked onto the man trying to kill my husband.

I leap, my feet leaving the ground, and I swing like I'm holding a bat, the helmet crashing into the side of his skull with a brutal blow.

He tumbles sideways, and I'm on him before he can suck in a breath, ignoring Ringo as he calls for me to stop.

I don't.

I *won't*.

I can't stop until every last person that means me or who I love harm, is dead.

I beat him, screaming with each hit, his face cracking open, but still I don't stop.

The thunderous crack of a gun echoes through the air close by, pulling me up short.

Panting, I spin to see a Rebel hitting the ground, a gun slipping from his hand to the leafy forest floor beside him.

It's then that I see the silhouette of a man behind him, a gun tight in his grip as a slither of smoke curls up from the barrel.

At first, I expect to recognise a Marx crewman, but that's not who I'm looking at, and I frown in confusion.

15

ABBEY

T his man… He's wearing a Rebel's cut. Did he just shoot his own guy?

"Stay back!" Jols pants, stepping up beside me, with Ringo and JD quickly flanking us as the man quickly holds his hands up in surrender.

"Don't shoot. I'm not here to hurt you."

"Dude, did you just shoot your own man?" JD asks what I'd been thinking, and the man shrugs, taking a step back.

"I'm not who they think I am."

"And who the fuck *are* you?" Ringo snarls, stepping forward, zero fear in his stance.

"I'm friend, not foe."

"Yet you wear a Rebel's patch," Ringo hisses, pointing to the logo stitched onto the cut he's wearing.

The man doesn't even flinch. "Like I said. I'm *not* who they think I am."

My eyes narrow, his words turning over in my head.

"Are you undercover or something?" I ask, and he breathes out hard, frustration flickering behind his calm.

"Look, I can't tell you *who* I am, but I won't stop you. Just go."

JD and Ringo exchange a weary glance before the man speaks again.

"Before you go, someone's gotta knock me out." His lips kick up in a smirk. "Gotta make it look real."

Ringo smirks, quickly closing the distance before pulling back and slamming his fist into the man's face.

The guy drops hard, out cold before he even hits the ground, and Ringo crouches and fishes through his pockets, pulling out his wallet and flipping it open.

"Blake Moore," he reads the name on his identification, taking out his phone and taking a picture of it.

"Never heard of him," JD mutters, stepping up beside Ringo to stare down at the man.

"Hey, you alright?" Jols' voice pulls my attention away from the men, and I nod, not entirely sure that I am.

"I kind of feel numb."

Ringo shoves Blake's wallet back into his pocket and turns to me, his eyes scanning over me from head to toe.

God, what must he see?

I can feel the blood coating my skin for the second time in the last eight hours.

He must think I'm a monster.

"Let's get you back to the safe house."

My reaction is delayed, my head a mess of images, like freeze-framed horror movie reels, flicking past my eyes.

Blood.

Bone.

Brutality.

I can see my hands inflicting it, but I'm struggling to believe that was really me.

"Angel?" Ringo steps closer, and I nod, glancing over my shoulder to the road where the SUV is still on fire and I can hear gunfire in the distance.

"Is it over?" I ask, turning back to find him right in front of me now.

"For us, it is. Riggs called in reinforcements. There won't be a Rebel left alive to come after us."

I swallow hard, bobbing my head.

There's been so much bloodshed. Too much.

All because of me.

It doesn't make sense.

"Come on. Let's get out of here," JD mutters, and I catch the worry in his eyes as he takes in the cuts and bruises marking Jols' face and neck.

I don't say a word. What is there to say?

They've all suffered yet again because of me.

We walk out of the forest, and on the side of the road, I stop to bend down and wipe the blood off my helmet, using the thick patch of grass before fitting it back on.

We mount up in silence, riding off to leave the Marx team behind to clean up the mess, and ten minutes later, we're pulling into the safe house on Redfield Lake.

By the time Ringo kills the engine and we've climbed off the bikes, my rage is back, hot and gnawing at me, my thoughts too dark to speak aloud.

Ripping off my helmet, I shove it into Ringo's chest. "You should burn this. I killed two men with it."

His brows shoot up, glancing at Jols for confirmation.

"They never stood a chance," she says simply, and I turn away, heading up the steps of the cabin.

Before I even reach the top, I stop and spin around, my glare molten as I stare at my three friends.

My fury isn't aimed at them, though. It's for my parents and that stupid, bloody church.

"Banes is the one willing to throw around serious cash to catch me, but I'm done running," I snap, jabbing my thumb into my chest. "No more running."

"What are you saying, Angel?" Ringo moves to the bottom step, looking up at me.

"I want to go hunting… for him. For all of them." I clench my fists as I struggle not to scream. "I'm sick of waiting around for other people to find intel on them while I sit here useless. I can't let more people die while I hide."

I brace myself, expecting Ringo to push back. For him to shut me down and tell me it's too dangerous. To tell me he won't allow it.

But he doesn't.

Instead, he nods.

"Okay. If that's what you want."

"It is."

My voice is softer now, some of the rage bleeding out of me, now that I know he's not going to fight me on this.

With that settled, the ache in my chest returns as I steel myself for what has to be done.

I don't want to. I really don't. But I have to.

After going to the compound today and experiencing the brotherhood. The grief they shared. And the honour they gave their men… well, it's time.

"There's something else I have to do first…" My voice cracks as I speak, and just like that, tears spring to my eyes and my lip quivers.

Climbing the steps, Ringo stops on the one just below mine, his big warm hands framing my face as I stare up at him, his touch working like magic to ground me.

"I know there is, Angel." His thumb swipes at my falling tears. "Just tell me how I can help."

Of course, he knows what I'm talking about. I've been avoiding it, shutting down every conversation that he tries to start about it. But I can't keep running from it anymore.

It's not fair to me… and it's not fair to Bobbi.

"I don't know how to organise a funeral." A sob lurches from my throat, and Ringo pulls me in, his arms wrapping around me, holding me tight.

"I'll help, Abs. We'll do it together."

"Thank you," I whimper into his chest, fisting his cut, scared he'll step away and leave me to feel the chill in the air.

But of course he doesn't. He never leaves me to suffer through this alone. Not even when I point a gun at him.

He's always there for me.

I really need to start returning the favour.

"Can I…" I pull back, releasing his cut to swipe at my tears, peering up into his whiskey eyes, now lit by the porch light. "I was wondering… and you can totally say no if you want… but I'd hoped…"

A warm smile tugs at the corners of his mouth, hidden just behind his beard.

"What is it, Angel? Just ask."

"I don't really have any family anymore… and well… you're my husband. For now, at least. And your family is so lovely. Your mum and sisters…" His brows shoot up, so I stop talking.

"I'm your husband, for now, at least? You planning on leaving me, Angel?"

I shake my head. "I mean, you said after all of this was over that I could divorce you, so I kinda figured that option was open for you, too."

Before I can blink, Ringo lifts me off the porch, and my legs wrap around his waist on instinct, carrying me up the steps.

"You're stuck with me, Angel. Actually, fuck that. I take back that statement. There's no fucking way I'm letting you divorce me when this is over."

Laughter follows us inside as JD and Jols listen to our exchange, but I pay them zero attention, not able to draw my gaze away from the fierce promise blazing in Ringo's eyes.

"Now that we've sorted that out," he sighs, "please tell me what you're trying to ask for."

Drawing in a steadying breath, I steel myself to say the words.

"Would it be alright if I bury Bobbi under the Jacaranda tree on your property? She doesn't have to be next to Hope… I just… well… I just don't want Bobbi to be alone."

Ringo's eyes glaze over, and he clears his throat before answering. "Say no more, Angel. Of course you can."

I swallow the lump that's lodged in my throat and lean forward, pressing my forehead to his, just like he loves to do with me.

"I love you," I whisper, and he hugs me closer.

"I fucking love you, too, Angel."

He closes the distance then, his lips claiming mine, and I melt against him, soaking in the calm he brings me. The rare sense of peace only he has the power to give.

"Uhhh, question," JD butts in. "If you two start fucking out here in the living room, because it's a shared space, we can totally stick around and watch, right?"

The low growl that rumbles up Ringo's throat is what breaks our kiss, and he shoots a glare in JD's direction.

"If I start fucking my wife *anywhere* and you or other people are in the fucking room, you all need to fuck right off! Got it?!"

"Except for when you're spying on us fucking, right?" Jols smirks, poking her tongue out as she strolls past into the kitchen.

A giggle slips from me before I can stop it, and even though I immediately feel guilty for it, I try hard to ignore the feeling clawing at me for having the slightest moment of happiness.

Ringo's frown softens into a grin at the sound, his eyes roaming my face before he heads for the stairs with me in his arms.

"I'm taking my wife to bed."

"Oh, I see how it is," JD huffs. "You'll yell at me but not Jols. I guess we all know who your favourite is."

As Ringo climbs the stairs, two at a time, I catch the smirk twitching at the corner of his mouth, yet he doesn't respond to JD.

He knows exactly how to annoy his best mate.

"Of course I'm his favourite," Jols snickers from over at the fridge as she grabs a bottle of water and cracks it open. "I'm prettier than you."

All I hear is a startled squeak from Jols as we reach the first landing, cutting off our view of the living area below. Then the sound of feet pounding on the timber floors follows, and their laughter echoes up to us.

"Fucking hell," Ringo groans. "They're gonna fuck on the kitchen table. I just know it."

I smile at that, and once again, guilt sinks in.

That's how it's going to be now. Every little glimpse of happiness will be tangled with grief.

This is my life now, I guess.

Up in our room, we peel off our clothes and slip under the blankets, our bodies finding each other like magnets as we curl together.

My mind is like a hamster on a wheel. A never-ending stream of thoughts as I replay everything that happened today in my head.

The funerals.

Wendy.

The shower and my milk.

The ambush.

In the last week, I've killed four people. Three of them were in the last twenty-four hours.

I'm not sure what to do with that.

Who am I becoming?

I'm not sure I like this version, but… well, now I feel like less of a victim.

Now I feel like the predator. Which makes no sense since I've had zero training. Just outbursts of blinding rage that hijack my body until I'm left standing in the aftermath, blinking at the carnage I've created.

It should repulse me. The violence by my hands should terrify me.

But it doesn't.

If Bobbi were still alive… and these people were trying to get to her… trying to hurt her… well, I wouldn't hesitate. I'd kill anyone who dared.

She may not be here now, but that doesn't change the fact that I'm her mother, and I'm not going to stop walking this path until every one of those monsters is dead.

And what happens after that? I have no bloody idea.

"I can feel you thinking, Angel."

Ringo's warm breath ghosts over my hair before he presses a kiss to my forehead, and I snuggle even closer.

"Sorry. A lot happened today. I'm just trying to process it."

"You wanna talk about it?" he asks quietly, and I shrug against him.

"Did any of the Marx crew die tonight?" My mind flashes to the man I saw on fire, screaming in agony.

"I haven't got a final tally from Griffin yet, but yes, Angel. There were some casualties on our side."

And there it is again. That sick, gnawing guilt.

I feel guilty for smiling. Guilty for the people suffering because they chose to help me. Guilty for every single life lost in my name.

"The men who work for the Marx family… are they like your club brothers? Like is the Marx crew *their* family? Or is it just a job, and they've got partners and kids waiting for them at home?"

Shifting next to me, Ringo's fingers hook under my chin, tilting my head up until I'm looking into his eyes.

"You don't need to worry about that."

"But I do," I whisper, knowing my voice will crack if I try to speak louder.

"I know, Angel." He leans in and kisses the apples of my cheeks, making me feel more cherished than I deserve.

"I need to know about the people risking their lives to protect me." I insist, and he sighs, nodding before he shifts us so I'm half-draped across his chest, my fingers immediately tracing small circles over his pecs.

"The men in the Marx crew are employees. It's their job. An extremely well-paid job," Ringo explains. "Their families are looked after for life if something happens. They know the risks. Most are highly trained ex-soldiers and special ops."

"So, they're here on protection detail, with us, and with your mum and sisters too?"

He stiffens beneath me. "How'd you know about that?"

"Jols told me," I admit. "And before you get shitty with her, just remember, she wouldn't have had to tell me if you had."

With my ear against his chest, I hear the deep rumble of his disapproval as much as I feel it.

"I didn't want to add to your stress," he pauses. "What else did Jols tell you?"

I shrug, like it's no big deal. "She told me where Wendy was being kept."

"For fuck's sake. *That's* how you knew where to find her?" he snaps, and I nod against his chest.

"If you tell her off for it, I'll stop speaking to you."

In an instant, Ringo flips us, pinning me beneath him, his naked body pressing into mine.

Goddamn this post-birth bleeding. I want my panties off and his dick inside me right now.

"You can try to stop speaking to me, Angel. But I can guarantee you'll be screaming my name in no time when I'm sucking on your needy clit."

I gasp, slapping his shoulder, and the bed shakes with his rumbling laughter.

"Even so, that's all you'll get out of me," I counter, but hell, who am I kidding? I'll be putty in his hands.

"You mean I won't have to listen to any wifely whining?"

My mouth drops open in shock as he snickers, so I pinch his nipples. Hard.

He yelps, laughing as he tries to bat my hands away, before catching my wrists, and pinning them above my head.

"Now look what you've gone and done." He grins down at me, and I can feel exactly what he means, his hard dick pressing into my thigh.

Heat unfurls deep in my core, and I grind against him without thinking. Only feeling. And a moment later, the familiar sensation tingling through my nipples has me stiffening.

"Shit," I hiss, and Ringo stills, leaning back to get a better look at my face.

"What is it?"

"I'm leaking again," I admit, sighing.

That unmistakable let-down sensation fizzles in my breasts, reminding me that my body is making milk.

Shifting back a little more, Ringo's gaze drops to my bare chest, and mine follows, seeing how tightly peaked my nipples are.

"They don't look full again," he acknowledges, looking a little confused.

"No… I think it's because I'm aroused."

A slow, cheeky grin lifts his lips.

"What a coincidence. So am I."

I snort a laugh, and he cups my breast, his touch like a soothing heat pack as I arch into him.

"I'm also really fucking thirsty," he rasps, licking his lips.

I shake my head. "I don't think we should—"

My words cut off the second his hot mouth closes over my nipple, and just like that, we're both moaning as we share a pleasure I never knew was possible until tonight.

16

RINGO

I have a constant fucking hard-on. I can't even look at Abbey now without picturing the way her face looks when I suck on her ripe pink nipples.

Fuuuck. It's become a thing. A thing we both didn't know we needed. Every time I do it, she tries to suggest it's a bad idea, but she doesn't have it in her to fight me off once I have my tongue on her nipple.

It's so fucking hot, drawing on her and feeling her warm milk spill into my mouth, so fucking sweet. She hasn't needed to express since the night of the funerals last week, because she's got me to take care of it.

"Did you know she probably feels a little pain when you do that?" JD asks quietly next to me as we sit on the deck watching Jols and Abbey stroll along the shore of the lake.

Well, *I'm* watching them. He's busy searching up lactation kink on his phone.

"Yeah, she told me." I pause to take a swig of my water. "Apparently, when new mothers breastfeed, it causes contractions in the uterus, which help it shrink back to its normal size, or some shit like that."

"That's fucking wild." JD glances up from his phone. "The fact a woman's body can do all of that… fuck, it blows my mind."

"My wife blows my mind."

JD chuckles at my remark.

"What does it taste like?" he asks, not able to help himself, and I grin at my best mate.

"It's sweet. That's all you need to fucking know."

"Fuuuck," he sighs, flopping back in the deck chair. "Now I'm hard."

"Stop thinking about my wife's tits!" I snap, and he smirks, holding his hands up in surrender.

"Wasn't thinking about *her* tits, man. Was thinking about *my* woman."

My brows shoot up. "She's your woman now? When are you gonna tell Smitty?"

"Fucking never!"

I laugh at his mortified expression until it morphs into a frown, and he leans forward in the chair, his eyes tracking our women.

"What's up with your wife?"

I follow his gaze to see her standing beside Jols, her head bowed and eyes on the ground as Jols chatters away to Vender, who's been patrolling the shore.

"You notice that too, huh?" I mutter with a sigh.

"Yeah, man. She doesn't do that with me, but she does it with the other men. Do you reckon she's scared of them or something?"

I shake my head. "Nope, not scared of them. I think it's more that she's scared of getting to know them and then something happening to them. Like with Mule."

"Fuck. Yeah, I didn't think of that."

We both fall silent as Vender walks away, and Abbey's chin lifts and she falls back into chatting with Jols like she hadn't just crossed paths with my club brother.

"She's too much of a sweet kid to be suffering through this kind of hell."

"Do me a favour?" I growl at my mate. "Don't call her a kid. Nothing about what I do with her indicates that she's a fucking kid."

"Okay, okay." JD smirks, standing from his chair. "You're a grumpy fucker today."

With a huff, I rake my hand over my face, feeling every one of my thirty-three years.

"It's the funeral plans for Bobbi. It's dragging up a lot of shit."

JD glances down at me and claps me on my shoulder. "I'm sorry, man. Is there anything I can do?"

Standing, I shake my head, my eyes glued to my wife as she chats to Jols, wondering what the fuck those two talk about while we're not listening.

"Everything's sorted. Ace helped with the casket once she picked what she wanted, and he's arranged for Bobbi's body to be taken to Ma's on Wednesday morning."

"Fuck. This is so fucked, man. I'm sorry."

I nod, because what the fuck else am I meant to do? This *is* fucked. It should never have happened.

"You know what you need?" JD wags his brows. "What *she* needs?"

I raise a single brow in question, waiting for him to say something dirty, but then he surprises me.

"You both need to get drunk. And she needs her friends." He points across the water. "Doesn't one of them live over there?"

I nod, looking at the houses seeming so small scattered along the shore across the other side.

"The ex-teacher lives over there. Tyler. I'm not sure who lives with him."

"Fuck, who cares. Let's give him a call. See if he can get Abbey's friends over here. It'd be a good distraction for everyone."

"A distraction would be good for her," I mutter, and before I can say another word, he's snatching my phone out of my pocket and making a call.

I don't bother telling Abbey what's happening. Instead, I sit back and enjoy the look of surprise on her face two hours later when a small boat pulls up to the jetty near our safe house, and her friends, Lexi, Rhys, Ayden and Tyler, step off.

I grin at the girls' squeals as they throw themselves into each other's arms, and then Abbey's big bright eyes find me.

Right then, I know letting JD arrange this was a good idea.

Sure she has me, but she also needs her friends, and not just Jols. But her old friends. The ones who knew her before I did.

"Hey man," Ayden greets me as he climbs the steps of the back deck. "Glad JD called. Lexi's been worried but didn't want to make things worse if someone followed her to see Abbey. Going to Tyler's first was a good call."

"The Marx crew has this entire area locked down." JD grins, pulling a few beers from the cooler before tossing one to Ayden and Tyler.

"I've noticed," Tyler grumbles, and I can't help but grin. This grumpy fucker reminds me of myself.

"Okay, I gotta ask…" JD starts, and I sigh, offering Tyler an apologetic look, because I already know exactly what he's going to ask.

"You really share your girl with four other blokes?"

"Yep." He shrugs, taking a swig of his beer. "Wasn't exactly how I imagined myself settling down, but then again, I never imagined she'd want me. The heart wants what the heart wants, I guess."

Ayden chuckles, and JD gapes like he's in awe.

"How the fuck does that work? Do you each have designated nights with her or…"

"Someone like Kitten doesn't do well with routine. She needs spontaneity."

"Kitten?" JD asks, and Tyler sighs.

"Shit, yeah, sorry. Rhys. She's only Kitten to me and Bossi."

"So you and Bossi like to share her… at the same time?"

"JD." I growl in warning, but he waves me off like I don't fucking matter.

"I'm curious. That's all."

"It's okay." Tyler lowers to one of the deck chairs as the rest of us do the same. "Most people have questions."

JD shifts forward on his chair like he's about to jump out of his fucking skin in anticipation.

"We were members of a sex club." Tyler watches Rhys as he speaks. "Her name at the club was Kitten, so it stuck with me and Bossi. The others have their own pet names for her."

"Fuck, was that the sex club at Vixen's Lodge?" JD asks, but I already know it is, so when Tyler nods, I'm not surprised.

"Let's move on, hey." I cut in, and JD sighs like he's just been told Christmas has been cancelled.

The women join us on the deck then, and we spend the next few hours drinking, chatting and laughing, the rest of my team eventually joining us.

After one drink, Abbey is relaxed enough to look at my club brothers. After two, she starts laughing with them. And after three, she, Lexi and Rhys are a blur of energy, huddling together, gossiping and in fits of laughter like they haven't had such dark experiences between them.

Jols stays back on the sidelines of their friendship, giving them space to catch up, and I chat with Ayden and Tyler, all while keeping one eye on my wife, enjoying my first time watching her get drunk.

When the sun is almost down, Murf and Stocky disappear into the kitchen to whip up dinner, and Abbey ends up on my lap, letting me feed her as she flashes me *fuck-me* eyes that I try fucking hard to ignore.

"You're cute when you're drunk." I smirk at her, and her playful smile widens.

"I'm not drunk. You are."

Chuckling, I draw her closer, burying my nose in her hair.

"I've only had a couple of drinks, Angel. You know I'm not a big drinker."

"I've only had a couple, too," she insists, and I laugh.

"Last count you'd had five. One more and I'll have to put you to bed."

"You can put me to bed now." She flutters her lashes at me. "You can do whatever you want with me in bed."

"What are we doing in bed?" Rhys pops up right beside us, and a squeak flies from Abbey's lips.

"There is no *we* in this scenario," I point out, jerking my head towards Tyler. "You've got enough to keep you busy."

Rhys grins mischievously, her teeth looking stark behind her black-painted lips.

"So you've been talking about my bedroom shenanigans." She wags her brows. "What was covered? Double penetration? Triple? A bit of spit roasting? Oh wait." She holds up a finger like she just thought of something brilliant. "Was it all of the above with some tit fucking thrown in?"

"Jesus Christ, Kitten. Stop giving everyone visuals," Tyler groans from next to me before landing a sharp slap on her arse.

"Sorry, *Daddy*," Rhys purrs, sticking her arse out towards him and giving it a little wiggle.

"Behave, or I'll push you to six hours."

Rhys gasps, straightening up as she glares at Tyler. "You wouldn't."

"I fucking would, and you know it."

Her eyes turn into slits, but then Abbey's voice cuts through the tension.

"Push what to six hours?"

When Rhys faces Abbey, her mischievous grin returns. "He's talking about edging me for six hours. Last week, we got to five hours and forty minutes before I snapped."

"Snapped? Edging?" Abbey frowns. "I'm confused."

"Nawww, you're so innocent," Rhys pouts, and Lexi giggles from my other side on Ayden's lap.

"Rhys, everyone is innocent compared to you," Lexi teases.

"True," Rhys agrees without hesitation, but then launches into a detailed explanation for Abbey, telling her what edging is and how Tyler likes to push her until she stops being a brat and falls apart.

"Why would you do that to her, Mr Foster?" Abbey blurts, her face twisting into an adorably angry frown. Nothing like the version of her that killed Wendy last week.

"Abbey," Tyler sighs, rubbing the back of his neck. "Please stop calling me Mr Foster. I'm not your teacher anymore. I'm not anyone's teacher anymore."

"Fine," Abbey slurs a bit, the alcohol clearly hitting her harder now.

"When Kitten… I mean Rhys… needs to be punished, I edge her," Tyler explains with zero embarrassment. "When she's a *good girl*, she gets rewarded."

Rhys bites her lip and wags her brows. "FYI, I love being punished just as much as I love being rewarded."

Abbey frowns. "I don't get it."

"That's because you haven't discovered kinks yet." Rhys smirks.

Abbey's cheeks blush bright red at Rhys' comment.

"I have kinks," she insists, a little too loud.

"Maybe you've had enough of this," I mutter, gently prying the almost empty bottle of fruity vodka from her fingers.

"What kinks do you have?" Rhys leans in, eyes alight with mischief.

"I'm kinda curious too." Lexi giggles, and Abbey's gaze darts over her shoulder to her best friend.

"Well…" Abbey hesitates. "I think it's a kink."

"We don't need to talk about this," I jump in quickly, but then, JD fucking opens his mouth.

"Ohhh, it's a kink alright."

If Abbey was sober, she'd probably be mortified about this conversation, but since her inhibitions are clouded by the effects of alcohol, she just chatters away like this is a normal conversation to have.

"It is?" she asks JD, before turning her big doe eyes to me. "We have a kink."

Her fucking smile is beautiful. I fucking love this playful side of her.

Sighing in defeat, I nod. "We do, Angel."

"Oh my God! What is it? Is it feet? Sy has a foot fetish. The things he has me do with his feet, or someone else's—" Rhys' words are cut off as Tyler clamps a hand over her mouth.

"Kitten, I don't think Simon would appreciate you sharing that."

"Are you serious?" Lexi squeaks. "Simon's into foot stuff?"

"Explains why he enjoyed rubbing your feet so much when you were in the hospital," Ayden mutters, clearly not happy.

"Our kink isn't feet." Abbey scrunches up her nose. "It's these." She points to her tits.

Fucking hell.

"Angel." I warn, but she fucking ignores me.

"Every guy loves tits, Abs. That's not a fetish." Lexi giggles, and Abbey shakes her head, staggering to her feet.

"I know that, Lex."

Before I can stop her, she cups her tits over her t-shirt, and fuck, they look full again. Swollen.

Shit, I guess it's been a few hours since I've had my mouth on them.

"It's the milk," she admits, and everyone falls silent.

If Abbey notices, she doesn't make it obvious as she continues palming her tits like they ache.

"My milk came in, and they hurt so bad. I have to express them so they don't get engorged."

Fucking hell. My heart just about stops as two dark wet patches bloom on her pink tee, spreading with every breath she takes.

"Angel," I rasp, moving to her, but she waves me off and tilts her chin up like she doesn't have a care in the world right now.

"Ringo loves the taste."

Groans rise up from my club brothers, and JD snickers, wagging his brows as his eyes meet mine.

"Oh, shit." Rhys jumps up, practically bouncing over, her gaze locked onto the wet patches on Abbey's t-shirt. "Can I taste?"

"No!" I bark, and Tyler curses.

"Kitten, back away. She's not yours to play with."

"But I've never tasted breast milk." Rhys pouts before glancing at me. "Is it sweet?"

I don't fucking answer her, my eyes fixed on Abbey as she finally notices she's leaking and everyone can see.

"Let's head inside," I murmur, reaching for my wife, but the wicked grin she flashes me has my club brothers groaning all over again.

"Is my husband thirsty?" she asks, her voice pure fucking sin.

"Who cares about him? I'm thirsty." Rhys waves me off like I'm no one to bother with, and Abbey laughs.

Tyler stands abruptly, closing the distance between him and Rhys before fisting her hair and jerking her head back.

"If you're thirsty, you can drink from my cock."

Abbey's mouth drops open, her eyes wide with a mix of disbelief and delight while my club brothers groan again, clearly missing access to the Doxies.

"Mr Foster!" Abbey squeaks. "That's so… naughty!"

Lexi and Ayden burst out laughing, but fall quiet the moment Rhys drops to her knees.

"Fill my mouth up, Daddy."

Abbey stumbles back, her expression curious but shocked, which gives me the perfect opportunity to snatch her up.

"On that note," I growl, smiling at my club brothers' cheers as I toss my wife over my shoulder.

When she squirms, I slap her arse and quickly duck inside before a fucking orgy starts up on the deck.

I'm not sure if that's what Rhys and Tyler are into, but I *do* know my club brothers won't complain.

As for Lexi and Ayden, when I glance back out the windows before heading up the stairs, I catch them rushing off towards the water.

I guess orgies aren't their thing.

"Your arse looks good from this angle," Abbey snickers, dangling upside down over my back.

"So does yours, Angel." I palm it roughly, giving it a good rub, my cock already stiff as a board.

"If you carry me the other way, I'd be level with your dick," she teases. "I could suck you off while you walk."

I chuckle at that, loving how playful she is right now, and hurry to our bedroom, closing us in.

"You're funny when you're drunk," I say just before flipping her off my shoulder to the bed.

She looks disoriented as I quickly strip out of my clothes, but when she sees me getting naked, she reaches out with grabby hands.

"I want. Bring here. In mouth."

I throw my head back laughing. "Angel, the first time you suck my cock is not going to be when you're half fucking cut. I want you sober and feeling every last inch of it."

She pouts adorably, but then presses her palm to her head, groaning. "The room is spinning."

Yep, she drank more than she should have.

Grabbing her a glass of water from the little ensuite bathroom, I insist she drink it as I peel her clothes off, and then refill it again and pass her glass number two.

"Drink all of that," I order, my gaze glued to her lips, "and then I'll drink from you."

"Ohhh, you're making me so horny," she moans, one hand slipping up her inner thigh as she chugs the water like a good girl.

She hasn't even realised she's not wearing panties. She's still bleeding, but not as much as last week, and I don't care if we mess up the sheet.

Fuck, I can't wait to eat her cunt. To bury myself inside it and *never* fucking leave.

When she's finished drinking, I refill the glass and set it on the bedside table, and before I can do anything else, my little minx has her hand wrapped around my cock.

"I want you in my mouth."

Fuuuck, I want that too. So fucking bad. But we haven't done that yet, and I don't know if it'll trigger her, so I want her fully present when we do that. Not drunk, frisky, and doing things she might not be ready for.

"Later," is all I say, gently urging her to lie back, and she flops back lazily, lips pulled into a drunken smile.

"Are you gonna fuck me?"

My brows hitch. "You're not too shy to say the word fuck while you're drunk."

She waves me off. "Maybe I should be drunk all the time. It feels good."

"I'm sure it does." I chuckle, shifting over her, drinking in her beautiful face, so free of the pain she's been suffering through. "But I'm not fucking you tonight. You have to wait four more weeks."

She pouts, and, fuck it's adorable.

"Are we gonna come, at least?"

Smiling, I nod. "You bet your arse we're gonna come." I palm her tit, and she arches into my touch, her lids fluttering closed. "You first."

Sliding down her body, I take my time before sealing my lips around her nipple. She gasps as I flick my tongue over the pebbled peak, her fingers lacing into my hair.

When I suck, feeling the rush of warm milk spray into my mouth, hitting my tongue as the sweetness rouses my taste-buds, she cries out, arching like she's trying to get her nipple deeper into my mouth.

As I suck, drawing milk from her, my fingers trail lower, to her clit. She parts her legs wide, a clear invitation, and rolls her hips trying to direct my fingers to her entrance.

Fuuuuck. Not yet.

I can't penetrate her yet. Despite how much she wants it. Despite how much I want it.

So I suck harder, my fingers circling faster as I dry hump the side of the fucking bed, every ounce of me aching for her. The moment she screams out her release, my cock jerks and I start coming too, spilling my seed down the side of the mattress and onto the fucking floor.

17

ABBEY

Wringing my hands together, I try to ward off the trembling that's getting worse as we turn down the road that leads to Ringo's house. We didn't take his motorcycle today. Instead, we're tucked inside one of Griffin's blacked-out SUVs. It's a Mercedes or something equally as fancy. It could be a rusted up old wreck as far as I'm concerned. I can't focus on anything other than what's about to happen today.

I'm not ready.

Fighting back tears, I stare out the window as trees blur past. The only thing keeping me from jumping from this speeding vehicle is the feel of Ringo's hand on my thigh.

I'm not ready.

"I need a distraction," I practically whisper, but Ringo hears, his big palm squeezing my leg as I continue. "Tell me about the

Marx crew. I've seen four groups of them since we turned down this road."

"Yes, they've been protecting my property since the night…"

He doesn't need to finish that sentence. I already know what night he's referring to.

The night I was taken.

I'm not ready.

"Why isn't your club handling it?" I ask, turning to him to find his eyes already on me.

He's been watching me more closely these past couple of days. I can tell he's worried, and I wish he didn't have to be, but the truth is, I'm not okay.

I'm not ready.

"My club is under attack too." His voice is low and calming despite the conversation we're having. "Satan's Rebels aren't just coming after you, Angel. They want my club. They want our turf, our connections, and our link to the Marx family. The dumb fuckers don't realise that even if they took every one of us out, the Marx family still wouldn't do business with them."

I already know why.

Apparently, the Marx family and the Southern Sadists have morals despite being criminals.

I, for one, can attest to that.

I'm not ready.

"There are a lot of Marx men here just to do this as a favour," I say, glancing down at the way his fingers brush over my leg. Somehow, that simple action is keeping me grounded. "Who's paying them? Is it your club?"

I'll have to figure out a way to pay them back. They wouldn't be under this threat if it weren't for me.

"*I'm* paying them, Angel. This isn't club business. This is personal." He gestures out the window as we pass yet another cluster of black-clad Marx crew, geared up with weapons, and probably more men lurking in the trees.

I'm not ready.

"How much money does it cost to have so many men guarding your home?"

His fingers stop moving on my leg, and I glance up to catch his gaze with mine.

For a few long moments, his eyes dance between mine, like he's trying to see past this mask of courage I'm trying to keep in place.

I'm not ready.

"I'm not paying them with money, Angel."

My brows shoot up. "Is it drugs or guns or something?"

"No," he mutters, not elaborating.

Ugh.

"Well… what is it then?"

"It doesn't matter." His fingers start moving again.

"The hell it doesn't. Don't keep secrets from me," I snap, not in the mood for games today.

I'm not ready.

Sighing, Ringo reaches up and cups my cheek, and I instantly melt into his touch, fighting to hold it together.

I'm not ready.

"I'm not trying to keep secrets from you. I'm sorry for upsetting you, Abs. I'm honestly not used to having someone to share this stuff with."

Abs.

I love it when he calls me that.

"I'm your wife now. I don't want there to be secrets between us."

"I know. Me either." He leans forward, pressing his lips to my forehead before pulling back to stare into my eyes. "Payment for their protection will be a favour. I'll owe them."

My brows shoot up. "Why don't I like the sound of that?"

"Probably because that payment will likely be something risky. Something big."

Tears sting my eyes at the thought of him being in danger. *I'm not ready.*

"You shouldn't have agreed to that. I'll pay them. I'll find the money somehow."

He shakes his head, a crooked smile kicking up his lips. "Money isn't valuable enough for the Marx family."

"But… what if…" I shake my head, not wanting to think of all the horrible things that could happen. "I don't want to lose you."

"You won't, Angel. The Marx family are ruthless, but they aren't cruel." He leans back as the car slows, his gaze drifting out the window. "It's nothing we have to worry about today."

When the car starts turning off the road, and I recognise the gates of Ringo's property up ahead, panic crashes through me so hard that I feel like I might stop breathing and die right this second.

"I'm not ready!" I blurt loudly, thankful there's a partition up between us and the driver.

Turning to the door, I reach for the handle, desperate to jump out, but Ringo stops me, his hand closing around my wrists, keeping me in place.

"Abs, look at me."

"No. I can't do this. I'm not ready!" I cry, hot tears spilling freely, my eyes already red, raw from crying myself to sleep last night.

Ringo's big, warm hands frame my face, gently forcing me to look at him instead of out the window.

"Abbey, listen to me. We're gonna get through this together. I'm here. Lexi's already waiting. Your friends are here too. We're all here to help hold you up, Angel."

A loud, choked sob lurches from my lips as unbearable pain grips my heart.

"I don't want to bury her," I cry, shaking my head still in his hands. "I don't want her to be gone, Cameron. Why is this happening? Why?!"

"Shhh, Angel." He pulls me onto his lap, wrapping his strong arms around me as I fall apart. "I've got you, Abs. I've got you."

"No!" I wail, feeling like my heart is being torn from my chest all over again. "I can't. I just can't!"

The door opens, and the chilly May air hits us, making me curl into Ringo's chest even more, wishing I could burrow under his skin and disappear forever.

"Give us a few minutes," Ringo says to someone outside, and the door closes again, taking away the chill.

For the longest time, Ringo holds me. Never pushing me to move. Never rushing me through my grief.

I don't know how long we sit there like that, but eventually, his steady strength anchors me, and my sobs subside.

I realise then that even though I'm not ready, I know I never will be.

Because what mother is ever ready to bury her child?

I will *never* be ready.

Using the tissues tucked into the back of the seat, Ringo wipes my face, and my sorrow hardens into cold acceptance that *this* has to be done.

I have to get out of this car and bury my daughter.

And then, I have to slaughter everyone who had a hand in her death.

When I'm finally ready to get out of the car, Ringo steps out first, offering me his hand as I rise on shaky legs to face a group of people who mean the world to me, all wearing yellow, just as I'd asked.

The moment my eyes land on Lexi, we stumble towards each other. My beautiful friend folds me into her arms as my knees nearly give way beneath the crushing pain in my chest.

"I have to bury my little girl today," I sob into her hair, and she shudders with her own tears as she nods.

"I know. I'm so sorry, Abs."

I feel Ringo at my back, and when we pull apart, I see Ayden at hers, ready to give her the support she needs.

God, I'm so glad she found him.

With Ringo on one side, and Lexi on the other, I face the crowd gathered. Some are my friends. Others are new acquaintances, members of the Southern Sadists, yet not a cut is in sight.

The Doxies are dressed in yellow sundresses, despite the cold air swirling around us.

The Southern Sadists are in their usual jeans and boots, but up top they have on yellow collared shirts, pressed and buttoned all the way up. A sight I never thought I'd see.

A week ago today, I attended the funeral of eight of their men, wearing the leather they all wear, and today, they are here looking like civilians, all for me.

For my little Bobbi.

Each of them holds a yellow rose in one hand, and a small gift for my little girl in the other.

"You ready?" Ringo asks softly, and even though I'm not ready, I nod.

We pass by the crowd, my friends and Ringo's mum and sisters amongst them, and we start walking towards the small orchard. Its path has been lined with small vases of yellow roses on the grass, and small wind chimes hang from some of the shrubs, tinkling gently in the breeze.

The crowd follows behind us, and with each step, my knees nearly buckle, but Ringo and Lexi keep me upright.

Keep me strong.

Keep me moving.

Halfway down the hill, the Jacaranda tree comes into view, most of the leaves already shed, and the few remaining are a bright, glowing yellow, as if the tree somehow knew what was coming before I did.

The closer we get, the harder it is for my legs to move as a small white casket resting above an open grave comes into view. Right next to Hope's.

"I'm not ready," I whisper, and Ringo and Lexi tighten their grip on me, being my strength when mine has been torn from existence.

There are seats laid out, but when Ringo and Lexi try to steer me towards them, I shake my head, breaking free of their hands and dropping to my knees beside the glossy white casket.

I cry and sob, draping myself over the top like I can somehow shield her from this cruel world.

No one tries to move me. They leave me to my grief, everyone taking their seats as quiet sniffles and sobs float through the air around us.

"Hear that, my sweet baby girl? Those tears are for you," I choke out. "For the love they never got to show you."

Time passes slowly, and eventually, I feel a presence on the other side of the casket, and I peer up to see Ringo, sitting on the damp ground with me. He has one hand resting on Hope's headstone, and the other on Bobbi's casket, his head bowed in silent respect.

This man.

This *warrior,* who has already endured so much.

God, I don't deserve him, but I'll never let him go.

Slowly sitting up, I cover his hand with mine, and he glances up, his whiskey eyes haunted by his own grief.

"I'm ready now," I whisper, and he nods, tears spilling down his cheeks.

"Okay, Abs. Do you want to stand?"

I shake my head. "I just want to stay here."

"Then stay here, Angel."

Nodding, I straighten a little, reaching out as Ringo places the folded paper in my hand, holding the words I cried my way through writing last night.

"Lex," I call softly to my friend, seated off to the side, reaching out for her.

She hurries over, sinking to her knees beside me on the damp grass, her hand moving to stroke my back as I brace myself for what I have to do.

Unfolding the piece of paper, I lay it carefully on top of the casket before clasping Ringo's and Lexi's hands, needing their strength to get through this.

Then, I clear my throat to begin.

"My sweet little Bobbi Cameron Musgrove. I never got to hear your laugh or see your eyes widen in excitement. I never got to learn what songs would make you dance, or how you liked your toast in the morning." I take a deep breath, needing a moment to let myself cry before blinking away the tears enough that I can read the words on the paper.

"You were here for what feels like a single breath, and then you were gone. But I need you to know, you mattered." I blow out a breath, taking another moment and feeling Ringo's gentle squeeze of support around my hand. A silent reminder that I'm not alone.

"You were loved the moment you existed. It didn't matter how you came to be. Not to me. And not to those who truly matter. And even though I'll never get to see you blow out your birthday candles, or kiss your scraped knees after you tumble off your bike, you will always live in my heart. I will carry this love for you every single day for the rest of my life."

A loud sob wrenches itself from me as the weight of those words sink in. I still don't understand how I'm here burying her when she feels so alive in my heart.

"I don't have stories to tell about your life," I continue, pushing through. For Bobbi. For myself. "So I'll tell the world who you were to me."

Ringo's hand tightens around mine, and I feel the way he's suffering too, sitting here, right next to the daughter he lost only a few years ago. I bet he's remembering the pain of that day.

"You were my daughter," I choke, my next words meant not just for me, but for Ringo, too. "You were *my* hope."

His eyes meet mine, flooded with tears, his lips silently forming the words, *'I love you'*, and I squeeze his hand this time, offering him the same strength he offered me.

"You were my little burst of sun who never got the chance to shine." I don't even need to read the paper anymore. I know what comes next.

"So today, we farewell you by wearing *my* favourite colour, yellow, and I gift you this blanket, so you'll always be wrapped in something I love."

Letting go of Ringo's and Lexi's hands, I slide the yellow baby blanket off my shoulders and drape it gently across the casket, lowering my head to it to take the moment I need.

When I sit back up, I swipe at my tears, accepting the tissue Lexi offers me, and I glance at Ringo, taking the hand he offers so I can prepare to say my final goodbye.

"Under this Jacaranda, where two babies now sleep forever, may the wind carry the lullabies of our hearts." I sob. "I will miss the lifetime we lost. But I will never, *ever* stop being your mum."

I collapse back over the casket, not ready to stand and leave her yet, crying as others join me, my heartbreak bleeding into the world around us.

No one speaks. They remain where they are, patient and respectful as my grief takes hold.

When my wracking sobs ease, and I work up the courage to move, I press a kiss to the top of the casket, and let Lexi and Ringo help me to my feet.

My whole body is trembling as they guide me off to the side, before Ringo clears his throat and steps up to speak.

"Thank you for coming today, and for the childhood gifts little Bobbi can keep with her always. Once the casket has been lowered, please step forward and place your gifts in the chest," Ringo gestures to a small toy chest that will be buried at the foot of Bobbi's casket, "and roses may be laid around the grave."

Through my tear-filled eyes, I watch my friends from Fox Pines step forward first. Marcus, Jared, Dee, Simon, Shaun, Garrett, Rhys and Tyler. They place books, a teddy, rattles and more in the toy chest, before coming to me and each pulling me into a hug I'll carry in my heart forever.

Lexi and Ayden go next, placing a pair of ballet shoes and a small ukulele in the chest.

The Doxies gift colourful kids jewellery, trinkets, and even a Cinderella dress-up costume. And the Southern Sadists place books, dolls, and even some Legos inside the chest.

Ringo's mum and sisters have so many gifts, I lose track. And Smitty steps up to the chest, unfolding a small piece of leather to reveal a mini biker jacket, turning it to show me the back with the Southern Sadists logo on it, and on the front, the patch says, *'Little Princess Bobbi'*.

It's overwhelming, and unexpected, and I don't think Smitty will ever truly know how much that means to me.

Jols steps up next, placing a motorbike helmet inside, and JD places a game of Twister in it.

All the gifts are truly wonderful, and I hate that little Bobbi never got to enjoy them.

Once everyone has stepped back, talking quietly amongst themselves, Ringo gives me a little squeeze, pulling my focus back to him.

"Will you come with me while I give Bobbi my gifts?"

My brows lift in surprise. I hadn't expected him to have gifts, and I wonder how he even found the time. But then again, I've been distracted a lot since we started planning for today, so it's possible he managed to arrange something while I wasn't looking.

I nod, and he holds me close as we slowly approach the toy chest, now practically overflowing.

"I bet she would have loved every single thing inside there," I whisper, and Ringo nods.

"Yeah, she would have." He clears his throat, reaching out to JD, who hands him a small paper bag. "I have three things for Bobbi."

Reaching into the bag, he pulls out a small picture frame and turns it to show me a picture of us on our wedding day. I'm on his lap, and we're both laughing and looking at each other, my hand resting against the ivory satin stretched over the swell of my stomach… over Bobbi.

"Oh… my…" The words catch in my throat as tears come again, the sight so beautiful and so heartbreaking all at once.

"I want her to always have a picture of the three of us," Ringo's small smile is warm as he locks eyes with me, "on a day we all felt safe and happy."

"Cam," I sob. "This is… so beautiful. Thank you."

Reaching up, he cups my cheek, his thumb brushing over my damp skin.

"There's another one upstairs in our bedroom for you."

In an instant, my arms are around him, and he presses a kiss to my hair as he bends us and places the picture in the chest.

"You'll like this next one."

There's a lightness to his tone that has me pulling back, and he reaches into the bag, and pulls out a CD, holding it up to show me the cover.

A laugh bubbles out of me as I stare at the cover of One Direction's Take Me Home album.

"I figured she'd probably have terrible music taste just like her mum," he teases, "so she'd probably like this garbage."

"Ringo!" I slap his shoulder, and he chuckles.

"It has that fucking awful song you walked down the aisle to."

I snatch the CD from him. "Saying things like that will get you divorced."

He winks. "You'll never leave me."

I shake my head, my smile fading as I hand it back, remembering why we are here.

"Thank you," I whisper. "She would have loved the CD, and not because of me, but because *you* gave it to her."

His smile is soft as he places the album into the chest before straightening and reaching into the bag one last time.

This time, when he pulls his hand out, there's a small velvet box resting in his palm.

I have no idea what it is, but by the look on his face, his eyes swimming with emotion, I have a feeling this is going to make me cry. Which, let's be honest, isn't exactly hard today.

"I know I'm not technically her dad," he starts, clearing his throat before continuing. "But I'd intended to raise her like she was my daughter, and I feel her loss just as much as I felt Hope's."

And here come the tears.

"So, I got her this." He opens the box, showing me the tiny bracelet inside before he lifts it out and dangles it before me. "I got it engraved."

Swiping at my tears, I try to clear the blur so I can see properly.

The bracelet is mostly silver, with gold detailing framing the front panel, and tiny silver and gold butterfly charms dangling at each end, with an inscription on the front.

Bobbi Cameron

"There's more on the back." Ringo's voice is choked up as he speaks, and I turn it over to read the back.

Love Dad xx

It's so simple, yet means so much, and a sob breaks free as I throw my arms around his neck, clinging to him.

"It's beautiful," I manage between my tears, and he squeezes me to him, my feet leaving the ground for a few moments as he buries his face in my hair.

18

ABBEY

There are moments when I feel completely numb, and moments when I feel everything at once, but the one constant is Ringo. Always at my side. Always touching me in some small way, keeping me tethered to him like he knows I'll crumble without his support.

Seeing Ringo's mum, Doreen, again made me feel like I was coming back home. She embraced me in what can only be described as a mum-hug, holding me through another wave of agonising tears, not letting go until I was able to breathe again.

I couldn't bring myself to leave Bobbi's graveside, so after roses were laid, and she was lowered into the cold earth, followed by the toy chest, both buried deep right next to Hope, everyone stayed under the beautiful Jacaranda tree, to just be.

Be still with me.

Be in tears with me.

Be in this agony with me, no matter how raw or ugly it was.

Doreen, Lani and Mills served finger food later, fetched blankets for people to picnic on, or huddle under as night began to fall.

Faint music played in the background. It wasn't anything I recognised, just a gentle hum of something pretty. Something that felt almost innocent, like my poor little Bobbi.

"I know this is a stupid question, but are you doing okay?" Ringo asks, the rumble of his voice meeting my ear, pressed to his chest as we huddle on a blanket at the foot of Bobbi's and Hope's graves.

"I don't know. Maybe?" It comes out as a question, but he understands that it really depends on the moment, and he gives me a squeeze.

"Abs." Lexi's voice draws my attention, and I glance up to find her standing before us with Dee and Rhys at her sides, holding an unlit lantern. "Are you ready?"

Tears are inevitable today, so I let them fall as I swallow thickly and nod.

The lanterns were Dee's idea, inspired by her favourite movie, *Tangled*. When she suggested it, through text, of course, I instantly loved the idea.

For one, I imagined little Bobbi loving that movie too. Perhaps she would have watched it with Dee. Hell, maybe Dee would have even taught her to dance.

Helping me up off the ground, I accept the lantern Lexi passes me, before she turns to the crowd.

"We are going to pass out lanterns and markers to everyone. Please write a word or more on the lantern you receive that you associate with little Bobbi." She holds up her lantern, showing everyone what she wrote. "Mine says '*Loved*.'"

Soft murmurs trickle through the crowd as my friends move among them with lanterns and markers, while I turn my focus to the one I'm holding, and with shaky hands I write a couple of words for my little girl.

My Heart.

When Ringo is done writing on his lantern, he clears his throat, gaining my attention, and holds it up for me.

My Daughter & Hope's Sister.

Both of us break then, holding on to each other as people write their own words for my little girl.

After a few minutes, once Ringo and I are able to pull away from each other and focus on what's happening, the process of lighting the lanterns begins. Marcus, Jared, Ayden, Simon, Garrett and Shaun slowly move through the crowd to assist, a beautiful warm glow lighting up the space around the tree, and once everyone's lantern is lit, Lexi speaks again.

"Tonight we send our love for Bobbi to the sky." She lifts her lit lantern, the glow illuminating her beautiful face. "And with them, our grief."

She turns to me with a sympathetic smile, and I know she's waiting for me to go first.

A loud sob tears free as I hold up my lantern, my handwritten words clear as I finally let it go.

Ringo follows, and I fall to my knees, my eyes on the dark sky, as more and more lanterns rise up, sending the words to the heavens.

> **Fighter.**
> **Precious.**
> **Sun.**
> **Cherished.**
> **Light.**
> **The Stars.**

It's the most beautiful sight, especially as the thick clouds part, as if Mother Nature herself knew they needed a clear path.

My friends join me and Ringo on the ground, all of us with our eyes fixed to the glowing lanterns in the sky for so long my neck hurts. But I don't dare look away as the lights grow smaller and smaller before finally floating out of sight.

When I finally look back down to Earth, my gaze catches Dee's, the vicious little assassin who keeps her voice locked away.

She shuffles closer until we are face to face, her big brown eyes brimming with tears as she cups my face so gently, it steals my breath. And then, she does something I never in a million years expected.

She leans close, so close that I can feel her breath on my chin, and she speaks, just for me.

"She'll always be with you, Abbey. So now you need to live fiercely and show her there can be beauty in this world."

I'm stunned at hearing her soft husky voice, yet I somehow manage to nod before Jared is leaning in to press his lips to her cheek, his gaze full of love as he admires his kickass girl.

When Dee glances back at him, they share a knowing smile, and I can see now, when she does speak, she saves her voice just for him.

The fact she just shared it with me means more than I can put into words.

More than she'll ever know.

When Ringo ducks inside to grab something, Helina and Casey steal a few minutes with me, sharing hugs and kind words.

I know it must be hard for them. Two of their own were taken the night of the ambush, yet they are still here in support, reminding me that I'm a part of their world now too.

When Smitty ambles over, the Doxies excuse themselves, leaving me to stand awkwardly with the club's leader.

"I… ahhhh…" He grabs the back of his neck, giving it a massage as he struggles to find the right words.

"You don't need to say anything," I offer him an out, but he doesn't take it.

"I feel like I should do something, or—"

"You know what you can do?" I cut him off, and his dark brows shoot up, not expecting the meek little mouse he likes to call Charity to be so rude.

"What?" he asks, looking more intrigued than annoyed.

"You can find Nessy and Darla. Have you even sent teams out looking for them?"

This time, his face hardens, and his eyes narrow into a glare.

"Of course I've had teams looking for them. You might wanna check yourself, girl."

I scoff. "Or what? You gonna slap me around? Kill me? News flash, Smitty. I don't have anything to lose, so do your worst."

A slow, sinister smirk stretches his lips. "You're wrong. You do have something to lose." His gaze shifts, and I follow it to see Ringo strolling back down the hill towards us. "You have him."

"Are you threatening my husband?" I snap, about ready to leap on him and start scrapping, but his chuckle pulls me up short.

"I know you're angry, darlin'. Just make sure you keep it aimed at the right people," he sighs as Ringo gets caught in a conversation with Murf and Stocky. "I don't normally discuss club business with the Doxies, old ladies *or* wives, but since you did us all a favour by killing Wendy, I guess it can't hurt to let you in on a little secret."

Smitty glances over his shoulder, checking if anyone is close enough to hear, and when he seems satisfied that there are no ears flapping nearby, he leans so close I can smell the beer on his breath.

"We've got a man on the inside. He's posing as a Rebel. We know exactly where they are currently hiding out with Nessy and Darla."

I jerk back, seeing Ringo notice in my periphery before he starts storming our way.

"Then why haven't you gone and saved them?" I hiss, my nostrils flaring in disbelief.

"It's not that simple. We need to wait for the perfect time."

"What's going on?" Ringo's deep voice cuts through the air, but I ignore him, my focus on his President.

"When the hell is the perfect time? When they've raped them so many times that they bleed for days? When they've tortured them until they confess things that aren't even real just to make it stop?"

"Who are we talking about right now?" Ringo snaps, but again, we both ignore him, our focus on each other.

"Twelve days," Smitty snaps, and my brows shoot up.

"Twelve days? What, you have it pencilled in your calendar because that's a good day for you?" I seethe, and he grits his teeth, his furious glare darting to Ringo.

"She needs a leash."

Ringo scoffs. "Just try to muzzle her and see what happens."

Smitty rolls his eyes. "You fuckers do your nuts over a chick and go soft. I swear I need to outlaw relationships."

"What's wrong with a week from now?" I butt in, ignoring them. "You have a hair appointment you can't cancel? What the hell is wrong with tomorrow? Nessy and Darla are suffering all because now's not a fucking good time?!"

My raised voice draws attention, but I don't care. Who's going to look out for them if he won't?

"Angel, stop." Ringo's tone is firm and demanding, and the submissive in me wants to snap my lips shut and drop my eyes to the ground.

But I can't.

Not for this.

Not when women are getting hurt.

"You trying to shut me up, husband?" I snap, whipping my glare his way, and he sighs.

"Just fucking tell her, Nate. She's one of us now. She knows how fucked up this world is. She can handle It."

I'm surprised Ringo used Smitty's real name, Nate, but it's hard to focus on that when Smitty sighs too, taking a moment to glance over his shoulder at the crowd now watching us.

"Well, Charit—" He holds his hands up in surrender when my lips part, ready to scold him for calling me Charity. "Abbey," he corrects, deliberately enunciating the name. "In ten days, the state will go into another snap lockdown. And in twelve days, when the Rebels are relaxed, partying and thinking they are safe because the law forces even the lawless to remain locked down, that's when we will hit."

My mouth opens, but then closes again as I frown, mulling over his words.

Another snap lockdown in ten days? What the...

"You can't possibly know that. Not even the Chief Medical Officer knows that yet. They have to wait for..." I trail off as Smitty shakes his head.

"Like most of the country, you believe the hogwash being fed to you through the media, which is tightly controlled by the Federal and State governments. Trust me, in ten days, on May twenty-eighth, Victoria will be thrown into a fourteen-day lockdown. And that, my love, is when we will get our Nessy and Darla back, and wipe out the entire Satan's Rebels State chapter."

All I can do is blink, because either this guy is completely delusional, or he's telling the truth. And if he is, then corruption in this country goes all the way to the top.

But to what end?

"Why would the government deliberately lock us down?" I look between Smitty and Ringo. "What do they get out of it?"

"Control," Smitty says quietly. "A way to force the majority of citizens to comply with strict regulations like vaccination mandates, check-in apps. Now they can track everyone. Some services have stopped accepting cash. Guess who benefits from that? The banks and the government."

"Most of the lockdowns have been sanctioned," Ringo cuts in. "But there are whispers that some of the more recent ones weren't. So when one of our sources tells us there's another one coming, we prepare. Because right now, it's more likely to happen than not."

I shake my head, turning to my husband. "This is so far-fetched."

"I know, Angel. But so is a cult church trying to force you into marriage."

My brows shoot up.

He has a point.

"It's not something to worry about now," Smitty mutters. "But you'll see. And when that lockdown happens, maybe then you'll believe me."

Sighing, I nod when all I want to do is roll my eyes at the insanity of it all.

It's then that I realise Ringo is holding something, my eyes dropping to the case in his hand.

"What's that?" I gesture to it, and his gaze softens.

"Well, I was hoping that I could sing a song. For you. For our girls."

Dammit. The bloody tears hit instantly.

"Yo-you want to sing to me?"

"Yes. If that's okay, Angel." He gestures to the seat JD has just placed down next to Bobbi's grave, and I nod quickly, swiping at my tears as a hush falls over the crowd.

Ringo pulls the guitar from the case while JD sets another chair next to Hope's grave.

When the background music cuts off, all that's left is the soft tinkle from the wind chimes, and everyone settles quietly to hear what Ringo has to sing.

I'm trembling as I sit, my anxious hands wringing together in my lap at the anticipation of seeing yet another new side of my husband.

He's never played his guitar for me before. There's something so special about him doing this, here on one of the hardest days of my life.

I'm not left sitting alone for long, my childhood friends coming to surround me. Lexi kneels beside me, taking my hand. Marcus settles on my other side, his fingers stroking my arm. And Jared stands behind us, resting a steady hand on my shoulder.

Then Ringo clears his throat.

"Please excuse how rusty I am. It's been a while."

He strums the strings a few times, giving it a quick tune.

My heart is pounding, but I can't tell why. Nerves. Excitement. Heartache.

Probably all the above.

"Sometimes, when I come to visit Hope…" He clears his throat, like he's trying to push away a clog of emotions. "I sing this song to her, imagining her with blonde curls, maybe six or seven years old, when her eyes would've sparkled with excitement for her future. For the possibilities that dreams can actually come true."

He takes a moment, drawing in a deep breath as he struggles to finish, but when he glances up and meets my gaze, all I see is strength.

"This song is all about her… *Hope*."

His fingers begin to strum, slow and hesitant at first, but he quickly finds his rhythm.

The chords are simple, and I immediately recognise them, tears blurring my view of how utterly handsome my husband is sitting under the tree, faint light casting soft shadows across his face, bent over his guitar as he parts his lips and starts to sing.

"*Why are there so many… songs about rainb…*"

Sobs ripple through the crowd, the gritty rasp in his voice adding to how hauntingly beautiful it is as he lays his heart and soul out for all of us to witness while he sings the lyrics for *Rainbow Connection*.

I can picture it then. Little Hope. Little Bobbi. Both with blonde curls, giggling as they skip under this tree, hand in hand without a care in the world.

"*Someday we'll find it,*" he sings, his eyes locking with mine, "*that rainbow connec…*" He winks, and I smile through my sobs as his voice grows stronger. "*The lovers. The dreamers… and me.*"

I'm barely holding it together by the time he finishes the final chord, my love for him so monumental that containing it takes more than I can muster.

The moment his fingers fall still, I'm up, nearly tripping over Lexi as I stagger forward.

Seeing my desperation, Ringo rushes to put the guitar aside, just in time to catch me as I launch myself into his lap.

My arms and legs wrap tight around him, and I bury my face in his neck, crying happy tears that blend with my grief.

"Angel," he breathes into my ear, his arms strong and steady around me like a shield against the rest of the world. "Do you wanna stay out here a while longer or—"

I shake my head against the curve of his neck, cutting him off.

"Take me to your room," I sob, and he gives me a gentle squeeze.

"*Our* room, Angel."

I nod, unable to speak, and he stands with me still clinging to him, excusing us, before carrying me inside.

19

RINGO

M y home looks like a fucking military base. Not that I'm complaining. I'm fucking grateful that the Marx family has stepped in to help me and my family after the last ambush, but it comes at a price.

Ewan Marx, the head of the Marx family, isn't someone who grants favours because he's a nice fucking guy. He's anything but. He wouldn't have agreed to this level of protection lightly, which makes me wonder what the fuck Griffin had to promise to get him to agree.

The steam from my coffee warms my nose as I take a sip, standing on the front porch as I count thirteen black-clad Marx security men guarding my property. And they are just the ones I can see.

There are more hidden in the trees surrounding the house. More again patrolling the boundary. And then, there are the crews stationed strategically on surrounding properties and roads, reaching as far as two kilometres away.

I knew the Marx family had a big private army, but I never expected *this*.

And I never expected they'd offer me more than a handful of men.

So yeah, I now owe the Marx family. And I owe them fucking big.

My eyes dart up at the low buzzing sound above the barn to find a drone floating by like a mechanical hawk. It's just another security measure they've got in place.

If the Rebels or that fucking cult church try anything, we'll have advanced warning.

"Don't get me wrong, I'm frothing at the mouth at all the hot testosterone walking around here lately." Lani's voice drags my eyes from the drone to see her standing beside me, her own cup of steaming coffee in hand. "But how much longer do you think this is going to take? They wouldn't even let me out on a Tinder date last week. I'm not happy about getting clam jammed."

"Fucking hell, Lans. I don't want to hear that."

She just shrugs. "You could always negotiate with some of the men to service me," she smirks, batting her lashes as she lifts her cup to her lips and takes a sip.

"I'm surprised you haven't already tried to lure one of them to your bed."

She nods, swallowing her morning brew. "Not for lack of trying. Either those men are gay, or they are the most loyal bunch of employees I've ever heard of."

I scoff. "Would it be so shocking that they are loyal?"

Her expression drops as she looks at me deadpan. "Mate, I walked into that barn wearing nothing but a G-string and a lace bra that barely contained my tits, and *not one* of those fuckers looked twice. Are they eunuchs or something?"

Biting back my smirk, I shake my head at my little sister, and return my gaze to a group of men that have just started sparring next to the barn.

"As far as I know, they haven't been neutered, Lans."

She sighs. "Looks like I'll have to pull out the big guns tonight."

"Dare I fucking ask?"

"Full nudity, brother." She claps my shoulder as she turns away, speaking over her shoulder as she heads back inside. "Might even have to bring out my Big Johnny Dildo and give them a show. Let's see how long they last then."

"For fuck's sake, Alana!" I spin to see her giggling as she disappears inside. "I'm gonna lock you in your fucking room!"

"Language, Cameron!" my ma calls from inside, and I hear Lans' laughter grow louder, like she's fucking happy I just got busted.

Little shit.

As I turn and stare out over the pond, movement to my right draws my attention to see my wife strolling up the hill. Her shoulders are slumped and her stride is small. Almost fragile. Her eyes remain on the ground as she walks around to the side of the house where I know she'll slip in through the backdoor unnoticed.

She's been down at Bobbi's grave again, after waking from another nightmare that had her drenched in sweat.

Okay, so *waking* isn't exactly the right term.

Blood-curdling screams ripping her from sleep is more accurate.

They started five nights ago, just after Bobbi's funeral, and have haunted her ever since.

She even tried to stay up all night last night, just to avoid them, but she didn't last past four in the morning before she was dragged into sleep, and then woke three hours later, screaming.

Going inside, I spend a few minutes with my ma, happy to see she seems to be getting a little better each day. She'd already had a lupus flare-up during the time I was away from Abbey, handling club business and hunting some of my Angel's rapists. Then the ambush happened, and she witnessed the violent brutality of my world, along with Jols and Millie getting shot in front of her… so yeah, she's been struggling.

With a plate of food in hand that Ma insisted I take for Abbey, I climb the stairs, two at a time, making my way to my room.

Up on the landing, I glance out the ceiling to floor window and I spot Millie over by the barn, sparring with one of the Marx crew.

If it were Lans, I'd immediately think she was trying to seduce the guy. But Millie isn't like that. She's over there because she's determined not to be a victim again. That's what she told me, anyway.

Fucking hell… everything is so fucked.

Sighing, I step into my room, hearing the shower running as I move deeper, and I place the plate of food on the bedside table before moving to the open bathroom door and leaning on the jamb.

"I can feel you watching me." Abbey's voice drifts from the shower, her body hidden by the fogged-up glass until her hand swipes across it, and her eyes meet mine.

"I can't really see you, Angel."

Her smile is small. Forced. She's been struggling to fake happiness since the funeral, but fuck, I wish she wouldn't even try with me.

I just want to see all of her. Even the parts that hurt.

"Oh well. Too bad."

Even her voice lacks the will to sound happy.

I chuckle anyway, trying to treat her as normal as possible.

"You need help expressing?" I ask, knowing that's why she's having her second shower of the morning.

It's easier for her to express milk under the hot water. There's less of it now, the engorgement not such a big issue anymore. She told me that her body will slowly stop producing it if she only expresses just enough to make herself comfortable.

The thing is, she can't seem to make herself stop.

"No, that's okay. I've got it." She shuts me down, not for the first time lately, and I fight the urge to fucking pout.

Clearly JD is right, and I've got a fucking lactation kink. I didn't even know it was a thing, but here we are. Although I'm pretty sure it only exists because it's her.

I've said it before, and I'll say it again. *She* is my kink.

"Ma insisted I bring a plate of food up for you. It's on the bedside table," I tell her, pushing away my disappointment at being shut down.

Ever since Bobbi's funeral, she hasn't let me draw from her.

Fuck it. Now my cock is getting hard just thinking about taking her nipple into my mouth and sucking until I feel the warm milk spill across my tongue.

A low growl rumbles in my chest, and before I can stop myself, I'm at the door of the shower, swinging it open to hear her squeak in surprise.

"Fine. I'll eat the food," she mutters, arms snapping up to cover her tits.

Fuck. I forgot I was talking about the food. My fucking head is too focused on her tits to think straight.

"I know you will, because you're not leaving our room until you do," I snap, my gaze trailing down the rivers of water streaming over her curves to the small patch of hair crowning her pussy.

Fuuuck. I've still got weeks to go before I can sink inside her.

"Someone's bossy this morning," she snaps back, and my eyes dart back to hers.

"Why are you covering your tits?" I dare to ask, and she sighs, looking defeated.

"I figured if you saw them, it'd be like dangling a lollipop in front of a toddler."

A slow smirk kicks up my lips. "Damn fucking right. But why is that a problem, Angel?"

Her gaze drops to the floor before she turns, giving me her back under the spray of water, yet she doesn't answer me.

For fuck's sake. She's gonna make me demand it, isn't she?

"Angel, turn around."

She doesn't.

"Turn around. Now," I growl, and just like that, she faces me, her eyes still trained on the tiled floor between us. "Eyes up," I snap, and they lift to show me the anger in them.

For the last five days, she's either been completely broken and wracked with tears, angry to the point of violence where the pillow or shoe or whatever is near cops her wrath, or she's in a quiet, numb, silence. And that's perhaps, the most worrying of all.

The rollercoaster of her emotions is giving me whiplash, but fuck, I don't blame her. I'm not angry at her. I just wish I knew how to help her.

My sisters have taken it upon themselves to teach Abbey how to fight and shoot a gun. I didn't point out that she already seems to know how to handle a gun after killing the Rebel in the hospital, and then what she did to Wendy.

Instead, I remind them to go easy on her, since it's only been a few weeks since Abbey gave birth. She has healed fast. She's kinda had no choice, but still, I fucking worry. My concern is met with nothing but death glares, though. Especially from Abbey.

The thing is, while she's training, she may be angry, but she's also focused.

The quietness and silent thinking are what truly unnerves me. I can't get a fucking read on her, and it's driving me fucking crazy. If she were an author, I'd say she was plotting her next bestseller. But since she's not, and now that Bobbi is buried, I have a feeling her plotting involves violence. Death. And a helluva lot of vengeance.

Not that I'm against that. I just wish she'd share what's going on inside her head with me.

"Why is seeing your tits a fucking problem?"

My question has her eyes dropping again, and my hand shoots up into her line of sight, my fingers gesturing for her to look back up at me.

Reluctantly, she does.

"Answer me."

"Fine," she snaps, clearly pissed I'm forcing her submissive side out. "Since the funeral, it hasn't felt right."

My heart sinks, because I immediately fucking think she's talking about us, but then I remind myself that we're talking about her tits and my enjoyment of drinking from her.

"Angel, if you don't enjoy it and don't want me to do *that* anymore, all you have to do is say so. It's your body, and I won't fucking do anything you're not into."

Her teeth appear briefly as she bites her lip, considering my words.

"That's the thing…" she practically whispers, all her anger gone as she looks at me with lost eyes. "I *am* into it. I *do* enjoy it, I just… my head's just not in *that* space right now."

"Fuck, Angel. I get that." I reach for her, and she steps into my open arms, pressing her naked, drenched body against my clothes, the hot water instantly soaking through.

"I'm sorry. I've just got a lot going on in my head," she mutters against my chest, and I press a kiss to her wet hair.

"You can talk to me, you know. About anything. I'm on your side, remember?"

She nods against me before pulling back, and my hands slide over her hot, wet skin before they fall away, and she steps back under the spray.

This time, though, she doesn't bother covering her tits.

A small smile pulls at her lips when she notices me staring at them, and she splashes water on me with a shooing motion, giggling.

"Get out of here, you pervert."

Chuckling, I step back, closing the shower door so she can finish, and I go and get changed since the front of my clothes are soaked through.

Once dressed, I head out to the barn, catching up with JD before we join church via livestream, which is fucking weird, but has somehow now become the new fucking normal.

Smitty is adamant that his government contact isn't bullshitting, and by the end of this week, we'll be back in lockdown again. And while I don't mind the idea of being locked away with my Angel, these fucking lockdowns are slowing down business and making it harder for the club to earn money, let alone how hard it is to hunt down the fucking rapists that need to eat lead.

Smitty explains that the man who saved our arses in the road ambush after the club funerals is apparently an old club associate, Blake Moore. He's a veteran who hung around the club when he rejoined society after three years in the Australian Forces, but he ended up in prison for manslaughter after a bar brawl. He'd only been out for a few months before this pandemic bullshit kicked off.

Unbeknownst to me, Smitty had reached out to Blake and offered him a deal to get fast-tracked into our club if he went undercover and tried to join Satan's Rebels.

It was a huge fucking ask, but since his family is estranged, keeping their distance because they can't handle his PTSD, the chance to join our club was the closest thing to having a family he was gonna get. And since he appreciates our moral code over the Rebels', he was happy to help.

When Blake saved us, I hadn't recognised him. His hair was dark, and he'd grown a thick, bushy beard, whereas before he'd been blonde with only stubble. But he'd killed Rebels for us and let us knock him out to make it look real, and because of getting away with that, he's been pulled deeper into their inner circle.

"So we have a confirmed location?" JD asks, and on the screen, Smitty nods.

"We do. I'll share that only when we're ready to move in."

I grit my fucking teeth.

He doesn't trust us. And fuck, he's probably right not to. If I let slip to Abbey where the Rebels were holed up, she'd go all fucking GI Jane and try to save Darla and Nessy herself.

"Has he confirmed the condition of our Doxies?" I ask, and Smitty nods.

"They are pretty banged up."

"And?" JD snaps, his fury bubbling to the surface.

"They're strong women," is all Smitty fucking says, and before I know it, JD hurls his can of beer across the fucking barn, the fucking thing clanging off the tin wall.

"Nessy hasn't even had her twentieth birthday yet!" JD roars. "She's not fucking strong! She's barely moved out of her scared-mouse stage, and those fuckers are raping her, aren't they?!"

"Hold on to that anger for the weekend, brother," Spud says, stepping into his VP role before Smitty flies off the handle for being yelled at. "Stay focused. Nessy and Darla need that fire pointed at the sick cunts hurting them."

JD bends in half, letting out a fucking howling yell, and the barn door bangs open, black-clad Marx men pouring in with their guns raised.

Fucking hell.

"Stand down," I call, holding my hand up to stop them. "Everything is fine here."

They scan the room quickly before nodding and lowering their guns, backing out of the barn.

"I'd still like to know what you had to do to get that level of protection from the Marx family," Smitty mutters. "I can't even get Leo Marx to call me back."

That's because the Marx men are businessmen. They don't like dealing with thugs, which is exactly how they see Smitty, with his God complex and fucking unhinged mood swings.

"I had to suck a lot of Marx cock." I grin, and Smitty actually smiles.

"You sick cunt. Get the fuck off my screen."

And just like that, he closes church.

JD is pacing, rage vibrating off him as he looks from the now blank screen to me.

"I want to punch the fucker."

I chuckle. "This about the Doxies, or the fact he's demanding Jols return to the compound?"

"Fucking Doxies, of course!" he yells, but when I raise a brow, his shoulders slump. "Fine. Some of it's about him bossing Jols around like he's got a fucking claim on her. He married her mum, and they barely see each other unless someone's getting married or buried." JD scoffs, starting to pace again. "You know, I should just tell him. Walk right up to him and tell him I'm claiming Jols."

My fucking brows reach my hairline. "*Are* you claiming her?"

He stops pacing. "Fuck. I don't know." He rakes his hand through his hair, leaving it a wild mess. "You think he'd kill me?"

I shrug. "Maybe. He's killed for less."

"Fuck," he mutters, then gestures to the far wall still dripping with his beer. "Sorry about that. I'll clean it up."

I chuckle as he grabs the cleaning supplies and starts scrubbing, and I leave him to it, going in search of my wife.

When I find her, she's at the dining table with my sisters and Jols, all of them bent over something spread out.

I approach quietly, suspicious as fuck.

"These are the locations they searched last time." Jols points to a map. "The circles are where they searched, and the crosses are who they killed."

Stepping up behind them, I see a map of Timber Valley pushed off to the side, with a map of Fox Pines their main focus, and it hits me what Jols is showing them.

It's the map I'd pinned up at the compound when my men and I were hunting for Abbey's rapists.

Somehow, Jols has fucking stolen it.

"What the fuck is going on?"

The four of them stiffen, their heads whipping over their shoulders to find me right behind them.

"Church over so soon?" Jols asks completely unfazed.

"Clearly it fucking is." I point to the table. "Why do you have that?"

"It's time to go," Abbey sighs, turning to face me fully, her arms coming up to cross over her chest.

Oh, I see what's happening. She thinks she's making decisions without me.

"It's time to go where?" I match her stance, crossing my arms over my chest as I stare down at her.

"To hunt the fuckers who took everything from me."

And there it is. This is what's been brewing. What she's been silently plotting.

She brought this up at the lake house before the funeral, and I guess now, five days after burying her little girl, she's ready.

Fuck, I'm not ready. I don't want to let her do this. It's fucking dangerous… but I can't stop her. I can't keep her from doing what she thinks she needs to do to heal.

After all, I did the same thing after Hope died, only there were no bad guys to punish, other than Kylie's drug dealer. So I took my rage out on whoever Smitty told me to.

I used to think it helped, but maybe I was wrong.

"You know where they are?" I challenge, knowing she doesn't. "You know the location of Daniel? Donny? What about Darnel?"

I'd already killed Tim, Michael, and Craig, which she knows by the red crosses on the map, thanks to Jols.

"Not exactly," she admits. "But I'm done waiting for someone else to figure it out." She drops her arms and turns back to the map, giving me her back. "You don't have to come if you don't want to."

"As if I'm not fucking coming with you, Angel," I growl, and she shrugs.

"Suit yourself."

I stare at the back of my wife's head in disbelief. Would she honestly go without me?

"It's not often I see you stumped, big brother." Lans giggles. "I think Abbey might be your kryptonite."

"I think you're right." Mills joins in, both of them laughing at my expense.

"Both of you will feel like shit if my wife gets hurt because you encouraged this," I snap, pointing a stern finger between them, and their smiles drop.

"Leave them alone, Cameron," Abbey sighs, bending over the table to study the map, and my eyes zero in on her arse, and fuck, how didn't I notice her dressed in those snug leather pants?

She's already dressed to go.

Fingers snap before my eyes, jolting me out of my daze, and I find Jols glaring at me.

"Eyes up, Sarg."

I fucking roll them, gently pushing Jols aside to reach my wife.

"So, if I had a problem with this, you were going to go anyway, weren't you?" I spin her to face me, staring her down as she shrugs, and I grind my teeth so fucking hard I swear I can taste blood. "How did you figure you were going to leave? Did you think you were gonna learn how to ride my hog in five minutes and steal it?"

She pulls a face like that's the most ridiculous thing she's ever heard of, scoffing, her eyes shifting over my shoulder before a mischievous smirk pulls at her lips.

"No. I was gonna jump on the back of JD's bike."

"Whoa." JD's voice comes from behind me as he strolls in, clearly hearing enough to know what's going on. "I know nothing about this, man."

Our eyes meet, and he's holding his hands up like he's trying to tame a beast. But it's too fucking late. She just mentioned riding on the back of another man's bike.

I'm fucking fuming.

Grabbing my wife's wrist, I yank her to my chest, a little gasp flying past her lips as I lean in close.

"You don't *ever* get on the back of another man's ride unless I give you *fucking* permission."

"Language, Cameron!" Ma yells from the other room, and I clench my fucking jaw, feeling like it's going to snap in half.

Snatching her wrist back from my tight grip, Abbey rubs at it, her glare zeroed in on me.

"You know when Rhys was talking to me about calling you Daddy, this wasn't the context I had in mind."

"The fuck?!" I snap, and she rolls her eyes.

"You're acting like you're my dad. Like you have a right to tell me what to do."

"And you're acting like a brat!"

The room falls silent as we remain locked in a battle of glares, the tension thick enough to choke on.

A moment later, JD's voice breaks the silent tension.

"Ahhh, maybe we should go for a walk." He reaches for Jols, but I shake my head.

"Don't bother," I spit, fisting Abbey's upper arm. "We'll go for a walk."

She gasps in disbelief as I start dragging her across the room, trying to tug herself free.

"Let me go!" she snaps. "Just because you're my husband doesn't mean you get to manhandle me!"

I spin on her so suddenly, a whimper escapes her as I seethe in her face. "Doesn't it?"

Before she can say another fucking word, I bend and hoist her over my shoulder, storming out the back door as she pounds her fists against my back.

20

ABBEY

He's turned into a caveman! I slam my fists against his back as he carries me out into the chilly May air, his grip tight around my legs as his hand comes down hard on my backside.

A squeak bursts from me, and I stop punching him and hang on as I watch the gravel path blur beneath us before giving way to tangled twigs, trying to ignore how much I liked the sting he left behind.

"Where are you taking me?" I ask, and a moment later he stops, and the world rushes past me as it goes from upside down to the right way up.

Stumbling back, I shake my head to try and focus, only to be shoved against a tree.

"What's your plan? How do you figure you'll find anyone?" he snaps, the fury in his eyes igniting the guilt I had this morning about not talking with him about this sooner. "Every time we leave to go somewhere, we get attacked. The Rebels try to kidnap you. And someone gets fucking shot."

And now the guilt hits like a sledgehammer.

Needing a second to breathe, I drag my eyes off him and glance around to find we're by the pond, and he has me pinned to the same tree he had me against on our wedding day… when he'd put his head between my legs and… had me as an appetiser.

The moment I feel the blush creep up my neck, I shove against his chest, trying to put some space between us.

"You're right. They'll be expecting motorcycles. We should take a car."

He rolls his eyes, stepping back just enough to let me breathe.

"You're not thinking clearly, Angel."

"Why are you trying to hold me back?" I snap, and confusion flashes over his expression.

"I'm not."

"It feels like it," I whisper, hating the hurt that flickers in his eyes.

"I'm just trying to keep you safe."

"I know." I nod, biting back the words I should have said sooner, but I just needed time to process everything that's happened. "I love how fiercely you love me, and want to keep me safe, but the thing is, I *won't* be safe until those men are dead. Until Darla and Nessy are safe. Until I have Tahli."

The burn of tears pricks my eyes, but I force them back.

I don't want to cry anymore. Not unless I'm visiting Bobbi's grave. For the rest of the time, I need to channel that pain into anger.

"Angel, you just buried your daughter last week." His voice is soft as he cups my cheek, his thumb gently stroking over my skin lovingly.

"That's right. I did. And now it's time for justice. Aren't you the one who said the MC gets to handle their own justice?"

He nods at my words, his eyes dancing between mine, concern blazing in their depths.

"So now, I need to get mine," I say softly, leaning into his palm.

"I feel like you've been deliberately keeping me out of your plans. Just like with Wendy." The truth of his words has guilt digging its claws in, but I don't deny it, and he sighs. "Would you have left if I had still been asleep or if I begged you not to go?"

"No." I shake my head, knowing this is the absolute truth. "I'm just so used to people deciding what happens to me. I got in my head about it, knowing you'd try to talk me out of it."

"I'd already agreed to it at the lake house," he reminds me, and my eyes drop with shame.

"I'm still learning how to trust."

My admission has both of us falling silent. The only sounds around us are the chirping birds and some sort of lawn mower humming in the distance.

"I'm always gonna try to protect you, Angel. But I don't want to stunt you. I want to see you thrive."

"I can see that now… I'm sorry," I admit, reaching up to fist his cut. "I just feel so out of the loop myself. I need to know everything, so I asked Jols because…"

"Because you didn't think I'd tell you," he finishes for me, and I shrug, staring up into his whiskey eyes, feeling like I might drown in them. "I'm sorry, Angel. I guess I've been holding back information too."

Offering him a small smile, I take his hand as he releases my cheek, linking our fingers.

"I know I'm acting crazy. I know this isn't… *me*. But I have to do *something*. I can't sit around and wait any longer."

"Okay," he nods, pulling me to his chest in a Ringo-scented hug. "Let me get a few things sorted, and we'll take my Landy."

"Landy?" I pull back, frowning up at him.

"Land Rover." His lips kick up in a cheeky grin.

"You have a Land Rover? I thought you only had a motorcycle."

"I also have a 1970s Ford Mustang locked away." His grin stretches, almost looking smug as he talks about his cars, something else I didn't know about him.

Before I can do anything else, Ringo's lips are on mine, stealing my breath as I melt against him out here in the open.

Well, not completely open, but with so many security guys walking around, I feel super exposed.

It's hard not to get carried away with each swipe of his tongue and the delicious heat of his body pressing me into the trunk of the tree. I could easily forget there might be people watching and let him devour me again right here, but things haven't settled *down there* yet, and well, if we can't get lost in sex, we may as well go on a killing spree… right?

When we come up for air, he leads me back to the house, and with a sharp slap on my arse, he strides away to get everything ready.

We hit the road a few hours later. Ringo, me, JD and Jols piled into his Landy, as he likes to call it, and two Marx vehicles with us. One up ahead, and one tailing us.

We drive back to the Timber Valley district. The closer we get, the more anxious I am, my leg bouncing relentlessly until it must start to annoy Ringo, because he presses his hand down on it, his warmth instantly calming the jitter.

We'd discussed strategy on the trip, and even though they had already been to the places marked on the map, there were a couple I wanted to see for myself.

It's just over an hour later when we're driving through Fox Pines.

My hometown.

It's weird being back here, my eyes taking in everything like I've been gone for years, when really it's only been a few months.

Everything looks different now, though. Probably because I see the world differently now. Nothing is the same. Where I used to see vibrant colour, all I see is meek dullness. Like a painting left out in the weather too long, and the colour has washed away.

Ringo seems to know my hometown well, something else I didn't know about him.

I'd never seen him before the night he stole me from my parents, so I'd just assumed he came to Fox Pines to get me, but I can see now he's been around these streets enough times to know them by memory.

The closer we get to my house, the more my heart thrashes.

He'd said it had been deserted when they came looking after Ian Allen took me from Ringo's home. That it looked like my family had left in a hurry. Yet still, the idea of walking back into that house has my stomach in knots.

Stay calm, Abbey. You need to do this. For Bobbi. For Tahli. For yourself.

The moment we turn onto my street, I stiffen, my hands clutching the seat as Ringo pulls up outside my neighbour's house.

"You don't have to go inside, Angel," Ringo reminds me, but I know I need to. I need to see it all. So I ready myself, forcing the bravest smile I can muster, and open the car door.

Our Marx escorts drive a bit further up the road, getting out to do a sweep, but I focus on my house as it comes into view with each step closer, the brown brick single-story home looking just the way it did before everything happened.

Ringo moves quickly to my side, with JD and Jols following behind as one of the Marx men, Riggs I think, approaches us.

"We are gonna park just outside each end of the street. Unless we were tailed without knowing it, there's no reason to expect a visit from the Rebels."

Ringo nods at the big guy. "Thanks, man. I'll text when we are coming out."

With another round of nods, Riggs leaves us, and we head up my driveway, Ringo taking my trembling hand in his.

When we reach the porch, Ringo beats me to a hidden key, my brows shooting up at the fact that he knew where it was, only it's not in its usual spot.

At seeing my confusion, he smirks and slides the key in the lock.

"Your little sister made sure to put it there after the first time your parents stopped keeping a key out."

"Huh." I smile. "She's a smart girl. When did she tell you about that?"

"She told Lexi." The door clicks open, and he releases my hand, pressing his finger to his lips before tugging out his gun.

It throws me off for a moment. The thought that anyone inside might pose a threat hadn't even crossed my mind, even after everything my parents put me through.

Have I been conditioned so much by them that I'd just walk straight into danger without thinking?

Jols takes my hand, holding me back as Ringo and JD slink inside, and we wait in tense silence, listening for a few minutes before the door swings wide suddenly, and JD flashes a grin past his scruffy beard.

"All clear, ladies."

I let out a breathless giggle, my heart hammering in my chest like a war drum, and when JD steps aside, I step inside the house I grew up in for the first time in three months.

I'm still trembling, but curiosity pulls me forward as I glance into the living room off to the side. The space dark but lit enough from the daylight filtering through the drapes, showing me it's spotless, just the way my mum likes it.

When I turn in the other direction, I spot Ringo leaning lazily against the wall by the hallway leading to the bedrooms, and a flash of the night he stole me leaps into my mind.

I'd been terrified of him. Of all of them. Their black ski masks and hulking bodies made them seem like monsters. But there was one moment that they didn't seem so scary. A moment I haven't forgotten, and now, staring at my kidnapper from that night, I can see that moment for what it was. A glimpse at the real man behind the mask.

"What are you thinking about?" he asks, and a small smile tugs at my lips despite the anxiety in my chest.

"I was terrified of you that night." I gesture to Jols and JD as well. "All of you."

The image of him kneeling in front of Tahli and talking quietly is ingrained in my brain.

"But then, when my little sister opened her bedroom door and I was sure you were going to hurt her, you lowered yourself to her level, and spoke to her. You even lifted your mask so she could see your face."

He nods. "That's right."

"What did you say to her?"

Pushing off the wall, Ringo closes the distance between us, my head tipping back as he towers over me, his fingers lifting to brush gentle knuckles over my cheek.

"I told her she was brave for reaching out to Lexi for help, and she asked me if I'd keep you safe, and I told her I would."

"She wasn't scared of you," I point out.

"She knew we were coming. She knew Lexi was sending help."

"But you must have looked like huge monsters to her." My eyes drop to his chest, remembering how he'd told her to go back to bed, and that our parents had been put in the naughty corner for a while.

"Probably." Ringo's voice draws me back to the present, and I blink away the memories so I can focus on the here and now. "You ready to take a look." He jerks his head over his shoulder, and I nod, taking his hand as he leads me down the hallway.

Tahli's room is tidy, but her bed is unmade, which means when they left, they probably grabbed her straight from it and ran.

I bet she was so scared.

My room still has the locks hanging from the outside of the door, and when I open it, everything is the same as before that night apart from some stains on the carpet over by the far side of my bed.

Bloodstains, I realise, remembering how I'd cut myself on the glass deliberately, smearing blood on my face in a twisted attempt to look scary, hoping it would keep my parents away from me when they came back.

The shattered window has been replaced, the outside shutter rolled all the way up, making the room look like a pretty teenage girl's space.

All I see is ugliness.

I rummage through my drawers, finding nothing of importance since Mum took everything from me.

I shove some clothes into a bag, happy I'll finally have something of my own instead of wearing other people's clothes, and then I hurry to the bathroom to get my personal items from there.

JD and Jols take my bags out to the car, leaving me and Ringo to continue our search of the house.

Maggie's room is pristine. Her bed is made, and I just know she would've helped Mum prepare to flee, leaving Tahli out of the loop.

A quick search of her room gives me nothing other than her notebook which has a few passages from the Script of Symme scribbled inside.

In my parents' room, their scent hits me the moment I step in, and my stomach lurches. What's even more surprising is how messy it is.

The bed is unmade, my dad's clothes scattered everywhere, which is unusual, and there are dirty plates piled up on his bedside table.

"That's different," I mutter, pointing to the dishes, and Ringo's brows shoot up.

"Not like your olds to leave dirty dishes around?"

I shake my head. "They never ate in here. Maybe that changed after I was taken from them."

Ringo frowns. "Maybe."

JD and Jols come back in, and Ringo chats to them while I dig through my mother's drawers, finding my old phone and charger, which I pocket, and my licence and bank cards.

She's probably drained what little money I had, but having access to the things that were mine is important to me, so I reclaim them, and keep searching.

I'm not sure what I'm hoping to find. Maybe any clues about where they could be, though I know it's a long shot.

I'm about to give up when I decide to look under the mattress and find what looks like an old scrapbook.

Frowning, I tug it out and drop it on the bed, gaining every-one's attention.

"What do you have there?" Ringo asks, and I can see him moving closer in my peripheral, so I open the cover to see my mother's name scrawled out in a purple marker.

Priscilla Louise Banes

My breath stutters as I re-read it.

Priscilla Louise Banes

Surely I'm misreading that. Her maiden name was Bates. I'm sure of it.

"Angel?" Ringo asks, concern lacing his tone, and I angle the book towards him and point to the name.

"Read this out to me."

His whiskey eyes flick to mine in confusion, his brows knitting together, but he nods, glancing down at the page.

"It says, Priscilla Louise Ba…" His eyes snap up to mine.

"Tell me I'm misreading it." I rush out. "It should say Priscilla Louise *Bates*. That's what she's always told me her maiden name was." I suck in a shuddering breath. "It says Bates… right?"

His eyes flick back down to the page, and he slowly shakes his head.

"Angel… it says Priscilla Louise *Banes*."

I jerk away from the scrapbook like it's going to burn me, but in the next second, I have it in my hands again, turning the page.

There in the middle of the page is a photo of a very young version of my mum. I know it's her. She's shown me pictures of herself as a child before, just never this one.

"Fuck," JD mutters over my shoulder, and I can feel him and Jols flanking me on one side, and Ringo on the other. "Is that…"

I nod before he can finish. "That's my mum," I whisper, pointing to the little girl in the picture. "And that man…"

I can't bring myself to finish, because surely this is some sick joke?

"That's Banes. Minister Banes," Ringo mutters in a deep growl, and I shake my head in disbelief.

A youthful version of Minister Banes stares out from the photo, and on his knee sits my mum. Probably only six or seven years old.

Shocked, but desperate for answers, I flip to the next page, finding a photo of my mum as an early teen, surrounded by kids a similar age. They don't look happy, but they don't look miserable either. Just eerily neutral, like it's a class photo where they weren't allowed to smile.

"That fucker looks familiar," Ringo growls, jabbing a finger at one of the boys in the picture, and my heart slams to a stop.

"Oh shit. That looks like that Daniel fucker," JD snarls, but I shake my head.

"Not Daniel. It's his dad. Karl."

"Did he and your mum grow up together? Go to the same school?" Jols asks what's running through my head.

"I… I don't know." I glance over my shoulder at Jols. "My mum never mentioned him, and when I first started seeing Daniel, it seemed like they didn't know each other when we introduced our parents."

The frown pulling at Jols' face matches mine.

This is just all too confusing.

Turning the page again, I find a picture of a woman with her back to the camera, wearing a white gown like the one my mum forced on me that day at the chapel.

It was a wedding dress, and as I look closer at the picture, I can see the woman in it is walking down the aisle of a church.

"What does that mean?" JD asks, pointing to the scribbled writing below the picture.

"One blood to bind. One womb to bear.
One heir to rise."

This will be me soon.

"It must be scripture," I mutter. Turning the page, I gasp.

In the centre of the page is a grainy photo of a naked woman standing in what looks to be a shallow barrel, with other women around her bathing her in a milky liquid.

"The fuck…" Ringo rasps next to my ear, leaning in closer as he reads out the script written under it. *"The body is not mine. The will is not mine. Let Symme shape me."*

I suck in a sharp breath as I read the words my mother has scribbled under the scripture. *"I'm excited to give myself to him."*

"Uhhh, I don't know about you guys, but this is giving me the creeps," Jols whispers like we are about to get sprung by a lurking spirit.

"That church really is a cult, isn't it?" JD asks, and Ringo lets out a low "hmmm" as I turn the page, my eyes going straight to the scripture first, reading it in my head.

"Before the Eyes of Flame,
we bind blood to blood.
Flesh to flesh. Womb to seed.
Obedience to order.
By right of line, let this vessel be claimed."

Today was Sally's ritual.
Soon it will be my turn.

A chill runs up my spine at the possible meaning of those words, and when my eyes drop to the picture stuck underneath, oxygen gets trapped in my lungs.

The photo shows a little girl, no older than fifteen or sixteen, lying on a table at the church altar. Her dress is hitched up. Her legs spread wide, and a man in a suit is standing between them with a blindfold over his eyes. Pain twists *her* face, and pleasure contorts *his*. There's no mistaking what's happening… he's having sex with her, perhaps taking her virginity with people watching on.

Minister Banes stands in the background, looking on with a pleased, almost proud expression. Behind him, the congregation is gathered, their mouths open like they're singing… or chanting.

"Please tell me that's not what I think it is?" Jols whispers, and I shake my head, too stunned to speak and tell her it's exactly what she thinks it is, so I turn the page, needing more answers.

This time, there are two more pictures staring back at me.

The first is of a man, bare-chested, being anointed with trickles of blood on his chest from a chalice. The picture next to it is of the girl on the table, teetering on the edge with her legs spread wide, and Minister Banes holding the chalice between her thighs…

"Oh my fucking God… is he getting anointed with her hymen blood?" Jols screeches, and all I can do is nod as I read the scripture and my mum's handwritten thoughts underneath.

*"**She bleeds for him,
so he may rise through her.**"*

I'm ready.

What the actual… I shake my head, bile rising in my throat as I shove the scrapbook away across the mattress, hearing it thud to the floor on the other side.

"This is sick. What is this?" I spin, completely freaking out as I face Ringo. "Did my mum grow up in this cult? That's it, isn't it? Otherwise, why would there be a photo of her on the Minister's knee? Is her maiden name really Banes? Please tell me it was just some sick fascination with the cult leader."

I'm losing it. Spiralling. Shaking my head, my stomach churning as I try to make sense of what this is. Yet as I line up what we just saw in that scrapbook with what happened in that chapel only a few weeks ago, I know the wedding ceremony they wanted me to be a part of was so much more. Something sick and vile.

"Shhhh, Angel." Ringo tries to soothe me, cupping my face. "Calm down. You're safe, remember."

I shake my head. "I might be safe, but Tahli's not. I need to find her!"

"We'll find her. I promise," he rasps, but then he stiffens, his head snapping up like he's caught a sound, and I force my ears to focus.

That's when I hear it. A car door slamming shut, right outside.

My eyes go wide, and JD hurries to the window, peering past the drapes.

“There’s a car in the driveway.”

Then, as the last word leaves his mouth, the front door swings open and slams shut with a deafening crack.

21

ABBEY

Trailing behind Ringo with his gun raised, we move in a tight pack towards the sound of someone in the kitchen. The way my heart thrashes has me worried I'm about to have a heart attack, fear coursing through my veins at the possibility of seeing my mother again.

Or worse. Ian Allen.

With a level of stealth I mimic from Ringo, Jols and JD, we slip into the kitchen and my eyes fall on a familiar man.

My dad.

He looks haggard, his greying hair sticking up haphazardly as he unpacks a few grocery items from a shopping bag.

Ringo still has his gun trained on my dad, so I step forward, taking the lead, knowing Ringo has my back if this goes bad.

"Dad."

My voice is louder than I'd expected, and his eyes snap up, a gasp flying past his lips as he finds me mere feet away.

"Abigail." He goes to move towards me, but then his gaze flicks to the people at my back, and the guns pointed at him. "Uhhh, sweetheart?"

His gaze flicks back to me, uncertainty flashing through them.

"Where's Mum?" I ask, and he shakes his head.

"I-I don't know, sweetheart."

"Don't call me that. You lost that privilege a long time ago."

He parts his lips to argue, but then snaps them shut, nodding, his gaze dropping to the floor.

Submissive.

That's all I can think as I stare at my dad, hot tears burning my eyes, but I refuse to let them fall.

Only for Bobbi. These people only get my anger.

"God…" I glance over my shoulder at my husband. "Was I that pathetic?" I point to my dad, and Ringo shakes his head, understanding my meaning.

"You've never been pathetic, Angel. What you're seeing isn't the same."

I want to believe him, but it's hard to tell the difference between the obedient daughter my mother shaped me to be and my pathetic father.

I hate her.

"I need you to tell me where Tahli is. *Please.*" I want to call him Dad again, but the word feels vile on my tongue when directing it at him.

"I don't know where they are exactly. Only that they are with Minister Banes," he offers, moving slowly to step out from behind the kitchen counter. "They were on the move. I tried to follow, but then some bikers chased me down, and well, this is what happened." He points to his face, and I see fading bruises as he steps a little closer.

"What bikers?" Ringo snaps, and my dad cringes back a step.

"I only remember the word Satan on those vests you guys wear." My dad gestures to Ringo's cut.

"Satan's Rebels," Ringo confirms, and my dad nods.

"Yes, that's it."

"Why aren't you with your wife and daughters?" Ringo asks, his lethal tone sending a chill up my spine.

He's a scary man.

My monster.

"I… They…"

"Fucking spit it out, old man," JD snarls, and my dad hurries a nod.

"I begged them not to make Abbey go through that at the chapel. They wouldn't listen to me."

I scoff. "I remember you begging on your knees, and when I asked where your balls were, you ran out of the chapel like a little bitch."

Ringo, JD and Jols snicker behind me, but my focus remains on my dad as tears flood his eyes.

"I didn't know how to stop it."

"Turns out I didn't need you. You've never been man enough to protect me. But my husband is."

His brows shoot up. "Husband?"

I jut my thumb over my shoulder. "I married the angry-looking one."

My dad's lips part as his eyes dance between me and Ringo, and I brace myself for the backlash, but it never comes. Instead, my dad nods.

"Good. I can see he'll do anything to protect you."

"He will. Including killing you if I ask him to."

If my words scare my dad, he doesn't show it. Instead, a strange calmness washes over him.

"I'm a coward. I know that, and I'm sorry." He shakes his head, anger lighting his eyes, but I can see it's directed at himself, not me. "I ran that day at the chapel, because I didn't know how to stop any of it. Pieces started falling into place, and I realised your mother's involvement with the church was bigger than I ever could have imagined."

"Let's not pretend that place is a church," Jols snaps from behind me. "It's a cult. There's no other word for it."

My dad nods in agreement, his shaky hand reaching out to grab the bench, like he's struggling to keep himself up.

"I should have run off with you and your sisters when Priscilla started going to Bible study a few years back. I could feel something wasn't right. She had so much trauma from her childhood, so I never in a million years thought she'd want to go back there." He cringes, his eyes falling distant like he's remembering a past I'm not privy to. "I didn't know, Abigail. She lied to me, and it was all too late when I found out."

A sinister chill ripples down my spine as my fears start to become a reality.

"Her maiden name is Banes, not Bates, isn't it?"

My dad's brows shoot high. "How do you know that?"

"I found a scrapbook under her mattress. The name in it is Priscilla Louise Banes."

My dad swallows thickly. "I only found out last month."

"Bullshit!" Ringo snaps. "You married her. It would have been on your marriage certificate."

My dad shakes his head. "My marriage certificate has her maiden name listed as Bates. She only revealed last month that she'd had her name legally changed to Bates when she got cast out of the church."

"Cult," JD snaps.

"Priscilla doesn't see it as a cult. She grew up in it. She sees it as a church." My dad's eyes shift from JD back to me. "I went back to the chapel that day. I got an hour down the road and turned around, determined to kidnap my own daughters if I had to… But by the time I got back, it looked like a war zone, and no one was in sight."

"Have you even noticed that I'm no longer pregnant?"

My dad's brows shoot up again, his eyes dropping to my flatter stomach.

"Oh, sweetheart. Where—"

"SHE DIED!" I scream, the words ripping from me without warning.

My dad stumbles back, his hand slapping to his chest as a sob lurches from him.

"Oh no." He shakes his head, tears bursting from his eyes. "No. No. No. No…"

"YES!" I storm towards him and shove him back, and he stumbles, nearly tripping over his own feet.

"The man you wanted me to marry raped me, Dad! He raped me and shared me with his friends so they could rape me too! And you did nothing but stand by and let Mum drug me and deliver me to them!"

My hand swings hard, my palm slapping his face so hard he tumbles into the fridge.

"I'm s-sorry, Abigail," he cries, and I scoff.

"Those men chased me down! I was almost eight months pregnant! Eight months! I couldn't even run properly. But I tried so hard to get away from them." Tears burst from my eyes as I remember the moment rough hands shoved me from behind, and I fell. "Daniel pushed me, Dad. He pushed me, and I landed on my BABY!"

My hand goes around his throat as I hold him against the fridge, knowing all too well that if he wanted to, he could overpower me. But he doesn't even try, his eyes overflowing with tears as I share the most terrifying moment of my life.

"I went into labour. I was bleeding. She was born right there in that fucking pine forest! In the fucking dirt!" I lean in, my lip curling with a snarl. "I only felt her alive for a few minutes, and then, I nearly died, and she DID DIE!"

I scream a vicious screech as my second hand wraps around his neck, squeezing hard.

"So you tell me, *Dad*. What was all that for? WHAT THE FUCK WAS ALL THAT FOR?!"

With another scream, I shove myself back, fisting my hands in my hair as I start pacing, too wild to even make eye contact with my husband and my friends.

"Abigail… I'm so sorry. My *sweet* Abigail."

"Shut up!" I snap, turning my glare back to him as he sinks to the floor against the fridge. "I don't want to hear your apologies. That can't bring my daughter back. The only thing you can do now is tell me everything, so I can save Tahli."

"W-what about Maggie?" my dad stammers, and I scoff.

"That cunt can die for all I care."

I don't know who I am right now.

I've never spoken like this. Even when I was a more unhinged version of myself that day at the chapel, I was never *this*.

"Is Mum related to Minister Banes?" I snap, needing to get the information and be done with him, and I watch as my dad nods.

"He… he is her father."

I stop pacing, the room turning eerily silent aside from my dad's sobs.

"Minister Banes is my grandfather?"

My dad nods.

"I didn't know. Your mother had always told me her father was dead."

"Jols." I turn to face my friend. "Can you please get the scrapbook?"

Jols nods and hurries deeper into the house as I pivot back and face my dad.

"So Banes is her father, and he is the leader of the cult. Correct?" I snap, and my dad nods. "She grew up in the cult, but then left?"

"I overheard Banes scolding her at the chapel the day that crooked cop brought you there," my dad sobs. "He told Priscilla there was a reason she was outcast, and he's not sure if what she's offering can redeem her." My dad shakes his head. "I don't know what that means. When I asked her about it, she ignored me and walked off."

"Here, Abs." Jols enters the room with the scrapbook, and I open it to the first page, holding it out for my dad to see.

"This is Mum sitting on Banes' knee, isn't it?"

My dad nods. "Yes."

Turning to the next page, I hold it out and point to the boy who looks a lot like Daniel.

"Is this Karl Stone?"

A sob lurches from my dad's lips as he nods. "Y-yes."

"Why is Daniel's dad there?"

Shaking his head, my dad starts sobbing uncontrollably, so I spin, holding my hand out for Ringo's gun, and even though he lifts a questioning brow at me, he hands it over.

When I turn back, my dad's eyes go wide as I point the gun at him.

"I didn't know. I swear, sweetheart. If I had known, I would have put a stop to it." He sobs, shaking his head, eyes pleading up at me. "It was Karl who got her back involved in the church. I wish I'd figured it out sooner."

"Stop fucking rambling and tell me who Karl is to Mum?!"

"Sweetheart, it doesn't matter. You don't want to know. Please trust me on this."

"Like fuck! It does matter!" I lunge forward, pressing the barrel of the gun to his forehead. "Tell me!"

"Okay, okay," he sobs, and I pull the barrel back just enough to leave a few inches of space between it and his head. "I only know what your mother told me. There's so much I don't know. Unless you're raised inside the church, you don't get the details of the inner workings until it's too late."

"What does that even mean?" I snarl through gritted teeth.

"I'm so sorry. I tried to stop it."

"Stop what? Stop talking in fucking riddles and tell me!"

"Y-you and D-Daniel." He shakes his head, trying to find the right words. "When I found out... I tried... but your mother...

she has these videos of me…oh my dear sweet girl. Please forgive me.”

I stumble back a little, trying to piece together what he’s saying.

Did my mum blackmail him? But why?

“Given what’s happened, it all seems so stupid now, but I was terrified of anyone finding out,” he stumbles over his words. “She used the videos against me to keep me silent.”

“Fucking tell her now, or I won’t hesitate to put a bullet in your skull!” Ringo booms from across the room, and the words finally fall from my dad’s lips.

“Karl Stone is your mum’s half brother. They have the same mum but have different dads.”

What.

Did.

He.

Just.

Say?

The world stops turning and crushes in so forcefully that my knees buckle.

“No…” I whisper as my knees crash to the floor. “You can’t be saying…”

“I’m sorry,” my dad wails. “I never knew Karl was your uncle. I would never have allowed you to date a cousin.” He shakes his head as a shudder rolls through him. “That’s just sick.”

Bile rushes up my throat, and I manage to scramble up in time to reach the sink as my body tries to purge the vulgarness from inside me.

I retch over and over, vomiting up the little food I've had today, hearing Ringo and my friends in the background, scurrying to help me and take charge of the situation.

It feels like it goes on forever, and once I'm through, I collapse into Ringo's arms in shattered disbelief.

No.

This can't be real.

Jols gets me a glass of water, and I sit on a stool taking a moment to recompose myself.

This can't be happening.

"Why…" I say quietly when I find my voice again. "*Why* would Mum allow that?"

"It's the church. Your grandfather," my dad mutters from where he's still huddled on the floor. "He's the head of it. He thinks he's something special. That all must bow to him." My dad cringes. "That sick fuck tried for years to get Priscilla pregnant. His own daughter! But she miscarried each time, and in his eyes she was a failure. That's why she was cast out. She was deemed unworthy if she couldn't conceive the spawn of her own father."

"I thought you said you didn't know why she was cast out," Ringo snaps, and my dad shrugs.

"I lied, okay. I didn't want Abigail to learn the sick truth."

"What do these words mean?" Jols asks, showing my dad the scrapbook pages and pointing to the scripture my mum had written as a teen.

"I don't know." Dad shakes his head. "Priscilla never trusted me with that information."

This is so much more than I expected. I thought I was being punished for bringing shame to the family by having premarital sex. But now I can see it has to do with the cult and their beliefs.

Daniel told me at the chapel that day that I had no clue what was really happening, and he was right.

I could never have imagined *this*.

"When they found out I was already married that day at the chapel," I speak up, my throat scratchy as a strange numbness washes over me. "They started talking about bloodlines. Do you know what that was about? Why Maggie offered herself up to marry Daniel?"

My dad frowns. "No, I'm sorry. I don't have a clue about that. I didn't even know that happened. Like I said, unless you're born into it, you only get told when things are happening and it's too late."

"And the reason you were finally trying to stop the wedding was because you'd just found out they were trying to marry me to my cousin?" Bile rises up again as I say the words out loud, but I manage to swallow it back down.

"Yes, that's right," my dad sobs.

This is just… *too* much.

"You didn't try hard enough to protect me. To protect Tahli." I stand from the chair, embracing the numbness as I stare at a man I no longer consider my father. "If you did, you'd either have Tahli with you safe right now, or you'd be dead from trying so hard to get her away from those sick cunts."

"Possum!" my dad cries, reaching out to me, but I just curl my lip in disgust.

"No, I'm not your possum. I'm not your sweetheart. And I'm certainly not your daughter." I lean in closer, jabbing a finger into his chest. "You never fought for me even when you knew what was happening was wrong. For that, I'll *never* forgive you."

Turning to Ringo, I eye the gun in his hand, which I must have dropped earlier.

"Do we have a spare one?" I gesture to his gun. "One you don't need?"

His brows shoot up, and he nods, holding his hand out to JD, who's carrying a number of guns on his person.

Taking one JD hands him, Ringo gives it a clean, making sure there are no fingerprints.

"Where do you want it?"

I gesture to the bench, and he places it down, his glare harsh as he directs it at my dad.

When my dad looks at me in confusion, an unhinged smirk spreads across my face.

"A gift. Feel free to use it on yourself."

And with that, I ignore the pain that contorts his face, walking out of my childhood home with Ringo, Jols and JD following.

The moment we reach the Landy and I open the car door, the loud clap of a gunshot pierces the air, sending magpies scattering in flight from the nearby gumtree.

22

RINGO

S he doesn't even flinch at the sound of the gunshot, her eyes catching on the flock of magpies that soar from the trees at the sudden disturbance. Something has flipped inside her. It was already teetering when she laid her heartache bare with her old man, making sure he knew the full extent of his actions. Or lack thereof.

But what she learned about Daniel… Fuck! Her own fucking cousin!

Yeah, that's the shit that tipped her over into this cold, dead version of herself.

My eyes meet JD's, and he gestures his head back towards the house, so I nod, and he turns, walking back inside.

Abbey watches him go, but doesn't say a word, just slips into the car and closes herself in.

"That was some heavy shit," Jols mutters quietly next to me, and I meet her concerned gaze and nod.

"People should need a licence to have kids. Her parents should never have been allowed to have them."

"Yeah, but then you wouldn't have her."

"Yeah." I let out a rough fucking sigh. "She deserved better than what she got."

"She's got you now. Us. Let's help her get through this, and then," Jols shrugs, her lips kicking up, "we all get to show her how fucking amazing life can be."

The slam of a house door draws our attention back to the house to see JD striding back towards us. When he gets closer, I lift a brow, and he gives me a single nod, telling me everything I need to know.

Colin Delany took the parting gift his daughter left him, and put himself down.

Slipping into the car, we all buckle up, Abbey's seat belt already in place as she stares out the windshield.

"Is he dead?" Her voice is empty, her big doe eyes flicking to me.

"Yeah, Angel. He's dead."

She nods once, settling back into her seat as I fire up the engine, and her gaze shifts out the window, staring at the houses on her street as we drive away.

"JD, shoot Riggs a message and get him to contact Officer Zimora," I mutter, my eyes meeting his briefly in the rearview mirror. "Tell him there's been a suicide and give him the address."

"On it." JD shifts in the backseat, taking out his phone, and I focus on the road as we meet up with our escort and wait for the second vehicle to catch up.

I consider that maybe what Abbey's learned today is already enough. Maybe even too much. That maybe we should head to the compound for the night, or the Redfield Lake safe house. But she's determined to find her sister, so I push on to the next stop on our list.

The Stone residence.

Abbey remains quiet, staring out the window as we drive through the streets of Fox Pines. Her leg isn't bouncing anymore like it was before we went to her house. She almost looks calm. Like she's in a trance.

The moment we pull up outside Daniel's house, she perks up, straightening in her seat as recognition flashes across her face. Before I've even got the car in park, she's unbuckled, her hand on the door handle, ready to leap out.

"Hang on, Angel. We need to think about what you want to do if anyone's in there."

Her eyes flick to mine, then drop to the console where I left my gun, and she gives a single nod.

"You're right."

Snatching up my gun, she's out of the car in a heartbeat, sprinting up the front path before I can even start cursing.

"Fucking hell," I snap, trying to unfold myself from the car faster than my bulk wants to move, with JD and Jols scrambling after me.

In my periphery, I see Riggs and his team piling out of their cars, but I'm locked on Abbey as she jabs the doorbell over and over.

"Angel!" I call, but she fucking ignores me as I charge towards her.

The next fucking second, the door swings open, and Karl fucking Stone appears, wide-eyed and gasping as he comes face to face with the barrel of a gun.

Shit.

"Hello, Uncle," Abbey snarls, shoving Karl, who stumbles backwards as my wife forces her way inside.

"She's a fucking badass right now," JD chuckles, wagging his brows as he rounds me and follows Abbey inside.

"You have to admit," Jols giggles as she follows JD while I stand frozen on the path, fucking stunned, "she's kinda hot right now. I'd do her."

"For fuck's sake," I mutter, raking a hand over my face before turning to Riggs, who's only a few feet behind me.

"Keep an eye on the street and have your men ready to leave in a hurry."

Riggs smirks, his gaze flicking to the door. "It's like a monster has been unleashed."

He's talking about my wife and I can't even deny it because he's spot-fucking-on.

All the pain Abbey has kept buried is spilling out, and fuck if her monster doesn't match my own.

Following my team inside, I close the front door, finding Abbey in the living room, looming over Karl as he shakes violently in his armchair, the barrel of the gun pressed to his forehead.

"When Daniel introduced me to you, did you already know who I was to you?"

"Y-yes."

"And you didn't think, *hey, these two are cousins, maybe it's not a good idea if they date*?"

Karl's head twitches in a tiny shake, his eyes pleading as he stares up at my Angel, who right now, resembles more of a demon.

"D-Daniel h-had d-done exactly w-what I'd asked h-him to d-do."

I can only see the side of my wife's face, but the way she tilts her head to the side is fucking creepy… and hot.

"And what the fuck did you ask him to do?"

Fuck, why do I love it when she swears like that?

"M-make y-you fall i-in love with h-him. T-told h-him that c-courting y-you would help h-him to move u-up the r-ranks in the c-church."

"It's a cult, Karl. Call it what it is!" she yells, and he flinches.

"It's not a c-cult, it's a churc—"

Before any of us know what's happening, Abbey snaps the gun to Karl's thigh, and pulls the trigger.

He howls in agony, which is the fucking opposite reaction to what I'm having.

Fuuuck. My cock is rising like a vampire rises for the setting sun.

"Stop whining," I snarl at Karl, flicking my eyes to JD. "Take Jols and search the house."

They nod and slip out, leaving the living room echoing with Karl's spluttering whimpers, his hands slick with blood as he clamps them over the gushing wound on his leg.

For a long moment, Abbey just stares at Daniel's dad, taking in his dishevelled appearance.

He was that way when he opened the door, and clearly Abbey is thinking the same.

"Is Daniel here? Your wife?" Abbey asks, and Karl shakes his head.

"J-just m-me."

"Why *are you* here?" Abbey lowers the gun to her side, her scrutinising gaze raking over Karl.

"I'm here because of you!" he seethes through gritted teeth, and Abbey's brows shoot up.

"Me?" she scoffs, pointing to herself.

"You fucked everything up," he continues. "All you had to do was marry Daniel, and this would all be over."

Abbey is quiet for a few long beats, and then she bursts out laughing, manically.

"Oh, *I'm sorry*." She slaps her hand dramatically to her chest. "I didn't feel like marrying my *fucking cousin!*"

The gun is quickly pressed to Karl's other leg this time, and she pulls the trigger again.

The bang is loud as fuck in this tight space, but my wife doesn't flinch. She just shoves the barrel up under Karl's jaw, forcing his head back.

"Stop," Karl sobs, his legs pissing out blood all over his fucking armchair, but my Angel's not stopping. She won't until he's dead.

"Why aren't you with Banes? Your stepdad, right?"

"That bastard cast me out!" Karl seethes, voice cracking. "After all the years I supported him! He fucking kicked me out because Daniel shared you with his mates, knocked you up before the sacred ceremony could be done, and then," Karl's lip curls, "you went and married another man. You ruined everything, and my beautiful…" He trails off on a sob. "My beautiful mother is the one who paid."

"Blame me all you want." Abbey snarls in his face, her caramel eyes wild. "As you can see, I don't give a single fuck. But I *am* interested in your pathetic story. So please tell me all about what my grandfather did to your mum. And why?"

For a long beat, Karl remains silent, his gaze flicking to JD and Jols as they return to report the house is clear.

Then, as if he knows his fate, he spills all the sick and twisted details.

"I did it all to save my mother," he sobs, his eyes going distant like he's remembering a different time. "He kept her locked up for years, using her as a fucking incubator for his spawn." His hands slip in the blood coating his legs as he tries and fails to stop the bleeding.

"When my step-father… Banes… learned Daniel might not be the father of your baby, I knew it wouldn't end well for my family. He needed the pure bloodline."

Abbey scoffs. "Don't you mean tainted? If Daniel was the father of my baby, her veins would be pumping with incest."

"Not in the eyes of the church," Karl rushes out. "In Symme, conceiving from the same bloodline is the purest form of creation."

A shudder ripples through my Angel as she takes a step back.

"So the cult is just one big incest ring?" she says, her voice dripping with disgust.

"Eve was made from Adam's rib," Karl mutters, his breaths heavy as he tries to ignore the pain in each of his legs. "They shared the same DNA. They then created life. Children, who then had children together. That is purity. The natural path."

For a long beat, the room is silent, Karl's eyes never leaving Abbey's. Then, to everyone's shock, she bursts out laughing.

"Fucking hell, Karl," she snickers. "Do you hear yourself? What a load of bullshit."

"It's not bullshit!"

"Yeah, it fucking is!" Abbey keeps laughing, and I catch Jols' and JD's eyes briefly, because shit, my wife is a little more unhinged than I thought.

"So, is Elizabeth your sister? Or cousin?"

Karl shakes his head. "No. My betrothed was meant to be your mother, Priscilla, but our father wanted to have a child with her first, and she kept losing them. When he cast her out, I had to go outside the church to find a vessel as my other female cousins were already promised to others."

"I think I just puked and swallowed it again, Karl. Because this shit you're saying is fucking sick." Abbey sighs, finally turning to face me. "Can you believe this?"

I shake my head, but it's not his words I can't believe. It's this woman before me. It's like she's become another person.

Not that I don't like it, but fuck, now I know pissing her off too much could have some dire fucking consequences for me.

"Where is your wife?" Jols asks, snapping me out of it, and I realise I've been staring at Abbey like a dumb fuck for way too long.

"She bolted when she learned the truth about Daniel and Abbey," Karl rushes out, his face screwing up in pain.

"So, Elizabeth didn't know Daniel and I were cousins?" Abbey presses, and Karl shakes his head.

"I had to tell her before the ceremony at the chapel. She slapped my face and fucking fled. I haven't seen her since."

"Where's Daniel?" Abbey asks, lifting the gun at Karl's head again.

"I don't know. He's with his mate Donny and his uncle. But I don't know where they are."

Abbey nods. "What about your stepdaddy?" she curls her lip. "You know where Banes is?"

Karl shakes his head. "No. He has hideouts all across the state, but I don't know where a single one is aside from the commune, which you bastards destroyed."

Karl gestures weakly to me and JD as Abbey turns to face me, lowering the gun from Karl's face.

"I really feel like a big, hot bonfire."

My lips twitch. "A really big one?"

She nods. "Ginormous."

JD chuckles, turning to leave the room, and calling over his shoulder, "On it."

Abbey returns her attention back to Karl.

"My baby is dead because of you and your fucked-up cult." Her head tilts, her words laced with venom. "So naturally, you have to die too."

"Wait, no. Please."

Abbey rolls her eyes and turns back to me.

"I think I also need a nail gun."

I smirk. "A fucking nail gun, Angel?"

"Yep."

Snickering, Jols walks past, "Leave that to me."

Karl spends the next ten minutes calling out to us from the living room as we ransack the house, looking for anything that might lead us to Daniel or Banes, but we come up empty.

JD returns with several fuel cans, and a few of the Marx security help him douse the inside of the house, while Jols produces the nail gun for Abbey.

"I'm almost scared to know why you want this." Jols grins, and Abbey shrugs.

"Didn't Jesus die on the cross?" Abbey asks, and when both Jols and I look at her in confusion, she points down the hallway to where a huge macrame seven-foot cross hangs on the wall at the end.

A slow smirk spreads my lips as I lock eyes with my wife.

"I'll get the dead man walking."

Riggs joins me in dragging Karl out into the hallway as he begs for his life, and we hold him up to the wall, positioning him on the cross as Abbey teaches herself how to use a nail gun, and proceeds to nail Karl's limbs to the wall.

It takes considerably more nails than it took for Jesus, given the size of them, but by the time she's done, Karl has pissed and puked and rivers of blood trickle from him in the close to one hundred nails Abbey pinned him with.

When she's done, she stands back and admires her work.

"I don't know, Karl. Maybe I should have been an artist."

All Karl can do is blubber incoherently, and she turns her back and walks to the front door.

We fall in behind her, with JD the last one out, drizzling petrol straight down the hallway to the open front door, before tossing the canister into the living room off to the side.

"I like your work, Abs." JD grins, and she nods like they're talking about a batch of fucking cookies instead of a man nailed to a cross. "You wanna do the honours?" He holds out a box of matches, and Abbey takes it, not even hesitating to strike the match.

Riggs and his men retreat to the street, and JD and Jols start walking to the car, but I stay planted at my wife's back, watching her end yet another life.

Holding up the match, she giggles and calls sweetly to Karl.

"See you in Hell, Uncle."

Then she tosses the match inside.

Knowing what's about to happen, I hook my arm around her waist and yank her back with me just as the hallway goes up in a whoosh of flames. A second later, Karl's blood-curdling screams echo from the house.

"I heard once that burning to death is the most painful way to die," Abbey mutters as I set her down, her big doe eyes meeting mine.

"I've heard that too."

She nods and starts walking. "Good."

As we reach the end of the path, the neighbours come bursting out of their house, eyes wide as they spot the smoke billowing up. I'm fucking shocked they didn't hear the gunshots.

"Oh my goodness!" the woman shrieks, and the man beside her fumbles with his phone.

"Hurry to the car, Angel." I pat her leather-clad arse, and she throws a glance over her shoulder at me before hurrying forward.

Drawing my gun, I focus on the neighbours.

"Get the fuck back inside! You didn't see anything! Mind your own fucking business!"

They gasp as I aim the gun at them, squeals flying from the woman as they both duck, like that will save them, scrambling back inside and slamming the door shut behind them.

23

ABBEY

"**S**top looking at me like that." I scowl at my husband, catching the worry in his eyes.

"What do I have to do for you to agree to stay here and wait? I'll do anything."

I shake my head firmly. "We're not having this conversation again, Cam. I'm coming with you, and so is Jols. That's all there is to it."

Twelve days ago, on the day I buried my little girl, Smitty told me our state would be going into another snap lockdown. I'd thought he was batshit crazy at the time, even when Ringo backed him up, so when it was announced a few days ago that yes, Victoria was going to be locked down once again, I realised I shouldn't underestimate the President of the Southern Sadists MC.

He might act like a nutcase sometimes, but he clearly has connections I never thought possible.

Right now, I don't give a damn about what's going on with the government or even the rest of the world. All I care about is vengeance, and saving Darla and Nessy. And right now, that's exactly what we are about to do.

Ringo's eyes darken and his jaw ticks as he stares at me. We've been stuck in this push and pull since the start of the week. Since I had a hand in killing my dad, even though it was his finger that pulled the trigger. And also, since the day I burned Karl Stone, my uncle, alive.

I am not myself. Or more like, I am something else entirely now, and maybe that's just who Abbey will be moving forward.

"I could chain you to the bed."

A rush of warmth shoots between my legs at the promise in his tone, and I want to call him out on using the one thing that seems to work to bend me to his will since everything that happened on Monday. But, as usual, I don't mention that I know exactly what he's doing to manipulate me, because deep down, all I want is to give him what he wants.

My submission.

"You could try." I shrug. "You might get hurt in the process, though."

That has his lips kicking up in a dark smile.

"Come on, Angel. I'm just trying to keep you safe. Leave this battle to me and my club."

My brows quirk at that.

"You told Smitty I was part of your club last week."

"You know what I mean, Angel," he snaps, his patience thinning. "What about sexual favours? I'll do anything you want if you agree to stay here."

I snort, standing and slipping the gun he gifted me at the start of the week into my bag. His gaze follows the motion before grazing up my thighs and coming to rest on the holster belt Jols gave me, which is secured around my waist, holding a knife.

I'd completely forgotten all about the knife Dee gave me weeks ago. I'd found it in the bedside drawer, and have been practising using it over the last few days, wanting to be better prepared in case someone tries to take me again.

I'm not stupid. I know this raid on the Satan's Rebels' hideaway is going to be a thousand times more dangerous than stumbling across my dad or visiting Karl Stone, but I wasn't lying when I told Ringo I was sick of waiting around.

This is my life now.

These are my people now.

I'll fight for them too, and the Rebels are a shared threat to both me and the MC.

"Okay… sure." I smirk at Ringo, knowing he absolutely won't do *anything* to get me to stay behind. "I'll stay here if you give JD a blowie until he cums down your throat."

"The fuck!" Ringo lurches up from the barstool as JD howls in laughter.

"Fuck yeah, man. Suck my cock like a good boy!"

Jols and I start cackling, but my lips snap shut the moment I see Ringo storming my way with fury in his eyes.

Spinning, a squeak flies from me as I try to bolt, only making it a few steps before his arms weave around me, snatching me up off the ground as I flail.

"It's about time I fucking punished you." Ringo's breath is hot against my ear as he carries me across the barn.

"No! Help! Jols! JD!" I plead.

"You're on your own." JD laughs. "Ain't no fucking way I'm gonna try to stop him when he has a raging hard-on."

"Traitor!" I screech, right as Ringo kicks open the bathroom door. "Stop! We have to go!" I yell, but my words are only met with his deep, dark chuckle.

"We'll go when I'm fucking ready," he snaps in my ear, the snip of the lock loud in the small space.

Shit. I'm in trouble.

The best kind, of course.

My heart pounds in anticipation, even though I should be shutting this shit down.

"You can't fuck me yet," I choke out, trying to pry his tight grip loose from around me, but he's already got my cheek smushed up against the wall, his body pressing into mine from behind.

"I'm not going to fuck you," he growls, somehow managing to wrangle both my wrists into one of his hands, pinning them above my head, while his other hand slides between me and the wall, starting to undo my black leather pants.

"Ringo…" I half-whimper, half-moan, annoyed at how desperate I am for his touch.

"You've been a brat all fucking week," he snarls, nipping at my earlobe as he finally gets my pants open and starts shoving them down. "I know what you learned about your family has been a lot, and you're fucking frustrated we don't have a lead on your sister yet." He wrestles my pants down to my ankles, the chill in the air hitting the places on me that feel like they are on fire. "But you need to remember *who* fucking owns your smart mouth."

I'm about to protest when he steps back from me, my wrists still locked in his grip, and a second later, the biting sting that explodes across my backside has me half-screaming, half-choking as his hand slaps down hard with a loud clap.

It stings, and burns, and shit, humiliation floods through me at being handled like this, but something else happens, too.

I heat. From the inside out. Deep in my core, rushing straight to my clit.

I'm on fire.

Trying to hold back my whimper, I fail, the needy sound escaping anyway, and Ringo leans in close again, his lips pressed right up to my ear.

"Colour?"

"G-green." I pant, not entirely understanding why I'm not red right now.

Being restrained like this, my top half still covered in my black clingy knit top, the holster belt snug around my waist, but my pants pulled down exposing my bare arse, should have me freaking out. I should be scared. Should have me feeling a thousand times *more* humiliated.

Yet all I feel is worshipped, and I know I'll do just about anything this man asks of me when I'm like this.

"Good girl, Angel."

His praise settles over me, a calmness sinking into my bones and making me feel a little drunk. When the heat of his body shifts back again, his hand running over the globe of my arse like he's trying to rub the pain away, my body responds, my back arching, my arse pushing out like it's his for the taking.

And shit… there it is, the familiar sensation of my milk letting down, sending filthy images through my head of him on his knees, mouth latched to my nipple, drinking me dry.

Dammit, I'm about five seconds away from asking him to drain my breasts again for the second time today. I'd been opposed to it after Bobbi's funeral, but after Monday's little killing spree… well. It changed me.

Again.

His hand smooths over my other arsecheek, almost soothingly, and I know exactly what's coming.

More.

"Even good girls need to be reminded of who's boss."

Normally I'd roll my eyes, but stuff that. He can be my boss. My king. My damn God, if he keeps this up. I'll kiss his feet if he asks me to.

When his hand comes down hard on my other cheek, my moan is loud, not even a hint of a squeal, his rumbling growl practically making me melt.

I'm acutely aware of how wet I am between my legs. Most of it's from the way he's making me feel. Some of it's from what I'm now calling my after-bleed, and I'm thankful it's so much lighter this week.

"Fuck, Angel. I like seeing the outline of my hand on your arse," he rasps, pressing into my back, his hand sliding around to my front, his fingers grazing over my sex. "Ahhh, fuck. You're soaked."

A needy whimper escapes me as he finds my clit, pressing into it with the pads of his fingers in a teasing way.

"You wanna come, Angel?"

"Yes," I rush out, trying to widen my stance, but my pants bunched around my ankles keep me locked in place.

"Such a pity that's not gonna happen."

I gasp as his fingers leave me, my wrists suddenly freed, and he spins me to face him, pinning me against the wall when I nearly trip over my own feet.

His shit-eating-grin is so smug I want to punch it off his face, and his low chuckle only makes it worse.

"You're a prick."

He shrugs. "And you're a fucking brat lately, Angel. I'm just matching your mood."

Rolling my eyes, I shove him back and try to bend so I can pull my pants up, but he stops me, his palm flat against my shoulder, pressing me into the tiles as he shakes his head.

"If you're not going to follow through, then there's no need for my pants to be down!" I snap, my anger flaring hot.

"One sec." He smirks, ignoring my rage as he pulls out his phone and snaps a picture.

"What the hell!" I screech, trying to lunge for his phone, but he holds it up high, out of reach. "Delete that now!"

"No."

I drop my hands to my sides, glaring at him and wishing I could set him on fire with my eyes.

"Delete it, *Cameron*."

"No, *Abbey*. I want this for my spank bank."

My face falls. "You want to get off to a picture of my humiliation?"

"This isn't humiliation." He turns the screen to me, and even though I don't want to see myself like that, I can't look away.

For a beat, I'm speechless.

Yeah, I'm standing with my pants down, my lady garden fully on display, but hell, with the rage on my face and the dark eye makeup that I've been wearing like a brand this week, and the way my blonde hair is a little tousled… I think… I look hot.

"Do you see it, Angel? How fucking hot you are?"

I nod, even though I don't mean to.

"So, no humiliation, but your throbbing little pussy will have to wait to be worshipped until I'm done punishing you."

And with that, he turns, unlocks the door, and walks out.

I growl out in protest, hearing his chuckle echoing back at me as he leaves me needy and aching for his touch.

I want to cry.

But fuck him. I can just get myself off. I don't need him.

The sound of car doors opening makes me stiffen.

"He wouldn't dare," I snarl to myself, and when I hear the car doors slam shut, I realise, he absolutely would leave me behind.

I hurry, dragging my panties up and yanking my pants into place, and bolt out of the bathroom, hearing the Landy roar to life as I fumble to zip my fly while running.

24

RINGO

The vans turn right ahead, and we follow in my Landy, while the rest of my MC, on their hogs, hang back, not wanting the rumble of our motorcycle pack to alert the Satan's Rebels of our approach.

My gaze meets the fury still burning in Abbey's eyes in the rearview mirror, and I shoot her a wink, earning me an eye roll for my trouble.

I could've left her with my ma and sisters, safely locked away with thirty Marx security guards watching over her. And maybe I should have. But, as much as I don't like the idea of her being put in harm's way, I can't deny her need to be involved.

She blames herself for the lives lost. For Darla and Nessy getting taken. She wants to help. She wants blood. So, I'll just have to work harder to make sure no one touches what's mine.

"Riggs to Sarg."

The crackle of the radio breaks the silence inside the car, and JD picks up the receiver.

"Speak," JD grunts, making his voice deeper, trying to impersonate me.

I glance sideways at him to see his fucking beaming smile, and I shake my head.

"I don't sound like that."

My Angel snorts in the back seat, and when our eyes lock in the mirror, she's smirking.

"We have confirmation from Moore. The gate is unlocked. The guards are out cold. We're a go."

"Roger that. Let's move," JD grunts deeply again, and this time, I can't help but chuckle.

"It's uncanny how much you sound like him," Jols snickers.

"Nah. It's not whiny enough," my wife fires back, shooting me a wink this time in the mirror.

"Yeah, I agree. I'll try to make it a little more nasally next time," JD says in all seriousness.

"You three fucking done?" I snap, trying to keep my focus on the road as the vans up ahead start to slow. "JD, text Smitty. Let him know we are about to breach."

They all fall quiet then, their attention shifting to what's about to happen.

"Remember, once we're through the gates, you two stay the fuck down until I tell you to move. You both listen to me or JD, and don't go fucking rogue."

"Got it," Jols agrees, and when Abbey doesn't answer, my eyes meet hers in the mirror again, and she fucking salutes me.

Jesus. I think we've created a monster.

"All teams alert!" Riggs' voice crackles through the radio again. "We're breaching in three, two, one!"

Dust kicks up from the vans in front of us as they hit the gas, and when I glance back in the rearview, Jols and Abbey are hidden from sight, giving me a clear view of the other vehicles in our convoy tailing us.

We're out in the sticks, north of Diamond Creek, and with the lockdown, the quiet roads make everything feel like a fucking ghost town. But that works well for us.

No witnesses.

I white-knuckle the steering wheel as my Landy rumbles over the cattle grate at the driveway entrance, the car bouncing us around as we speed up the pothole-riddled dirt road.

"Hold on to your tits!" JD yells from next to me, clutching the hand grip for dear life as we're tossed around from the fucking shit conditions of the driveway.

"Engage!" Riggs roars through the radio, and the next second, I hear gunfire erupt up ahead.

That word means two things.

It's time to shoot shit, and time for the pack of hogs to join us.

The old farm property is littered with rusty car wrecks, scrap metal, and all kinds of junk.

Three of the vans ahead veer off to the right, towards the old shed Moore confirmed is the clubhouse, while we follow behind Riggs and two more Marx SUVs, taking the road that snakes around to the back of the property where a house sits, junk lining the fence along a vacant paddock and dam.

"Cars two and three, secure the house," Riggs barks through the radio, and I have to slam on the brakes as the vans veer sharply left towards the old, weathered farmhouse, where several Rebels are already spilling out.

"Stay down!" I yell right as bullets start pelting the car from the house.

A squeal comes from the back seat, and I know it's my Angel, and fuck, she'd better be alright or I'm gonna go fucking apeshit.

Planting my foot on the accelerator again, I steer us away, following Riggs and another car around the back where Moore said Darla and Nessy were being held.

"Bus up ahead," Riggs informs, and I spot it past the cars. The old school bus Moore said would be there.

The red flash of taillights has me slamming on the brakes, just before Marx security pour out of their cars, guns raised and shooting.

"Stay down!" I bark, slamming the car into park and gripping my gun.

JD and I lock eyes, and the second I nod, we're both out the doors, guns raised, firing at anything wearing a Rebels' cut.

Most of the Rebels are fighting on the other side of the clubhouse, but a few have slipped out here, heading for the same place as us.

The old school bus.

With the Marx team backing us up, I barely need to squeeze off a shot, and it's only a matter of minutes before the coast is clear.

"Angel!" I shout, fucking stunned she's not already right behind me.

Jols and Abbey scramble out of the Landy, guns up, eyes scanning for any remaining threats.

"Now you follow instructions," I growl, and even though she looks like some sort of dark golden angel with her blonde messy hair and those fucking sexy, smoky eyes, when she moves up to my side and glances up, I see the vulnerability flickering in her gaze.

My little submissive is still in there.

And then, she ruins my little wet daydream by fucking speaking.

"Yes, Sarg."

Jesus fucking Christ, the way the corner of her pink lips kick up, her doe eyes peeking up at me through the fan of her dark lashes, paired with those two words, has my cock fucking springing to life like the traitor it is.

"Every day, I like that chick more and more," JD snickers, ignoring the deadly glare I throw his way.

Shaking off my sassy wife's words, I refocus on the old bus, my gun raised as I creep closer.

JD flanks me, while our women follow behind, and we only make it a few steps before the back door to the clubhouse bursts open with a bang, and three bodies spill out.

Spinning, we swing our guns towards the movement, my finger about to squeeze the fucking trigger when I realise it's friend, not fucking foe.

"The fuck, Brody!" JD snarls before I can even open my mouth. "We nearly fucking shot you!"

"Have you found her?" Brody blurts, his eyes darting frantically over our shoulders to the school bus.

"What the fuck are you doing?" I snap, glaring at Brody, Vender and Mex. "You're meant to be securing the clubhouse!"

"Is she in there?" Vender demands, stepping forward and ignoring my fucking question.

"Who, Darla?" JD asks, knowing Darla is a crowd favourite.

"Well, yeah. But no," Mex chimes in. "We mean Nessy. Is she in there?"

Nessy?

The fuck is going on?

"Nessy!" Mex calls, trying to shove past JD, but JD blocks him with a hard shove.

"Why the fuck are we standing around? Nessy needs us!" Vender barks, lunging past me this time, and I fucking let him, confused as fuck as he starts for the bus.

He's only made it a few steps when the bus doors spring open, and all I see is my Angel with her back to the bus, confusion etched across her pretty face as she watches three of my club brothers storm forward.

She has no clue a fucking Rebel is stepping out of the bus with his gun raised.

I swear my heart fucking stops when that barrel starts to level at her, but then, three loud pops ring out, and Brody, Vender, and Mex drop the Rebel with shots to the chest before he can even blink.

Abbey gasps, spinning to face the threat she didn't even know was there, and we watch, stunned, as Mex drags the dead Rebel off the steps while Vender charges on board, gun ready for the next motherfucker.

"Good to see your men know how to follow orders." Riggs chuckles beside me, and fuck, I can't even be mad right now, because I'm just too fucking confused.

My three men disappear on the bus, so JD and I follow, stepping over the dead Rebel discarded on the gravel, climbing the steps to find my three club brothers fawning over Nessy.

"Well, I didn't see this coming," JD mutters over my shoulder, and all I can do is grunt, watching Darla roll her eyes.

"Oh sure, don't worry about me," she snaps, still sounding strong despite how beat up she is.

Fuck. I don't want to think about the torture they've suffered through.

A rough shove sends me staggering as Jols pushes past with Abbey on her heels. They head straight for Darla, untying her while three grown men act like they're Nessy's dad... or big brothers... or... lovers?

No, that can't be right. Sweet little Nessy looks fucking terrified right now. She's a meek little thing. The greenest of our Doxies, still learning the ropes. Still getting used to public sex displays and group orgies.

Nessy is trembling so hard I worry she's about to have a seizure, reminding me of the night I stole my Angel away from her parents.

Fuck, that feels like a lifetime ago now.

Vender cups Nessy's face with a level of gentleness I never imagined him capable of, and his touch and whatever quiet words he's whispering works to snap her out of her panic, her shoulders relaxing as she climbs into his arms.

That, I get.

She needs security. And we fucking take care of our Doxies. But when Brody and Mex step in for a group hug, I'm left even more fucking confused.

"The fuck is going on?"

"I'd say these three have done their nuts over our sweet little Nessy," Jols says as she and Abbey help Darla limp towards us, "and decided to share her… maybe?"

"For now," JD mutters, reaching out to take Darla from Abbey. "That's gonna end fucking badly. Three of them can't claim her."

"It didn't end badly for Rhys," Abbey points out, watching JD and Jols lead Darla towards the steps. "She has five men to keep her happy. Seems to work for some people."

"She's not in a fucking MC," JD chuckles, while my eyes narrow on my Angel as she glances back at the love triangle… or is it a love quad? Fucked if I know.

"You need more than me, Angel?" I ask because, yeah, apparently I'm fucking insecure about that shit.

Her brows arch as she looks back at me, shaking her head with a frown.

"Hell, no. You're all the man I need."

Fuck. I let out a breath I didn't fucking realise I was holding on to.

"Naww, this is such a beautiful moment," JD coos, and I fucking glare at my best mate, pointing to the open door.

"Fuck off. Let's get the girls outta here."

JD and Jols laugh at my expense as they help Darla off the bus, and I lead Abbey down, giving my three club brothers a fucking moment before they finally carry Nessy out.

As Nessy and Darla get loaded into one of the Marx SUVs, my Angel moves to my side, a frown creasing her brow.

"You wondering how Nessy is going to handle those three guys?" I chuckle, but she shakes her head, her big doe eyes flicking up to mine.

"I don't understand why they are here," she says, gesturing subtly towards Riggs. "This is a club thing, not a *me* thing."

"You're here in a dangerous situation, so they are here." I shrug.

"So they are like my bodyguards? Even for club business?"

"Yes." I nod, watching her frown twist into anger.

"Ringo, we need to talk about this arrangement. I know you said it's not a financial cost, but the cost to you has to be huge. I don't want to think about what you'll owe them after this is over," she snaps, jutting her thumb towards Riggs. "Tell them to stand down. Now."

"Nope," I mutter, starting towards the Landy.

"But—"

"No, Angel," I cut her off, yanking open the car door for her. "It's not up for negotiation."

"But—"

"Look, now's not the time for this conversation," I snap, turning to reach for my door.

In my periphery, sudden movement bursts from the bushes, and I'm reaching for my gun again. By the time my eyes lock onto the Rebel, his gun aimed at me, it's too late… the loud crack is deafening as the gun explodes with a flash.

25

RINGO

P ain explodes through my side, the force of the bullet caus-ing me to stumble back against the car. I can barely focus as another loud crack rips through the air, and I stare at the Rebel, now dropping to his knees as blood trickles from his lips, and blooms across his chest.

"That was for shooting my husband!" Abbey snarls, stalking the Rebel and pressing the barrel of her gun to his head. "And this is for being on the wrong team!"

She. Doesn't. Even. Flinch.

Her finger squeezes the trigger, blood and brain matter spraying from the back of his skull before he topples over.

My little monster.

"Fuck, man. You alright?" JD rushes up to me, barely glancing at the carnage my wife just unleashed. "Where'd you get hit?"

"Fuck," I growl, batting his fussing hands away. "It's just a flesh wound."

Abbey whips around to face us, her big eyes wild with rage.

She's fucking beautiful.

Her gaze snaps to my left side, where JD has my cut and tee hoisted outta the way to check the damage, and I catch the flicker of fear in her eyes.

"I'm okay, Angel."

Shoving me to the side, JD checks my back. "Fuck. It went straight through. You'll be alright. Just gotta pack it until we get you home."

"You drive, JD. I'll handle this," Abbey insists, grabbing his shoulder and tugging him back.

"Yes, ma'am." JD grins and salutes, and Abbey rolls her eyes at him as he beams.

He's been too fucking playful lately. This thing between him and Jols is making him soft.

Abbey helps me into the back seat before sliding in next to me, looking calmer than I thought she'd be.

"You're getting used to this life," I mutter as JD starts up the Landy and shoves it into drive.

Abbey shrugs, rummaging through the first aid kit. "Surprisingly, despite your caveman ways," her eyes flick to mine as one corner of her mouth kicks up, "I feel more in control of my life than I ever have."

Fuck. I love hearing that. Knowing this sheltered sweet girl from the country is comfortably slotting into the wild fuckery of MC life with me has warmth settling in my chest.

It feels like coming home.

"Don't get too comfortable bossing me around," I tease, loving the way she rolls her eyes and scoffs, handing me some gauze that I reach around and press to my back.

I always knew there was more than a wounded, fragile woman inside her. I knew there was sass. And I'm fucking glad for the banter we have.

While I do love her submissive side, I definitely prefer that behind closed doors when it's just the two of us.

I want her to feel in control. Powerful. Like the warrior she is.

"Don't act like you don't secretly love it when I do," she shoots back, shoving my shoulder playfully, and my lips kick up this time. Her gaze tracks to motion before locking with mine. "And do me a favour. Try to avoid getting shot. It's honestly a pain in the arse."

JD bursts out laughing, clearly listening in as he drives the Landy to the front of the property where my club has a line of Rebels kneeling on the ground while Murf and Stocky set fire to the building.

As Abbey starts packing gauze into the wound, through JD's open window I hear Spud demanding information from the few Rebels they spared, and I stare out at the scene, dead Rebels everywhere.

"Is that Moore at the end?" JD asks quietly, and my gaze shifts to the man kneeling farthest away, a snarl twisting his face.

He's in character right now.

"It is," I confirm, watching Smitty limp up to the car.

Looks like a bullet nicked his thigh.

"You gonna live, Ringo?" he asks, bending down to peer at me through JD's open window.

"Yep. Bullet didn't hit anything vital," I grunt, nodding his way. "You get hit too?"

"The Rebels President had a fucking go. Not a good enough one, though." His lips kick up in a savage grin.

"Where's he now?" JD asks, and Smitty jerks his head towards a pair of legs sticking out from a pile of bushes.

"He's gone to Hell. Let's see how the ones that got away handle not having anyone in leadership."

My brows shoot up.

"You got their VP too?"

Smitty's eyes gleam as he holds a finger up, telling us to wait, and then a gunshot cracks through the air, and he grins. "There goes the VP."

Glancing back out over the line, I see the barrel of Spud's gun smoking and the man who was kneeling now lying dead in the dirt. Then Spud steps to the next Rebel and pulls the trigger.

Darting my gaze to Abbey, I see her watching, not a flicker of regret or pity in her eyes.

It's like she's somehow switched off the part of herself that made her so human. So caring, even for monsters.

I mean, she still cares for me, but the woman she used to be is either gone or buried so deep it'd take a miracle to bring her back.

Another loud crack of Spud's gun snaps my gaze back out the window to see two Rebels left kneeling.

One's a dead man. The other is our informant.

Moving to the second-last Rebel, Spud points and shoots, like it's just a typical fucking Sunday, and then he moves to Moore, fisting his shirt, and drags him through the dirt towards Smitty.

"What's he doing?" Abbey asks quietly.

"Gotta make it look real in case there are Rebels hiding and watching," I explain, watching as Smitty draws out his own gun and presses it to Moore's forehead.

"How many do you think got away?" he asks Moore quietly, but his expression is stone cold so anyone watching would just see a club President intimidating an enemy.

"Maybe half a dozen. They'll probably reach out to Panda and get picked up by him," Moore offers softly.

"Who the fuck is Panda?" JD butts in through the window, but Moore doesn't take his eyes off Smitty.

"Panda has a team of twelve Rebels with that snake, Allen, and his nephew."

Abbey sits taller at the mention of Ian Allen's name, her hand still holding the gauze in place.

"No one knows where they are, but after what's happened, they'll look to Panda for leadership. He's the only one remotely smart enough to take over now that you've wiped out the others." Moore cringes when Smitty shoves his barrel harder against his forehead.

"Find the stragglers. Get the location and report back the second you have it."

Spittle flies from Smitty's lips as he snarls in Moore's face, who nods like he's terrified, but fuck, he's nothing but a good fucking actor.

He's not scared of Smitty or anyone here. Not even when Smitty shifts his gun and presses it to Moore's bicep.

Knowing what's coming, I have a split fucking second to grab Abbey's head, pressing my palms over her ears before Smitty pulls the trigger.

Being this fucking close while we sit in a goddamn box, the sound of the shot amplifies, my ears explode with pain before they start fucking ringing.

With my eyes locked on my Angel's, I can't hide the pain twisting my face, and she quickly shoves my hands away from her ears, leaning over me to wind the window down.

"Jesus, Nate! You couldn't have done that over there?!"

I barely catch her words through the ringing in my ears, my heart fucking pounding with fear that my unhinged President might turn the gun on her.

"Why hello, sweet Charity," Smitty drawls, bending to peer in at my furious wife. "So nice to have your opinion. Which I *didn't fucking ask for!*"

"Maybe you *should* ask for it, since you clearly need to learn how to read a room!"

"Okay!" I hold my hands up, trying to block Smitty's view of my wife. "Let's just calm the fuck down."

"No, *husband*. I won't calm down. He nearly burst your eardrums!"

Smitty simply smirks. "Ha-ha! Never thought I'd see the day someone wrangled your nuts, Ringo. She's a fucking keeper."

"Fucking hell," I mutter as JD chuckles up front, one finger jammed in his ear.

"I like your fire, Charity." Smitty continues to taunt my wife, who takes the bait.

"How many times do I have to tel—"

"Next time, I think I'll keep you by *my* side." Smitty continues like she wasn't just talking. "Let you do the slaughtering for me, since you've got a taste for it now."

"Like fuck," I snap, while Abbey scoffs.

"I'm not one of your men, Nate. I don't answer to *you*."

Smitty falls eerily silent, and the moment his head tilts to the side as he studies my wife as she presses her hands back to the gauze, I know I need to get her the fuck out of here.

"Don't you?" he asks, brows hitched. "Because all of this," he gestures behind him, "started because of *you*. And let's not forget, there are fucking *suits* coming on raids with us now, something fucking unprecedented until you showed up. So, my *sweet* Charity, if there's *anyone* who should be bowing to me, dear child, it is absolutely *you*."

"That's enough!" I snap at Smitty, bracing for his fucking wrath, but all he does is smirk, and when I glance at Abbey, I know why.

She's feeling the weight of his reminder. Blaming herself for everything that's happened once again. Her glassy eyes and grim expression say it all.

For fuck's sake.

It's like we take one step forward and thirty thousand steps back.

"We gotta go," JD mutters from the front, his eyes tracking the smoke billowing from the clubhouse.

Smitty, clearly pissed at the way my wife keeps speaking to him like he's nothing, angles his head towards JD, and then to Jols in the front passenger seat.

"Leave my stepdaughter behind. She's coming back to the compound with me."

JD stiffens, and Jols snarls over her shoulder.

"You're not my dad, Smitty. How many times do—"

"Either get out of that fucking car, Jolene, or stay away from *my* club."

Smitty's harsh snap brokers no argument, and he knows it, straightening up as he mutters something to Spud, who starts rounding the car.

Fuck.

"I'll call you," Jols whispers to JD, who looks about ready to lose his shit.

"Jols, you don't have to go with him," Abbey says urgently, reaching into the front and laying her free hand on Jols' shoulder.

"Actually, I do."

Abbey's hand falls away, and for a brief moment, Jols and I lock eyes, and I see her worry.

It's not for herself. It's for JD.

"Babydoll," JD whispers, but Jols doesn't even spare him a glance. Probably because she can't or she'll break, and then Smitty will know what he probably already suspects, which is exactly why he's demanding she go with him.

When Spud opens the door, Jols slips out of the Landy, being led with an iron grip by our VP over to Smitty's hog.

"I'm gonna kill him," JD mutters quietly so only we can hear, and I reach forward, giving his shoulder a firm squeeze.

"I need to get home, man. This gauze ain't gonna stop the bleeding for long."

JD's eyes snap to mine in the rearview mirror, and with a nod, he slowly pulls away from Smitty and the carnage that man leaves in his wake, merging with the Marx convoy.

Abbey hurries to get her seatbelt on before applying pressure again to the gauze, doing her best to stop the flow of blood as we hit the road.

Since we are in another lockdown, and the freeway should be like a ghost town, we avoid it, sticking to the back streets so we don't draw too much attention.

By the time we reach the south-eastern suburbs, I'm starting to feel woozy, and know I'm going to black out soon.

"Angel," I grunt, as the darkness closes in. "My phone's in my pocket. Text Mills. Tell her to have blood ready."

Abbey's eyes widen. "JD!" she snaps over her shoulder. "He doesn't look good."

"I know. Just do what he asked," JD mutters from the front. "I'll get us there as fast as I can."

I feel the Landy pick up speed, and one of Abbey's hands slips into my pocket, fishing out my phone.

Her frantic fingers move over the screen as she struggles to send the text with one hand while keeping her other hand pressed to me, and even through the haze, I can't help but smile at how fucking pretty she looks in the glow of my screen light, even with smears of my blood coating her chin and cheek.

"I love you," I whisper, finding it hard to speak any louder, and her eyes dart up to mine.

"Cam?" She sets the phone down, shifting closer, her delicate hand cupping my cheek. "Stay with me."

I think I smile. It's hard to tell.

"You're the only thing I want to see when I take my last breath."

"What? No, Ringo, you're not dying. Right?" she snaps over her shoulder. "Tell him, JD. He's not dying."

I smile, I think. She's so fucking adorable, those big doe eyes frantic as she looks over me.

I blink a few times, each one heavier than the last, and the darkness starts swallowing me until the last thing I see is the tears springing from her eyes.

26

ABBEY

Trailing the tip of my finger over the dusting of hair that leads from Ringo's navel, I watch his face to see if he's awake.

I did this a few months ago, when everything was new and I was struggling with my trauma. He'd been asleep, and I was curious. I somehow trusted him not to hurt me, even though I don't think I really knew that at the time.

He'd been rock hard in my hand, and I loved the feeling of being responsible for turning him on. For making him feel good. For making him come.

Now, I want to do it again. But this time, I want more.

His breathing is even, telling me he's still asleep, so I ease the sheet down, revealing his package.

For a dick that's soft, it sure is big. His erect size had terrified me at first, reminding me of... nope, not thinking about *that* arsehole. But as always, Ringo made sure I was well prepared, and the first time he sank inside me… well, now I'm all hot and flustered.

Sitting up, I get comfy next to him, careful not to disturb him too much, and I gently graze my fingers up and down his sleeping dick, applying a little more pressure after a few strokes, watching him slowly harden.

My eyes flick to the dressing on his side, reminding me that he was shot five days ago when we raided the Rebels' compound. Maybe now isn't the best time to be doing this.

But then again, we were dry humping last night, and he had no issue coming all over my stomach so…

A flush springs to my cheeks at the memory, and the way he latched onto my nipple and drank from me, yet again.

I know him doing that is delaying my milk drying up, but I just can't bring myself to stop. I know it's a weird thing to want to do, but in a twisted way, making milk still ties me to Bobbi, and I know that's not healthy. But it feels so damn good, and it's something beautiful and erotic to us. So I just can't ask him to stop.

Not when he loves it so much.

Focusing on his dick, I'm fascinated, watching it grow and thicken, lengthening at the same time. When it's hard enough to gently pick up, I wrap my hand around it, gripping it firmly the way he taught me, and slowly pump it up and down, from base to tip.

"Angel," he mumbles, the words barely passing his lips, and I can tell he's still mostly asleep.

Shit. Why does this turn me on so much? Arousing him while he's half-conscious?

I still have two weeks until we can have penetrative sex, but the idea of making him so hard in his sleep and sinking down onto him while he's powerless to stop me has me burning with need.

God, I want to do that so much.

I won't, though. Not this morning. Not today. But I will be taking him inside me.

Inside my mouth.

I've been nervous about it. It's never been anything but brutal torture for me, in the worst possible way. But I know he'd love to feel my lips wrapped around him. To feel my tongue swirl around the fat head of his dick. And I'm ready to make this memory with him, even if he doesn't get a say, since I haven't asked his permission.

Maybe I should've, but he loves me exploring his body, and I know he'd tell me to stop if he wanted me to. So I pump his dick one more time before lowering my head and flicking my tongue over the bead of pre-cum.

His dick jerks, and he mumbles something again, but it's incoherent. So I flick my tongue again.

When his hips lift a fraction, I know he's going to wake fully soon, so I part my lips wide, and guide his dick into my mouth.

I only take in his tip, sucking on his head, swirling my tongue, before sucking again.

"Abs," he mutters louder this time, and I know he's waking, so I open wider and swallow him deeper, until I know if I take anymore, I'll gag. "Fuuuck, Angel. What are you doing?"

I don't answer, because obviously he can feel exactly what I'm doing, but my eyes flick up his body to find his whiskey eyes blinking open.

With my hand tightly around his base, I keep my eyes locked on his and I suck, pushing myself to take more of him, fighting the urge to gag.

"This is the best fucking way to wake up," he groans, his hand fisting gently in my hair, but shit… I stiffen.

"Relax, Angel. I'm not trying to control you. I'll let go and put my hand above my head if you want?"

"Mo." I try to speak around his dick and shake my head, making him chuckle.

"Okay. Fuuuck. Okay."

The way the whiskey colour of his eyes is nearly swallowed by his blown pupils drives me wild.

This.

This is what I love.

The power I have over him.

The power to make him feel *this* good.

The power to shatter him into a million pieces under my tongue.

Heat pools between my legs, and I whimper as I suck him in deeper, now ravenous to feel him hit the back of my throat, even if it *does* make me gag.

Shit. I think I want that. I want to *give* him that.

Popping him free, I move to straddle one of his legs, his hand loosening in my hair as I shift.

He never takes his eyes off me. His heated stare is fixed, like he's in a trance and only I can command him.

"Is your pussy wet, Angel?"

"Yes." I nod, pressing my panty-clad pussy to his thigh before lowering my lips back to his dick, and sucking him back in.

"Fuuuck, I'm gonna come way too fast. Your hot little mouth feels so fucking good wrapped around me."

I moan around his tip, gliding my tongue over it, then sinking him deeper again.

As my tongue, lips and hand work together to build his pleasure, I ride out my own over his thigh, grateful I'm only down to a thin precautionary panty liner now since my bleeding is practically gone.

"You like my cock in your mouth?" he asks, knowing I can't answer, but when I take him in further, gagging around him, he knows exactly how much I do.

I never thought I'd be able to do this again. Never thought I'd handle that feeling, but I want everything with this man. So much so that one day soon, I hope I can give him all the control to use my mouth exactly how he wants without me slipping into a PTSD episode.

"Fuck, Angel. I'm gonna come soon. You might wanna stop if you don't want it in your mouth."

I don't stop. If anything, his warning sets me off, and I suck and gag and pump him while grinding on his thigh, a frenzy tearing through me.

"Fuck! Fuck! Fuuuuck!" he roars, his hips thrusting up uncontrollably, choking me deeper as his control snaps, and he fists my hair, holding me down.

I wait for the terror. For the flashback. For the panic. But all that comes is blinding pleasure shooting straight to my core as he thrusts and I suck him like a starved animal.

"I'm coming!" he roars, his body going rigid, and the moment the first spurt of cum hits the back of my throat, I grind myself so hard on his legs that I shatter.

I cry out around his pulsing dick, my mouth flooding with so much cum it leaks from the corners, but I don't stop sucking, desperate to milk every last drop from him, just like he does with my nipples.

"Angel. Baby. Fuck, stop… ahhhh." He groans and jerks, his dick clearly oversensitive, so I ease up, swallowing what I can, the rest oozing from the sides of my mouth and down my neck as I gasp for breath, his dick popping free.

"Was that okay?" I pant, my chest heaving as I wipe at my mouth with the back of my hand. "Did I do it right?"

"Right?" He makes a strangled choking sound. "I think my soul left my body, Angel."

My lips kick up in a slow smile.

"So what you're saying is, I'm God?"

A laugh bursts from his lips, and he sits up quickly, grabbing me and pulling me back down to the bed with him.

"Wait. I'm covered in your cum," I protest, but it doesn't faze him, and he does something I never expected him to do.

He flattens his tongue to my neck and licks up one of the trails of his own seed.

"Mmm. I taste fucking good on you."

"Shit," I pant, grinding myself against him, and he chuckles.

"Does it turn you on to watch me lick up my own mess, Angel?"

I nod, slamming my lips to his, tasting his cum on his tongue as our mouths clash in a ravenous battle of need.

This man has the power to turn me into the filthiest, most depraved woman on Earth, and I'm not even mad about it.

We roll and tumble on the bed, my pussy and his dick not getting the memo that they've just had an orgasm, and I blindly hook my fingers into my panties, trying to shove them down.

"Uh-uh," he mutters into my mouth before breaking the kiss and pushing up to loom over me. "No sex yet. You've got two more weeks."

"I'm fine. I'm ready now."

"Doctor said six weeks, Angel. I won't fuck you a minute before."

Huffing, my arms flop back onto the bed, and I pout.

"You're no fun."

His smile is gentle as he brushes my wayward hair off my face.

"You didn't think that a minute ago."

I roll my eyes, but the sudden sound of his phone ringing has us both freezing.

It's three in the morning. Calls at this hour are never good.

Shifting off me, Ringo reaches for his phone on the bedside table, his brows shooting up as he looks at the screen.

"It's your friend."

He turns the screen to me, the name 'HUSH' flashing across the display, which is weird, since she's not verbal. She usually just texts.

Then I notice it's actually a video call, and my pulse jitters as I sit up, quickly patting my hair down and wiping my neck in case there's any cum left.

Then I hit accept.

The screen flickers, the frame frozen for a few seconds before Dee's face comes into view.

"Dee? Is everything alright?"

She smiles and nods, giving me a thumbs up.

"Uhhh, what has you calling me at three in the morning?"

She grabs a notepad and scribbles something on it before holding it up to the camera.

'It's only 2:30 in the morning here.'

My brows shoot up, and Ringo's head pops into the frame beside mine.

"Where are you?"

She scribbles again, then turns it to us.

'Darwin.'

I stiffen. "Darwin? As in the Northern Territory? *That* Darwin?"

She nods, her smirk almost shit-eating.

Again, she writes on the notepad before showing us.

'Look who I found.'

My heart pounds. I already know who it is, but there's no need to answer because she shifts the camera until it lands on someone in the background, strung up to an overhead beam, his naked body covered in cuts and bruises as he quietly whimpers.

The notepad pops up in front of the screen again.

'Do you wanna watch? All g if you'd rather not.'

I don't know why she's there. I didn't ask her to go, and from the look on Ringo's face, neither did he.

Darnel was one of my rapists. Like Tim, he wasn't as brutal as the others. Almost hesitant, like he was scared of what would happen if he refused.

But he and Tim still could have helped me. Stopped Daniel, Donny, Craig and Michael. But they didn't. They joined in. And they must have liked it to some extent since they got hard enough to rape me.

While I want him dead, the need to do it myself isn't as dire as it is with Daniel and Donny.

"I want to watch," I rush out.

"Abs, you don't wanna see that," Ringo objects next to me, but I just shake my head.

"Yes, I really do. I *need* to see it. I need to know he suffered. That he's gone."

Dee pokes her tongue out at the camera, an obvious fuck you to Ringo, and he sighs, throwing his hands in the air.

"Whatever."

"Don't be like that. I promise I'll suck your dick again afterwards."

A strangled sound bursts from Dee as she covers her ears and stomps her foot, glaring at me before scribbling on the notepad and holding it up.

'If you keep talking like that, I'll hang up and do it without you watching.'

"Meany!" I pout, but her glare dares me to give her a reason to end the call. "Fine. I'll behave. Please proceed." I wave a dismissive hand, and she nods before scribbling one last thing.

'The only information he knows about Daniel and Donny is that they're with Donny's uncle somewhere. And that Daniel's dad is dead and his mum is missing.'

"Okay. Thanks for that," I announce, and she tosses the notepad aside.

Grabbing the phone, Dee carries it over to Darnel, giving me a closeup of his face and battered naked body. The bruising and cuts are far worse than I'd thought, and it's clear that she's been torturing him.

Propping the phone up on a stand or something, she makes sure I can see everything, and then approaches him.

Sobs spill from his lips as she unsheathes a huge knife, twirling it through her fingers like she's been doing circus tricks with sharp blades since she was three.

Hell, maybe she has. I wouldn't know.

Turning back to the camera, she smiles in a way that's more disturbing than anything, and then she picks up his flaccid, shrunken dick between two gloved fingers, waggling her brows at me.

"Fucking hell. I don't think I can watch this part," Ringo mutters beside me, but he doesn't move, like we are sitting here streaming a horror movie.

For a second, I think maybe she's just messing with us, but then she moves so fast the blade is a blur, and his screams crackle through the phone speaker as blood starts gushing from the short, pathetic stump where his dick used to be.

She holds the severed piece up, dangling it close to the screen, and once she's sure I've seen it, she climbs onto a chair and shoves the severed appendage into his screaming mouth.

"Fucking hell," Ringo hisses, turning away, but I keep watching, needing to see Darnel suffer.

He jerks against the chains, a choked gag tearing from him, and when Dee can't cram it in any deeper, she slams the hilt of her knife against his stuffed mouth, over and over, so savagely that I finally have to look away.

The sounds spilling from him make me gag, and Ringo snatches the phone, yelling at my friend, who I swear I will never underestimate again.

"Get the fuck on with it, Hush!"

She stops mid-swing, glaring at the screen like he's just ruined her fun, and for a moment, I wonder if Jared truly knows who he's sleeping with.

With a bored shrug, Dee hops down from the chair and kicks it aside, and a second later, she plunges the knife into Darnel's chest, dragging it downward and opening him up as his insides spill out.

She steps back quickly, dodging the ropes of intestines hitting the floor, before her eyes lift to the phone…

I swear I can't breathe.

I can't talk.

I can't even move.

You think you know someone.

Moving to the phone, Dee picks it up and walks over to a door before pulling it open to reveal an unhappy-looking Jared sitting on the floor outside in the hallway.

"You done?" he snaps, and she must nod, but I can't see it with the screen pointed in Jared's direction.

With a huff, he stands, dusting off his arse before stepping into the room.

"Fucking hell, Dee. You just needed to kill him for her." He sighs, taking the phone and spotting me and Ringo still on the screen. "Uhhh, sorry about that. She kicked me out of the room and locked the fucking door. Told me rapists need to choke on their own cocks before they die, so…" His arm shoots out and gestures to what's left of Darnel Rivers.

"She certainly did that," Ringo croaks, his voice scratchy, and I bet his balls have shrunk all the way up after witnessing that.

I feel kinda sick, but also relieved.

Another one is dead now.

Another rapist is gone from this world, and the list is getting smaller.

That thought makes me relax.

"Dee," I call into the phone, and she pops up behind Jared, not looking like she gives a shit about his disapproval of her methods. "Thank you. It would have been hard for me to get to Darnel. I appreciate you doing that for me."

Peeling off her gloves, she kisses two fingers and flicks them towards the screen before Jared carries the phone out into the hall.

"You know if you even try to leave her, she'll kill you before you even reach the door, right?" Ringo tells Jared, and the wicked smile Jared flashes the screen makes my stomach flip.

"Don't you worry about me. I know how to handle my girl," Jared snickers. "You just keep Abs safe."

With a few more brief words, we end the call and sit frozen for a beat.

"I'm not gonna be able to sleep after witnessing that," Ringo admits, and I nod in agreement.

I can't unsee or unhear what we just saw. A part of me is disturbed by it, but perhaps even worse, another part of me remembers what I did to Karl, and I grin.

There's just something intoxicating about getting retribution on people who use their power to commit the worst sins.

Suddenly, all thoughts of Dee's call vanish as the adrenaline coursing through my veins turns to something else entirely.

My eyes flick to Ringo, leaning against the headboard, bare-chested and looking good enough to lick, and I wonder if maybe I've finally snapped.

"Stop looking at me like that, Angel. Ain't no fucking way I can get my cock up after seeing that."

I pout, shifting over his lap to straddle him.

It's hard to believe my daughter died only a month ago. Each minute, each day, each week brings a tornado of emotions.

Somehow, I've managed to save my tears for my morning showers. I cry under the spray of water. I ask myself what I'm still doing living in a world without her. And then I remind myself that I have a job to do.

Losing Bobbi shattered me in more ways than I can count. I know I'll never be the same. But it's also freed me from giving a shit about what people think.

I can't believe I let myself be ruled by that for so long.

Sure, I was conditioned to care. Now, I've been conditioned to stop.

The need for vengeance fuels me. Helps me shut off the tears, step out of the shower, dry myself off, and harden the hell up.

It's also ignited a level of desire in me I never saw coming.

It's not the hormonal neediness I had when I was pregnant.

It's not even the twisted kink Ringo and I share.

It's something darker. Something wicked, and I have to wonder if falling into the lap of a man from a club with the name sadist in it isn't a coincidence.

That's the only way to describe the heat pooling between my legs as I stare at Ringo and remember Karl's screams as he burnt alive.

I've turned into a sadist, and I'm not even mad about it.

"Challenge accepted, husband," I smirk, loving the way his fingers dig into my hips as I grind against him, and before I know it, he flips me, and his lips crash into mine.

27

RINGO

er sobs are so fucking guttural as she cries in the shower. Something that's become a daily ritual. Even if I shower with her, she always stays behind and asks for ten minutes alone, and then she breaks.

It's hard not to go to her, but she's adamant that she wants that time alone, so even though it fucking guts me, I give it to her. I don't go far though, standing right outside the door, enduring the sounds of her pain until they fade. And when the water finally shuts off, that's when I leave my room.

Six hours ago, we watched that mute assassin friend of hers slaughter Darnel Rivers.

Not gonna lie, I've done some fucked up shit to the people I've killed or tortured, but that… what she did… fuck. I don't think I'd have it in me.

As hard as it was to watch, I could tell Abs was relieved that he was dead. But that relief turned into something more carnal afterwards, and she spent a good hour trying to trick me into burying my cock inside her, even though the six weeks aren't up yet.

I made her come twice, and fuck, I was even able to get it up again and spilled against her cunt as she screamed her release. But… and there is a big fucking *but*… as much as I love getting lost with her, I can't help but be concerned about the level of darkness creeping into her sweet soul.

I don't want to change her. I'll take her however she wants to be, but I'm still fucking worried that when this is all over, she'll come out the other side in such a dark place that she won't even think twice about following through with her promise to Bobbi.

That she'll *join* her.

"You look like shit," JD mutters, shovelling a spoonful of milky cereal into his gob as I enter the kitchen.

"So do you," I grunt, grabbing a banana from the bowl on the counter and wincing a little as my healing wound pulls.

"Yeah, but I've got a fucking reason. My bed is still fucking empty."

"I told you I'd come and warm it," Lans giggles as she walks through the living room with a basket of laundry.

"You stay the fuck away from his bed," I snap, pointing a stern fucking finger at her, and she pokes her tongue out in response.

"No thanks, Lans," JD mutters, his tone so fucking mournful. "Only one woman belongs in my bed, and her stepdad is cock-blocking me."

I gotta say, when I first suspected something was going on between JD and Jols, I thought it was nothing but a bit of fun, but now I know it was so much more than that.

"Still haven't heard from her?" I ask him, peering down the hall that leads to my ma's room to see the door open and her legs stretched out on her bed.

Fuck, she's struggled to get over the last flare-up.

"Fucking nothing," JD snarls, dropping his spoon into his bowl with a clang. "Brody hasn't even seen her since Smitty rode in with her five days ago. He's *heard* her though."

My brows shoot up. "How so?"

"Every night, when Smitty goes in for the night, everyone can hear them fighting. He said it gets pretty heated, yet she never steps foot outside."

"The fuck," I snap, and JD stands abruptly.

"We gotta go get her. What if he's chained her up or something?"

"Smitty's a crazy fucker, but he wouldn't do that… would he?"

"Do what?" Abbey's voice joins us as she steps into the kitchen, her hair wet, her eyes red, but her shoulders are back, and her head is held high.

She's had her moment, and now she's ready for the day.

"You should take Abbey there." JD ignores my wife, pointing in her direction with his eyes locked on me. "Tell him she wants to visit her friend. He can't deny her. Plus, Abbey doesn't give a shit about him and his fucked-up rules. He won't say no to her."

"I'm assuming we're talking about Jols?" Abbey asks, pouring herself a glass of juice.

"Ain't no fucking way I'm taking her anywhere near our Prez right now." I snap at JD, giving up on the banana I'd half peeled, my fucking appetite vanishing. "You saw what happened between them at the Rebel's raid."

"Shouldn't I get to decide that?" Abbey snaps, but JD keeps ignoring her.

"She's one of us now. He won't hurt her, but he might hurt Jols. Fuck, what if he's hurting her?!"

Suddenly, JD's head jolts to the side as a mandarin slams into his cheek.

My eyes snap in Abbey's direction in time to see another mandarin flying my way.

"Fuck!" I duck just in time for it to splat against the wall, my fucking disbelieving eyes locking onto my wife as I grip my side, sure I might have fucking opened up the stitches one of Riggs' men did.

"You rude fuckers deserved that. I'm right here, and you just ignored me three times!" She storms over to me, snatching my peeled banana off the benchtop, snapping her teeth into it like she's imagining it's my cock. "If you'd taken a moment to spare me the decency of a conversation," she mumbles around the banana she's chewing, "then I could have told you Jols is fine."

She strides out of the room, and my eyes land on JD, who is wide-eyed, his mouth hanging open like he's waiting for me to toss him some fucking food. Then he snaps it shut, his gaze meeting mine.

"Your wife is scary. But also *sexy* when she's mad."

I scoff at the idiot as he barges past me in chase of my absolutely sexy wife.

"How do you know she's okay?" JD barks as he chases her out onto the porch, and I follow, needing to know that too.

"I'm not sure you deserve to know," she scoffs, finishing up with the banana and licking her fingers.

I fucking love watching her eat. The way her tongue sweeps out and…

Fuck. This woman is such a distraction.

A fucking good one.

"Come on, Abs. I'll do anything," JD begs, sounding like he's about ready to drop to his knees, and then the fucker actually does it.

My brows shoot high as he shuffles towards my wife, his hands clasped together, already begging.

Fuck… he really has it bad for Jols.

Abbey smiles down at him for a long beat, leaving him hanging, then tilts her head as she studies him.

"I think I like you down there on your knees—"

"You'd better not mean what I think you mean, Angel!" I snap, storming closer, and she rolls her eyes at me.

"Not everything is about sex, Cam. I just mean I like him grovelling." Her glare is harsh, doing absolutely nothing to get my head out of the gutter because yeah, I fucking love her feisty side.

"Ignore him," JD whines, waving me off. "How do you know Jols is okay?"

"I spoke to her," she shrugs.

"What? When?" JD shuffles closer, still on his fucking knees.

"Just before I came downstairs." She's being vague on purpose. Probably to piss us off, given we ignored her before.

Note to fucking self: don't ignore my wife.

"How?" JD barks. "Brody said Smitty took her phone away."

"He did." Abbey nods, glancing out over the pond at the Marx men patrolling the other side. "But Celina still has a phone, and she called me back."

"Hold up. I'm confused." JD lifts his hand in a stop signal. "How'd she call you? On Ringo's phone?"

"No," I jump in to answer. "She has her old phone back. Took it from her mum's drawer."

JD's brows shoot up as he glances between me and my wife. "Oh… shit, so Celina called you and put Jols on the phone? Like you actually spoke to her?"

"Yes, *Jimmy*. I actually spoke to her." She grins, using his real name, but he doesn't even notice. "You shouldn't worry about her. She's hell-bent on making Smitty's life hell."

She's right.

Jols doesn't take well to being controlled. I can't imagine her letting him walk all over her.

"Do we wanna know what she's up to?" I ask, gripping JD's arm and helping him to stand.

"He told her she couldn't leave until she made his shipping container house look like a home," Abbey shrugs, "so she's been sleeping most of the day, and doing all the work at night just to piss him off."

"Oh, my Babydoll!" JD throws his head back, laughing. "Ha! She's fucking perfect. Fuck, I can just imagine Smitty's face each night when he comes in expecting to get some fucking sleep."

My lips lift in a wide smile, my gaze locking with my wife's as she laughs too.

It's nice to hear her laughter. I only wish her eyes didn't give away how much pain she's still in.

Nothing can hide it. Not really. Not if you know to look for it.

JD's mood is lighter now, but I'm sure it will crash again when his bed is empty for another night.

"When is your next church thingy?" Abbey's question has me frowning.

"Church thingy? You mean our meetings?"

She nods. "Yeah. When's the next one?"

"In a couple of days. On the weekend." I shrug. "We'll just attend via video link again," I remind her, but she shakes her head.

"No, you'll go in person."

"Will we now?" I cross my arms over my chest, lifting a brow at her, and she matches my stance, doing the same.

"Ahhh, is this foreplay? It's hard to tell with you guys," JD mutters between us, but I don't take my eyes off my wife.

"Yep. You'll go to that, and I'll visit Jols."

I can see JD nodding in my periphery, looking between us like this is the best idea he's ever heard, but I know my wife better than she thinks I do.

She's cooking up something inside that head of hers. Something I'm not gonna like.

"And what will you and Jols do while we're in church?"

She shrugs innocently, dropping her hands to her sides. "Braid each other's hair."

I roll my eyes. "You can't kidnap her from Smitty."

Her lips kick up. "Can't I?"

"*Angel.*"

"*Cameron,*" she challenges, using only my first name.

"I think Abbey's idea is perfect." JD claps and rubs his hands together.

Sighing, I tip my head back, my eyes tracing the cobwebs on the porch ceiling.

Shit. I need to clean those away for Ma.

"Thanks, Jimmy. I think it's perfect too." Abbey giggles.

"It's flawed as fuck, Angel. How do you think you're gonna get her outta there? I guarantee the gate guards have been warned not to let her leave."

Shrugging, Abbey moves down the steps and calls over her shoulder, "If they don't let us pass, I'll just shoot them."

"Yes. Brilliant idea!" JD claps his hands again.

"No! Not a brilliant idea, you dick." I shoulder past my mate. "You're talking about my wife shooting our club brothers. What do you think is gonna happen then?"

JD's face falls as it sinks in. "Smitty calls for her head."

"Exactly," I mutter, going down the steps after my wife. "You shoot a club brother, and there's a new target on your back, Angel."

"Just add it to the others," she snaps, crossing the yard to the barn where Riggs is chatting with a few of his team.

"I'm not gonna stand by and let you do that," I growl, and before I know what's happening, Abbey skids to a stop and whirls on me, rage twisting her face.

"And I'm not gonna sit back and let a father abuse his role!" she yells so loud that silence falls over the yard. "It's a form of abuse, Ringo! He's abusing his power and holding her against her will because he knows she's sleeping with JD! And before you remind me your club has their own set of rules, let's get one thing clear." She slaps her hands to my chest, fisting each side of my cut and she stretches closer, getting right in my face. "No man or woman, king or queen, prime minister or president *ever* has the right to control someone like that. Our bodies, our hearts, our souls are not available for other people to dictate what happens to them. And the longer you stand back and look the other way while your *President*, or *any* of your men do that, the less respect I have for you!"

She shoves me back, and air gets trapped in my lungs. Not because of her shove, but because of her *words* and how fucking true they are.

"Angel, I—"

"You should find a new name for me," she practically seethes, "I'm no angel anymore."

Spinning on her heel, she storms away, heading straight to Riggs, who nods as she says something, and a moment later he follows her into the makeshift fighting ring they've been using to keep up with their training.

"You okay, man?" JD asks quietly, coming to stand beside me.

"I don't think so," I admit, feeling every bit of guilt I should, because fuck, what sort of delusional world have I been living in?

I've been blinded by my lifestyle of killing and living on our own terms, and although the Southern Sadists have some fucking morals, we are far from perfect. Fuck, even the fact I held Abbey against her will is wrong, despite me meaning well.

But more than all of that, the fact she's losing respect for me… fuck. I don't even want to begin to unpack that.

But I should.

I fucking should.

"She's starting to hate me," I mutter to JD, watching as Riggs shows her a defensive move they were working on yesterday.

"She'll never hate you, man. She's just angry at the world. You know what that's like."

Yeah, I fucking do, which is how I know I need to be a better man.

"I don't want her to look at me like that ever again." I swallow thickly and glance at my best mate.

"Does that mean we're attending church in person on the weekend?"

Fuck.

I rake my hand through my hair and nod. "We are. But she's not gonna be the one to get Jols free. You are."

His brows shoot up. "You want me to break her out? I'll get shot on the spot."

I shake my head. "No, man. It's about time you and Smitty have a chat."

His face falls. "Again… I'll get shot on the spot."

"Looks like you're getting shot either way then, because Abbey is right. Smitty shouldn't be doing that. But what she's wrong about is thinking it's up to her to fix it. It's *not* up to her, it's up to *you*." I clap him on the shoulder. "So figure out what you are gonna say to lessen the blow. It's time for you to man up."

I leave JD looking stunned in the middle of the yard and head over to where my wife is sparring with another man. Not that I have a problem with Riggs teaching her. He's a good man despite who his boss is, but right now, I want my wife's attention. I don't want it on another man.

Riggs notices me approaching and steps away, like he already knows I want this time with my wife.

When her eyes fall on me, there's no hate, but I also don't feel any love right now, either.

"Let's spar, little demon."

Her brows shoot up. "Little demon?"

I nod. "You said you're no angel. So I guess you're a demon then."

She smirks. "Sounds legit."

I huff a laugh, pulling on some MMA gloves to match the pair she's wearing, silently hoping my wound is okay. I guess I'll just have to worry about that later.

Once I'm done, we circle each other a few times, eyes locked, yet neither of us makes the first move.

Typically, the few times we've sparred over the last few weeks, it's turned into us needing to hurry behind closed doors.

This time, however, I'm not sure what will happen given the way she looked at me before.

Fuck. I can't get that image out of my head.

"You gonna start?" she asks, her hands held up ready.

I shake my head. "You looked like you wanted to punch me before. Here's your chance."

Her shoulders drop, and her hands fall to her sides.

"I didn't want to punch you."

"You sure? Your words sure packed a punch."

Guilt flashes across her face. "That... what I said... the respect part. I didn't mean it."

Shaking my head, I reach out and lift her hands back in place, needing her to spar with me.

"Yeah, you did. Don't apologise for speaking the truth, Ang—little demon." I correct, and the corner of her mouth quirks up.

"You make me sound like I'm going to sprout horns."

"I think you already have." I tap my gloves to hers, and this time, she starts moving and we circle each other again. "Now, before you ask or yell at me again, I can confirm that we'll go to the compound for church on the weekend, but *you* will not be breaking Jols out."

She opens her mouth to argue, so I swing at her, and she dodges at the last second.

"JD is responsible for sorting that shit out with Smitty. Not you," I rush out, blocking her swing with my arm.

"So what? JD's gonna kidnap her?" she asks, lunging for me and nearly falling when I slip out of the way, gritting my teeth as my side burns from the sudden movement.

Ignoring any pain I feel, I seize my moment, crashing into her and sending us down to the ground, pinning her in place with her face pressed to the grass.

"JD is going to talk with Smitty." I breathe against her ear, feeling my cock leap to life at the way it's pressed into her arse, the pain in my side forgotten. "And if that doesn't work, JD will either be dead or running for his life, at which point he'll probably drag Jols with him."

Abbey giggles. "That's your plan?"

"That's my plan." I press my lips to her cheek, and she relaxes under me, not even trying to get me off her.

"What are the chances of you sending the men away so we can have some privacy?" she whimpers, pressing her arse back onto my hard length, and I groan.

"You're killing me, Angel."

"I thought I was your demon."

"No," I nip at her ear. "No matter what you say, or how demonic you act, you'll always be my Angel."

A loud whistle has my ears pricking before I hear Riggs call to his men.

"Mikey, pull the van up here. Everyone else, inside for a briefing."

I fucking grin.

Riggs, my man. I'll have to thank him later.

"What's happening?" Abbey asks as I roll my hips, getting a better feel of her arse against my cock.

"Riggs is giving us some privacy."

The sound of the van pulling up draws our attention as it parks and blocks the view of the house, which means I can't scare my ma when I make my wife come.

I can feel Abbey's breathing deepening as we watch Mikey's feet get out of the van and hurry into the barn, and the moment I hear the door shut, I lean over awkwardly, giving my Angel a heated kiss.

"Cam," she breathes as our lips clash is a messy, frantic attempt, my hands roaming down her sides.

"Lift up so I can get to you," I mutter, breaking the kiss as she lifts her hips as much as she can with me on top of her, and I slip my hand down the front of her gym pants and into her panties. "Fuuuck, Angel. You're so slick for me."

I know she still has a bit of spotting, but I can tell the difference between that sort of wetness and the one her body produces when she's turned on.

"Just take them off and fuck me here in the grass," she begs, thrusting against my hand, my palm pressing into her mound as my fingers tease her entrance.

"You're not having my cock yet," I growl, thrusting against her from behind, wishing like fuck we were both naked and I could give her what she wants.

Only a couple more weeks.

"Just fuck my hand the way you want," I rasp, getting fucking carried away. "I wanna feel you drench it."

She grinds so hard onto my hand that my fingers nearly slip inside her, my lips pressing to her ear as I fucking pant like a dog in heat.

"Please. Cam. Please put them in," she begs, and fuuuck, I can hardly hold back.

Would half a finger be bad? How about two fingers just inside so I can get to her G-spot and give her the relief she needs?

Fuck, she grinds on my hand over and over, panting with need, my fingers slick with her juices. I know they would slide inside her so easily.

"Please. I'll do anything," she begs, her restraint gone as she grinds my hand into the fucking earth.

There's a big chance she's gonna break my fingers soon. Not that I'd care. I'd happily tell people how I broke them, but…

Fuuuuck.

Reaching back, her hand digs into my hip, pulling me to her like she can't get enough, and fuck, I guess she can't.

This was always going to be a quickie. A wham-bam-there's-your-orgasm kind of thing, but I want to give her at least *something* she needs.

"Two fingers. Okay? And if it hurts, you fucking shout red, you hear me?"

"Yes. Yes. Please. Yes." Her desperation grows as she shifts her legs wide, giving me better access.

The moment I slowly ease them inside her is the moment she cries out, spasming around my fingers as she comes hard. I don't even get a chance to press against her G-spot before I feel her climax rip through her, but I milk it longer by massaging it, feeling it for the first time in fucking weeks. And as a second orgasm piggybacks her first, I join her, my nuts going tight before I cum in my fucking pants right there in the grass beside the fucking barn.

28

ABBEY

There's a swarm of butterflies beating against my chest today, and they're definitely not the good kind. I was nervous throughout the whole ride here. Not just because I was clinging to Ringo on the back of his motorcycle again, and worried the whole time that we'd get ambushed again by some Satan's Rebels. But also because we were coming back onto the compound and knowing I'll be seeing Smitty again leaves a sour taste coating my tongue.

Every new encounter with that man makes me like him less and less. And today, I can't even summon the energy to pretend to be nice.

The Marx convoy is waiting out on the road for us, staying in their cars as the June winter weather turns bleak.

There's an icy chill in the air, probably rolling off the snow-capped mountains, leaving the compound looking deserted as everyone hides indoors.

"No plotting," Ringo reminds me, ushering me up the steps of Smitty's house. "Leave it to JD. He'll get this shit sorted out."

I roll my eyes, because I don't know how he's gonna talk a man like Nate Smith around. But whatever. We'll try it their way first, I guess.

When the door to Smitty's cabin swings open, Jols' eyes dance between us before shifting over Ringo's shoulder to where JD stands in the yard, rubbing his hands together as steam drifts from his parted lips.

"Hey, Babydoll," he calls, but doesn't come closer.

"Hey… you." Jols shifts anxiously from foot to foot, so I step up to her and slip my hand in hers.

"Show me what you've been up to," I say with a smile, and she nods, her eyes still glued to JD, who shoots her a wink as Ringo gives my arse a playful tap.

"Behave."

I flutter my lashes at him, earning me a smirk before he stalks off, leaving me with Jols, and the guys hurry over to the barn.

"Has he been okay?" Jols asks, tracking him as they get further away, and I nod.

"Show me what you've been doing to turn this tin box into a home for Smitty."

She smirks. "He doesn't know it yet, but I've left little surprises hidden around the place that he'll find over time, and remember me."

I giggle, following her inside, relieved it's cosy and warm enough to take off my thick coat and gloves.

Something I didn't know about Jols is that she's quite the handywoman.

She knows how to use tools like tradies use to build houses. I have no idea about any of that, but she does, and it shows in every corner of this place.

There are pictures hanging on the walls, and she lifts each one to show me a message scribbled in black marker directly on the plaster.

They are messages basically telling Smitty to go fuck himself. I howl with laughter as she reveals each one, telling me that Celina knows about them too.

"Why is she with him? He's such a pig, and she knows he's married to your mum."

Jols shrugs. "My mum's relationship with him is purely transactional. She's actually got a girlfriend, so she's happy with the arrangement. As for Celina…" Jols flops back on the couch. "She's top Doxy because of her relationship with him. Maybe that's why she puts up with his bullshit. Or maybe she actually likes him."

I scoff. "She might need her head checked if that's the case."

Jols smiles, but it looks forced.

Shit. Maybe I shouldn't be bagging her father figure. He did save her.

She has a strange relationship with him, and maybe she puts up with his crap because she feels like she owes him.

But that's her prerogative, right?

"Sorry. I know you care about him. I'm sure he can be a decent guy."

"Let's not talk about him anymore. Tell me how you are."

I cringe. "I'd rather talk about you."

Jols snickers. "Geez, we're a pair."

Sighing, I stare at the TV playing a muted footy match, then tip my head onto Jols' shoulder.

"Not knowing where Tahli is is turning me into a horrible person," I admit, and Jols slips her hand in mine, giving it a squeeze.

"You need to cut yourself some slack, Abbey. You've been through more shit than most people can handle. If you're moody because you're stressed about finding your sister, that's completely understandable."

"I told Ringo I was losing respect for him," I whisper, but Jols hears, straightening to face me.

"And are you?" she asks, and I shake my head.

"No. It was a heat of the moment thing that actually had to do with you and Smitty and… I guess parents who dictate are a trigger for me."

"You know Ringo would see right through your outburst, right?"

I shrug. "You didn't see his face. My words… they hurt him."

"Did you apologise?"

I nod, but then shrug. "Kinda, I guess."

Her brows shoot up. "What does that mean?"

"It means I told him I didn't mean it, and we sparred, and then Riggs had to send everyone away so Ringo could… you know… pleasure me, right there on the grass next to the barn."

Jols throws her head back, laughing. "Abbey, come on. Just say what he did," she laughs again. "Did he fuck you? Finger you? Eat your pussy? Like what sort of pleasure are we talking about here?"

Even after everything, my cheeks flare to life, burning from the outside in.

"You don't need to know."

"Hell yes, I do! I've been stuck with just my hand and my imagination. Give me some details, *please*."

Giggling, I wave her off, like what I'm about to say is no big deal.

"He used his fingers. It was the first time he slipped them inside since…" I trail off, my smile falling as I think about Bobbi.

"Shit. Yeah, sorry. I didn't think about that."

I shrug. "It is what it is."

"Still… was it good?"

"Oh my God, yes!" I blurt out, making her laugh again.

"Jesus, I hope I'm not around when he finally impales himself in you again. That's gonna blow your damn mind."

She wags her brows which has us both cracking up, and I realise how much I've missed this. Missed *her*.

"So, is there any news about your sister?" Jols asks, sinking back into the couch beside me.

"That inside man, Moore, managed to send a text a couple of days ago. Said the word is Minister Banes is still in the Timber Valley district, hiding in plain sight in one of his safe houses. But that's over four thousand square kilometres of area to search. I think Ringo was gonna bring it up at church today. See if Smitty is willing to help put feelers out to his local associates."

"I'm sure he will. I know you don't believe this, but he actually does want to help. This life isn't easy to wrap your head around when you're new to it, but you'll see. Smitty always has a plan, and the club's best interests at heart."

Voices drifting from outside draw our attention, and Jols gets up to peek out the window.

"Church is out."

I jump up, eager to see how JD's chat with Smitty went.

Shucking on our coats, we slip outside onto the porch, watching as the men hurry across the yard to a new sheltered carport area where a fire is burning in a steel drum, all of them shoving at each other to get closer to the warmth.

"I can't remember the last time it was this cold," Jols whispers, hugging herself.

"Why aren't they out yet?" I ask, meaning Ringo and JD, since most of the others are already outside.

"Is everything okay in there?" Jols calls to Vender as he hurries towards us with Mex at his side.

"We'll know soon enough," Vender grins.

"Yeah, no gunshot means he's still alive," Mex chuckles, and my mouth drops open.

"Oh my God. Don't say that!" I rush out, and Jols waves me off.

"Smitty won't shoot him."

"You sure about that?" I ask, catching her eyes, and unease flickers through them.

"Is JD really in there talking to Smitty about me? About us?"

"Yep," I nod. "I was just gonna sneak you out while church was on, but Ringo shut that idea down."

Jols scoffs. "Good. You would have gotten yourself killed." Then she gulps. "Oh man, JD's gonna get himself killed."

"Maybe," I admit, and Vender and Mex both bark out a laugh.

"Abbey, you're not a very supportive friend right now." Jols glares at me and I shrug.

"At least you know I won't lie to you."

"She has a point, Jols," Mex grins, leaning against the porch railing.

Jols huffs, her eyes staying trained on the barn door as we all wait, and after a few minutes of conversation involving footy scores, the barn door swings open.

We all straighten, standing taller as we wait for someone to emerge, and finally Smitty and Spud step out first, with Ringo and JD trailing behind them.

"Oh, thank fuck," Jols sighs, but as JD steps out into the light, even from here we can see a dark trail of blood trickling down his chin. "Jesus." Jols rushes down the steps, and I follow right behind her.

A bell clangs, and I spot Spud holding an old school handbell, ringing it over and over, drawing the attention from the club brothers huddled under the shelter, while Doxies start streaming out of a couple of the houses.

"What's happening?" I ask, confused as everyone moves to gather at the front of the barn.

"He's gonna kill him," Jols snaps over her shoulder. "That's what's happening."

"Wait… what?" I hurry to catch up to her. "Seriously?"

"Why else would he want an audience?"

I gulp, because shit.

Is she right?

Surely not.

Shoving through the crowd, Jols and I push to the front to find JD standing with Smitty on one side and Ringo on the other, with Spud, who has finally stopped ringing the bell, standing on Ringo's other side.

My eyes lock onto Ringo's. He's staring right at me, his expression cold and unreadable, giving nothing away.

"Sorry about bringing you all out into the cold," Smitty starts, before jabbing a finger at JD. "But *this* fucker just copped a knuckle sandwich. Anyone wanna guess why?"

When no one speaks, I open my big mouth.

"Because you wanted him to kiss your arse, and he told you to shove it, so you threw a tantrum?"

Smitty's glare snaps to me instantly as a few snickers ripple through the crowd, and I hear Ringo mutter a curse as he shoots me a glare of his own.

"Good to see you again, *Charity*," Smitty drawls, using that name on purpose to piss me off, which works, and I grit my teeth, hearing Jols snicker next to me.

"You asked for that," she whispers.

"Whatever," I mutter, watching Smitty's gaze shift to Jols.

"When my stepdaughter started living with the club, you all were told the rules," he snarls, his voice sounding a little unhinged. "Hands off. She's off fucking limits!"

A shiver runs up my spine, and not from the cold. It's the savage note in his tone that has me on edge, and I have to wonder if Jols was right. Is Smitty actually going to kill JD for touching her?

"This fucker must have been hard of hearing!" Smitty hisses, fisting JD's cut and shoving him to the ground where he crashes to his knees.

Jols and I both gasp, and Ringo moves to step in, but Spud and Tups dart forward, grabbing him and holding him back.

I see red.

My vision tunnels on my husband and the bastards daring to lay hands on him. I lunge forward, but Celina and Casey snatch me by the arms, keeping me back.

"It'll be better for everyone if you don't interfere," Celina whispers in my ear, and I have half a mind to slap her, but freeze when Jols barrels past me.

"Stop this!" she snarls at her stepdad, who just shakes his head.

"Nope. He knew the rules." His eyes drop to JD, still on his knees, but JD doesn't look scared at all.

His eyes are glued to Jols, burning with fury that says he's ready to die for her.

"Tell everyone what you told me in there," Smitty snarls, and my heart thrashes wildly at knowing this was the wrong way to go about helping Jols.

We should have just kidnapped her and run.

"I told you," JD snaps, "and I'll happily tell everyone here now. I *want* Jolene. She's mine."

JD's words have Jols staggering back a step, while Smitty nods and glares down at him.

"And then you ate my fist, right?"

"Yeah, and you had a right to do that." JD looks up at his President. "But come on, man. I'm claiming her. I'm making her mine."

"JD, no," Jols hisses, stumbling as close as Smitty will allow before he throws a hand up, stopping her cold, and just like that, she freezes.

"Yes, Babydoll." JD keeps his gaze trained on her. "I fucking am. You're mine. That's all there is to it."

"Babydoll," Smitty snarls, the word like poison on his tongue. "You call my daughter, *Babydoll*?"

"Stepdaughter," Jols snaps. "We're not blood, Smitty. Stop this."

Smitty shakes his head, eyes burning as he stares JD down. "I'll give you *one* chance. Retract your claim and save your life. Otherwise… you die."

"This has gone far enough!" Ringo roars, thrashing against Spud and Tups, while another big guy steps in to help hold my husband back.

"Hey! Let him go!" I scream, ready to launch myself over there and go crazy bitch on their arses.

"No!" JD yells, breaking through the chaos, getting everyone's attention. "I won't retract my claim. I love her. I loved her before she even knew I was interested. I'd do *anything* for her. Even die here today, because I will *never* retract my claim on her. She will *always* belong to me. *Even* in death."

"Oh my God," Jols gasps, tears streaming as she stumbles forward a step. "Jimmy, no. He's going to kill you. I'd rather you were alive than live in a world without you! Even if it means we can't be together!"

The moment the words leave her lips, Smitty cocks his gun, the cold click loud as gasps ripple through the crowd.

I can't watch this.

I can't witness someone else I care about die!

Squeezing my eyes shut, I hold my breath, and flinch when the deafening crack of the gun tears through the air, my heart shattering into a million pieces all over again.

29

RINGO

Screams rip through the crowd, and in my peripheral, I can see my Angel thrashing against the Doxies, trying to break free to run to Jols, or perhaps to me.

A strangled cough catches in my throat as I stare at my best mate on the ground. His eyes are wide, still locked on Jols, not even flinching when faced with death.

I scan JD's body, desperate to see where he's been hit, and it takes a long fucking second for my brain to catch up to what's actually happening.

Where's the blood?

My gaze flicks to Smitty, a wide smirk split across his face, his arm raised… above his head.

He… The gun… It's fucking skyward!

I cough as air rushes from my lungs, finally realising Smitty didn't shoot JD.

He didn't fucking shoot him!

Jols lunges forward, a sob tearing from her lips as she skids to her knees in the mud, throwing her arms around JD.

In an instant, his arms are around her too, hugging each other hard before they pull back, cupping each other's faces to murmur a few words… then they are kissing.

"He's not dead!" someone yells, and the crowd erupts in cheers as Spud and Tups finally release my arms.

I double over, bracing my hands to my knees as I try to calm the fuck down.

"I had to be sure you'd die for her," Smitty says over the noise, tucking his gun into the back of his pants. "This is cause for celebration! My stepdaughter has been claimed!"

The crowd cheers, but I'm ready to punch the fuck outta my Prez. His fucked-up mind games are gonna get him killed. Most likely by one of his own.

My gaze snaps to my wife, and I straighten as I see the rage twisting her expression. Her face red, fists balled, and eyes zeroed in on Smitty.

Fuck.

I move at the same time she does, knowing I need to stop her before she gets herself killed. I practically leap over JD and Jols still on the ground, closing the distance as Abbey charges straight for my Prez.

An oomph flies from her when I collide into her side, and I bite back a hiss from the burn of my healing wound as I wrap her up in my arms and shove us through the crowd.

"What are you doing?" she protests, nearly tripping over her own feet as we break through the rear of the crowd.

"You're gonna get yourself hurt, Angel. Just leave it," I mutter, needing to pick her up as she starts struggling to break free of my grip.

"I won't leave it! That arsehole is crazy. Someone needs to stop him!"

I keep moving, carrying her across the yard, heading for the nearest tree.

"In his own twisted way, Smitty felt he had to test JD," I try to explain, the only thing I can come up with myself. "What greater declaration of love is there than a man willing to die rather than give her up?"

A sob escapes her lips as she falls slack in my arms, so I stop and set her down so I can see her face.

Tears spill free, streaking through the dark eye makeup she's wearing as she breaks.

"I thought we'd lost him," she whispers, the agony of that thought clear in her eyes as she stares up at me. "I can't lose anyone else, Cam. I can't bear it."

"Fuck," I hiss, feeling the pain of her words slam into my chest and grip my heart in a tight fucking fist. "I know, Angel. I know."

I pull her to my chest right as the heavens open up, and heavy drops of ice cold rain begin to fall.

Scooping her up, I hurry under the big oak tree, getting us out of the rain.

When I go to put her down, she whimpers, her arms tightening around my neck, so I squeeze her close and lean back against the trunk, just fucking soaking up the feel of her and taking this moment to be fucking thankful JD is still here. And now, he can be with Jols freely.

I stare out over the yard as everyone scatters. Most run inside the barn, while others dart for their bungalows or the carport to gather around the fire drum.

JD and Jols stay put, both of them on their knees, kissing in the rain and mud.

"Angel, look," I urge, tilting her so she follows my gaze, finding our friends.

"Oh… wow, look at them," she whispers on a sob. "Have you ever seen anything more beautiful?"

My eyes fall to her tear-streaked face. "Yes."

Those caramel pools flick up to mine, and a soft flush blooms across her cheeks.

"Stop. I probably look a mess right now." She swipes under her eyes, smudging her eye makeup, which she notices on her finger when she pulls it back. "Oh, God. Has my makeup run?"

"Yes." I smirk.

"That's not beautiful," she sniffs, wiping under her other eye.

"It is to me. I love seeing you all made up and perfect. I love seeing you completely natural with nothing on your skin. And I love seeing you all messed up. Mostly after I've had my way with you, but still," I brush my thumb over her black tears, "I love seeing how much you trust me to fall apart in my presence."

Even as more tears pop free, she keeps her eyes pinned to mine.

"I was a bitch to you the other day. I'm so sorry for saying I was losing respect for you. I didn't mean it," she rushes out. "I'm so in love with you it hurts."

She bursts into sobs, and I hug her close, pressing my lips to her forehead as I struggle with my own fucking emotions.

"I know you didn't mean it, Angel. Things got heated and… well, you're passionate about something that's a very serious matter, and it's a conversation more men should be having."

Pulling back, she blinks up at me, swiping at her eyes.

"You really believe that?"

"Fuck, yes. I know I say I own you. Hell, I've even told you I'll never let you leave me, but let me be clear." I cup her face and lean in, pressing our foreheads together. "*You* own *me.* And I'll never let you leave me because I'll do *whatever it takes* to be the kind of man *worthy* of your love."

"Shit," she sobs before pressing a salty kiss to my lips. "I'll never leave you."

I claim her lips in a deeper kiss, lowering her feet back to the ground and spinning us so I can press her against the tree. She paws at me like she can't get close enough, and I fucking wish we were at my place instead of this fucking compound where privacy is a fucking myth.

"Fuck," I breathe as I pull back, practically panting with the need to bury myself inside her.

It's got nothing to do with scratching an itch and everything to do with being close to her. Losing myself in her touch, her words, her kisses.

Glancing over my shoulder, I see JD and Jols disappearing down the road that leads to the row of bungalows, and know I can't go to the one we share.

They need alone time now more than anyone.

Looking back down at my wife, I cup her precious face and swipe at the tears drying on her cheeks.

"I don't have anywhere to take you to be alone right now. JD and Jols just headed down to my bungalow."

Her lips twitch into a small smile. "I hope they don't come up for air for days."

I chuckle. "I fucking hope so too."

I consider our options and realise the barn is the only place we can go right now unless we want to catch a fucking chill.

"What are the chances you're gonna try to kill Smitty if we go into the barn?"

I swear the fucking devil has possessed my wife's body with the way she smirks at me.

"I'll only try to kill him a little bit."

I bark out a laugh at the way she flutters her lashes like she's fucking innocent.

"Okay, little demon. Let's get you cleaned up." I press a quick peck to her lips as she giggles and lead her out into the rain.

She's carefree as she skips beside me, arms out, spinning as she looks up into the falling rain.

Fuck.

If I could save an image of her, this would be it. Her blonde hair darkened by the rain, the black smudges of her dried tears getting wet again as she blinks those long dark lashes.

"Do you think she's up there?" she asks, not looking at me as she stops to stare past the tumbling drops. "Do you think she's watching? That she sees what I've become?"

It's then that her head lowers and those caramel eyes lock with mine.

"Do you think Bobbi sees the monster I've become?"

"I think she's up there." I nod. "I think she's in every raindrop that falls. In the sun that warms the Earth. In the leaves on the trees, and in every breath of wind. But most of all, I think she's in *you*, Angel." I step up to her and brush a clump of wet hair off her cheek. "And Bobbi sees the same thing I do. A fighter. A warrior. A beautiful woman who loves with all of her heart, and fights for what's right."

She stares at me for a long moment, her eyes dancing between mine before she speaks.

"I really hope she doesn't see me in those moments when I change."

"Change?"

"Into the monster. Into the rage that consumes me."

"I think she's watching when she needs to, Angel. And you need to do what you feel is right, no matter who's watching."

A small smile tugs at her lips as she gives me a nod.

"I think Hope is with her."

"Yeah, me too, Angel. They've got each other." Leaning forward, I press my lips to her wet hair. "Come on. Let's get you inside."

When we step inside, I ignore everyone until I've got Abbey safely in the bathroom so she can clean up. Given what's happened here today, she's surprisingly light-hearted by the time we step out again, and I reluctantly let the Doxies lead her away to huddle in front of the fire, chatting to her like she's an old friend.

Shit. I hope she finds friends among them. Family even. A found family, just like the one I found when I needed it the most.

"How many bodyguards do I need?" Smitty's voice has me turning as he hands me a stubbie.

"To protect you from *me* or my *wife*?"

"Pfft." He rolls his eyes. "Your wife, of course. You, I can handle. Her..." We both glance across the room to where she's smiling at Darla, who seems to be recovering well. "She's fucking scary."

I bark out a laugh. "You're scared of that little thing?" I lift a brow his way, and he nods.

"In my opinion, there are two kinds of crazy," Smitty rasps, taking another swig of his drink. "The kind that's obvious in everything someone does. Like me." He flashes me a toothy fucking smile, completely proud of that. "I know I'm a crazy fucker. *You* know I'm a crazy fucker. It's no fucking surprise. But the kinda crazy your wife is…" He blows out a breath. "Man, that's the sort of crazy you don't see coming. It's calculated, and full of unforgiving rage. No fucking way do I want to be alone in a room with her."

I know he just called my wife crazy, but honestly, I'm fucking proud.

Her crazy wasn't born in her. It was created from her environment. She's learning to adapt. To evolve. And I'm glad she's embracing it, because it makes her so much stronger.

"Well, man," I clap my Prez on the shoulder. "Guess you'd better watch your back then."

His smile falls, and he leans in. "Really? You think she'd really come for me?"

"Dunno. She's fucking crazy. I never know what she's gonna do next." I lie, and his eyes widen.

"Why the fuck did you marry a crazy woman?" he hisses, and I shrug.

"Seemed like a good idea at the time."

"Well, now, I can't fucking kill her, can I?" Smitty huffs. "Not without declaring war against you, and you know damn well I'd never do that."

I chuckle, shaking my head at my deranged President. "Should I remind you that *you* were the one who demanded I marry her?"

Smitty's shoulders drop. "Fuck. I did, didn't I?"

"Yeah, man. You fucking did." I chuckle at his expense.

"So how do I get her on my good side?"

"Not threatening or pretending to shoot my friends is a good start."

Smitty stiffens at my wife's voice, and fuck, my smirk grows wide.

"Fuck… she's right behind me, isn't she?"

I nod, glancing over his shoulder to the blonde head of hair, now dryer than it was before.

"Better be careful. She's carrying a gun *and* a knife."

Smitty's brows shoot up, and he leans closer, whispering loudly.

"Why the fuck would you give her a gun?"

"So I can do this," she says, and he stiffens like a board, his hands shooting up.

She moves behind him, and his back arches like she's running something up his spine, and a moment later, her hand appears on his shoulder, her finger pointed against his cut before she stretches up to press it to his temple.

"Pew-pew," she giggles, and he chokes on a cough before spinning to face her.

Those around us burst into laughter at the sight of her holding up her finger gun like a badass bitch, while Smitty shakes his head.

"Uh, Prez. Looks like she got you," Vender laughs, falling against Mex, who's too busy recording the whole thing on his phone.

"Charity—"

"Uh-uh." She shakes her head, pressing her finger gun to the middle of his forehead, and this time, Smitty laughs.

"Fine! Our dear *Abbey*. Please join me for a drink." He gestures to the bar, which looks like it's been extended since the last time I was here.

"Fine. But not that harsh stuff. I like the sweet stuff, thanks."

"Of course," Smitty beams, leading her to his table, and I follow, hoping like hell he can get on her good side for longer than five fucking minutes.

We all sit, and Casey brings over the bottle of Jack, a bottle of Moscato, and some glasses, and we settle in to drink.

I refuse the shot of Jack Smitty insists I down, sticking with the beer I've got, knowing it's the only alcohol I'll touch today, while I watch my wife enjoy a few glasses of the sweet stuff as she and my Prez finally take some time to get to know each other.

It's amusing watching her walls drop as the alcohol starts to take effect, but she stops at three glasses, telling Smitty if she has any more, her knife skills will suffer if she has to stab him. That sends them both into fits of laughter, and I swear their energy spreads throughout the barn, infecting everyone for the first time in a long time.

JD and Jols make an appearance after about three hours, everyone cheering like they've just walked into their own fucking wedding. Abbey hurries to Jols, throwing her arms around her neck, and they hug and talk into each other's ears as they sway to the music like they're fucking dancing.

Fuck. I love seeing her like this.

With my friends.

They are her friends now.

It's been nearly four months since Abbey came into our lives, and look how loved she already is. Look at the friendships she made. I wonder if she realises she's already got a new family.

"You have a weird, nostalgic look on your face right now. It's creepy," JD chuckles as he sidles up to me.

Dragging my gaze from my wife, I stare at my best mate.

"Glad you didn't die," I mutter, and he beams.

"You would have cried."

"Maybe a little." I bump his shoulder with mine. "So what's the plan? You staying here with your woman, or?"

"Where you go, I go, brother," he reminds me.

It's not really a club pact unless we're in trouble. We are each other's wingmen, but what he's talking about is nothing more than two mates having each other's back.

"Well, alright then. I'll have Lans make up the guest room in the house for you. No need for you two to worry about Riggs and his team out in the barn while you're in your honeymoon phase."

JD laughs. "Lans might leave tacks in the bed."

I shrug. "Probably, but she likes Jols, so maybe just on your side of the bed."

"Probably," he laughs. "You know your sister offered to join me and Jols."

I hold my hand up to his face. "Don't say another fucking word. I don't want to hear what my sister gets up to."

JD chuckles. "You don't have to worry about me and her, man. She has all the Marx men she needs to satisfy her libido."

"I'm not fucking opposed to punching you!" I snap.

"Fine. Okay. I'll stop."

Glancing at each other, we both burst out laughing, right as my phone starts ringing. Taking it out, I see Griffin's name flash across the screen, and show JD who it is before I hit accept, moving through the crowd to step outside.

"Speak," I bark, hearing him chuckle.

"I swear, sometimes I have to check my phone to see if I called Barrett. You two are the same fucking person."

"That's why only one of us can be in the country at once. Too much fucking awesomeness and all that."

Griffin scoffs. "Fucking hell. You both have the same ego, too. Why the fuck do you sound like you're in a good mood?"

"Just am. What can I do for you?"

"It's more like what I can do for you. Or more specifically, your wife."

My smile drops. "I'm listening."

"I've been showing pictures of your wife's cunt mother and her sisters to my girls at the club, and Minnie came in earlier and said she's positive she spotted them at the Redfield supermarket this arvo."

"Fuck. Really?" I ask, my heart speeding up with the possibility.

"Yeah, it was a few hours ago. I fucking tore into her for not calling me straight away, but she said she wasn't sure it was them."

"Fuck." I rake my hand through my hair. "So how do we find out?"

"Already sorted." Griffin chuckles. "Had one of my hackers get into the store cameras. It was them."

"Okay. Well, that's a start. Is there any way to track them?"

"Nah, we tried that. Redfield isn't exactly high tech. We lost them as they crossed Murray's Bridge."

"Fuck," I huff, my shoulders dropping.

I would have loved nothing more than to give Abbey this information and be able to tell her we know where they are.

"I know it's not exactly what you were hoping for, but it does mean they are close. And I *can* tell you where they will be next Sunday around two in the afternoon."

My brows shoot into my fucking hairline. "The supermarket?"

"Yep. We went back through the footage. For the last four Sundays, the mother has come in with both daughters, filled up a shopping cart, and left again, heading over Murray's Bridge."

"Fuck. Yes!" I grin wide.

"Wish I could be there to see your wife's face when you tell her." Griffin chuckles.

"Shit… I can't tell her." I groan.

"Why the fuck not?"

"Well, what if we go there on Sunday and they don't show? I can't fucking bear to disappoint her."

"Well shit. Good luck in keeping that secret."

Fuck. I'll need all the good luck I can get.

30

ABBEY

As far as lockdowns go, this one wasn't so bad. Probably because the Southern Sadists still spent it together, and you just don't feel so isolated with your family around.

That, and the fact Ringo's property is still crawling with Marx security guards. It makes it hard to believe the streets across the state are like ghost towns when it's bustling here.

A week ago today, Jols and JD declared their love for each other, and no one died. It was a beautiful day, and it wasn't even a wedding or anything. Just a celebration of love, which had me getting a little tipsy. It made for a tough hour-long ride on the back of Ringo's bike when we finally headed home though.

I'd been nervous about potentially getting ambushed by Satan's Rebels again, but the ride there and back was, thankfully, uneventful.

I guess Ringo's club really did wipe most of them out the day we raided their compound to save Darla and Nessy.

The week has been quiet, and I've been getting antsy just sitting around doing nothing, but Ringo kept assuring me there'd be an update today. Something that might finally bring us closer to finding my sister.

"Don't the Doxies usually do this?" I ask through the protective layer of the face mask as I stare down at the shopping list on Ringo's phone.

They are all ridiculously random things that Smitty apparently asked us to grab on our way to the compound this afternoon.

"Yeah, but since we were out, I offered." Ringo readjusts his mask with a grumble. He hasn't stopped complaining about having to put it on.

It's been a while since I've worn one. Most of the last few months, I've spent hiding away, but today, we're out in public like there's not a massive target on my back.

It's hard to care though, because this all feels so… normal.

I smile behind my mask as Ringo pushes a shopping trolley through the entrance of the Redfield supermarket.

This feels very domestic.

The thought makes me grin.

I never thought I'd see the day Ringo and I would go grocery shopping together.

I mean, I know that's what married couples do, but we aren't exactly like normal married couples, and our life in general isn't exactly normal.

Not right now, anyway. Hopefully, one day it will be.

"What the hell is a Zipper Dipper?" I ask, glancing up from the screen to my husband, catching him frowning as he steers the trolley along the top of the first aisle.

"No fucking clue."

"Maybe they mean Zooper Dooper?"

His frown deepens, almost comically, those warm whiskey eyes flicking to me. "What the fuck is a Zooper Dooper?"

I stop walking, my mouth dropping open behind my mask as I stare at my husband in disbelief.

"You don't know what a Zooper Dooper is?"

He throws a hand up, shaking his head. "No fucking clue."

"It's those different coloured icy poles in the long, narrow plastic sleeves."

His brows lift in understanding. "Shit. Never knew that's what they were called."

I giggle. "Stick with me, husband. I'll teach you all about unimportant things."

Chuckling, he shakes his head at me before stopping, his eyes turning serious.

"What?" I ask, confused, as he leans in closer.

"You know that information we were waiting on about your sister?" he asks quietly, and I nod quickly. "Well, I need you to stay calm. Just stay here with me, but turn around."

My mouth drops open as my heart thrashes wildly in my chest, and I slowly turn around.

My frantic eyes scan past the people walking out of the aisle we're standing in front of, right down to the other end where I see… three familiar faces.

Oh. My. God.

"Tahli," I whisper, feeling Ringo's arm slip around me from behind, his grip firm, keeping me in place.

"Surprise, Angel." His mask-covered lips brush my ear. "Now we have to be smart about this. I've got men outside the store, and some inside, but we want to try and avoid a scene."

I nod, knowing he's right, even though every fibre of me is screaming to run to Tahli and snatch her up right now.

"You got her?" Jols' voice breaks through the chaos in my head to find her approaching with JD.

"You knew about this?" I snap, and she shrugs.

"We all did."

I spin to face Ringo, glaring at him as he tries to explain.

"I just didn't want to tell you until I knew it would happen. I didn't want to disappoint you if it fell through."

Gritting my teeth, I jab a finger into his chest. "You're not getting a handy off me tonight."

JD barks out a laugh as Jols giggles, but Ringo shrugs.

"If all goes well, Angel, you'll have your sister to entertain. I doubt your hand will be anywhere near my cock for a while."

"Huh." I nod. "You have a point."

"They're about to turn and take the next aisle," Jols points out, and I glance over my shoulder to see both of my sisters, and my mum, round the corner.

"We'll take this one." Ringo gestures to the aisle my family just left. "You two take the one they're in."

I pout, wishing I could be the one to go down *that* aisle.

Jols and JD move to do as ordered, and Ringo leads me into our aisle, where I rush ahead, trying to see through to the other side.

"Angel," Ringo whisper-yells, but I ignore him, peeking through the shelving until I finally spot them on the other side, and my heart sinks.

Tahli looks… awful.

She's pale, with dark circles under her eyes, yet Maggie looks perfectly fine.

Tahli walks with her head down, eyes trained on her feet as Maggie and Mum chat about the shopping list.

"Oh, Tahli. Grab one of those pasta sauce jars your grandfather likes. You're going to cook for him again tonight."

She's going to what?

My sisters obviously know Minister Banes is their grandfather now, but why the hell is Mum making Tahli cook for him?

My stomach rolls at the possibilities.

Tahli stiffens at Mum's words, nodding without looking up, before her eyes snap to this side of her aisle, scanning further down.

I move with her, tracking every step as she edges away from Mum. When she stops, I shift the packets of chips aside so I can see her better.

Her eyes look dead. Like the life's been sucked straight out of her soul. It makes me want to scream. To slaughter everyone who dared to do this to her.

As her hand lifts to pick up a jar of sauce, I steel myself and tug my mask down, revealing my face.

"Tahli," I whisper, and when she doesn't hear me, I say it louder. "Tahli."

Her eyes flick up, locking with mine through the grates in the shelving, and she flinches, the jar slipping from her fingers.

I cringe, pressing my finger to my lips in a 'shhh' gesture, bracing for the jar to smash, but someone catches it.

"Whoops. You nearly dropped this." Jols' voice is like music to my ears as Tahli looks away from me to my friend.

"Oh my goodness. Thank you. My daughter is such a klutz." My mum rushes forward, quickly wedging herself between Tahli and Jols, making Tahli look like an idiot.

"Don't sweat it," Jols says, though I can hear the strain in her voice.

"Come along, sweetheart." Mum ushers Tahli to the other side of the aisle, where Maggie grabs her arm like she's leading an invalid.

My blood boils.

I want to rain hell down on them, but I see Jols' and JD's chests move past as my mum urges my sisters forward, so I bite my tongue and keep following from my aisle.

When my eyes meet Ringo's, I see him speaking quietly into his phone and wonder when I gave it back to him.

He probably took it back without me noticing while I was in shock at seeing Tahli.

He stays on my tail as I creep along, hiding at the end of the aisle when Mum and my sisters leave their aisle and move to the next one.

I dash out, peering down the aisle as JD and Jols reach the end, and they glance back, giving me a nod.

I don't know what the nod means, but when they start moving up the same aisle as my family, I edge forward and peek around the corner.

My mum has stopped a third of the way up, helping Maggie load tins of food into their trolley, while Tahli glances at JD and Jols before looking over her shoulder to see me.

Again, I press my finger to my lips, my mask still sitting under my chin, and she nods, slowly trailing behind Mum and Maggie as they start moving again.

With their attention in the other direction, I rush forward, my eyes locked on Tahli, desperation crashing over me so hard I start sweating despite the cold day.

As I get closer, I press my finger to my lips, holding my other hand out to her, frantically wiggling my fingers, begging her to come to me so I can get her out of here.

She steps towards me, her eyes dropping to my stomach, and I see the moment she realises I'm no longer pregnant by the way her brows knit together in confusion.

'Come on,' I mouth, needing her to meet me halfway, and she nods, about to move when Mum suddenly turns around.

Time slows.

Everything around me moves in slow motion.

Jols and JD approaching from the other end, their strides long, but slow…

My mum's expression changes at a snail's pace as recognition flickers across her features, morphing into a deep frown.

Maggie, taking a few more slowed steps forward before stilling and looking back over her shoulder, realising Mum has stopped.

Tahli, stiffening, her eyes slowly widening in terror as Mum's shriek tears through the air.

"No!" she screams so loud, time speeding up once again, and I know other shoppers must have heard her.

"Run, Tahli!" I yell, watching the horror in her eyes as she panics.

I sprint forward, no longer scared of my mother, only terrified she will hurt Tahli.

My mum lunges, grabbing Tahli before I can reach her, just as Maggie comes charging our way.

With rough hands, Mum yanks Tahli backwards, her small frame so easy to move as she slams into Maggie, who catches her in a death grip, and my mum whips around to face me, rage twisting her face.

"You can't have her. She's mine. Not yours."

"You're not fit to be a mother," I snarl, closing the distance fast, enjoying the panic that flashes in her eyes, and the way she stumbles back. "Tahli is coming with me. Do whatever you want with Maggie. I couldn't give two fucks what happens to that bitch!"

"No!" Mum lunges for me, and I brace myself for the impact, but it never comes.

Instead, Ringo's hand shoots past me, fisting the front of Mum's blouse as he leans close, his voice a deadly growl.

"What the fuck did I say to you last time?" he snarls, walking her backwards towards my sisters. "I told you I'd make you go missing. I wasn't fucking joking, *Priscilla*."

When my mum's calves hit the trolley, she gasps and tries to slap at Ringo, but he ignores her attempts, his eyes snapping to my sisters, who are now boxed in by JD and Jols behind them.

"You remember me, Tahli?" he asks calmly, and as I peer around him, I see Tahli nodding. "It's time to come with us now. Abbey will take better care of you than your so-called mother ever did."

"You can't have her!" Maggie snaps, fisting her hand in Tahli's hair and yanking it back so hard that Tahli cries out.

"Let her go, Maggie!" I storm forward, but Jols reaches her first, grabbing Maggie's hair and giving her a taste of her own medicine.

The moment Maggie cries out, she releases Tahli, and my little sister bolts for me, flinching as she passes Mum, who tries to grab for her, but Ringo's grip on her is ironclad.

And just like that, Tahli is in my arms, her frail, trembling body collapsing against me as she falls apart.

"Let's go," Ringo snarls into my mum's face. "You're coming with us too."

Part of me doesn't want Mum and Maggie anywhere near us. I don't even want to see their faces, but I know we need to deal with them, and we can't do that inside a supermarket.

"No! Stop! Help! I'm being kidnapped!" my mum shrieks, her voice high and panicked.

Ringo curses, looking like he's a breath away from knocking her out. And I kinda wish he would.

"Someone call the police!" a woman screams from somewhere, and I know this situation is about to turn bad, and fast.

"Leave them!" I call over my shoulder, clutching Tahli tight as I hurry down the aisle. "They'll keep."

"You sure?" Ringo asks, and I nod.

"Let's just get Tahli out of here," I say, and Ringo nods back before shoving my mum into the shelves, while Jols does the same with Maggie.

Then, we run.

I know there are cameras in here, but I don't care. My face has been splashed all over the news. Let them run their fake stories again. I know the truth, and so does Tahli.

"Do it now!" Ringo barks, his voice low and deadly as he sprints next to me, snapping orders into his phone.

I have no idea who he's talking to, but the next second, a window-shattering boom explodes from the carpark as a car goes up in a ball of fire.

Screams echo around us, shoppers scattering, the distraction now drawing attention to the blast. People run and hide like the supermarket is under attack, giving us the perfect cover to get away.

Now I understand why Ringo insisted we take the van today. He planned this from the start, prepared to haul more people with us than what we came here with.

The door to the van flies open, and Vender leaps out, rounding the front and diving into the driver's seat.

Ringo reaches the van first, turning to me, but then his eyes go wide as he looks over my shoulder, and my stomach drops.

A second later, Tahli's hand gets ripped from mine.

31

ABBEY

My mother's manic eyes lock with mine as she drags Tahli away. The entire parking lot is chaos as people run for their cars, black smoke billowing up as a car burns out of control. Yet she doesn't seem to care that bystanders can see her fist Tahli's hair, forcing her from me as Tahli screams.

I don't know where Maggie is, and frankly, I don't care. All I care about is getting my little sister to safety.

"Give her back, and I'll let you live," I snarl, matching each one of my mum's steps as she hurries backwards.

"You can't kill me here. Not with all these witnesses," she hisses, like that will work in her favour.

I tilt my head, stalking her, my eyes never once breaking from hers.

"Why not? What do *I* have to lose? You already *killed* my daughter. The only thing I have left is Tahli, and at least I know she'll be safe with my husband and my friends. Unlike with *you*. So yes, *Priscilla*," I hiss her name, my satisfaction spiking when her face contorts with rage. "I will *absolutely* kill you right here, right now, in broad daylight, with cameras and witnesses watching."

And there it is. The flicker of panic. I really do love seeing it on her face.

To prove my point, I reach behind me and slip my gun out from under my coat.

She gasps as I lift it towards her, and just like I knew she would, she jerks Tahli in front of her, using her as a human shield.

"You'll have to kill Tahli first!" Priscilla yells, but I storm forward, done playing.

"On your six, Angel," Ringo's voice comes from behind me, and I know he's got a gun trained on my mum too, so I seize the moment, lunging forward to snatch Tahli free.

Priscilla's hands shoot up, trembling in the air as she watches Tahli wrap herself around me, and I back away, holding my sister tight, before passing her off to Ringo once we're clear.

"Let's go," Ringo orders, and even though I nod, I don't move when he does. I stay rooted, my gun trained on my mum.

It would be so easy to just pull the trig—

A body slams into my side, sending me crashing sideways, my gun going off with a loud pop. I hit the ground hard, and before I even process who's on top of me, a wild female screech explodes in my ear, fingernails tearing at me in a frenzy.

"Abbey!" Tahli cries from somewhere, but I can't see anything as I fight to get this rabid bitch off me.

"I hate you! You've ruined everything!" Maggie screams, her voice wild and unhinged, and somehow, I manage to twist a hand free, and land a punch straight into the side of her head.

Car tyres squeal as I right myself, sitting up to see my gun has slid under the car next to me. I scramble for it just as Maggie pushes herself off the ground, tears streaming down her face.

"You shot Mum!"

My brows hitch, and before I reach my gun, I spot Mum clutching her upper arm, blood soaking through her coat.

"It's her arm. She'll live," I snap, quickly snatching the gun just as the van screeches to a stop beside me, the side door already open and Ringo's hand reaching out.

"Time to go, Angel," he urges, and I glance to my mum and Maggie and nod.

He's right. It's time to get the hell out of here.

Maggie doesn't try to stop me again as I leap into the van. She just rushes to my mum's side like the woman is dying.

A girl can dream, I guess.

As the van speeds away and the door slams shut, I'm left in the back with Ringo and my terrified little sister.

"Chook…" I whisper, tears spilling as I pull her into my arms. "I've got you."

God. How many times has Ringo said those three words to me? And now it's my turn to step up. To be the adult and reassure my little sister that she's safe now.

As she crumbles in my embrace, my eyes find Ringo's, and I mouth a silent *thank you,* knowing I could never have done this without him, or the danger he and his club have willingly stepped into for me.

He answers with a wink and a crooked smirk before reaching behind him to grab a blanket.

I settle back with Tahli as he tucks it around us, and spend the next hour just staring into his eyes, hoping he can see every bit of love I have for him in mine.

Tahli doesn't speak during the drive. Eventually, her tears fade, and she cries herself to sleep in my arms.

I don't know where Jols and JD ended up until we pull into Ringo's property and I see them climbing out of one of the Marx security vehicles. I have a million questions about how the hell today came together, but there will be time for that later.

Right now, I need to focus on my sister.

Tahli is a little dazed as I help her out of the van. Her eyes scan Ringo's property, jumping from the barn to the orchard to the house, before landing on the pond.

"Are there ducks in the pond?" she asks hopefully, and I smile, and ruffle her hair.

"Yeah, Chook. There are. We can feed them later if you like?"

Her eyes light up, and she nods. "I'd like that."

"This must be Tahli." Doreen's voice catches me off guard, and I glance up to see her coming down the porch steps.

She's really struggled with her last lupus flare-up, but seeing Tahli has her eyes lighting up and her arms open in a welcome that warms my heart.

"Yes, Doreen, this is Tahli, my little sister."

"Oh, sweet girl." Doreen stops in front of us, her eyes turning sympathetic. "You look like you've had a tough day."

Tahli nods slowly, a little unsure.

"Well, I've just cooked a fresh batch of cookies." Doreen gestures to the house. "Would you like to come inside and have some? Maybe a hot chocolate, too?"

Tahli's eyes go wide as she looks from Doreen to me.

"It's okay," I reassure her. "This is Ringo's mum, and this," I gesture around the property, "is your new home."

Her lip starts to wobble as tears spring to her eyes. "It-it is?"

"Yes." I slip my arm around her shoulders. "Let's go have some cookies."

With a teary smile, Tahli nods, and we follow Doreen inside, Ringo right behind us.

I don't exactly know if what I told my sister is right. Ringo and I haven't discussed what would happen when I got Tahli back. Where we would live. How we'll make this work.

Shit. I'll need to get a job. Make sure I can earn enough money to feed her. Support her.

Suddenly, doubt claws at me. I know Ringo would never kick us out on the streets, but surely he has thoughts about this. Surely he knows I'll do whatever it takes to pay my sister's way.

Shit. We need to have a talk. And soon.

For instance, where is Tahli going to sleep tonight?

I know they have spare guest rooms, but I don't want her to be alone. Maybe I'll have to move into one of the rooms with her.

There's so much to consider.

Inside, Ringo's sisters warm to Tahli instantly. They are kind and gentle. Yes, even Millie. They show Tahli around the kitchen, telling her she doesn't need to ask if she wants something to eat, that she's welcome to eat whatever she wants, whenever she wants.

It's such a simple thing, but it instantly has Tahli relaxing, and I take a moment to try and understand how daunting this must be for her.

Just this morning, she thought she'd have to endure another day living with our mum, Maggie and… *him*.

Ugh. The thought of Minister Banes anywhere near Tahli makes me feel sick.

The gentle brush of fingers on my thigh pulls me from my spiral, and I shift my gaze to Ringo, finding him watching me closely.

"What's going on inside that head of yours?"

I smile, though it's tight. "So much."

His lips kick up, and he lifts his fingers to graze over my jaw.

"I can just imagine."

"Should I find a lawyer?" I lean in close, keeping my voice low so I don't worry Tahli as we sit around the large dining table. "Like… how likely is it the cops will turn up? I did shoot my mum. There must have been cameras."

"You don't have to worry about that. It's all been taken care of," Ringo says quietly, making me frown.

"How?"

"Griffin's hackers wiped every bit of video footage from the store and within a five-kilometre radius. Jason Zimora is fielding any reports coming in. He just happens to be the responding officer."

"Convenient." I smirk, and Ringo winks. "What about my mum? Has she reported Tahli missing?"

"No. Not yet. Apparently, she was nowhere to be found by the time law enforcement arrived."

"I should have shot her again," I mutter, and Ringo chuckles.

"She'll get what's coming to her in time, Angel. For now, just enjoy having your sister back."

Smiling, I glance at Tahli, who is listening eagerly to a story Alana is telling about her days as a ballerina.

Worrying my lip between my teeth, I turn back to Ringo to find he's still watching me.

"We never spoke about this." I gesture subtly to my sister. "About what would happen when I got her back." My eyes drop to my lap, and I swallow the lump forming in my throat as I speak quietly. "I'll get a job to help pay for her expenses. And she's really a good kid. Super helpful around the house. She loves to cook, so she can help in the kitchen and—"

Ringo's finger presses to my lips, silencing me.

"Angel, remember when I said I wanted to raise Bobbi as my own?"

When I nod, a tear pops from the corner of my eye, and Ringo sweeps it up with his finger, holding it between us.

"Same goes for Tahli. I want to look after her. I want to look after you. Don't worry about money, food, or clothing. Or... whatever it is girls like or need. It would be my honour to take care of you both. To give Tahli a safe space to heal and grow and thrive. My ma and sisters want the same too." He pops his finger in his mouth, swallowing my tear. "I want this to be *your* home. Always."

Completely overwhelmed with the barrage of emotions swirling through me, I fist his cut, yanking him forward until our noses brush. "How'd I get so lucky to find you?"

"You didn't." He nips at my lips. "I'm the lucky fucker who found you."

He claims my lips in a kiss that sends heat spreading through my entire body, and a second later, the clearing of a throat has me stiffening, my eyes snapping open.

"Whoops," I whisper against his lips, feeling his smile curve against mine before we pull back.

"Don't worry. You'll get used to them sucking face." Millie rolls her eyes as laughter ripples around the table.

"Is he really your husband?" Tahli asks, her eyes wide, gaze dancing from me to Ringo, and I nod, holding out my hand.

"Mum or one of those cult crazies stole my wedding ring, but we still have this."

Tahli takes my hand, eyes tracing over Ringo's name tattooed on my finger, then glances at his hand, seeing my name inked there too.

A small smile tugs at her lips as she glances up at Ringo, but when her gaze returns to me, pain flickers behind them.

"Where… where's your baby?"

The words cut like a dagger, and I know she sees the flinch I can't hide in time.

"It doesn't matter. You don't have to answer that," Tahli rushes out, her eyes dropping to her lap in such a way that looks achingly familiar.

I feel like I'm looking at myself.

Conditioned.

She's been conditioned the same way I was, and I didn't even notice it until now.

Probably because I'm aware of it now.

"My baby…" I start, my voice cracking as I clear the lump from my throat. "She died."

Tahli's head snaps up, tears flooding her eyes. "No."

"Yes," I whisper, taking her hand in mine. "She only lived for a few minutes, I think, but I got to hold her." I press my hand to my chest, feeling her there still, even after all this time. "I called her Bobbi Cameron Musgrove."

"That's a really pretty name." Tahli sobs, trying to stop her tears with the sleeve of her jumper, and Doreen hurries over with a box of tissues, placing it on the table in front of us.

I offer her a nod in thanks, grabbing tissues for Tahli and then myself.

"I named her Bobbi after my husband's brother, who died a couple of years ago," I explain, pointing to the picture on the wall. One Doreen told me all about during those weeks I was here without Ringo. "He was actually the guy who saved Lexi once."

"He was?" Tahli asks, eyes wide, and I nod.

"Yeah. I wanted to name her after him, and I thought Bobbi was kinda cool for a girl."

"It is." Tahli smiles, dabbing at her tears with the tissue.

"And her middle name is Cameron. After Ringo." I jut my finger in Ringo's direction. "His real name is Cameron, and he's the man who saved me."

"I love that, Abs." She sobs again, so I squeeze her hand. "And Musgrove?"

"That's my married name. Ringo's surname."

"Oh." Tahli sits taller. "Abigail Eloise Musgrove."

"Yeah." I giggle, pulling her in for a hug, but when we pull back, she cringes.

"I hope you've let Harry Styles know you won't be marrying him anymore."

Laughter explodes around the table, and even Ringo lets out a bark of amusement as everyone remembers my wedding day. Tahli has no idea how perfectly she hit the mark.

As the afternoon fades into night, I give Tahli a tour of the house, and with Ringo's encouragement, I take her to my room and show her where she'll be staying for the meantime.

Ringo suggested that keeping her close for a while until she feels safe again would be best, and he agreed to crash on the couch so I could share our marital bed with my sister.

We join Doreen in the kitchen and help her cook. It's mostly for Tahli's sake, knowing her love for cooking will help her settle in, and after dinner, we retreat up to our room and watch a movie in Ringo's suite before bed.

Tahli is absolutely buggered by 9pm. She takes a quick shower and snuggles into bed while I take my turn to shower.

I have to express the milk buildup, and part of me wishes I could invite Ringo in here to help, since he loves assisting me with it so much. But I can't exactly explain that to a twelve-year-old. So I hand-express, and quickly finish up, returning to the room to find Ringo sitting on the end of the bed, telling Tahli about our wedding day as she holds the photo he had framed for me.

"Now I understand why everyone found my Harry Styles comment so funny before," Tahli giggles, as I climb into the bed beside her. "Did you really walk down the aisle to One Direction?"

"Yes." I grin, and when my eyes meet Ringo's, he shoots me a playful wink.

"You're crazy." Tahli yawns, so I take the picture from her and pop it back on the bedside table.

"Crazy in love, apparently," I tell her, and she makes a dramatic gagging sound.

"Don't be gross, Abbey." She shuffles down under the covers, settling onto my pillow before glancing up at Ringo. "Are you sure you don't mind sleeping on the couch? I feel bad that I kicked you out of your bed."

Ringo nods as he stands. "It's totally fine. Your big sister needs you close right now. And when you're both ready, you can pick one of the guest rooms downstairs and we'll turn it into a Tahli paradise."

Her smile is huge as her lids flutter closed. "I like the sound of that."

As she curls on her side facing me, Ringo rounds the bed and presses a soft kiss to the top of my head. "Get some sleep, Angel. It's been a big day."

I want to protest since it's still so early, but my body betrays me and I yawn, deciding that it's okay to sleep now that Tahli is back.

Now I feel like I can breathe again… just a little bit.

Ringo retreats around the corner to the lounge, and I snuggle against Tahli, holding her close, and fall asleep to the quiet hum of the TV in the background, and Tahli's gentle snores.

For a while, everything is peaceful.

There's no one chasing me in my dreams tonight.

No blood pooling at my feet. Or cries of a baby I can hear, but can't find.

There's just plain nothingness. Deep and heavy, weighing me down in a restful slumber.

At some point, though, something changes.

I dream of fireworks cracking overhead. Pop, pop, pop as colour bursts through the darkness, before a loud bang jolts me awake.

I sit up with a gasp, my hand pressed over my racing heart, and I glance to the side to see Tahli sound asleep.

What the…

Pop. Pop. Pop.

My heart flips, and not in a good way.

I scurry out of bed, dashing around the corner into the lounge area, which is completely dark except for the faint glow coming from the ceiling to floor windows.

I stagger back, my heart hammering when my eyes land on the silhouette of a man standing in front of the windows, a gun hanging at his side.

32

RINGO

A faint gasp sounds behind me, and I glance over my shoulder to see the shadow of my Angel standing across the room.

It takes me a moment to register what's happening as she stumbles back, and I mutter a curse under my breath, realising she's probably just seeing the silhouette of a man and not recognising it's me.

"Angel. It's me." I hold up a calming hand, knowing that with no lights on in the room, I must look fucking scary standing by the windows.

"R-Ringo?" she whispers, and I grin, even though she can't see it.

"No, it's Harry Styles."

A relieved giggle escapes her as the tension eases from her shoulders at my teasing, but it's short-lived, because a beat later, more loud pops crack in the distance.

"Is that… shooting?"

"Yep." I wave her over and turn back to the window, peering out into the dark night.

"Shit. Should I get my gun? Get your mum into the panic room? Shit, what about Tahli…" Her voice climbs higher with each word as she comes closer, so I snatch her wrist and pull her in tight, pointing out the window.

"I know it's hard to see in the dark, but if you look out that way, every thirty seconds you'll see a small green light flashing."

Pressing close to me, she glances in the direction I point, and we wait quietly until it flashes again.

"I see it."

"That's one of the signals in place to tell us we're still safe. If it starts flashing red rapidly, then it's time to brace for an attack."

Shifting, she glances up at me, our faces only just visible in the glow filtering in from one of the barn's exterior lights.

"But I can hear someone shooting."

"They are. It's coming from out by the main road. The sound is travelling on the breeze, but so far, Riggs and his team have it handled."

"But what if they don't? What happens then?" Her panic is understandable. She has her sister here now, so naturally, she's desperate to keep her out of harm's way.

"There are men posted every hundred metres along the road leading to the property, and men every fifty metres surrounding it. It would take a lot to get through them, and if they did, they'd still have to deal with the thirty men stationed around my house.

Plus, in addition to that, they've got twenty drones in the air at any one time, all armed. And the house has had so many upgrades it's practically a fortress now." Leaning forward, I press my lips to her hair. "I'm not worried, Angel. If I were, we'd already be gone."

"Is it the Rebels?" she asks, refocusing on the spot she saw the green light flash.

"Riggs confirmed it's some Rebels and crooked cops. About eight to ten, best they can tell… well, though by now, I reckon there's probably only a few left."

I feel the tension drain from her body as she melts into my side, and we stare out into the darkness for a long while in comfortable silence.

A few of the drones I told her about buzz overhead, and a small laugh slips from my wife's lips.

"What's so funny?"

She pulls away and moves to the couch, flopping down onto the blanket I'd been under before the gunfire woke me.

"It's these men." She flicks her hand towards the window as I take a seat on the coffee table in front of her, placing my gun next to me. "The level of security is just so… extreme."

"I thought you'd be happy about that."

"Oh, I am," she sighs. "It's just… where did they come from? Are they like some sort of special ops team? They are more than just security. It feels like something straight out of a movie."

Leaning closer, I place my hands on her thighs and part them, lowering to my knees between her legs.

"They've all had special training. Most were in the military," I say, sliding my hands higher, disappearing beneath the oversized t-shirt she's wearing, and her breath hitching at my touch. "Some are ex-cops. Riggs makes sure his men are the best."

"I guess they're putting their skills to good use protecting us," she breathes, parting her legs wider to give me better access.

I take that as the invitation it is, grazing my fingers over her panties, a whimper passing her lips.

"Cam," she breathes. "We can't…"

"We can if you're quiet." I smirk, watching the way she sucks her lip into her mouth and rolls her hips, so I start to rub over her clit.

"I don't know if I can be quiet," she purrs, reaching for me. "Not with the way you make me feel."

I fucking love this side of her. The way she melts so easily for me. The way she loses herself under my touch, even after everything she's been through.

"Be careful, Angel. Talk like that and you'll make me feel like a god." I let her pull me closer, her nails digging into my nape as her breath ghosts across my lips.

"When it comes to my body, you *are* a god," she whispers, a slight giggle spilling out of her lips before she crashes her mouth to mine.

I moan into her mouth as she arches into me, one of my hands on her back and the other still working between her legs, our tongues clashing in a desperate, hungry dance.

I hadn't planned on more than touching her, but like always, our bodies take over, and I fucking give in. Give in to the need coursing through my veins and shooting straight to my cock.

"Cam," she whimpers, breaking the kiss, her lips trailing across my beard to my ear, where she sinks her teeth into my lobe. "Fuck me."

"Fuuuck, Angel," I growl as she wraps her legs around my waist, grinding her core closer. "We can't. Not yet."

"Three days. It's only three days until I have the all clear. That's just a guide," she whines, grinding her panty-clad heat against the hard bulge straining behind my boxers. "Just take it out and slip it in."

She follows this by sliding her palm down my abs, her fingers dipping under my waistband, immediately wrapping around my cock.

"Fuuuck, you don't play fair, Angel."

"I'll be a good girl. I swear. Just stick it in," she begs, shoving my boxers halfway down my arse with her free hand, freeing my cock and giving it a pump. "*Please*. I'll do *anything*."

I try to pull back from her, but her legs are wrapped tight around me and her hand is unrelenting as she tries to steer my cock to her entrance, still covered by her panties.

"Fuck, Angel. I do love the sound of you begging."

"I'll beg. I'll grovel. I'll do *anything*." Then she sinks her teeth into my neck.

Fuuuck, she's feisty.

I smile into her hair and grind my cock against her soaked panties, her teeth sinking in deeper as she lets out a soft whimper, obviously trying to keep quiet so we don't wake her sister in the other room, which, I might fucking add, doesn't even have a door separating us. Technically, we're in the same fucking room, just around the corner.

This was a bad idea.

Abbey's nails are biting as they claw into my skin, so sharp I know I'll have marks I'll have to lie about if my ma sees them.

I wanna push Abbey back and free her tits. Suck the hard peaks into my mouth until the warm milk rushes down my throat. But she's too far gone right now, clutching my neck and cock like her life depends on it, her fist a vice as she pumps me and grinds onto me at the same time. Her panties are so fucking wet. I can feel the swollen bump of her clit pressing against the head of my cock through the fabric.

"Please," she pants into my ear. "In… me."

The way she positions my cock at her panty-clad entrance again has me fucking snapping, and I thrust against it like I'm trying to tear through the barrier to get inside her.

And fuck, maybe I am.

Maybe I want to forget what the doctors said and just sink into her, feel her heat wrap around me, the hot silk of her cunt sucking me in and…

"Fuck," I choke out as quietly as I can. "I'm gonna come."

"Yes. Yes," she whisper-yells into my ear, her hips frantic as she grinds faster, and I can't fucking hold back.

I come *hard*.

Holding my breath, I jerk and fucking shudder as pleasure detonates inside me, cum shooting from my cock into the fabric covering her entrance.

The strangest hushed sound I've ever heard Abbey make comes from the back of her throat as I jet cum into her panties, her cunt spasming and teasing the head of my cock, right down to the rim.

Fuck.

Frowning, I ease back, trying to pant quietly but sure I'm fucking failing as I glance down between us. There's only just enough glow from outside light illuminating the yard for me to see that even though I was fucking Abbey's panties, I still managed to get the head of my cock, covered by the fabric, just inside her.

"Shit. Did I hurt you?" My gaze flicks up to Abbey's as she flops back panting, a grin pulling at her lips as she lazily shakes her head.

"Hell no. That was hot."

My brows shoot up. "You liked me fucking you with a barrier between us?"

She nods quickly, biting her lip. "It was like a tease… but with penetration. Kinda."

"Damn. That gives a whole new meaning to *just the tip*."

A giggle slips from her lips, and she slaps her hand over her mouth, a look of horror contorting her expression.

"Oh my God," she whispers. "What if Tahli heard us?" Her head darts in the direction of my bedroom.

"Tell her… it was the TV?"

Her hand drops away, and she looks at me deadpan.

"She's twelve, not an idiot."

"Well, I don't know. This is new for me," I admit, sitting back and wondering how the fuck to start cleaning up this mess.

"I know. I'm sorry," Abbey whispers, reaching for me. "Hey. I love you."

My eyes lift from her cum-painted panties to her face, her hand pressing to my beard and cheek.

"I know," I grin at her. "And you know I fucking love you more than… well, fucking anything."

"I know," she giggles.

"Promise I didn't hurt you?"

"You didn't hurt me. It felt good. I feel good."

"Well, good." I nod, pointing to her crotch. "I made a mess, Angel. Want me to lick it up?"

Her lips drop open. "Yes… but no."

"Which is it?" I chuckle.

"No," she says regretfully. "That's way too hot for me to handle quietly. There's no way I won't end up impaled on your dick if you do that."

A growl rumbles from me as I scoop my hands behind her back and pull her to my chest. "Three days, Angel. Then I'll be buried inside you for fucking weeks."

Her smile is huge as she nods eagerly, and I close the distance to claim her mouth in another heated kiss.

We get carried away for a few minutes, to the point my cock starts to think it has the fucking stamina to go again, but then a whimper drifts to us from my bedroom.

Abbey stiffens, and I pull back, her head tilting towards the bedroom, and a second later, a piercing scream rips through the air.

Abbey shoves me back, staggering up and stumbling as she quickly shoves her drenched panties down, kicking them towards me.

"Get rid of them," she hisses, leaving me with the cum-soaked fabric as she runs into my bedroom.

I quickly right myself, picking up the panties as I hurry after her just as light fills the room.

When I round the corner, I see Abbey on my bed, cradling a sobbing Tahli to her chest as she mutters words I can't make out.

I quickly toss Abbey's panties into the hamper and notice her bare arse peeking out from under the oversized tee she's wearing.

I wonder if I should tell her.

"Shhh, it's okay. You're safe," she tries to calm Tahli, who obviously had a nightmare.

"I didn't want to do it," Tahli cries, clinging to Abbey.

Fuck. I don't like the sound of that.

"Do what, Chook?"

"She said I just had to sit on his knee and give him a kiss. That he was more than my grandpa. So I did what she said." Tahli pulls back, and I finally get a glimpse of her face, so much like Abbey's, but her features a little darker.

Her cheeks are beet red and blotchy, soaked from the tears streaming down her face as she shakes her head, a shudder rippling through her.

"It's not right, Abs. Kids and grown-ups aren't supposed to kiss like that."

I freeze, my heart practically staggering to a stop, but it's nothing compared to how still Abbey is right now. If it weren't for the rapid rise and fall of her chest, I'd think she'd stopped breathing.

"Are you saying…" Abbey can't finish, but Tahli nods, shame washing over her features.

"We'll find them, Angel," I say, dragging her attention to me, her gaze cold. Distant.

"Abs?" Tahli murmurs on a sob, her little hands coming up to cup her big sister's cheeks. "I'm sorry."

That snaps Abbey out of the cold trance she was in, her eyes going wide.

"Chook, you have nothing to be sorry for." Abbey shakes her head, dragging Tahli back to her chest. "What they did is wrong. Everything they have done is wrong. But don't you worry. You're

safe now, and I won't let anything bad happen to you ever
again."

33

ABBEY

I feel like I'm losing myself. A month ago, I wouldn't have cared. I was happy to flip the switch and turn into a badass with barely any feelings, because it was easier than letting the crushing weight of them drown me.

But now I have Tahli to think of.

And if I'm being honest, I have Ringo to think of as well. He means more to me than I ever could have imagined, and while he does like the darker side of me, it's not something I want to subject Tahli to.

Not that she hasn't already seen glimpses, but that's not necessarily a bad thing. She needs to learn how to toughen up too. She just maybe doesn't need to see me go full psycho like I wanted to when I realised what she was telling me two nights ago.

Banes, that fucking prick, had Tahli on his knee… and he kissed her. Like *kissed*, kissed.

The thought makes me want to hurl.

My poor sweet Tahli.

I guess I should be happy it didn't go beyond that. Tahli assured me that was it. And aside from cooking for him and serving him dinner, nothing else happened, but she was scared it would.

Mum had started preparing her. Tahli told me that Mum was teaching her how to be a wife.

Ugh, that bitch is going to die. And soon.

If we ever find them.

"She'll be fine out here with Millie and Lans." Jols shoulder-bumps me, dragging my attention away from my little sister as she paints rocks by Bobbi's and Hope's graves.

She wanted to make the ground pretty for them, so Riggs, of all burly men, wandered around the pond with her and helped her collect a bucket of rocks. Now she's painting them with rainbows and butterflies and flowers on their smooth surfaces, laying them in the grass around the graves.

"Look, I'm the last person who wants to talk about my brother's sex life," Lans leans in on my other side, lowering her voice like it's a secret. "But he needs to get laid, and *you* definitely need to get laid. You've been a moody bitch the last couple of days."

I grin, shaking my head. "You know why I've been moody."

"Well, a little bump and grind will take your mind off things for a while." Lans wags her brows, and we all giggle.

"I'm glad Tahli can't hear what you're saying." Millie grumbles as she steps closer, and I roll my eyes before looking to Lans.

"You sure she'll be okay?"

Alana nods, her smile wide as she hooks her arm around her sister. "Mills and I will paint rocks with her. We've got her covered for at least an hour."

I bite my lip, glancing at Jols, who beams.

"He's down in the garage, working on that old car of his." She holds up a bag. "You'll need this to get him over the line."

Taking the bag, I peer in to see a girthy dildo and a small bottle of lube.

"Ahhh, am I using this on him? Is there something about my husband I don't know?"

Millie makes a gagging noise, and Lans bursts out laughing as Jols starts to explain.

"Can't say I know about *that*, but he's been refusing to stuff your bun until the six weeks are up, which is literally tomorrow, and knowing him, he'll make you wait until tomorrow and then add another week for good measure. So that," Jols points to the bag, "is what you use as an ultimatum. Either *he* fucks you, or you'll use that."

A laugh babbles out of me, and honestly, it's a brilliant plan, aside from one thing.

"What do I do if he doesn't cave?"

"Girl, you fuck that dildo like it's your last day on Earth." Lans slaps my shoulder, and we all roar with laughter, gaining Tahli's attention.

"What's so funny?"

"Oh… nothing." I giggle, hiding the bag behind my back. "Will you be alright here with Aunty Millie and Alana for a while, Chook? I have a few things I need to do."

Smiling up from the ground, Tahli nods, looking the happiest I've seen her since she came here.

I ruffle her hair before heading towards the back of the barn, where the old garage is, and Jols hurries up to my side.

"Just in case you were wondering, that's brand spanking new. Straight out of the pack, washed and ready to use." She does a little shimmy as she walks, and another laugh falls from my lips.

I'm thankful to have these women around me. It'd be easy to sink into the dark hole I'm walking the edge of lately, but Jols, Lans and Millie won't let me fall in.

It's so nice to have friends again.

Not that Lexi isn't my friend. She is, but I don't get to see her as much as I'd like.Hopefully, once all of this is over, that will change.

I ignore the Marx guys sparring next to the barn, paranoid they've got X-ray vision and can see what's inside the bag. When we reach the garage, Jols skips in, whispers in JD's ear, and he drops the spanner in his hand, muttering something about leaving the iron on before chasing Jols out and closing us in.

"I swear those two act like they're on their honeymoon," Ringo grumbles from under the hood of the old car.

"I wouldn't mind being on a honeymoon," I say, dragging my finger along the cold metal panel of the car. "I'd love some Ringo time."

His head tilts in my direction. "I gave you Ringo time in the laundry room this morning."

I pout. "Dry humping is getting old." I sigh. "I want to be filled."

A low growl rumbles in his chest as he straightens. "Not yet, Angel."

I sigh, scanning the space, and deciding over by the work-bench is my best option for now, so I move over to it and place the bag on the counter.

"What's in the bag?" he asks, using a rag to wipe his hands.

"Oh nothing. Just a little gift for me," I say innocently, taking off my coat as I turn to him, discarding it on the stool. "Your sisters are looking after Chook for a while."

His brows shoot up. "Why?"

I grin at the curiosity in his voice.

"Oh, you know, so I can have some alone time with my gift."

His brows hitch, so I start stripping out of my clothes.

With a smirk, he slams the hood of his car closed, crosses his arms over his chest, and leans on the bonnet.

"What is my wife up to?"

I shrug, batting my lashes innocently as I toe off my boots, shuffle my pants and undies off, and quickly tug the shirt over my head.

"Angel," he warns, but I just bite my lip, cupping my breasts before unhooking my bra. "What's going on here? They feeling full again?"

"They're always ready for you to suck on." I palm their heavy weight, giving each one a little squeeze until a drop of milk beads on the tip of each nipple.

"Fuck, Angel. You do realise you're completely naked right now, right?"

I nod. "Yes, and I'm *aching* to feel you inside me."

"We can't."

"It's one day," I whine, and he shakes his head.

"One day is one day, Angel."

I pout, realising I really am going to need to pull out the big guns.

Turning, I fish out the lube and hold it up so he can see.

"Making my cock slippery isn't the solution. One more day."

I roll my eyes, sighing, and reach into the bag, wrapping my hand around the pink, glittery silicone dildo.

It takes everything in me not to burst out laughing as I drag it out, watching his expression twist in horror at the sheer size of it.

Jesus, does Jols really think I can handle this thing?

"The fuck are you doing with that?" he snaps, and I shrug, using my teeth to flip open the lid on the lube before pouring a good portion over the tip of the dildo, watching it ooze a trail down.

"If you're not gonna fill me, husband, then I'll do it myself."

The words sound surer than I feel as I set aside the lube and meet Ringo's eyes, finding his brows raised.

"Well, go ahead then."

That fucker!

He's calling my bluff, and I have half a mind to throw this monstrosity at him, but then it might get dirty, and well, now that I'm looking at it, if he's not gonna stretch me, then this thing may as well.

When my eyes meet his again, there's a hint of a smirk tugging at his lips. He really doesn't think I'll do it.

Granted, neither did I, but when in Rome or whatever…

Biting my lip, I consider how I'm actually meant to do this. There's really nowhere for me to lay, and I could sit on the stool, but the old thing looks rickety, and I might break it.

This was a bad idea.

"What's wrong, Angel? Having second thoughts?"

His shit-eating-grin is getting on my nerves.

"No," I snap, and decide to be honest. "Just trying to figure out how to do this standing up."

Maybe I should have watched some porn first. Learned how to seduce my husband from there.

"Pop your foot onto the stool's foot support." He gestures to the stool beside me, so I do as he says, thankful for his instruction.

Putting my foot on the timber rail, it opens me up, and I catch the flare of his nostrils, realising this is affecting him more than he's making out.

Maybe this *will* work.

"So what now?" I ask sweetly, waving the glittery object in front of me. "Do I just slip it in?"

He nods, his chest rising and falling faster as he watches me lower the dildo between my legs and line up the sparkly tip with my entrance.

"Like this?" I ask, biting my lip as I press it against myself, realising I need to open myself up more to take it in.

Ringo rumbles something like a yes in response, so I try again, bending my knees to give the dildo more access and press the tip of it gently—

"Stop!" he roars, hurrying forward to rip the dildo from my hand, his hands rough as he lifts me and my arse meets the workbench behind me.

"Nothing fucks you but me," he growls, his voice laced with a possessiveness that sends tremors of pleasure rippling up my spine as his whiskey eyes turn black with lust.

"Then fuck me. Give me what I need."

His hands grip the bench on either side of me, his breathing deep and ragged as he fights for control, pressing his forehead to mine.

"I don't want to hurt you," he admits, his gravelly voice sending shivers through me and turning my body into molten need.

"Not fucking me *is* hurting me, Cam. I ache for you. So bad."

Before I even know what's happening, he lets out a feral growl, his hand fisting the hair at my nape before he slams his lips into mine.

We both moan into the kiss, my body lighting up in anticipation, my hands grappling at his clothes as he helps me strip them off him.

We barely break apart as each item comes off him, my hands then fumbling with his fly as I desperately try to get to him.

He pulls back, breaking our kiss to help, shoving his jeans down and freeing his hard cock as he grips it at the base.

"This is going to be fucking quick, I'm sorry," he mutters, his eyes roaming over every part of me as I sit with my legs spread on the workbench.

"I don't care. Just get inside me. *Please*," I beg, and he steps forward, both of us watching where he presses the fat head of his dick to my wet folds, running it up the seam, teasing my clit and extracting another moan from me.

"I've missed this," he rasps, biting his lip, his nostrils flaring as he slowly nudges his tip against my entrance.

"Yes," I gasp, arching into him, making him sink in a little. "Give it to me. Give me *you*," I beg, and with a feral groan, he finally does. He drives himself deep inside me.

Our moans are loud as he stretches me, pushing all the way to the hilt.

"Colour," he chokes out, like talking is nearly impossible right now.

"Green. A huge fucking green," I pant, and his lips spread wide in a smile before he slowly eases halfway out, and then sinks back in.

My fingernails bite into his shoulders as he starts to thrust, the feel of him inside me too much, yet still not enough.

We kiss in a frenzy. A messy, desperate clash of lips and tongues, and before I can process it, he's hoisting me in his arms, carrying me. Shuffling us over to his car, he nearly trips on the pants tangled around his ankles, but manages to get us safely to his car where he lays me on the hood. The chill of the old metal makes me arch with a gasp, but the new position allows him to slam into me deeper and harder as he watches where we are joined.

"You feel so fucking good," he rasps, his face twisting with a mix of pleasure and pain.

His eyes shift from where we are joined up to my breasts, bouncing with each thrust, and a moment later, his mouth latches onto my nipple, drawing on me. Drinking from me.

I cry out, the combination of his mouth on me and his dick filling me sending shockwaves through my body, more intense than anything we've ever shared. I shatter around him, a pulsing orgasm that seems to last forever until he's following me over the edge.

"Fuuuck, Angel," he pants, releasing my nipple and jolting with each ripple of pleasure, his back arching and his head thrown back as he fills me. "I've fucking missed this."

Even as tears sting my eyes, I force them back, refusing to ruin the moment with my messy emotions. I've craved being this close to Ringo for weeks, and I know my feelings make sense, but I'm just damn tired of crying.

"I've missed you," I admit to Ringo, and his whiskey eyes lock with mine as he leans over me, bringing us nose to nose.

"I know. I get it. I've fucking missed you too."

I smile. "It really makes no sense. It's not like we haven't spent time together… doing stuff."

His lips press to mine in a gentle peck. "It's not the same as this." He gestures between the two of us. "Nothing beats getting as close as two people can get. Nothing will ever top that."

Reaching up, my fingers weave through his hair as I stare into his eyes.

"You're the best thing that's ever happened to me, Cam. I hope you know that."

His smile is small but warm. "I do now. And I feel exactly the same about you, Angel."

We kiss again, slow and tender, even as I feel him still nestled deep inside me, his release beginning to leak out.

Oh shit.

He's leaking out of me.

"What?" he pushes back, eyes wide with panic as he feels me stiffen. "What's wrong?"

"Uhhhh… we didn't use protection, and I'm not on birth control."

His face softens instantly, a smile tugging at his lips. "Oh, that's fine, Angel. Don't worry about it."

My brows shoot up, and I shove at his chest. "I'm not ready to have another…" I trail off, unable to even say the word *baby* right now.

"Shit. No." He shakes his head quickly, gently easing out of me. "I didn't mean that, Angel. I just… well… I know for a fact Lans has a stash of morning-after pills."

My shoulders slump as relief floods me, and I finally breathe again. "Ohhhh. Okay. Good. I guess I'll go ask her for one then."

He chuckles, helping me sit up. "We should probably talk about this kind of stuff, huh?"

I nod, letting him help me down off the hood of the car, and together, we start cleaning ourselves up and slipping our clothes back on, the comfortable silence between us making the moment more intimate.

"Where the fuck did you get that from?" He nods at the pink, sparkly dildo lying forgotten on the workbench.

"Jols." I snicker, unable to hold back my grin, and he rolls his eyes.

"Of course. Should've known."

"I think your sisters were in on it too," I add, giggling as I scoop up the dildo and toss it back in the bag.

"Great," he mutters with a scoff. "Just what I need. Lans thinking she orchestrated me getting laid."

I giggle again, but the sound is cut off by a piercing scream tearing through the air outside.

I'm running before I can blink, my feet carrying me like a bat out of hell towards the sounds of Tahli's screams as I burst from the garage and sprint across the yard.

Marx men are already ahead of me, charging in the same direction, and I hear Ringo shouting something behind me, but none of it registers. My mind is focused on only one thing.

Getting to my sister.

I don't think I've ever run so fast in my life as I bolt through the orchard, towards the Jacaranda tree, finally spotting a group of black-clad men standing around Tahli, their guns raised at something, or someone, off to the left.

"Tahli!" I scream, and her head snaps to me instantly before she wrenches free from Millie's grip and sprints straight into my arms. "What happened?"

"A-a-a m-man," she sobs, her voice breaking as she clings to me, and I glance up, straining to see past the wall of men blocking my view.

Passing Tahli off to Jols, who appears at my side, I shove my way through the Marx security to find a man bleeding on the ground.

"Who are you?" I demand, then bark to anyone that will listen, "What happened?"

"He came out of nowhere," Alana blurts out, rushing to my side. "Like he was hiding in the grass or something."

Frowning, I glance to where she points, and Riggs storms in that direction to investigate as I turn my attention back to the man.

"You look familiar," I snap, and his lip curls as he glares up at me.

"You stabbed me once," he seethes, and my brows hitch, memories slamming into me of the night Officer Allen and his cronies ambushed this place and took me.

But not before killing some of the Southern Sadists, and then shooting Jols and Millie.

"Fucking hell," Riggs sighs, drawing everyone's attention. "He fucking tunnelled in."

My brows climb into my hairline as I spin to find Ringo. "They are tunnelling in now?"

"That must've taken fucking days," Ringo snarls, shoving through the Marx men to come to my side.

"Like I had a fucking choice," the man on the ground rasps, his voice cracking in desperation. "That fucking cult, and Allen, they've got my son. If I don't come back with one of the Delaney girls, then my boy is fucking dead."

"You and you, down the tunnel," Riggs barks orders to two of his men. "Find where it leads and call it in."

They nod without hesitation, lowering themselves into a man-made hole that could very well cave in on them at any moment.

Jesus. No one could pay me enough money to do that.

Tahli's whimpers float to me from where Jols is trying to comfort her, and everything inside me screams to reach for a gun and shoot this bastard in the head, but Ringo is my voice of reason.

"Take him to the barn," he orders, glaring at the thug on the ground. "Let's show him the very best of hospitality until he coughs up a location for Banes or Allen."

When Ringo's eyes meet mine, I nod and flash him a mischievous smile.

"I wonder if Hush might like to help," I murmur. "That sort of hospitality seems right up her alley."

34

RINGO

Eight fucking days. That's how long it took for the arsehole who tunnelled his way onto my property to finally crack.

I've gotta hand it to him. He was fucking tough. But I suppose almost any father would suffer the most brutal torture if it meant keeping his son safe.

So what was it that made him crack?

The same twisted shit Hush did to Darnel.

The threat of having his dick severed.

Turns out some fathers just don't have the balls to see it through after all.

Mind you, Hush told us from the start that the fastest way to get answers was to go for the cock, but we didn't want to believe her. So she spent days torturing him in other ways. She even dug out one of his eyeballs with a pair of fucking tongs.

Turns out losing a dick is a helluva lot scarier than losing an eye.

Who fucking knew?

That was two days ago, and ever since, we've spent every second planning.

Surprisingly, Abbey didn't insist on rushing in guns blazing like I'd expected. Instead, she wanted to plan, determined to make sure we get this right.

One of our biggest concerns with this raid is that Moore has gone radio silent.

We don't know if he's been made. Or if he's even still breathing. We're walking into this blind, and one wrong move could have all of our heads on spikes.

Today, the hogs are left behind for vans again, but this time we've got more Sadists riding with us than Marx crew.

Abbey made it fucking clear her sister's safety comes before anything else. That's why we've only got one team of four Marx crew with us on the ground today, with the rest on high alert on my property, just in case.

We may have fewer Marx men with us, but we've got their eyes in the sky. Some of their drones are buzzing over the airfield right now, getting us some much needed intel.

We've gotta get this fucking right.

"We have heat signatures in hangars seven, eight and eleven. All the rest are cold," Riggs' voice cracks through the radio earpiece, relaying the data they are getting from one of their drones.

"Do you know how many?" I ask, pressing the button on my sleeve that connects my voice to the comms.

"Hangar seven has five. Eight has three, and eleven has one," Riggs confirms.

"Roger that," I mutter, hating the fucking radio lingo, which Abbey must pick up on because she smirks at me from where she's huddled in the back of the van, her eyes glinting.

"You sound so professional, Sarg," she teases, and I narrow my eyes until my own smirk breaks free across my face.

"Yeah, *Sarg*. You sound so professional. And *sexy*. I'd do you." JD gets all up in my ear, and I elbow the fucker away as he laughs.

"Get in line," Abbey deadpans without missing a beat, and JD howls with laughter.

"I was in line long before you showed up, darlin'. He was watching my balls slap against—"

A shoe smacks him square in the head, and his glare shoots to Jols.

"What was that for?"

"I don't want to hear about *who* your balls were slapping against. As far as you're concerned, you were a virgin until I came along. Got it?" she snaps, her blue eyes narrowed on my best mate.

Slowly, JD's lips spread in a fucking toothy grin that even his scruffy beard can't hide.

"I love it when you get all possessive over me."

Jols rolls her eyes, fighting a smile as Abbey giggles beside her.

"You two are hilarious."

"No, they're not, Angel. Don't fucking encourage them," I snap, and my wife pokes her tongue out at me.

A sudden jolt rocks the van as it flies over a bump, reminding us that we're about to go on a fucking deadly mission, and one wrong move means body bags.

We need to keep our heads in the game.

Riggs' voice cracks through the earpiece again, confirming little activity outside the hangars, and a few minutes later, the vans are speeding through the gates of the private airfield, heading straight towards hangar seven.

Suddenly, every instinct in me is screaming to call it off. To turn the fuck around and get Abbey out of here.

But I know she'd never forgive me if I tried to stop her again.

"Get ready!" Vender shouts from the front, and we all tense, mentally preparing for the moment we need to jump from the fucking van.

Brody is up front with Vender today, and I can tell JD is worried about having his little brother with us. Ever since the ambush at my place, Brody has been more focused and dedicated to what we do. He insisted on coming today. To do his part.

Stocky, Murf, Trunk and Mex are cramped into the second van, while Trigger, Ace, Tups and Spud are squeezed into the third. All good men. Brothers I'd bleed for.

I just hope none of them die today.

Fuck, this shit is hard.

It's like my head and heart are splitting in two. Half of me is worried about my men, and the other half about my wife. Both sides of my worry tearing at me.

Shifting my foot, I nudge Abbey's boot with mine, and her gaze darts to me.

"Remember. On my six. At all times," I snap, my voice low and edged with steel, and for once, she doesn't give me the eye roll

I'm expecting. Just a tight nod, her eyes burning with the same fear and fury I feel.

"Just remember too, no one kills Daniel and Donny but me."

I nod this time, happy with the arrangement we have in place.

I agreed to let her be the one to kill Donny and Daniel, if she leaves Ian Allen up to me.

That sick fucker raped my wife. Ain't no fucking way he's dying by anyone else's hand but mine.

The van screeches to a stop, all of us bracing as the door whooshes open, and JD and I leap out first, guns raised, eyes sweeping for threats.

The other two vans speed off towards hangar eight, while the black SUV sticks with us, and Marx men pour out, boots pounding the pavement as we run for the hangar door.

Outside the entrance door, two of the Marx team swing the access door wide and toss in a smoke bomb. The flash flares bright, the clap echoing as the space fills with choking white smoke.

Checking over my shoulder, I see Abbey ready with her gun, eyes darting around, right as the first bullets rip through the air.

As much as it nearly fucking kills me, I wait, forcing myself to hold position until my team is inside, working on securing the inside. Every second we hang back is like fucking acid in my veins, but Abbey's safety is my first priority.

There's shouting, more gunfire, and then something we weren't prepared for.

An explosion.

Hangar eleven behind us goes up in a hot ball of fire, the shockwave knocking us off our feet as part of hangar seven's wall caves inward.

"Angel!" I bellow through the smoke and chaos, my lungs burning, heart ready to fucking cease to exist if I can't fucking find her.

My ears ring with gunfire and screams until a dainty hand claws my arm, and I quickly blink through the haze to see her on the ground next to me, dazed as she sits up.

"I'm okay!" she gasps, her eyes wide as they flick around the carnage. "What the hell just happened?"

Gunfire pops closer, and I shove myself to my feet, about to pull her up when a body crashes into me, knocking the breath from my chest.

A fist crunches into my nose, hot pain exploding across my face, and my fists fly automatically, trying to fight whoever the fuck is on me. We scrap like rabid dogs, rolling over the harsh gravel in a feral, bloody scuffle.

"No!" Abbey screams, and at first I think she's yelling about the fucking thug beating on me, but then her voice comes again, sounding further away. "Come back, you son of a bitch! You're gonna die today!"

Fuck.

I throw my elbow into the thug's jaw on top of me, feeling bone crunch under the hit. He tumbles off me, and I shove myself up, my fucking heart thundering as I search for my wife, just in time for a bullet to rip through my thigh.

"Fuuuck!" I roar, heat flaring down my leg, and through the swirling smoke, I catch a glimpse of someone who looks a helluva lot like Allen, turning and bolting away.

Rage ignites in my chest, and I snatch up my gun and fire at the Rebel crawling back towards me. The shot lands dead centre, between his fucking eyes, painting the gravel with his brains.

Keeping my gun raised, I scan the smoke-choked space for the next threat.

No one is there. Just shifting shadows amongst the smoke. Voices yelling somewhere deep in the haze, every plan we had in place completely gone to shit.

"Abbey!" I bellow, staggering up as I slip my belt off and cinch it tight above the bullet wound, hissing through clenched teeth. "Angel!" I roar again, needing to hear her beautiful fucking voice.

But nothing comes. Just more gunfire. More screams. And more fucking chaos.

35

ABBEY

The sight of Donny Allen has the opposite effect on me as the last time I saw him.

It's not fear this time. It's raw, electric anticipation.

I'm ready for him, and from the flicker of panic flashing in his gaze when our eyes locked, he bloody knows it.

Donny bolts for another hangar. It's not one of the ones we had planned to ambush, but the second he slips in through the access door, I know that's exactly where I'm going.

I don't have one of those fancy earpieces like Ringo and JD have, but I can't risk Donny getting away while I waste time finding backup.

I'm ending this today.

I'm ending him, so I can finally breathe again.

With a shaky grip, I wrench the door open, storming in with my gun raised high.

It's dark, but not pitch black. There's enough light filtering through the skylights to see the two light planes parked inside, and the bottom of Donny's legs as he scurries across the hangar floor.

Got you, motherfucker!

Charging forward, I duck under the wing and around the plane, the barrel of my gun trained on Donny's back as he runs.

Just as I squeeze the trigger, a hand snatches my ponytail in a brutal yank, jerking me backwards, and the shot goes high.

I scream, my feet leaving the ground before my back slams onto the cold concrete, knocking the wind from me.

A vile laugh that I never wanted to hear again cuts through my panic, and I look up to see the familiar eyes of Donny's uncle Ian.

"You really thought you had him, didn't you?" Ian Allen looms above me, his own gun now trained on my chest as I gasp for air.

"He'll…" I cough, "keep." I snarl the second word, and Ian's brows hitch in surprise.

"The girl finally has a bit of fight in her," he laughs, low and mean. "This is going to be fun."

Slowly, a smug grin unfurls on my face as my hand wraps around the hilt of the knife at my hip, and I nod up at him.

"Yeah. It is." Letting out a war cry, I slam the blade into his ankle, and he instantly howls in agony.

Blood spurts from the wound, causing him to slip, and his head cracks against the concrete floor with a sickening thud, his cries instantly cutting off.

"Hey! Get away from him!" Donny roars from somewhere, and with Ian now unconscious at my feet, I scramble for my gun, scooping it up and whipping around just as Donny skids to a halt, his eyes going wide.

"Fuck!" he hisses, spinning on his heel and bolting back the way he came, but this time when I squeeze the trigger, my aim is true, and the bullet tears into his back.

He stumbles forward, a strangled cry ripping from his throat as he crashes to the floor.

A rush of triumph surges through me, the heat of it flooding my veins. But it's not enough.

Not yet.

Not until he's dead.

Standing, my legs are trembling as I keep my gun trained on him, slowly approaching as he tries to crawl away, his blood smearing the concrete.

"I would have liked this to be slow," I tell him with an icy chill to my voice as I reach his side, planting my boot on the bullet hole weeping crimson.

He screams, the sound like music to my ears, reminding me of the day Karl Stone died.

Karma always comes. Don't they know that?

"I've dreamed of this day, you know," I murmur, leaning down so he can hear the hate in my tone. "I really wanted to see exactly how you'd like a taste of your own medicine." I grind my boot down harder, drinking in every ragged scream that falls from his lips.

"Stop! P-please! I'm s-sorry." He sobs, his voice breaking.

I scoff. "No, you're not. You loved every minute of raping me, Donny. Don't you dare pretend you regret a thing."

"P-please I'll d-do anything," he begs, and I sigh, lifting my foot from his back and shoving him over so I can see his ugly, pale face.

"Anything?" I ask, letting the word drip from my lips and smiling when he nods frantically.

"You're not gonna like it," I say, almost sweetly, as I aim the gun at his shoulder and pull the trigger.

He howls, blood splattering up my legs, and without hesitation, I shift my aim to his other shoulder and fire again, the second shout tearing another guttural scream from his lungs.

He's a sobbing, broken mess. "P-please… s-stop…"

"Do you remember me begging, Donny?" I ask, dropping to my haunches. "Do you remember me pleading with you to stop?"

He cries out something I can't make out, so I press my gun to his lips, watching his tear-filled eyes go wide.

"Open wide, Donny," I say, nudging the barrel against his lips. "You know how this goes, don't you? It's exactly what you did to me." I shove the cold metal between his teeth, his muffled cries vibrating against the barrel. "Yeah, I know. You used your diseased dick instead of a gun. But the thing is, Donny, it might as well have been a gun for me." My lip curls into a feral snarl as I ram the gun deeper until he gags, choking wetly around the steel.

"What were the words you said?" I taunt, his pathetic whimpers stoking the fire inside me. "You said, '*take all of it, you cunty whore, and fucking choke!*'"

I shove the barrel so far down his throat he splutters, his eyes rolling back as he starts to violently choke.

As much as I want to drag this out, to watch him die a thousand deaths, I know he's not worth a second of my life.

So I squeeze the trigger.

Blood and brain matter literally explode around my hand, up my arm, and over my face.

A rush of pure, soul-deep satisfaction rolls through me at the knowledge that Donny Allen is finally dead, and for a long beat, I just stare at the place his face once was.

A noise behind me snaps me back to reality, and I spin on my knees, my gun raised as I catch a bloody trail smearing the concrete where Ian Allen was moments ago.

With my heart in my throat, I scurry up, following the crimson trail, spotting my knife on the floor on the other side of the plane. My eyes track the bloody path until I see Ian Allen limp-running for the exit.

I point and shoot, but I miss, his deep yell echoing in the hangar before he bursts through the door, vanishing out into the chaos.

I sprint after him, my boots pounding the concrete as I dodge the slick trail of blood he left behind, and when I reach the door, I burst through it, stumbling into a war zone.

It's utter chaos. There's gunfire coming from every direction. I can't tell if it's friendly fire or the enemy. There's smoke and flames from the hangar that blew up, plus a plane burning out in the open.

Scanning the swirling smoke, I finally spot Ian Allen limping towards another hangar, and not far behind him is Ringo.

My shoulders relax at seeing my man moving like a predator, his sights set on the man he wants to kill.

I take off in their direction, desperate to reach my husband, to watch the moment he ends that fucker, once and for all.

I've barely covered a few metres when movement flickers at the edge of my vision. I try to pick up speed as the bulky form charges for me, but it's too late. Their heavy footsteps thunder closer, and a second later, I'm tackled hard to the ground, my gun skittering across the pavement out of reach.

"You're coming with me, bitch!" the man snarls against my ear, his weight crushing me into the pavement.

The moment he yanks me upright, I whip my knife around and slam it backwards into his hip with all the strength I can muster.

He howls in agony but refuses to let go, his fist slamming into the side of my head and rattling my brain.

Darkness rims my vision as stars burst past my eyes, and I grit my teeth, fighting the urge to collapse as I thrash in his grip.

"Let me go!" I screech, and he laughs like I said the funniest joke.

"No fucking way am I letting you go," he growls, spittle hitting my cheek. "You know how many men have died trying to get the fucking bounty the cult freak put up for your capture? I'm gonna fucking claim it, bitch."

I start laughing, loud and unhinged, feeling him stiffen like I hoped he would.

Men really can't handle a crazy bitch.

"You idiot. He doesn't have any money to pay you," I lie, because hell if I know whether my grandfather does or not. "Once you hand me over, he'll kill you. Why are you so dumb?"

"The fuck?!" He releases my hair and spins me to face him. "Did you just call me dumb?"

"If the shoe fits."

"You fucking—"

Blood sprays across my face in a thick and chunky shower as the echo of a gunshot fades away.

"Fuck! Abbey, are you okay?" Jols hurries up to me, her eyes tracking over all the blood covering me, her hand gripping the gun she just used.

"None of it's my blood," I say, tugging off my hoodie and using it to wipe off my face with shaky hands.

"Thank fuck." Jols sighs, her shoulders slumping in relief.

"Where's JD?" I ask, and she tenses again. "I don't know. I lost him in all the smoke and shooting."

Nodding, I turn to face the hangar that Ringo chased Ian Allen into.

"Ringo chased Allen in there." I point to the hangar, and then it erupts in a deafening explosion.

The force throws us back, and we land a few feet from where we were standing as air gets trapped in my lungs.

I sit up, tears stinging my eyes as I stare in disbelief at the blazing wreckage before me.

"NOOOOOO!!!" I scream, scrambling to my feet and sprinting towards the mangled, flaming inferno.

I barely make it a few steps before hands wrap around me from behind, yanking me back.

"Abbey! No!" Jols cries, but I fight and struggle against her hold, tears searing my cheeks.

"RINGO!!!" I scream, my heart ripping from my chest so savagely that I know I'll never survive this. "RINGO!!!!"

I wrench free of Jols' grip, trying to bolt closer, but the searing heat lashes across my skin like whips of lava.

"Stop, Abbey!" Jols cries, and the agony in her voice only twists the invisible knife deeper in my chest.

Ringo went into that hangar.

It blew up… with him inside.

My knees buckle, sending me and Jols to the pavement as a wailing scream explodes from the pit of my soul as the truth of what's happened starts to sink in.

Colour starts to seep from my world. Nothing but greys and blacks closing in as ice creeps into my veins. Through the blur of tears, I stare at the rolling smoke, every breath ragged as I completely shatter.

My cruel mind plays tricks on me, imagining a figure striding through the flames, plumes of smoke billowing around him as he moves with unyielding power and purpose, like an immortal being.

"Abbey…" Jols whispers at my ear, her arms loosening around me. "It's him."

No, this is too cruel. Why would my mind play tricks on me like this?

"Angel!"

I jerk at the sound of his voice, swiping furiously at my eyes as Jols helps me to stand. A gust of wind whips between us, blowing aside the thick smoke revealing my husband, his clothes torn, his skin streaked with soot, but his steps moving with the same unstoppable purpose that first made me fall for him.

"Cameron?!" I cry out, my voice breaking, and the moment he starts sprinting towards me, I take off for him. "Cameron!"

"Abbey!" he roars, like it's him who feared I was the one who died, and we charge towards each other, sobs ripping from me right as we slam together like two magnets that were never made to be apart.

I wrap myself around him as our lips clash in a fierce, desperate kiss, the taste of my tears mixing with it as we grapple at each other.

"Fuck, Angel," Ringo gasps, pulling back just enough to press his forehead to mine.

"I t-thought y-you w-were d-dead," I sob, and he swipes at my tears with his gentle thumbs.

"Gotta be honest. I thought I was too for a second there," he admits, and I kiss him again, clawing at his beard to bring him closer.

"You're not allowed to leave me." I sob, pulling back and slapping his shoulder, and his smile makes the agony in my chest start to ease.

"It'll take more than bullets, knives and explosions to keep me away from you, Angel. That I fucking guarantee."

A giggle bursts from me, and I hug him so tight I feel his heartbeat slamming against mine.

"Did you get Ian Allen?" I ask, and Ringo's smile fades.

"The fucker got away. There was a four-wheeler parked behind the hangar. But his time will come, Angel. Don't you worry."

Nodding, I smile, excited to tell Ringo the news. "I killed Donny."

His brows shoot up. "Really?"

"Choked him with the barrel of the gun first, and then I blew his head apart. Literally."

A savage grin spreads across Ringo's face. "Fuck, there's my little demon."

"Ahh, guys…" Jols steps up, her eyes focused on something to our side, and we turn to see JD dragging someone across the gravel by their hair.

"Oh sweet Abbey," JD sings, his eyes gleaming. "I got you a pressie!"

Ringo lets me go as I push back from him, my boots hitting the ground just as JD shoves the whimpering man at our feet.

"Thought you might want to do the honours." JD grins wolfishly, gesturing to the pathetic, sobbing form on the ground.

A sickening chill ripples up my spine at the sight of my ex-boyfriend, Daniel, who is actually my cousin, and I have to fight the urge to throw up.

"Abbey. Please," he pleads, blood-streaked snot running from his nose.

I shake my head slowly as disgust curls my lip. "It's funny how you are all sooo sorry when it gets to this part." I roll my eyes, extending my hand with my palm open, and Ringo places his gun in it without hesitation.

I check the chamber with steady hands, the metallic click ringing louder than Daniel's pathetic whimpers.

Then I level the gun at his forehead, pressing the barrel hard enough to leave an imprint.

"Wait! Don't kill me! You need me!" he cries, his voice trembling with panic.

I scoff. "What I need is you dead!" I start to squeeze the trigger.

"No, wait!" he shrieks. "If you kill me, you'll never find her!"

"Find who?" I snap, pausing on the trigger as I tilt my head, studying the terror twisting Daniel's face.

"Your baby didn't die, Abbey. She's still alive."

***

Is little Bobbi really alive?
Find out in BEAUTIFULLY SAVAGE, Secrets & Scars Book 4 - the
final instalment.
https://geni.us/secretsandscars4

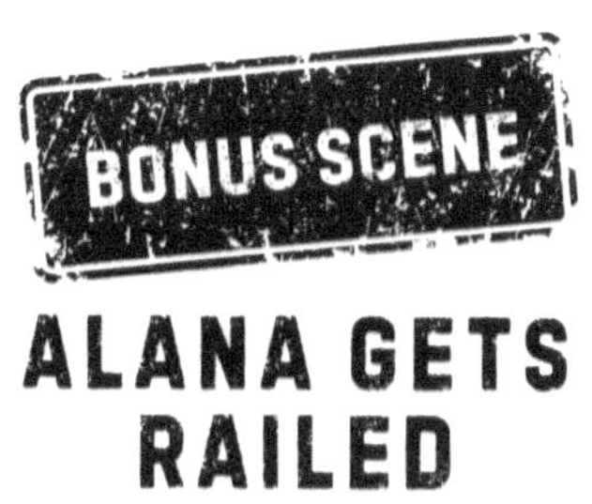

ALANA GETS RAILED

Want to know if Alana finally got laid and who by?

Get your bonus copy of
Alana Gets Railed now.

<u>Secrets & Scars Book 3 Bonus Scene -</u>
ALANA GETS RAILED
https://BookHip.com/NMCNTZN

By downloading a copy of Alana Gets Railed, you will be signing
up to Sarah JD's Darker Shades of Romance Newsletter.
(Please note: if you are already signed up to Sarah's newsletter,
you can still access the bonus scene
by completing the same process.)

https://sarahjdauthor.com/books

STALK ME!!!

Want to join the conversation about your fav characters?
Join my Facebook Readers Group
SARAH'S VICIOUS KITTENS

JOIN HERE!

https://www.facebook.com/groups/
sarahjaneduncanreadersgroup

For more information on books & book signing
events please visit:
https://sarahjdauthor.com

STALK SARAH HERE:

SARAH JD

Sarah JD, also known as Sarah Jane Duncan, is an Australian dark romance author living her best life with her high school sweetheart, Mr Duncan.

Sarah can be found in her writing room plotting out her next smut filled romance, packed with angst, violence, and themes so dark you should probably question why you love it so much.

Sarah enjoys torturing her characters. There's nothing easy about their stories. They are hard, gritty, and painfully heartbreaking at times. But what doesn't kill us makes us stronger, right? And when you throw in a swoon worthy guy, or an alphahole you just want to slap, but also fall to your knees and obey, it's the recipe for a rollercoaster ride.

So buckle up. Read the warnings. And let yourself get lost in the dark stories Sarah creates.